C000221578

The Long Game

Kerry Costello

Kerry Costello Books

KERRY COSTELLO
B O O K S

CONTENTS

CHAPTER 1

The early February drizzle gave way to a weak, watery sun and a biting wind. The woman looked to be in her mid-fifties, had a hangdog, weary face, and lank dark hair. She closed the door of the grimy red brick terraced house, stooped down, put the key under a plant pot by the door, stood, and buttoned up her coat. She took a packet of cigarettes from her handbag and lit a cigarette. The first inhalation of the toxic smoke wrote a hint of pleasure on her otherwise miserable face.

She slowly, gently, blew the smoke out, in the practised way of a long term smoker. Then she walked out of the garden gate, and towards Agecroft Road, to catch her bus home. He watched from his car, as he had done, for most mornings, for over a week now. He assumed she was a cleaner or a home help. She was punctual. Arrived nine thirty on the dot every weekday day, ten on Saturdays. Tomorrow would be the day.

*

SATURDAY MORNING

Billy was down the mine, gasping for breath, suffocating. He panicked and woke up. The morning light leaked through a gap in the curtains. He was confused, then remembered. Another nightmare. He lay in bed trying to clear his mind of all the jumble. His breath rasped, as he tried to hitch himself up into a sitting position. He got halfway, gave up and slumped back against the pillows. He felt frightened, but why? Then he remembered. First Geoff, then Joe. Was he next? Then he forgot what he was frightened of but remained anxious. He needed to pee. Billy huffed and puffed, as he manoeuvred his legs over the side of the bed, and eventually made it to a sitting up position.

He remained a while, sitting on the edge of the bed. Then he stood up, and slowly shuffled the short distance to the lavatory, muttering and cursing quietly with every step. He relieved himself, then made his way back to his bed and lay back down, pulling the covers up and closing his eyes. The effort of going had occupied his brain and temporarily suspended his anxiety. He slipped into a peaceful doze.

The nondescript man walked down Regent Park West, stopped at number seventeen and retrieved the key from under the pot.

Was that the key in the door, Mrs Littleton, she's

early, cup of tea? Billy suddenly realised he was thirsty. He kept his eyes shut and waited for her to shout hello, nothing. Then the bed moved slightly, and suddenly he felt the huge crushing weight on his upper torso, his arms trapped.

He opened his eyes and wanted to shout, scream, but nothing came out. The intruder, sitting astride him, smiled briefly, before slowly pulling a plastic bag down over his head, firmly twisting the ends to form an airtight seal. The plastic bag misted as Billy struggled to breathe, shaking his head from side to side. Then, the last rattling breath, and his body relaxed. The intruder waited a while longer, then held the top edges of the bag between his fingers and thumbs and slid the bag off the dead man's head.

He got off the bed, and stood beside it, looking at his victim for a few seconds, making absolutely sure. Finally satisfied, he tidied Billy's hair with his gloved hand, checked there were no marks on his victim's neck or face, and no signs of a struggle. Then he straightened the bedclothes, patted them down and left quietly, closing the front door behind him and replacing the key under the plant pot.

CHAPTER 2

TWO WEEKS LATER

G ibson left the clinic in a foul mood and drove his black Saab 900 to the station. He parked and looked across at the stark, grey bleak building. Pebble dashed sections of concrete tied together with steel rods to create a nondescript square block, *resembled the East German Stasi HQ, rather than a British police station.* He thought. *How could anyone in their right mind have designed or built such a god awful ugly edifice? It made you depressed just to look at it, never mind working in the place. Its only redeeming feature,* thought Gibson, *was its proximity to the Buckley Arms where you could get a decent pint of bitter.*

Taking a deep breath, he got out of his car. The sharp winter rain stung his face, as he ran the short distance to the covered entrance.

'The DCI was asking after you a few minutes ago,' said the duty constable as Gibson passed through reception.

'Thanks Taylor.' *The one morning I'm late, and he's on my tail, well he'll just have to wait till I've had a cup of tea and something to eat.* Gibson made his way to the canteen, which was empty, other than for Big Betty, who seemed to be getting ready to leave. She wasn't fat, she was just big, in every sense of the word. Jet black hair, and a huge bosom. She glowered at Gibson as he entered the modern, white painted room, with steel topped counters, and metal tables and chairs to match.

'Morning Betty, a mug of tea and two poached eggs on toast please, runny.'

'Bit late for breakfast, aren't we? My shift was over ten minutes ago?'

'Sorry about that, hospital appointment.'

She poured his tea then put the mug down in front of him, liquid slopping over the top of the mug.

'Sit yourself down,' she said, muttering under her breath as she fired up the gas ring on the stove.

Gibson took his tea, found a newspaper and sat down at a table to read, while his eggs were being prepared. He stroked his chin as he read, then out of habit, ran his fingers over the texture of his mildly pockmarked face, the result of puberty triggered acne. Although he wouldn't call himself handsome, he'd never had any problems attracting the opposite sex. He had a good head of dark brown hair with flecks of grey starting to appear, a well proportioned face, a crooked nose, and a small scar under his right eye, thanks to a minor fracas early in his police career. The scar added to his slightly rugged look, but his thoughtful blue grey eyes softened the effect. He stood five foot eleven, had a spare physique, liked to dress smartly, and always wore a suit to work. Betty arrived at his table with his plate of eggs on toast

'You're looking a bit off colour if you don't mind me saying so,' she said.'

'Just a bit tired, I'm okay.'

'Well, you should tell that wife of yours to start looking after you properly.'

Gibson was minded to tell her to fuck off and mind her own business, but he was wise enough to know you kept well in with anyone who serves your food. So he said nothing, and got stuck into his eggs. They were overcooked. He read on for a while, then finished his toast. He had a last swig of tea and looked at his watch. *Shit, forgot all about the DCI.*

'Thanks Betty, lovely eggs,' he lied as he got up to leave.

'You're welcome I'm sure' she replied disingenuously and went back to clearing up.

He hurried to his office. Unusually for a Detective Sergeant he had his own small office. Not favouritism, just the way it had worked out with the available space. He sat down and was just about to call the DCI, when his phone rang.

'Taylor here, front desk, a Mrs King here to see you. Said she has an appointment at ten.'

Shit, I forgot.

'Look Taylor, apologise to her will you. Tell her I'll come and see her later this morning. There's no real point in me seeing her until I've seen the DCI anyway. Just take her telephone number and address and tell her I'll call her within the hour to arrange to come and see her, okay?'

'Will do.'

Gibson put the phone down, then picked it up again and dialled the DCI's extension.

'You wanted to speak to me sir?'

'Yes Gibson, having a problem with your alarm clock?'

'No sir, had to go for a blood test, took a bit longer than I thought.'

Gibson thought back to how his day had started. He'd planned to be at the clinic early, but a car crash on the A57 made the twenty minute journey considerably longer. He arrived at the hospital haematology department, took a ticket from the dispenser, and sat down on one of the chairs, arranged theatre style in the waiting area. He was number thirty six. The red digital light display suspended from the grubby looking white ceiling showed the number eighteen. *So much for my early start!* His headache was getting worse; for twelve hours, he'd had no food, not even a cup of tea, just water. He felt uncomfortable and tetchy. Jill had made him go to the doctor, said he was looking 'peaky'. And he had felt a little off colour, *then again*, he thought, *I have been hitting the sauce a bit lately.*

'Okay, so I like a drink, but that doesn't mean I'm an alcoholic,' he'd replied when Jill had asked him if he realised how much he'd been drinking lately. 'Lots of the lads at the station drink much more than me. I consider myself a moderate drinker, compared to them.'

'Georgie Best would be considered a moderate drinker compared to that lot,' she'd countered.

So he'd gone along to see the GP, who asked him, amongst other things, how much he drank. Despite lying by approximately half about his intake, the doctor tut tutted and suggested he get a liver function test. And his 'other bloods' whilst he was at it.

He looked around at the others. All ages, shapes and sizes. Then his gaze fell on a lady who looked so like his mother, he felt a lump come to his throat. Memories came flooding back.

'Thirty Six,' said a loud and impatient sounding woman's voice. Gibson realised she'd shouted the number previously, but he'd been in a trance.

'Yes, sorry, me.' He followed the nurse through the plastic curtain.

'Take your jacket off, roll up your left sleeve and sit down. Have you got a card...?'

He tuned back into what the DCI was saying. 'Blood test, what for? Never mind I don't want to know, just come to my office now and tell me why the fuck you've left this William Bowie report on my desk.'

Gibson sighed. 'William Bowen, I think you mean sir'.

'Bowie, Bowen, whatever, just come and tell me why you want to waste valuable police time on this.'

Detective Chief Inspector Tom Watson put the phone down and leafed through another file while he waited. He looked out of the window at the sleet and rain. He hated February. Tom Watson was stocky, overweight, balding, cantankerous, and seemed permanently ready to erupt. He sometimes appeared distracted and vague but was not to be underestimated. Some made that mistake and had learned a hard lesson. He was a tyrant and glory thief.

Gibson knocked on the door and entered. He looked around, *so much paper, files all over the place, how does he manage to work in all this mess?*

'Sit down Gibson. So what's this all about?' Watson said, pointing to a folder on his desk, 'as far as I can tell, this man died a natural death with no suspicious circumstances, and no reason for any investigation. So please explain, why this is cluttering my already overburdened desk – and brain? Both of which have limited capacity to cope with more – more stuff,' he hesitated looking around at his cluttered office, searching for a better word but couldn't think of one. 'Yes, stuff,' he repeated, more to himself than to the hapless Gibson.

'Well?'

'Yes sir, sorry. I agree, that on the face of it, it seems pretty straightforward. But his daughter is very insistent that we look into his death, in a bit more detail. She claims he was expecting it, er, his death that is.'

'I think I can say with some certainty Gibson, that "we're all expecting it".' Watson snorted at his own wit. 'So why did she think "he was expecting it"?'

'Well sir, the daughter, Mrs King, she says he was worried. Claims he'd been saying things like he was next, stuff like that. Said he seemed troubled and scared. Then he died, and she won't accept that he died a natural death.'

'He wasn't at all well, according to the information in your file.'

'No, he wasn't. He had a bit of dementia, but had long periods when he was very lucid, according to his daughter He did have a couple of other medical conditions as well, emphysema and a bit of a dickey heart apparently.'

'Anything suspicious, about the death, I mean other than the daughter's concerns, any evidence to suggest anything untoward about the way he died?'

'There was no post mortem. The doctor who attended, specified natural causes on the death certificate. Heart failure I think it said.'

'And where did he die Gibson?'

'At home, he had help.'

'Help?'

'Visits from a home help I mean. Twice a day, plus his daughter visited when she could.'

'Who found him?'

'The home help,' Gibson looked at the file, 'a Mrs Littleton,. She called twice a day, once in the morning, got him up made his breakfast and all that, and then once again in the late afternoon, to make his evening meal. She found him dead in bed. Said he often stayed in bed till late morning on a Saturday.'

'And how did this Mrs Littleton get in, if he wasn't able to answer the door? No, don't tell me Gibson I can guess, a key under the mat.'

'More or less sir Under a pot actually.'

'Jesus Christ Almighty! Why don't they just put a fucking sign on the door, inviting any passing villain to come in and rob 'em? You know Gibson, sometimes I wonder, I really do.... people are just so....' Watson shook his head and sighed in frustration, then carried on. 'So, had he fallen out of bed, anything like that?'

'Apparently not sir. The report says he was just lying in bed, looked as if he was asleep. She tried to wake him up, the home help, then she realised.'

And is this, er...' Watson consulted the file, 'Mrs King, the daughter, is she the only child?'

'As far as I know, yes, yes I'm pretty certain she is.'

'So no one else who might benefit from his death? Wills and relatives that sort of thing? Insurance pay-outs on his death, sale of the house etc?'

'I, er, I haven't checked that yet sir,' Gibson rushed on before the DCI could bollock him for not checking the obvious. 'Billy Bowen was a widower, I know that, and the house was rented so nothing there. My guess would be that there's no insurance pay-out either. I can't imagine he would be leaving much in the way of money, some small savings maybe, but I'll check it all out and make sure.'

'Yes Gibson, you know what they say "where there's a will there's a relation". Did the daughter say if he'd had a row with anyone, any sort of dispute with a neighbour, anything like that?'

'No sir, but I haven't really questioned her properly, I thought I'd better pass it by you first.'

'Well as far as I'm concerned Gibson, it looks pretty straightforward. And in the circumstances, unless someone administered a drug overdose or something, which seems highly unlikely. I suggest that it was, as the doctor stated, a natural death. But, I sense that you harbour some scintilla of doubt.'

'Well, I'm not sure. if I'm honest. But the daughter, she's so insistent. And she's not a nutter, quite the opposite.'

'I take it from that, that you mean she's a good looking woman, and she's got you on a sympathy kick? Look, just put it down as a natural death, fob her off and let's get back to clearing some of the backlog, instead of pissing about with some highly strung neurotic woman with a stupid idea about her father being done in.'

'With all due respect sir, I think I should have another chat with her. I mean it wouldn't look good if she starts complaining that the police didn't take any notice. Remember that case last year sir, the old lady, the one that complained about the man running round her garden at night, naked. Our lads put her down as barmy, but it turned out she was telling the truth. Took a reporter to stake out the place to prove it, and then he made us look like complete twonkers. It was a bit embarrassing, to say the least.'

'Yes, yes, okay Gibson, point made. Well go and have another chat with the daughter if you must, and let me know if she can come up with any valid reason why she thinks he was killed. Jesus H Christ, if it isn't enough having to deal with real crimes, now we're having to investigate imaginary ones.'

'Yes sir.'

'Off you go Gibson. Hang on,' said the DCI looking at the file, 'This William Bowen lived in Regent Park West, Pendlebury I see.'

'Yes sir, lived there all his life. Why, has that got some significance sir?'

'No not really Gibson, just that I grew up just a stone's throw away from there, that's all.'

'Oh right sir. Well, I'll go back to my office then, if there's nothing else?'

'Right Gibson, off you trot.'

He closed the door and winced at the DCI picking him up on not finding out if there were any other beneficiaries.

CHAPTER 3

Back in his own office, Gibson sat down, picked up the phone and called Mrs King. He apologised for missing their appointment that morning, and told her he'd come along and see her at midday, if that was okay.

'I'll be here,' she said in a brusque voice, and put the phone down. It clattered in his ear. He replaced his own receiver and frowned. He thought about what the DCI had said and wondered again if this was all a complete waste of time. He understood her distress at losing her father. She was upset, and no one could blame her, but as for there being something sinister about her father's death? Well, he'd go through the motions, now he'd got the okay from the DCI. Then, like the DCI said, try to get her to accept the obvious, and hopefully, she'd leave him in peace.

Gibson grabbed a quick coffee before leaving. He had plenty of time to get there on time, but got delayed by the front desk, questions about a recent case. He found her house, rang the doorbell and looked at his watch, ten minutes late *shit..*

Mary King opened the door almost immediately.

'What a surprise, you're late. But at least you've turned up, so that's something, I suppose.'

She showed him into her front room. She was blond, slim, and what Gibson would call petite. She wasn't difficult to look at, and certainly didn't look her age, which he knew to be forty five. The house was a post war semi-detached, situated on a quiet road on the Westwood Estate in Pendlebury, a couple of miles or so from where her father had lived. They both sat down. Gibson spoke.

'Look, I'm sorry I couldn't see you at the station this morning, but I was tied up. So, what did you want to see me for?'

'Well obviously, I want to know if you'd made any progress. As in, have you found anything out yet?'

'No I haven't Mrs King. As you know, the doctor who issued your father's death certificate stated that he died of natural causes. Heart failure, or myocardial infarction I believe was the precise term used I understand he'd been suffering with heart and lung problems for some time. Is that correct?'

'Yes, like I said before, he worked in the mines till he was well into his fifties, then he got ill, like a lot of miners, emphysema. It was that that led to his bad heart, the doctor said, that and him being a bit overweight. Anyway, he had to give up work and lived mainly on the social from then on, until,' her voice cracked, 'until he died.'

She dabbed at her eyes with a tissue and thought back to happier days.

Every Sunday, her dad would take her to the big field by the canal. There were whippets, miners and miner's wives, milling around.

The men made a big fuss of her, but stopped when the race was about to start. Then it was all business. She remembered a man with a big blackboard, dogs names chalked on it. He shouted all the time before the race and people placed their bets.   Their dog was called Perfect Lady, or just Lady when she was at home.

'You stay there with yer mam and let's see if Lady here can win us a few bob, c'mon Lady in you go.'

The men coaxed their whippets into their home-made narrow wooden traps. Then went round to the front, and walked backwards down the track waving bits of rag. Lanes were marked out with thin rope and tied at intervals to stakes in the ground. The whippets yelped excitedly pawing at the slatted doors of the boxes, desperate to get out and race to their respective owners.

As soon as the dog owners reached the end of the track, the man near the traps signalled with his arm and a whistle The front of the traps sprang open, and the dogs were off. The dog owners at the end of the long lanes, bent forwards, batting their thighs furiously and frantically waving their bits of rag, shout-

ing at the tops of their voices to their dogs, spurring them on to even greater speed.

The bedlam and general pandemonium electri-fied the spectacle. Dogs accelerating to astounding speeds, their legs lost in a blur of spectacular momentum.

'Mrs King, are you okay?' The policeman's voice brought her back to the present.

'Oh, sorry, I was… never mind, what was it you asked again?'

'I was asking about his medication. Was he good at taking, whatever he needed to take?'

'Yes, he never missed his meds. He had them in a pillbox, all marked up so he would know which ones he'd taken each day, he was very methodical. I hope you're not suggesting he died, just because he forgot his meds?'

'I'm not suggesting anything. Just that con-sidering his general medical condition, and I don't want to seem insensitive, but in the circum-stances, maybe it's not really that surprising that he suffered a heart attack, is it?' I mean sixty eight wasn't a bad age for someone who had the prob-lems he had.'

'I don't accept that. I think he could have gone on for a few more years at least. And, like I said, lately he'd been frightened, kept saying he was next, and then he died so suddenly. It just seems connected. A bit of a coincidence, don't you think Sergeant?'

'Well there's no physical evidence that anything untoward caused his death, but let's put that on one side for the moment. Let me ask you some more questions, and see where that gets us?'

'Okay, like what?'

'Well, when did your father start expressing these, er, fears, about "being next" and did he say what "being next" meant, did he think he was going to be harmed physically, killed? I mean, are you sure it couldn't have been something else he was referring to, such as just dying from his heart problems? People do become more aware of the inevitable as they get older, especially if they're not well?'

'He never said what he was afraid of in that much detail, no. I asked him what it was all about, and he sort of wafted me away. I don't think he wanted me to worry. He said I wouldn't want to know, and things like that. Then sometimes he'd forget all about it. His mind did wander a bit at times. Like I said, the doctor said he had a bit of dementia. But most of the time he could talk about things in a perfectly normal way, remember stuff, better than I could.'

'Okay, let's talk about his life before he became ill. What did he do when he was young? Was he in the army, in the war?'

'No, being a miner, he was in what they called a reserve occupation I think, which meant he didn't have to join up. Although he always said he wished he had joined the army, said it would have been better.'

'What did he mean, better?'

'I don't know, he never really explained. I thought at the time he meant he felt he should have been out there fighting the Germans. Perhaps he meant he felt he hadn't pulled his weight. Funny when you think about it, but it might have been healthier for him in the end.'

'How do you mean?'

Tears welled up in her eyes as she began speaking.

'I mean, if he'd been a soldier, he might have been wounded, killed even, but maybe that would have been preferable to the years he'd had struggling to breathe and not being able to walk very far. I nursed him during the bad times, when he got a cold or a chest infection. It broke my heart to see someone who'd been such a strong able man, brought to his knees, literally sometimes, by fucking coal dust.'

Mary King obviously found it difficult to carry on speaking and bowed her head, sobbing quietly. Gibson couldn't think what to say, so he kept his mouth shut. He waited, but found her distress hard to take and had to fight the urge to get up and give her a hug. She recovered.

'Sorry about the language. I don't normally swear like that.'

'You've no need to apologise. I'm only sorry to

put you through this, but I need to have as much information as possible, you understand?'

She nodded. Gibson carried on.

'So what did he do, after he'd retired?'

'Not much, well he liked to bet a little bit on the horses, and sometimes he'd get the bus to the pub to meet up with Joe, an old friend of his, at the Pack Horse, up on Bolton Road. Then I think Joe moved away, had to go into a care home or something and he lost touch. I'm not even sure if Joe's still alive, but anyway, Dad didn't go to the pub that often anymore.'

'Did he have any arguments, fall out with anyone, disputes, rows with a neighbour, anything like that?'

'No, not that I know of. Look, I know my Dad, and he just wouldn't say anything like that without a good reason. He was worried, someone was going to do him harm.'

'I understand, but let's finish these questions. I assume you're the only child and that there are no other beneficiaries to anything he might leave, in a will, that sort of thing?'

Mary King laughed derisively.

'No, there are no other "beneficiaries" as you put it. Dad wasn't in a position to leave anything of value. Well, not money anyway. Some old pictures, the odd bit of furniture. The house was rented so...'

'Okay, I understand. Well that's about it for the

time being,' said Gibson starting to put his note-book away, 'but you must appreciate, that unless you can come up with a more compelling reason than you have so far, as to why we should inves-tigate your father's death, I'm afraid I can't really take this much further. I understand that you're upset and you have my deepest sympathy for your loss, but without more to go on, I'm afraid we can't justify spending any more time on this, I'm really sorry.'

Mary King stood up suddenly, arms straight by her side, tears welling up in her eyes again. Her face was taught, eyes blazing, Gibson blanched.

'Look here Mr, Sergeant Gibson, or whatever your bloody title is, I'm not prepared to accept that my Dad died a natural death. Now you go and find out what happened to him, or I'll take my case to the papers, the chief constable, my MP, to anyone who'll listen. So, please get off telling me how sorry you are, stick your sympathy, and get out there, find out what really happened.'

With that she fled out of the room in tears. Gibson heard her running up the stairs then she stopped and shouted down,

'See yourself out.' A door slammed upstairs, shaking the house. Gibson stayed seated for a minute, stunned.

'Bloody hell', he said out loud, then got up and left.

He sat in his car outside the house and reflected

on Mary King's outburst. Gibson laughed to himself and shook his head in admiration. *She certainly knows how to make a point, that's for sure. Now where did she say her Dad went for a drink, the Pack Horse? Good excuse to go for a half on my way home, all in the line of duty of course.*

Gibson went back to the station and managed to catch up on most of his paperwork. He was pretty well finished by five, by which time he felt ready for a beer. He drove towards Pendlebury and soon came to the pub he was looking for. Remarkably it was still called the Pack Horse, the brewery or whoever owned it now, had apparently resisted the growing trend to rename the pub, for the time being at any rate.

The pub's original grand façade, a mixture of grey stone with red brick inserts, looked faded and dilapidated in the miserable orange glow of the street lighting. He turned into the pub car park and stopped. The lights were off and the place looked deserted. *Maybe a bit too early for the evening drinkers?* He turned the car round and was just driving away, when he spotted a man in his rear mirror walking across the car park and into the pub.

Gibson turned his car around again and parked up. He got out and went through the heavy wooden doors and into a large cavernous room, with a bar running along the left hand side. It was empty. He stood there wondering where the man

23

had gone, when he heard a noise coming from behind a door in the corner. He went through it and found a smaller, well lit room, with a pool table, dart board, and five people variously sitting at the bar and playing pool.

It was like going back in time. Behind the bar, was a huge gold framed mirror on the wall, and peeling mauve paint on the walls. There were various faded old signs hanging on the wall, 'Guinness – think what toucan do', 'Mackeson milk stout' and 'I'd love a Babycham'.

The barmaid was sitting on a stool behind the bar, smoking and watching the men play pool. As Gibson walked over, she turned towards him, got off the stool and smiled. She was slightly overweight, had plenty of makeup on her pretty face, and wore a very low black dress, revealing an impressive cleavage. Gibson tried hard not to stare.

'Yes love?' she said in a pronounced local accent

'Just a half of bitter please.'

The barmaid tapped the ash from her cigarette into a huge red ashtray then left her cigarette balanced there while she pulled his beer.

'There you are sweetheart' she said putting the half pint of bitter on a beer mat in front of him.

He thanked her and paid. She picked her cigarette up, took a long drag, turned away, put her elbows on the bar and went back to watching the men playing pool.

'Excuse me , but could I ask you a few questions?'

She turned back to Gibson.

'Yes love, as long as they're not too personal,' then she looked him up and down and said 'mind you, good looking bloke like you, I might make an exception.'

Gibson smiled. It was hard not to like her cheeky reply, and he could see why she was a barmaid. Some people just had the personality.

'Did you know a man, a customer, called Billy Bowen?'

Two older men who had their backs to the bar turned round to look at Gibson.

'Old Billy,' she said 'yes, poor love, kicked the bucket recently I heard.'

'Yes I'm afraid he did. Did you know him well, I mean did you talk to him at all?'

'And who's asking?' she said, not unpleasantly.

'Well I'm a police officer, but this isn't really official, just checking a few things that's all. So, what did you know about him?'

'Used to come in fairly regular, Tuesdays mostly I think, met up with his pal Joe. But that was quite a while ago, he didn't come in that much lately, not since Joe moved away. Last time I saw him, he'd gone a bit miserable. Not like he used to be, no idea why. I know he had a few medical problems so maybe they were getting on top of him.'

'Bloody obsessed, thought there was some sort

of conspiracy agin him,' said one of the men listening at the bar.

'Lost his marbles if you ask me,' said the other one, then went back to sipping his pint.

Gibson turned his attention to the two men. 'What sort of conspiracy?' he asked.

'Well since his mate Joe died last year, he kept saying he was next, wouldn't say anymore. If you asked him why, he'd just clam up, barmy bugger.'

'Oh, I was told this Joe had moved to a nursing home. Is that where he died?'

'That's what we 'eard, moved to a care home or whatever they call 'em. Somewhere near to where his son lived. Eccles way I think'

'Did Billy have any other friends, or old workmates, anyone else that you know of?'

'Not that I'm aware of, what about you Fred?' said the man, turning to his drinking partner.

'Nope, just his old mate Joe. It was just after he jossed it that old Billy started goin' on about being next. Thinking about it though, he was right, wasn't he?' Both men laughed heartily.

Addressing the two men and the barmaid, Gibson asked.

'What was Joe's surname?'

'Martin,' said one of the men, 'I always remember 'cos he had two first names, Joe and Martin.'

'I don't suppose you know anyone who might be able to tell me where this care home is, that Joe moved to?'

'Sorry love', said the barmaid.'

'No idea,' said one man, the other shook his head.

'Like I said, somewhere Eccles way but I don't know any more than that,' said the other.

'Do you know where he lived before he moved then?'

'Ay,' said the man called Fred, 'he lived not far from here, Connor Street, number twenty four. Helped him home a couple of times, when he got a bit the worse for wear, if you know what I mean?'

Gibson wrote the address in his notebook.

'Connor Street. I think I know where it is, but can you give me directions anyway?'

'Turn right, carry on towards Manchester, for about quarter of a mile and it's on your right, can't miss it, newspaper shop on the corner.'

'Okay and thanks for your time,' said Gibson turning to the barmaid and finishing his drink.

'Anytime sweetheart,' she said, giving him a smile and a big wink.

He drove back along Bolton Road and found Connor Street without too much trouble. Holes in the tarmac exposed large patches of the original cobbles. Faded red brick terraced houses faced each other, with cars parked on either side of the narrow street making his passage tricky. He found number twenty four but was forced to park some distance further down the street.

He walked back and knocked on the door. It

was opened almost immediately by a pretty little girl with a dirty face, blond hair and pigtails. She was no more than seven or eight years old.

'Is your Mummy or Daddy in?' he asked and wondered at people who would let such a small child answer the door.

'Who is it Trace?' came a loud female voice from inside the house. The little girl ran back into the house leaving the door open, then a woman appeared cigarette in hand. She wore a tight yellow stretch tee shirt showing every contour of her body, tight jeans and dyed blond hair, going dark at the roots, no makeup.

'Whatever you're selling, we don't want one,' and she slammed the door firmly in his face.

Gibson gave his hard police knock, the door opened and the woman was ready to give him a mouthful. Then she saw the warrant card he was holding up. Her shoulders slumped.

'Okay what is it?' she asked in a resigned manner.

History there, thought Gibson.

'My name's Gibson, Detective Sergeant Gibson and I'm making enquiries about the previous occupant of this house.'

'Don't know how I can help. I don't know anything about the bloke who lived here before.'

'That's okay; I just wondered if you had a forwarding address, for sending mail on, that sort of thing.'

'Oh right, yes I think we did have something his son gave us, but I'm not sure if it got thrown away. I mean it's been a while since we moved in.'

'Could you have a look please?'

'Yeah, okay, just wait there, I think it might be with the rent book stuff.'

She went upstairs and came back down a few minutes later.

'Is this what you want?'

It was a piece of paper with the name Joseph Martin printed on it and the address of a care home in Eccles called Fairview Gardens.

'Perfect, thanks. I'll take this. I don't think you'll need it any more, Mr Martin died last year I'm afraid, but I can make you a copy if you want.'

'Nah, we never got any stuff for him anyway, so keep it. Can I go now, my hubby's back in a bit and if I haven't got his tea on the table there'll be ructions?'

'Right okay, well thanks and goodbye.'

'Yeah, bye,' she shut the door.

Gibson drove home wondering once again why he was pursuing this matter. He had plenty of other cases on the go, but something kept niggling away at the back of his mind. Perhaps it was the dead certainty of the daughter that something wasn't right about her father's death. Tomorrow, he'd pay a visit to Fairview Gardens and if that didn't turn up anything, he'd tell Mrs King he couldn't do any more unless something new came to light.

He put the matter of Billy Bowen to the back of his mind, turned the car radio on to catch the news and started to wonder what he'd be having for dinner. Thursday, so it could be steak and kidney pie, and the half of bitter had just put that extra edge on his appetite. He'd been married previously for a couple of years but it didn't take. Not her fault, he always said, it was the job, he told people if they asked, or if he could be bothered to tell them.

Now he was married to Jill. They'd met two years ago at a friend's dinner party, he'd been going through a rough patch at the time and nearly didn't go to the dinner, but at the last minute he decided to make the effort, try to get back to something like normal. They'd hit it off right away. As soon as he laid eyes on her he felt she was different. He didn't believe in all that 'love at first sight' stuff, but with Jill, it was as though they already knew each other. He instantly felt at ease and sensed she felt the same. She was slim, had auburn hair, an oval face, expressive brown eyes, and full generous lips.

She reminded him of an old fashioned film star - classical, if he had to choose one word to describe her. It wasn't long after they met that they moved in together. They married a year later and Gibson thought they were doing okay so far. She was a qualified pharmacist and had chosen to work in a city centre at a twenty four hour chemist. She hated normal routine and enjoyed shifts and the odd hours, and the odd characters she met there, she said. This fitted in quite well with Gibson's own unruly hours. She was a great cook, and he'd put pounds on since they moved in together, but what the hell, he thought, happy days.

*

The man sat on the sofa with a copy of the local paper and the Manchester Evening News. He read through each paper carefully. No mention of the death of Billy Bowen. Nothing, nor had there been since the third of February. He smiled to himself. He wondered if the police would ever catch on, he doubted it. He was safe, he would never be caught, he was far too clever, but then again, he would like some acknowledgment, some appreciation of why he'd had to kill. He'd think about it, maybe write to the police anonymously, tell them what it was all about, and still they wouldn't be able to catch me - I'm already dead. He laughed out loud and went into the kitchen to make himself a cup of coffee.

CHAPTER 4

'**M**orning Sherlock'

'Morning Sir' Gibson replied as DCI Watson entered his office.

'Any headway with the 'mystery' of Mr Bowen's death?' The DCI said the word 'mystery' in an exaggerated manner. Sarcastic bastard, thought Gibson.

'Not so far sir, I went to see Mrs King and she couldn't really offer me any more reasons than she already had, but she did tell me where I might be able to talk to someone else who knew him, mates that sort of thing so I went to the pub he used to go to.'

'And?'

'Not much, just that he'd told them a similar story, that he was next. Been saying it since his drinking pal died a year ago or so, bloke called Joseph Martin, friends since childhood apparently, but then Joe moved away to a care home near Eccles a while ago, where I'm told he died.'

'So what's your next move?'

'Well I got the address of the place he moved

to from the people who moved into Joe Martin's old house, so I thought I'd try to clear my desk of the more urgent stuff, call the care home then pop along there early this afternoon, confirm the details of this Joe Martin's death, then I can go back to Mrs King and tell her we've looked into everything we can and, well nothing, no suspicious circumstances etc., etc., and put the lid on it. What do you think?'

'Yes Gibson, might as well go, then at least we can get his sodding nuisance of a daughter off our backs. In fact I think I'll come along, I've got plenty on, but a trip out of the office and away from that bloody desk is just what I need.'

'Of course sir, you're more than welcome.' *What's the old git up to, he wants to make sure we ditch this investigation as soon as possible.*

'And on the way, we can make a bit of a diversion, go and have a quick look at Regent Park West where your mystery murder took place. Did I tell you I grew up not far from there Gibson?'

'Yes sir you did mention it.'

'Did I? Right okay, well let me know when you're ready to go.'

'Will do sir.'

It was nearly midday before Gibson had got up to date with his case files. He called the DCI and they drove to Pendlebury in Gibson's Saab. The DCI gave directions and soon they were turning off Bolton Road, and driving down Agecroft Road into the Irwell Valley. DCI Watson began a nostalgic commentary.

'That war memorial we just passed on the left Gibson, that was erected to the miners from round here who died in the First World War, colliers they called them then, no reserved occupation for that lot poor sods, and all these houses Gibson,' said Watson gesturing to the left as they drove further down the hill, 'are built on the fields I played on as a kid. Slow down, turn right here, this is Regent Park West.'

They drove slowly along a pot holed road with terraced houses on each side, the houses on the left finishing halfway down the street, the ones on the right continuing to the end of the road.

'Stop here Gibson, and look over there, you can still see Agecroft Colliery, all but finished as a working mine. They say it'll be demolished in the next couple of years.'

Gibson stopped the car and looked at the area Watson was pointing to. He could see some big concrete towers, some fields and what looked like industrial buildings, but it looked bleak and derelict to him. It was obvious that Watson could see a quite different picture in his mind's eye. The DCI carried on speaking.

'When I was a little kid, the original mine only occupied a smallish area on the far side, over there, and the rest of that land was made up of fields and Chapman's farm. Then eventually the mine expanded, took virtually all of the land, and the fields and even the farm got gobbled up in the process. Further over there were the woods where we used to go birds nesting, Oats's woods, which were actually the old grounds of Agecroft Hall. And would you believe Gibson, someone bought the Hall in the nineteen twenties, dismantled it and shipped it over to America and re-built it stone by stone in Richmond Virginia.'

Gibson said nothing, it was all very interesting but hardly had any bearing on his investigation, still it was useful to get a feel for the area he supposed. As if reading his mind Watson said.

'C'mon Gibson enough of this nostalgia crap, let's go and see this old peoples' home or whatever it is.'

They drove out of Regent Park West back up Agecroft Road up a steep hill that Watson said the locals used to call Smithy Brew. They made their way to Eccles and eventually arrived at the Fairview Care Home. The place looked deserted. They parked and entered through the double doors of the neat modern building and the first thing that Gibson noticed was the smell, or the lack of it.

He'd been in a few old people's homes in his time and the most depressing thing was the smell, musty and stale piss, but not in this place. There was a small unmanned reception desk with a front door type bell push screwed to the top. Gibson pressed it and heard the distant ding dong sound somewhere in the building. A small neat woman appeared as if from nowhere.

'Can I help you gentlemen?'

'Yes, said Gibson, 'I called earlier, Sergeant Gibson, and this is DCI Watson.'

'Ah yes, they said you wanted to ask some questions about a previous resident I understand.'

'Yes we do, is there anywhere we can talk in private?'

'Oh sorry, I've just got so much to do at the moment, I'm not thinking properly, please come in here. Would you like a cup of tea or anything?' She showed them into a small ante room. They both declined the offer of a drink and sat down.

'My name's Dorothy Green, I'm the care home manager, so how can I help you?'

Gibson looked at Watson who nodded for him to take the lead.

'Well it's just an informal enquiry at this stage, but it's about a Joseph Martin who we understand was a resident here and passed away last year?'

'Yes, that's correct. Poor Mr Martin, Joe, he passed away at the end of January, or was it February? My memory's not what it used to be. Have there been, er, developments?'

Watson looked at Gibson and raised his eyebrows, Gibson looked confused.

'Sorry, developments?'

'Well I always thought it was unsatisfactory, accidental death my left foot.'

'Sorry, I assumed he'd died in here, I mean….,'

Gibson immediately felt foolish and realised he should have checked to see what Joseph Martin had died of before coming out here, especially as he was accompanied by the DCI – shit again, I can't believe this! He had a name and address and it wouldn't have been that difficult. He looked at DCI Watson who was smiling his nasty smile. Watson took over.

'Er, Mrs Green was it? We're not from the local police so we're not familiar with what happened to Mr Martin. We're here informally, on a related matter but we're not looking directly into the circumstances of Mr Martin's death, so maybe you could tell us briefly what happened.'

'Oh I see, well he, Joe went out for his usual walk along the canal and fell in, according to the police. They said he died of shock and, what's that word…, hypothermia, said he must have slipped. I know it was freezing cold that day, but Joe was good on his pins and he wouldn't have been stupid enough to go near the edge. Truth is, he was an old man and it was easier for the police to put it down as an accident. They dismissed the idea of him being attacked or anything, and I know there was nothing stolen but still….' She trailed off.

Watson and Gibson sat there in silence letting the information sink in. A loud jangling noise suddenly started up.

'Oh dear, that's a patient alarm, urgent, I'll have

to go, sorry gentlemen, please call back if you find out any more.' And with that Mrs Green left.

'Well Gibson, what excuse do you have for not checking the cause of death? Made us look like a right pair of idiots.' Watson said as they drove away from the care home.

Trust him to be with me every time I make a cock up!

'Yes, sorry sir, I should have checked on how Martin had died, I mean it might not make any difference, probably a genuine accident despite what the lady says, but still, it just throws a bit more doubt into the pot.'

'Yes Gibson, on both counts, and you should have checked, you really must be more thorough, you're never going to get that promotion if you carry on like this.'

Gibson couldn't think of anything to say. The DCI continued.

'You see Gibson, you have to be methodical. Establish the facts then analyse, consider and evaluate. So, let's think about what we have, which is two deaths, about a year apart, one officially an accident and the other stated as natural causes by the doctor. The only link being that they were both friends, both miners who worked together, but they were both old men as well, so two old people died who knew each other and worked together. If we used that as a basis for investigation we'd be well and truly overwhelmed, so why should we take this any further Gibson?'

'I take it you're playing devil's advocate here sir?'

'I am indeed the devil incarnate some people would say, so convince me Detective Sergeant Gibson, why waste any more time on this?'

'Okay, well there's Mary King, who said her father knew he was next, and he did die.'

'Big deal, no evidence - and?'

'Well obviously the death of Joe Martin, which the lady in there says she doesn't accept was an accident, but okay,' Gibson said weakly, 'nothing else really, but having gone this far, I think we might as well look more closely into the cause of death of both men, after which we may be in a position to close the file or possibly take matters further.'

The DCI sighed an exaggerated sigh and shook his head from side to side. 'Well I'm not convinced Gibson. All we have now is yet another woman with suspicions, but again, absolutely no proof'

Gibson thought about the dressing down Mary King had given him, and his own instinct that maybe something wasn't quite right about these deaths.

'I really think I should do a bit more digging sir. I'll go and talk to both doctors who issued the respective death certs and go and have a chat to our colleagues in Eccles, see if they have any doubts about whether the canal death was an accident.'

'Hmm, sounds like you're chasing your bloody tail to me. Okay, but if you can't come up with any tangible evidence soon, that's it, understand Gibson?'

'Yes sir, I understand.'

'Okay then let me know how you go on and we'll take it from there.'

'Yes sir will do.'

Watson spent the journey back telling Gibson about his previous cases and how he'd cracked them. Gibson feigned interest, but having heard most of the stories before, found himself having to resist a yawn, covering up by having mild fits of coughing each time he felt a yawn coming on.

'You should get that chest seen to Gibson.'

'Yes sir.'

CHAPTER 5

The next morning Gibson wrote up the file on Billy Bowen, keeping opinion out and simply recording the facts. He started a separate sheet within the same file for Joseph Martin, so if there were developments in the Martin case he would be able to use the sheet to open a separate file. After concluding that he'd listed all the information correctly, he turned his attention to his other cases. He found that focussing on something else completely always had a beneficial effect on his view of a particular case when he returned to it.

He soon became absorbed by his other work and the next time he looked up at the clock it was lunchtime. He asked one of the office girls to get him a sandwich, deciding to work through his lunch hour. Having finished his other work, he picked up the Billy Bowen file, taking out the sheet on Joe Martin, then picked up the phone and dialled the division that looked after the Eccles area.

'Hello, D S Gibson here, Salford North, can I

speak with someone about an accidental death, one Joseph Martin, fell into a canal in Eccles Late January, early February last year?'

'Hold on sir, won't be a minute.' The girl came back on the line 'I'm putting you through to Detective Sergeant Pollitt, I believe he was involved in that incident.'

'Pollitt here.'

'Yes Sergeant Pollitt, DS Gibson here, Salford north, I'm calling to see if you can provide me with some details about the death of a Mr Joseph Martin. I understand he died in an accident last winter, apparently as a result of falling into a canal, I'm told you handled the case.'

'Yes I did, hold on I'll get the file.'

'Thanks.'

Pollitt came back on the phone. 'So why are you asking about this case now, nothing new come up has it? I hope it's not that daft old bat at the care home making a fuss again?'

Sounds like the "daft old bat" hit a nerve, wonder why?

'No, nothing like that, it's just that we're looking into the death of another man called Billy Bowen, an old friend of Joe Martin. They used to meet for a beer occasionally.'

There was a pause while Pollitt thought about what Gibson had said. 'Okay, but how would that link these two deaths, how did this Billy Bowen die?'

'A heart attack, natural causes the doctor said, and we're not linking the deaths as such, just that Joe Martin was a pal of Billy Bowen, and so we're just tidying up any possible loose ends really.' Gibson felt awkward and decided to tell half the truth to deflect any further difficult questions. 'Truth is, the daughter, Billy Bowen's daughter that is, she's putting us under a great deal of pressure to look further into her father's death so we're just going through the motions, looking at everything, you know how it is sometimes?'

'I'm not sure I do, all sounds a bit odd to me. You holding anything back?'

'No really Sergeant Pollitt,' said Gibson, involuntarily pulling a face as he lied 'there's nothing sinister going on, just casting around at the moment. So, can you give me some brief details of what happened to this Joe Martin?'

There was a heavy silence, then Pollitt spoke.

'As far as we were concerned it was pretty straightforward. The old man went for a walk by the canal, freezing cold day, slipped, banged his head, fell into the water, or slipped, fell into the water and banged his head, slight difference same result, and by the time he was found, he was all but dead. I think he managed to keep his head above water, the canal isn't that deep in places, but in the end he died from a combination of hypothermia and shock, according to the PM.'

'Oh, so there was a post mortem?'

'Yes, the woman who ran the old folks home where he lived wouldn't accept that he had slipped and my boss said he thought it safer if we had a PM.'

'Safer, you mean there was some doubt about how the accident happened?'

'No, like I said, we were sure enough about what happened and the PM didn't turn anything up to the contrary, so that's the way it went, okay?'

'Yes, okay, but I'd like to see a copy of the PM, can you send me a copy?'

'Why? D'you think we got it wrong or something, what exactly are you suggesting here Sergeant Gibson?'

'I'm not suggesting anything, just doing my job.'

'I'm not sure I like this, what exactly are you inferring?

'Sorry, I phrased that badly. I didn't mean to infer you hadn't done your job, I just need to double check, my boss is a stickler for detail and if I don't do a thorough job, then I'll get an almighty bollocking, okay?'

'Yeah okay,' Pollitt replied grudgingly, 'but I don't like this, where do I send the info to, Salford North you said?'

'Yes, thanks Sergeant Pollitt.'

'You're welcome I'm sure.'

'Oh just before you go, what date did Joe Martin die?'

Pollitt sighed, impatient with Gibson now and anxious to end the exchange. 'Right, let's see, it's here somewhere, February third, nineteen eighty nine, a Friday, okay, anything more you want know, 'cos I need to go and do some proper work?'

Gibson sat back in his chair and blew out a long breath. The same date as Billy Bowen's death, just one year earlier, bloody hell!

'You still there?' came the exasperated voice of Sergeant Pollitt.

'Sorry, yes, you sure about the date?'

'For fuck's sake Gibson, yes I'm sure about the date, why?'

Gibson thought Pollitt would erupt if he told him about the coincidence of dates so he replied as casually as he could and tried to keep the excitement out of his voice.

'Oh nothing, just wondered, that's all, thanks again for your time Sergeant Pollitt.'

'Yeah okay, anytime.' And with that the phone clattered down

Gibson put his own phone down gently and began to wonder.

He looked in the file, found the number he was looking for and called the care home.

'Is Mrs Green free please? Tell her it's Sergeant Gibson Greater Manchester Police CID, I'll hold thanks.'

'Dorothy Green here.'

'Yes Mrs Green, Sergeant Gibson we came to see

you yesterday.'

'Oh yes Sergeant, sorry I had to dash off like that.'

'No problem, but we didn't quite finish our conversation. You indicated that you didn't believe Joe's death was an accident, said he was good on his pins etc., was there anything else that made you doubtful?'

'No not really, nothing specific anyway.'

'Okay, well how was Joe before he died, I mean was he ill or anything, depressed, happy, was there any change from his normal demeanour?'

'No, not really, although thinking about it, I suppose he didn't seem quite as jolly as he did when he first arrived here.'

'Can you think of any reason why he wasn't as "jolly", as you put it?'

'Well, just after he came to us Joe became religious. I don't think he'd been a churchgoer previously, but he suddenly started going to mass on Sundays, sometimes during the week as well. I mentioned this to his son early on, when he visited, and he was a bit surprised. He said he knew his Dad had been brought up a Catholic, but he couldn't remember him ever going to church.

I told him I'd seen it before, you know as people get older and realise they're not going to live forever, they sometimes think harder about what happens when they pass on, but with Joe, there seemed to be something else going on as well.'

'Something else, what do you mean?'

'I don't know, but he had a visitor, a man, not long after he arrived here. I remember because it was the only other person who ever visited him, apart from his son that is. After that, he seemed a bit troubled, thoughtful, I don't know maybe it's just my imagination, although I do know he also went to confession, at least once.'

'How's that?'

'Well one of our part time ladies is a devout Catholic and she mentioned she'd seen Joe at confession one Saturday morning, said she hadn't realised he was a Catholic till then.'

'Interesting,' said Gibson but he wasn't sure it added anything.

'Do visitors have to sign in Mrs Green?'

'I'm sure he would have been asked to, do you want to hold, it won't take a jiff to check the visitor's book, hold on.'

Gibson held the phone tapped his teeth with his pen. After a few minutes Mrs Green was back on the line.

'I've found the entry in the register, but the signature is an unreadable scrawl and I can't decipher a name. I can tell you the date though, twelfth November nineteen eighty eight.'

'Okay, I don't suppose you can remember what the man looked like?'

'No, I never actually saw him and I'm not sure any of the staff would've taken much notice either, although I think I recall someone saying he was a foreigner, spoke with a funny accent, but maybe that was another visitor, sorry to be so vague.'

'No not at all, did you ask Joe who this visitor was?'

'I think I did at the time but it didn't seem important then, and from memory Joe wasn't very forthcoming.'

'Right, just one more question, did Joe ever mention an old pal of his called Billy Bowen?'

'The name rings a bell, but I can't be certain, I remember he did go to see an old friend of his he used to work with and who still lived in Pendlebury, but I don't know if it was this Billy Bowen. I remember arranging for a taxi as the bus connections weren't very good from here, Agecroft I think it was. I remember because I think it was the only time Joe forked out for a taxi.'

'Did he go to see this friend of his, before or after the visit from the man?'

'Let me think, after, or was it, yes definitely after.'

'Did he mention anything to you about the visit, afterwards?'

'No, never said a word.'

'Okay Mrs Green, you've been very helpful.'

'Anytime dear.'

'Oh, before you go, could you let me have Joe's

son's contact details, and a phone number if you have one?' A couple of minutes later, Mrs Green came back to the phone and gave him the information.

Gibson sat thinking for a while, then opened the Billy Bowen file and found the copy of the death certificate. It was signed by a Dr Ernest Stemp, St Mary's Medical Centre, Pendlebury. Gibson picked up the phone and dialled.

'This is Detective Sergeant Gibson from Greater Manchester Police CID, Can you put me through to Dr Ernest Stemp please?'

'I'm sorry Dr Stemp is with a patient at the moment, could you call back?'

Gibson called back ten minutes later and asked again.

'I'll just try his line and see if he's free.' There was a short silence then a voice answered.

'Dr Stemp speaking.'

Gibson introduced himself and asked him if he recalled the death of William Bowen.

'Yes, I certainly do, Billy was my patient for quite a few years so I knew him well, why do you ask?'

'Well his daughter has expressed some doubts about his death; she claims he was afraid that something was going to happen to him.'

'Yes I recall she mentioned that to me at the time, but I couldn't see anything untoward about his death, and it wasn't entirely unexpected you know, he was quite a sick man.'

'So I understand. Look, I hope you don't mind me asking this, but is it possible that his death wasn't from natural causes? Could it have been, well, enhanced in any way, but to make it look like natural causes?'

'Well, there are ways of making a death look natural when it's not, but there would have to be other circumstances, evidence of motive or something to suggest foul play, to justify a post mortem which might uncover such a thing. All we ordinary doctors can do is make a logical judgment based on what we see and what we know of the patient's condition prior to his death etc. and I certainly didn't see anything that could have justified a post mortem.

You see, Billy's condition was such that he could have dropped dead any minute, or lasted for years, there was no telling really.'

'Okay doctor, but just for the sake of argument, what are the possible ways you could think of that might be used in such circumstances to fake the cause of death?'

'Well, I'm not really happy to speculate, I mean there are obviously certain drugs that could be used, but really Sergeant Gibson I can't see how or why.'

'What about suffocation?'

'Yes, in theory it's a possibility, but not as easily done as you'd think, the pressure required suffocate a normal person, with a pillow for instance, like you see in films, would be such that you'd probably do some obvious physical damage, a broken nose, perhaps bruising, that sort of thing. And the person being suffocated would undoubtedly resist, causing other possible tell-tale signs. Admittedly with someone as poorly as Billy was, it's more feasible, but I think we're getting into the realms of near fantasy here detective and I have a waiting room full of live patients to attend to. So, please forgive me, but I have to go.'

'Yes sorry doctor Stemp, and thanks for your time.

CHAPTER 6

Gibson finished updating the Bowen file with the latest information and sat back. *Maybe I'm getting obsessed here, smothering people with pillows, seen too many detective films, but still, those dates, a bit weird to say the least.*

'Okay, try to look at this objectively.' He said out loud. Just then there was a knock on the door and DCI Watson walked in, he looked around.

'Talking to yourself Gibson?'

'Yes sir, helps me focus sometimes.'

Watson plonked himself down in the chair opposite Gibson. 'C'mon then, what've you got to tell me about Mr Bowen and his friend Joe martin, both murdered by some arch fiend maybe?'

'Yes sir, got him all locked up in the back, beat a confession out of him in no time.'

Watson smiled. 'Taking the piss now are we Gibson?'

'No sir, just my little joke.'

'Well jokes aside, do we have anything concrete?'

Gibson filled him in on all the new information, including his phone call with doctor Stemp.

'What do you think about the dates sir, big coincidence isn't it, both dying on the same date third February?'

'Could be Gibson, but so did Buddy Holly.'

'Sorry sir?'

'Buddy Holly, died with the Big Bopper and Ritchie Valens on the third of February nineteen fifty nine, you know, The Day the Music Died? Just making the point Gibson, what I'm saying is, don't get too hung up on them dying on the same date, maybe it adds up to something, but it's not evidence of anything sinister, not yet anyway. If there was something else then maybe, but....'

'No sir,' said Gibson finding it hard to understand his boss's lack of enthusiasm about this remarkable coincidence. He's trying to rile me, I won't rise to the bait. Change the subject.

'Tell me sir, how did you know what date Buddy Holly died?'

'Big fan, Gibson got every record he made, some of them in the old vinyl. Don't write 'em like that anymore, then of course there was Don McLean and American Pie.'

'I'd never have guessed sir.'

'Well Gibson, there's a lot you don't know about me. Now let's look at this situation again. We're spending a considerable amount of time on this, and so far all we've got is speculation at best. I just can't see how I can justify going forward without some evidence of foul play involved in either of these deaths.'

'Yes I understand sir but I have a suggestion or two, on how we might get some better information.'

'Go on Gibson, enlighten me.'

'Well, the first is a bit tricky, but worth a try. Are you a Catholic Sir?'

'Why do you ask?'

'I have a good reason, I need to ask someone with knowledge of the Catholic church.'

'Well as it happens I am, well was, I'm what they refer to as lapsed. I sort of grew out of it, but I was quite, well quite devout at one time you could say, so c'mon Gibson what do you want to know?'

Gibson tried to imagine the DCI as a devout religious person and struggled. 'Well sir, I think I should try to find out who the priest was who heard Joe's confession and see if he's willing to give me anything.'

'Hmm, I suppose you could try, but you realise he'll be bound by what's called, the inviolable secrecy of the confessional. That means that what's said in a confessional is sacrosanct. The priest can't say anything to anyone about what he's heard, regardless of what's been confessed.'

'You do know a lot about this sir.'

'I do Gibson, in my early youth I briefly entertained the idea of joining the priesthood.'

'Never, you - you're pulling my plonker – if

you'll pardon the expression sir.'

'No Gibson, all true, I told you there's a lot you don't know about your Detective Chief Inspector.'

'I don't have to refer to you as Your Holiness now, do I sir?'

'Careful Gibson, be very careful now.'

'Sorry sir, no offence meant, so anyway, getting back to this priest, you don't think there's any point in going to see him then, I mean, what if someone said they were going to murder someone, you mean he couldn't tell us, the police I mean?'

'Nope, he can't tell anyone.'

'Bloody hell, that's a bit rough, so no point in going to see him then?'

Watson got up and walked around the small office contemplating.

'Well maybe there is Gibson, maybe there is, you see, not that it releases the priest from his obligations, but now the penitent, this Joe Martin, is dead, he might be prepared to, as it were, give you a steer, for example, you might ask him if anything Martin said might have made him a target for anyone. Tell him in strict confidence that we have some suspicion that Joe Martin's death might not have been an accident and see what gives, worth a try anyway. '

'Yes, I see what you mean, thanks for that sir.'

'You're welcome Gibson, but I still think you're on a wild goose chase. You said you had two suggestions I think, so c'mon, what's the second one?'

'I think I should go and talk to the pathologist who carried out the post mortem on Joe Martin and see if he believes that there's any possibility that it wasn't an accident, see if he has any doubt at all about the cause of death.'

'Hmm, I suppose that's worth a shot, anything else?'

'Well, I intend to interview Joe Martin's son at some stage, see if he has anything relevant to tell us?'

'Okay, anything else that might convince me that this isn't all a complete waste of valuable police time and resources, God knows what the CC would think if he knew you were playing Sherlock Holmes instead of catching some real villains.'

'Well the way I see it, is that if someone did kill these two men, then it has to be as a result of something that happened in their past, payback for something they did to someone, punishment or revenge, the latter as you are well aware sir, being the most common motive for murder.

'Yes I am well aware of that Gibson, don't try to teach your grannie to suck eggs.'

'No sir.'

'So, any ideas on what it could be, this 'thing in their past' I mean?'

'No, but it seems highly unlikely that the two of them have been up to no good in the last few years, due to their age and physical condition etc.

I suppose they could have been involved in some way in the miners' strike. That was about five years ago, so they wouldn't have been involved directly, they'd have both been too old, and well retired by then, but still, they might have been involved in some way, organising, that sort of thing? I don't know if you remember sir, but I seem to recall that it was particularly nasty at Agecroft Colliery.'

'Yes I do Gibson, only too well. It was a huge drain on police resources at the time and some of my colleagues were injured by those strikers, vicious bastards they could be I can tell you. And it wasn't just us they were fighting, they fell out with each other.

Jesus, you've never seen anything like it, beating the shit out of each other if they got half a chance, I'd 've left 'em to it if it'd been up to me. Some of the miners voted to strike and some were against, so they had these picket lines and we had to try to police them. Lots of miners and families who'd been friends for years fell out big time, in fact, one of the miners at Agecroft was convicted of killing his best mate during the dispute.'

'Yes I remember that now you mention it.'

'Anyway, going back to your train of thought Gibson, I suppose it could be worth finding out if either of these two men were involved in any way in the strike, even on the side-lines.'

'Yes sir I agree, but maybe there could be other

events in the past that caused someone to be so pissed with these two, that they killed the pair of them, so I'll see what I can dig up.'

Watson sighed, then made to go towards the door.

'You'd better come up with something soon, otherwise.'

'Yes, sir, I'm sure I will. I'll also go and see the daughter again and ask her if she can recall any pertinent events in her father's past life, including the strike, and I'll do the same with this Joe Martin's son, see where that gets me.'

'Okay Gibson, you've got two more days. If you don't make any progress by then, you drop it, understood?'

'Understood sir.'

CHAPTER 7

It had been a long day and Gibson was looking forward to getting home. He'd called ahead to make sure Jill was still going out for a drink with her friends. United were playing that night and he was looking forward to a night on his own by the TV *Just the thing to clear my mind, a few beers, a takeout curry and United on the telly, what more could a hard working copper want?*

He opened the front door, and shouted up the stairs.

'I'm home…, Jill…,' No answer, she did say she might go out straight from work. He shouted again, louder, nothing.

There was a note on the hall table.

"Opened the envelope as I could see it was from the doctor. Your blood results say you need a new liver so I'll get some from the butchers on my way home tomorrow, do you want pigs or lambs?
Love Jill xx x x
PS just kidding, your bloods are perfect.
PPS Don't wait up I'll be late."

He smiled, picked up the envelope and read the letter from his GP, all readings within normal range it said. *So it's not the end of my drinking career thank God.* He went into the kitchen, put on the kettle for a cup of tea, suddenly realising how thirsty he was. Plenty of time before the match starts, *now where did I put that Indian take away menu?* He found the menu and phoned his order through. Delivery would be in an hour, they said, as they were very busy because of the football. Gibson made his tea in the cup, poured in some milk and went to sit down in the living room. He sat sipping his tea and his thoughts wandered back to his sister.

He got up, took his tea upstairs, found the box of old photographs he'd stored in the cupboard over the wardrobe, sat on the bed and went through them. There were lots of prints showing him and his sister when they were small children, then some on family holidays in Devon. He found one of him and his father when they'd gone out walking together in Derbyshire, just him and his father, and Jenny their black Labrador. Gibson guessed he would have been aged about ten at the time. His father looked so happy.

He found another shot of himself studying, homework by the looks of it, he thought. It was a candid shot, taken without him being aware. It showed him typically stroking his chin in deep concentration, something he did without noticing whenever he had to think hard. He laughed remembering, his first wife used to mimic him doing it when they were first married. That was when things were okay, before it all fell apart. Ah well, he rummaged some more and found the photo he was looking for, then put the rest of them back in the box.

The photo was of him and his sister Sophie at a friend's wedding, the last one taken of them both together he reckoned. Their father had died as well by then. Everyone said he'd died of a broken heart, never having got over the death of their mother. Gibson knew that to be true, having heard his father crying alone in his bedroom on a number of occasions after she'd passed away. Apart from his obvious grief in the immediate aftermath of their mother's death, their father never confided his emotions to him or Sophie about her passing, probably thought it would be too upsetting for them, but they were grieving as well. It was a shame we didn't all share the grief, thought Gibson as he looked again at the picture of him with his sister.

He decided to take the photo to the station and keep it in his desk drawer. Just then the doorbell chimed. There's the take away, great, I could eat a horse, course I might well be doing just that shortly. And he laughed at his own joke as he went downstairs to open the door.

The next morning Gibson made his way to St Bartholomew's church in Eccles, it was a Tuesday so he thought the priest shouldn't be too busy. He'd established that the parish priest was called Father Madden, but hadn't called ahead as he didn't want to warn the priest what he wanted to see him about. He'd also taken the DCI's advice and checked that it wasn't a saint's day or anything, so he was hopeful he could get an interview without too much trouble.

Parking outside the church gates, he got out and saw that the presbytery was directly across the road from the church. He walked up the path and knocked on the big shiny black painted door using the heavy brass knocker. He was about to knock again when the door was opened by a small elderly woman wearing a white pinafore over a black dress. She had permed silver hair, fine features and a fierce look about her. The smell of baking instantly transported Gibson back to his childhood.

'Yes, can I help you?' she asked impatiently in a brisk but unmistakable Irish accent.

'Yes, my name's Detective Sergeant Gibson, Greater Manchester Police CID, is Father Madden available please?'

The little lady looked him up and down, then said sternly

'Have you an appointment?'

'No I'm afraid not, is that a problem?'

'I'll see if the Father is free to see you young man, but you should make an appointment, he's a busy man you know, wait there.'

Young man - that put me in my place.

She came back, opened the door wider and asked him to follow her. She walked briskly along a small badly lit corridor and knocked on a heavy oak door.

'Come in,' said a gravelly voice, another Irish accent?

Gibson went in and the priest got up from his desk and held out his hand.

'Detective Sergeant Gibson is it, now what can I do for our protectors and guardians on this fine day?'

Gibson was thrown a little by the greeting. Was he taking the mickey or was the flowery language just the way he spoke. He decided the latter; the smile on the priest's face was genuine enough, the handshake firm and strong. Father Madden looked more like an old fashioned prize fighter than a priest he thought. The priest was a little smaller than Gibson, stocky with grey grizzled hair, big features and hooded eyes with big bushy eyebrows.

'Please sit down won't you?' The priest pulled over another chair for Gibson and sat down again. He was dressed in a priest's traditional black cassock and white clerical collar.

Can I offer you anything Sergeant, cup of tea?'

'No thanks, you're very kind, but I had a coffee at the station before I left.'

Father Madden leaned back and gestured for Gibson to speak.

'Well Father, I'm here about one of your parishioners, a man called Joseph Martin, he er, passed away last year, February.'

'Ah yes, Joe Martin, very sad, so how can I help you?'

'I understand he only started going to church again a short time before his death.'

'Yes, that's correct, he hadn't regularly attended church for many years.'

Gibson wondered how to frame the next question. 'I understand he also came to confession.'

'Yes, that's correct also.'

'Was it you who heard his confessions Father?'

The priest frowned. 'Well now you're getting into a very tricky area Sergeant, and, with all due respect to your office, I'm not sure I can carry on with this conversation. You'd better tell me what it is you want.'

'Okay Father, cards on the table. We have some doubt that Joe's death was an accident, although no hard evidence so far, and though we have our suspicions, we're having a bit of a problem trying to find a motive, for anyone wanting to kill him that is.'

'And...?'

'Well we wondered if anything he told you, in

or out of confession, could possibly involve something that might cause someone to want to punish him for something he'd done, in the past.'

The priest held his hand up in a gesture of stop there. 'I don't know how familiar you are with the Catholic Church Sergeant, but we have something called the inviolability of the confessional. Do you know what this means?'

'I do Father, but...'

'But nothing Sergeant, this conversation is over.'

Gibson tried a different tack. 'Look I understand, and I wouldn't for one moment expect you to reveal anything that Joe told you in your confessional, but if Joe had done something in the past, something that might have caused someone to take revenge, then it might mean that another man, an old friend of Joe's, was also murdered, so all I'm looking for is some indication, I mean anything at all that could tell us we might be on the right track, that's all.'

The priest closed his eyes and sat very still. Gibson sat quietly, waiting for what seemed an age. The priest's eyes eventually opened and he spoke.

'I'm sorry, but can't give you the answers you want.'

Gibson nodded his head in acceptance and understanding and made to get up from the chair, but then the priest said. 'What I can give you Sergeant Gibson, is my blessing and a little advice.

65

Rely on your instinct, a very useful asset in your profession I should think. Now it's been very nice meeting you Sergeant, do you think you could find your own way out?'

'Yes of course and thanks for your time Father.'

'My pleasure Sergeant, goodbye and God bless you.'

Gibson sat in his car outside the rectory and replayed the conversation in his mind. I think I'll take that as a yes.

Father Patrick Aloysius Madden leaned back in his chair, closed his eyes, pinched the bridge of his nose between his finger and thumb and sat for a while, deep in thought. He got up went to the door, opened it and shouted.

'Mary, I'll have that cup of tea now please?' He'd been about to have his morning tea when Gibson had turned up.

A voice came back from the area of the kitchen. 'I'll be along presently Father.'

He went back to his seat and resumed his contemplation.

Poor old Joe, he did a wicked thing and suffered for it for the remaining days of his life, and then in turn, he became the target of revenge himself, does it ever stop Lord? He reached for the bible on his desk, turned to Romans 12.19 and read out loud to himself.

'Avenge not yourselves, but rather give place unto wrath: for it is written, Vengeance is mine; I will repay, saith the Lord, Amen.'

CHAPTER 8

G ibson went back to headquarters and added details of his interview with the priest to the Bowen file, then called the number Mrs Green had given him for Joe Martin's son. He didn't really expect an answer assuming the son worked, and planned to call again that evening to arrange an interview, but the phone was answered on the third ring.

It turned out that Frank Martin worked as a porter at Manchester Airport and was working late shifts that week, so they arranged to meet at Martin's house at eleven the next morning. Frank Martin lived in a smart semi on a new housing estate in Monton, just a few miles from the Fairview Gardens nursing home. Gibson checked the house number and parked his car. As he got out, he took note of the neat and tidy front garden. The day looked promising, though still quite cold. A clear blue sky and the early daffodils in the Martin's garden promised spring. *Course it could snow this afternoon.*

The door was opened before Gibson could knock. Frank Martin also looked tidy, shirt and tie. He was well groomed and had an open friendly face.

'Sergeant Gibson is it?'

'Detective Sergeant Gibson if you want the full title. Mr Frank Martin I presume?'

'Yes it is, please come in.'

'I was just admiring your garden.'

'Yeah, not me, the wife, she's got green fingers. Please, come in here and sit down. Would you like a cup of tea, coffee, or anything?'

'You're very kind but no thanks.'

Gibson followed him into the living room. Once they were both seated Gibson took out his notebook and pen.

'You said this was about my father, his death presumably, have you found out something new?'

'Not exactly Mr Martin, we're just following up a line of enquiry to see if it leads anywhere. A friend and old workmate of your father's died recently and it's thrown up some questions that's all, probably come to nothing really, but I just need to ask you some details, about your father's past, that sort of thing.'

'Is it Billy Bowen you're talking about, the other death?'

'Yes it is.'

'I heard he'd passed away, hadn't seen him for years. I used to call him Uncle Billy when I was a kid, he was always in our house, the two of them were thick as thieves. He had a daughter, Mary, we used to play together as kids, haven't seen her for years either. Sorry, I do gab on a bit, please ask away I'm happy to help if I can. What would you like to know?'

'Well we know that your father and Billy Bowen worked together down the mine, Agecroft Colliery, and they lived in the same street for most of their lives. Can you recall any incident that might have put them in conflict with someone, some row, or incident, a big fall out with anyone at all?'

Frank Martin looked perplexed.

'No I can't think of any particular thing like that, I mean there were squabbles, life was hard in those days, miners were a tough lot, and they liked a drink, so there was plenty of instances of fights, that sort of thing, but – serious stuff, not really, why?'

'No particular reason, as I say, it's just a tidying up exercise really. These days we have to be very thorough, hence these questions, which are probably irrelevant, but need to be asked.'

Frank Martin frowned and stroked his chin.

'Okay, carry on then.'

'Right, so any disputes at work that stand out in your memory, anyone blame your Dad or Billy for anything, any accidents they were involved in. It was a dangerous occupation so there must have some incidents...'

'I'm still not sure what you're getting at, but, well there was the big one, in fifty eight.'

'Big what?'

'The accident, you must remember, went worldwide, the news and all that? '

'I'm afraid I was only four years old then, so it wouldn't have registered, so tell me what happened.'

'Well there was a terrible accident, some bloke in charge made a mistake and I think at least one man died and a lot of others were badly injured. They said there was some misunderstanding and that the men at the top thought the miners down below had already left the mine, so they began blasting and sent a load of rubble down on to the poor sods below, I'd never seen my Dad cry before that, but I remember him being inconsolable that day. I was fourteen at the time and I didn't know how to help. I just couldn't comprehend what had happened. Took Dad a long time to get over it though.'

'Were he or Billy Bowen directly involved?'

'Not that I know of, no I'm pretty sure they weren't, at least Dad wasn't, I can't be absolutely sure about Billy, but I think my Dad would have said if he had been.'

'What about the miners' strike?'

'What about it?'

'Was your father involved in that?'

'No, he was well out of it by then. He used to shout at the telly whenever Scargill came on though, never trusted him, said he was in it for his own glory, the miners were just cannon fodder to him, he said.'

'So he wasn't a militant then, didn't believe in the strike?'

'I don't think you'd call him a militant. He wanted some action to stop the pits closing but he said they were going the wrong way about it, playing into the government's hands, said the government had planned it that way, Thatcher wanted Scargill to bring 'em out on strike, so she could break the miners hold on the UK, payback for when they held the conservative government to ransom, in seventy four I think it was, when we had that three day week.'

'Yes even I remember that, I was just turned twenty at the time and not interested in politics, but when the lights went out, it made an impact.'

'Yeah I think everyone remembers that. But then a friend of Dad's was murdered during the strike and that really did it for him.'

A friend of your Dad's you say?'

'Yes, he was an old pal of Dad's well they were both old pals, both miners and neighbours of ours. One killed the other, well supposedly. You must have heard about it, it was in all the papers?'

'Yes, I did, but I can't remember the details,' Gibson said, 'tell me all about it.'

'Well these two blokes, been best friends all their lives, part of my Dad's gang when they were kids.'

'Gang, what gang?'

'My Dad used to tell me about their gang, they'd all grown up together, all born in the same street – same place I was born, Regent Park West. Anyway these two, er, Geoff his name was, yes Geoff Brown, and the other bloke, hang on a minute it'll come to me, Freddie, yes Freddie… Exan, well one was for the strike and the other one was against it. You can't imagine it now, but the split in the miners was fierce. The ones that crossed the picket lines were called scabs and worse. People stopped talking to each other and not just the blokes themselves, but their families, people who'd been friends for years but it didn't matter.

There were arguments and fights, it was worse than anything I'd ever seen, or seen since, except maybe for all that shit in Northern Ireland. Anyway this Geoff Brown, he was found dead in his house. His wife came back from work and found him, mutilated they said, and Freddie was standing over the body. There was a knife on the floor. Police said it looked like he'd been tortured he was so badly injured. So they pinned it on Freddie, who always said he was innocent, and my Dad says he was too. He said they might have had a big fallout with each other but there was no way that Freddie killed Geoff. Even the wife, Geoff's wife, said she didn't believe Freddie had done it either, but he went down for it anyway.'

'This was in what, eighty four?'

'Eighty five, I'm pretty sure it was eighty five. I remember the strike ended not long after Geoff was killed, so it was eighty five.'

'Okay, now tell me more about this gang you father talked about.'

'Right, the gang, well, there were five of them all told. Dad said they used to call themselves the five musketeers when they were kids.'

'Five, I thought there were only three musketeers?'

'Yeah there were, but I think they just liked the name, musketeers, and there were five of them so that was that. They were all similar ages and all ended up as miners, which was natural enough in those days. Dad said they did everything together when they were kids.'

'Can you remember who the five were?'

'Let's see, there was my Dad, Billy,' Frank Martin stopped 'you sure you want to know all this?'

'Yes, it's very interesting, please go on.'

'Okay but I'm getting a bit thirsty, all this talking, so if you don't mind I'm going to have a cup of tea, do you want one?'

Gibson broke his normal rule and said he would love a cup.

'Milk no sugar please, thanks.'

While he waited for Frank to make the tea he

flipped through his notebook and thought about what he learnt so far, quite a lot really. He wasn't sure where this was leading but it was all very interesting. Frank came back, they both sipped their tea and Frank resumed.

'Okay, where were we?'

'The gang, and who was in it.'

'Right, well like I said there was my Dad, Billy Bowen, the man who was killed, Geoff Brown, that's three.'

'Sorry, is that Jeff with a J or Geoff with a G?'

'With a G I think.'

'Okay carry on please.'

'Then there was the bloke that was supposed to have killed Geoff, Freddie, Freddie Exan, that's four, then there was… nope, can't remember the last one sorry.'

'Not at all, I think you did well.'

'Got it, d'Artagnan, that was it.'

Gibson looked up from his note taking, quizzical look on his face.

'Sorry, just my daft sense of humour.'

Gibson forced a simile.

'Jones it was, Barry Jones, how about that for a memory?'

'Excellent, well done,' Gibson looked at his watch, 'now tell me a bit more about your Dad, if you have time.'

'Okay but this is taking longer than I thought,' me too, thought Gibson. 'I'm going to have to go in a bit.'

'Right, well just tell me a bit more about your father and then I'll contact you again if I need any more information, okay?'

'Okay, well we got on really well. I used to love him telling me stories about the old days. I was born in forty four, just before the war ended, so I was too young to remember anything about it, but Dad, he could tell you some stories. He used to tell me about food rationing and how there was a sort of black market in stuff, ciggies, meat and all that sort of stuff, even booze. A couple of the blokes who lived on the street were Dockers, worked at Salford Docks, and my Dad said they'd bring all sorts of stuff back that they'd knocked off. He said, but that all stopped when they brought in containers. Anyway, in those days, people who lived on the street were so poor, they used to go and steal vegetables, spuds mostly, at night, from Harry Chapman's farm which was just across the fields.

Some of them used to take old prams and fill them with spuds he said, they used to nick coal as well, from the slag heaps. I thought we were quite poor when I was a kid, but Dad said we didn't know what being poor really meant. People don't starve any more, he said, but they did then. They didn't have holidays or anything like that, but, and I thought this was hilarious, they used to move houses, swap with each other, flit.'

'Flit?'

'Yeah, as in moonlight flit. The miners and their families would change houses with each other, even in the same street, when the fancy took them. Dad said they did it sometimes just to have a change of scene, but, sometimes to avoid people they owed money to.

'That's a new one on me I must admit,' said Gibson, and waited, feeling that Frank Martin enjoyed telling stories himself, and sure enough he carried on talking.

'Yeah, then there was the time they got bombed in the war. He said the Germans were really after Trafford Park, but they also went after railway lines 'cos they thought they were supply lines for the Park, so one night they bombed the railway line at the back of the houses in Regent Park West. One of the bombs, maybe more, missed the line and destroyed a house, wiped out nearly a whole family. My Dad says that he and Mam should have been the ones killed, but they'd done a flit the day before and had moved from the house that was bombed. I think he always felt guilty about that, relieved that they'd moved, but guilty 'cos the other family got bombed.'

'What a sad story, do you know what year that was by any chance?' 'No 'fraid not, Frank Martin looked at his watch. Listen, I'm sorry but I'm going to have to go now or I'll be late for work.'

'Yes, no problem and thanks for your time, it

helps me build a picture of your Dad and his past.'

Frank Martin got up and went to get his jacket from the hall. He opened the front door to let Gibson out.

'You never really said what this is all about, do you think there was more to my Dad's death, was it not an accident like they said?'

'No, I mean yes, Gibson lied, 'We really don't have any reason to suppose it was anything but an accident at this stage, but these days we have to look at everything in great detail, you know how it is, but if anything different turns up I'll let you know. Thanks again for your time, oh, and the tea, oh, and if you don't mind I'll call you again if I need any more information, is that okay?'

Frank Martin didn't look entirely convinced but said. 'Yeah no problem, actually, I enjoyed it, talking about my Dad and all that.'

They bid each other goodbye and Gibson drove back to the station. The weather had changed back to winter with driving sleet and rain slowing the traffic down

.

CHAPTER 9

Gibson had great difficulty making arrangements to see the pathologist who'd carried out the post mortem on Joe Martin, but eventually managed to get an appointment for eight thirty on Wednesday morning. The pathologist's over protective secretary had made it plain that she considered a request from the police to see Dr Forbes-Mackay as a bit of an affront.

'It's all there in his report if you want details Sergeant Gibson.' she told him.

Gibson held his tongue.

'Yes I appreciate that, but I'm afraid I will need to meet with Dr Forbes-Mackay to ask him some further questions, so please tell me when I can see him.'

'Well he's a very busy man you know.'

'Yes Miss...?'

'Miss Welch.'

'Well Miss Welch, I appreciate he's a busy man, but so am I.'

'Hmm, well I've got an eight thirty Wednesday

morning, but he won't be able to spare you much time so you'd better be brief.'

'Okay I'll take that.'

'You know where to come?'

'Yes thanks.'

'Well don't be late.'

And with that she cut the line, which was fortunate as Gibson had just boiled over and was about to tell her what a disrespectful, cheeky, ignorant cow she was.

He took some deep breaths, calmed down and went back to the file on his desk. He decided it was now appropriate to start a separate file for Joseph Martin so he took out the relevant papers from the Bowen file and put them in the new file, marked it up, then consulted his notes from his interview with Frank Martin and wrote up the new Joe Martin file.

He decided not to update DCI Watson until he'd been to see Dr Forbes-Mackay and in the meantime he would go and have another chat with Mary King. He made the call and she agreed to see him later that afternoon. That gave him time to clear up some issues on other cases he was working on.

He cleared his desk just in time to have a quick cup of tea before heading out to see Mrs King.

'Hello again,' said Gibson when she answered the door.

'Yes Sergeant, come in, I hope this visit means

you're taking me seriously now,' she said, showing him into the dining room.

They sat at the dining table and Gibson took out his notebook with the details of his recent interview with Frank Martin.

'Well?'

'Well first off, thanks for seeing me again, and I do take you seriously, it's just that.... look, I won't take up too much of your time, I just wanted to go over a few things.'

'Okay Sergeant, but you must have some reason for coming back.'

'Well yes, sort of, nothing definite, but since we last spoke I've been doing some digging and I've also been to see Joe Martin's son Frank, I believe you played together as kids.'

'Frank, yes, I haven't seen him since, well since we left Regent Park West. I'm not sure who left first, I think it was me, so what has he got to do with anything?'

'Well you were right, Joe Martin did go into a home, but he died last year.'

'Oh, how?'

'Accident, fell into the canal, in the winter, slipped apparently.'

'Poor bugger, so, go on, what has this got to do with my Dad's death?'

'Nothing really, it's just that they, he and your Dad, were friends, so I thought I'd go and see if his son could tell me anything, background, that sort of stuff, so anyway, I had a long chat with Frank. They spoke a lot it seemed, his father told him lots of stories about the war, working down the mine, all the things that went on in Regent Park West. It was quite interesting, they were obviously quite close....'

Gibson saw Mary King's expression change into a hard stare and he realised the implication of what he'd just said.

'I didn't mean to imply that you and your father weren't close, I....'

She waived away his feeble attempt at an apology. 'Was he able to throw any light on why someone might want to harm my Dad, or his Dad for that matter?'

'No he wasn't, not directly, but he did give me information that I need to follow up, to see if it reveals anything that might possibly be a motive for harming either of them.'

'So you now believe someone killed my Dad?'

'No, I'm sorry, all we can do at this stage is to establish if there was anything unusual about your Dad's death or the death of Joe Martin, to see if we should take things further.'

'But you wouldn't be spending all this time on something if you didn't believe you had some justification.'

'Well let's not jump to any conclusions. I need to gather more general background information, try to see if there could be any reasons why someone would want to harm either of them.'

'Such as?'

'Well, for instance, Frank Martin told me about the mine accident in fifty eight, when a man died due to some misunderstanding. Something about thinking the miners had left the shaft when they hadn't. Do you remember the incident, and was your Dad involved in any way?'

'Yes I remember it, Dad wasn't involved at all, but he was upset, everyone in the street was. I think the man who died was from Farnworth, a good few miles from Agecroft, so not really a local man, but the mining community was very tight knit and when one was hurt they all felt it, that is until the strike.'

'Yes that was my next question, was your father actively involved in the strike in any way, I realise he would have been retired by then, but did he help out in any way, organising, that sort of thing?'

'No, he supported the strike in principle, but he was already quite poorly by then and was in no condition to do anything really. Mam was ill as well then as well so he was a bit busy you could say.'

'Erm, when did your mother...'

She finished the question for him. 'Die? Five years ago, just after the strike finished, lung cancer, they all smoked like chimneys, people from that era, I seem to remember all the parents smoking when I was a kid, fags hanging out of their mouths, even when they were cooking, talking, anything really.'

'I'm sorry.'

'Yeah, me too.' Mary King looked down at her lap.

Gibson gave her a minute to compose herself. 'Okay, what about the man who was convicted of killing his friend during the strike?'

'You mean Freddie, Freddie Exan, no one believed he'd done it. Him and the man he was accused of killing, they'd been friends forever.'

'If everyone thought he was innocent, then who did they think killed him?'

'Good question, there was no one else that had any reason. The man who was killed, murdered, Geoff, everyone liked him, he was a bit of a scallywag, always selling bent gear that sort of thing, nothing serious, but everyone liked him. My Dad and him had been friends since they were kids as well, but Freddie and Geoff had fallen out about the strike apparently, and that was what the police said was the reason, that, and his wife finding Freddie standing there next to Geoff's body, well I think he was still alive actually.'

'Still alive?'

'Yes, well that's what I was told. I'm sure you can find out properly yourself, but apparently Geoff's wife came home and when she went in she found Freddie standing over Geoff, and he he'd been stabbed, multiple stab wounds apparently, blood everywhere they said. Brenda, his wife, said Freddie was just standing there, looking shocked. The police found a knife on the floor. Freddie said he found Geoff like that, but they didn't believe him and he went to jail. Funny though, even though she saw what she saw, she didn't believe Freddie had done it, but....'

Gibson made a note and ticked off one of the items on his list.

'Right okay, thanks for that, now, different subject, do you know anything about the house that was bombed in the war, I mean I appreciate you're not old enough to have been around then, but did your Dad tell you stories about it at all?'

'No, we all knew that's why there was a gap in the houses, and what happened, but my Dad never talked to me about it. He didn't really talk to me much about the past, I mean about the time before I was born, least not until he got older and then he would reminisce sometimes. Tell me all sorts of things they got up to as kids. I encouraged him to talk about the past, I thought it would help with his dementia and it did, I like to think so anyway...'

'Did he ever tell you about the gang he belonged to as a kid?'

'Yes, a little bit,' she laughed, 'the five musketeers they called themselves. I think they always considered themselves part of that gang, even much later in life.'

'All right', said Gibson closing his notebook and putting his pen in his inside pocket, 'that's all for now, thanks for your time. I'll let you know if there are any developments.'

Mary King looked disappointed.

'Are you any closer to finding out what really happened to my Dad?'

'No is the honest answer, but we have some interesting information, we just need to see if it has any bearing on your Dad's death. I know you won't like me saying this, but I still think you have to be prepared to accept that he did just died of natural causes, but I promise I'll do everything I can to find out if it was otherwise.'

'You just do that Sergeant, because I won't be fobbed off. I know you lot think I'm just some neurotic woman who's upset about losing her Dad, and I am, upset I mean, not neurotic. I know there's more to his death, call it intuition, call it anything you like, but I want the truth and I won't settle for anything less.'

'Yes, Mrs King, I've got the message, loud and clear.' He got up and she showed him to the door. Gibson sympathised with Mary King and although she made him feel uncomfortable, he couldn't help admiring her resolve. He drove back to police headquarters thinking about all the new information he'd got in his last two interviews, broadly consistent, so that helped.

He decided to avoid trying to come to any con-clusions until he'd written up the file. He found that writing up the file, then having a break, then reading the file from start to finish in one go, al-ways adjusted his perspective on a case. He also wanted to avoid coming to any interim conclu-sions until he'd met with the pathologist. But that was tomorrow and Jill was taking him out to the Italian tonight, it was her birthday treat, might get lucky, who knows, he thought, and smiled.

'Buona sera Signore, Signora Geebson.'

'Buona sera Franco, how are you?' Gibson re-plied.

'Bene bene Signore Geebson, please follow me, I 'ave a lovely table for you and your beautiful wife, please...' Franco gestured for them to follow him and led them over to a corner table, they sat down. Franco lit the candle and replaced the glass cover. The restaurant was simple and very traditional, dark wood furniture, dimly lit tables, red and white gingham table cloths, Italian music playing in the background, Gibson loved the place.

'And now a little aperitif Signora Gibson?'

'I'll have a Punt e Mes with ice please Franco.'

'And Signor?'

'I'll have a Peroni please,' said Gibson.

'Perfect,' said Franco, then handed menus to each of them and bustled off to get their drinks. Gibson smiled at Jill. She leaned across to Gibson and spoke in a low voice.

'Don't tell Franco it's my birthday or I'll kill you, got it? I'd rather die than have everyone singing happy birthday to me.'

'Got it, any idea what you're going to order?'

'Who cares about food, it's worth coming here just to be called beautiful.' She replied.

Gibson laughed and Jill made a pretend hurt expression.

'You're supposed to say – that's because you are so beautiful my dear, you know, like they do in the movies?' Then she laughed.

'Okay,' said Gibson, and assuming a serious camp expression, he leaned over the table and took her hand in his.

'Shall I compare thee to a summer's day? Thou art more lovely and more temperate …'
The waiter arrived and put their beers on the table.

'One Punt e Mes and one Peroni. I will return momentarily for your order, cin cin.' Then Franco spun on his heels and disappeared again.

'Carry on,' said Jill, laughing. Gibson took his hand away from hers, and turned to address his glass of Peroni.

'Shall I compare thee to a glass of British bitter, Or art thou art a more lovely, superior glass of Italian lager..'

'Bugger off Gibson,' she said, still laughing, 'and let's order, I'm starving.'

Just then, Franco arrived back at the table with a flourish. 'Okay, so what are we eating tonight?'

CHAPTER 10

He was ten minutes late for his meeting with Dr Forbes-Mackay, the one person Gibson didn't want to be late for. If his secretary was such a pain, then what would he be like? He drove around the hospital car park, getting more and more frustrated and eventually found a parking space. He'd forgotten just how busy hospitals were at this time of the day. After wandering through an interminable labyrinth of corridors and asking directions twice, he eventually found the right door and knocked on the opaque glass panel displaying the doctor's name.

'Enter' said a loud Scottish voice.

Gibson entered a small cluttered office and sitting behind a chair writing up some notes was the missing link, possibly the yeti, certainly not your average human being. The man was huge, no massive, thought Gibson. The man stood up and extended his hand. Gibson took it, and his own hand disappeared in the huge paw which was surprisingly soft. The grizzled bearded being spoke.

'You'll be Sergeant Gibson I take it?'

'Yes Doctor, sorry I'm late.' The doctor sat back down, his chair audibly creaking.

'No worry son, pull up a chair. Gibson dragged a chair across the small room to sit opposite the doctor.

'Gibson, now that can be a Scottish or an English name.'

'Yes, I believe my father's grandfather was Scottish, a crofter by all accounts.'

'Ay well there we are, almost family. Now, what did you want to know about...,' he found a file on his desk and consulted it, 'about this Joseph Martin?'

'Well, we're investigating a related death and there might be, and I stress, might, be some suspicious circumstances and we wondered how certain you were that Joe Martin's death was an accident.'

'Hmm, well that's not easy to say in the circumstances. In the absence of any evidence to the contrary, it would seem to be an accident, but I suppose it is possible his death could have been otherwise. Mr Martin died of shock and hypothermia due to immersion in extremely cold water and the fall preceding it, of that there is no doubt, but what caused him to fall into the water is the question I suppose.'

'Were there any injuries?'

'Yes there was bruising to the body as you'd expect, and a cerebral contusion which could have occurred by him striking his head on the edge of the canal bank as he fell, or caused by a blow with a blunt instrument, it's impossible to say, especially in the absence of anything found at the site that could have been used to deliver a blow to match the injury. But in any event, it wouldn't have been necessary to knock the old man on the head to cause his death, just pushing him into that freezing cold water would have done it, providing he wasn't rescued and pulled out within a few minutes, and I mean a very few minutes. People don't realise just how quickly you can die of hypothermia. In very cold water, your blood pressure increases dramatically and you usually suffer cardiac arrest within three minutes or so.'

'That quickly?'

'Aye, never worry about drowning in freezing water, the hypothermia will get you first, every time.'

'So Doctor, off the record, what would your guess be, accident or foul play?'

The doctor laughed heartily and the room seemed to shake.

'Now you're the detective son, not me, but if I were to make a guess, off the record mind you, and just between us two Scotsmen,' he smiled conspiratorially, 'I'd be relying more on his general condition immediately prior to the event, how likely he was to have lost his footing in such a way that he fell into the canal? I see from the notes of the ambulance men who pulled him out, that he was a little distance from the bank, perhaps not as near as you might expect if he'd just slipped, I don't know.'

'And how good was he on his legs? It was a very cold day and the banks would probably have been icy. All I can say is, in the absence of any evidence to the contrary,' Gibson remembered the exact same words used by Dr Stemp, 'it was an accident, but it is possible he was pushed, or knocked on the head and pushed, but I couldn't say from the results of the post mortem. All I can tell you, is what he died of, not if a third party put him in the circumstances that caused his death.'

'Okay Doctor Forbes-Mackay, I've taken up enough of your valuable time, thanks very much'

Gibson got up to go. The doctor got out of his chair, loomed over Gibson and extended his hand once again. They shook.

'No problem Sergeant, anytime. Just one thought though. If someone was looking for an opportunity to kill someone without it looking like murder, those circumstances were ideal, if a little opportunistic.'

'How do you mean?'

'Well, if you knew when the old man took a regular walk along the canal, then along comes the freezing cold weather, it creates an ideal opportunity wouldn't you say?'

'Yes Doctor, I would say, thanks.'

'No worries son, Goodbye and good luck Sergeant Gibson.'

Gibson got lost trying to find his way back to where he'd parked his car. All the corridors looked the same. Eventually he had to ask a passing nurse. *Good job she doesn't know I'm a detective he thought, can't even detect where I left my own car.* He drove back to headquarters in the tail end of the morning rush hour and felt pity for people who worked regular hours and had to endure driving every day in traffic like that. He arrived at the miserable grey stone police headquarters building, parked and went in. On his way to his office, he bumped into his boss DCI Watson.

'Morning sir, would you have time to see me in about an hour, I'd like to bring you up to date with the Billy Bowen and Joe Martin situation, nothing exciting yet but if you have a few moments?'

'Yes, okay Gibson, I can spare you about fifteen minutes maximum,' Watson looked at his watch. 'My office in about an hour, let's say eleven, okay?'

Yes sir, see you then.'

Gibson went to his office, wrote up the details of his interview with the pathologist, then went and got a coffee, went back to his office, put his feet up on his desk and read the Billy Bowen and Joe Martin files from start to finish. Satisfied he now had a comprehensive impression of all the relevant information, he gathered up the files and went to see the DCI.

He knocked and entered his boss's office. Watson was on the phone.

'Take a seat Gibson I won't be a tick.'

Watson listened, nodding and making the occasional 'hmm,' noise and 'yes I see sir, absolutely, will do,' then ended the call.

'Okay Gibson what've you got for me, I could do with something more stimulating than being told about roster changes and being given a bollocking for allowing too much overtime.'

Gibson told Watson all about his interviews with the various parties; often referring to the file to make sure had had the right details and dates etc. The DCI listened intently in silence.

'So what are your conclusions Gibson, so far I mean?'

'Well in terms of reasons why someone might want to kill either of these two men, historically I suppose there are a number of events that might fit. The pit accident in fifty eight where one man died, the miners' strike in eighty four five, the murder of Geoff Brown during the miners' strike, ostensibly by his pal Freddie Exan, but if he was innocent of the murder, as a number of people seem to think, including the victim's wife, then obviously someone else killed Brown which adds a complication. Then there was the miner's wife and children killed when the German planes bombed that house in nineteen forty two. Joe Martin told his son it would have been their family who'd have died if they hadn't swapped houses with the ones who were killed in the bombing, so did someone think he, Joe Martin, was to blame?'

'Okay Gibson, quite a few situations which might give rise to someone wanting to take revenge, but so long after the event, particularly that last example, the bombing of the miner's house in forty two, I mean do people really harbour resentment for that length of time?' Watson said, more by way of thinking out loud than asking a direct question, but nevertheless Gibson replied.

'Yes I've been thinking about that too, and I agree it's a long time to bear a grudge, but people sometimes do. Jill was telling me her mum's sister, her auntie Sandra, she hadn't spoken to Jill's mum for over twenty years, because of some fall out over nothing. A forgotten birthday I think she said it was. Words were exchanged and that was that. Then they bumped into each other in Manchester a couple of weeks ago, went for a coffee and made up. Twenty years wasted. So yes people do harbour grudges for a long time.'

Watson looked at Gibson.

'Your wife's auntie Sandra – you're suggesting we base our assumptions on your wife's Auntie Sandra? Tell me Gibson, did she kill anyone for forgetting her birthday?'

Sarcastic bastard. 'No sir I don't believe she did, all I was doing was giving you an example of human behaviour, I know that's not in the same league as this, but it's just by way of an illustration of how people can bear a grudge for a long time, that's all. I agree that normally people don't do anything about grudges, when the heat's gone out of a situation as it were, but maybe if there's an event in their lives that acts as a trigger, then maybe they decide to settle old scores, right wrongs as they perceive it.'

'What sort of event Gibson?'

'Oh I don't know, maybe they realise they're getting on and only have so much time left to do something. Maybe the bloke convicted of Brown's murder, this Freddie Exan, maybe he's just got out of jail and he's carried on where he left off as it were? That's a bit too pat I realise, but...'

'Well we can check on that one can't we, but what other reasons can you give me for justifying carrying on with this case Gibson?'

'Well, there's the big hint dropped by the priest about Joe Martin, and then the comments from the two doctors who issued the death certificates for Bowen and Martin. Both said that it was possible that the respective deaths could have been other than natural causes or accident, and finally, the coincidence of them both dying on the same date, but just one year apart.'

'Yes Gibson, intriguing if nothing else.'

They both sat in silence for a while, Watson contemplating all that Gibson had told him.

'Any suggestions on what to do next sir?'

'Yes, find out if, whatshisname, the person who went down for the murder of his pal, Freddie somebody was it?'

'Freddie Exan.'

'Yes, go and see him, in jail if he's still there or if not, the prison authorities will know where he is if he's been let out on parole, let's see what he has to say.'

'Okay, and?'

'Try to trace any other members of this so called gang, see what's happened to them if you can.'

'Well I think there's only one other member not accounted for actually,' said Gibson.

'Oh, okay well go and find out where he is then. That's probably enough to be going on with, in addition to your other workload, but keep me up to date with anything you find on this. I have to say I still think it's all a complete waste of time Gibson, nevertheless, I'll give you the benefit of the doubt for the time being, but not for much longer, not without something a bit more concrete than the ranting of some hysterical daughter and a couple of coincidences.'

'Yes sir'

Gibson went back to his office, quietly fuming at the DC's attempt to make him feel silly about his wife's auntie Sandra example of grudge bearing, *I'll show him grudge bearing all right and he'll be on the end of it this time.* Gibson had calmed down by the time he reached his office and sat down to consider the situation. Try to be objective he told himself. It was no good, his gut told him there was something to this and it wasn't down to coincidence. All the DCI was interested in was facts and results, *but surely detective work is a combination of facts and instinct. Then again, maybe I've let myself become too personally involved, am I being swayed by my sympathy for Mary King? No bollocks, I'm right and I'll prove it to that miserable curmudgeonly old bastard.*

He consulted the files and made a list of the 'gang'

'Let's start with Billy Bowen,' he said out loud to himself, and he wrote the names down as a list.

Billy Bowen – died 3rd Feb 1990

Joe Martin – died 3rd Feb 1989

Geoff Brown – murdered 1985

Freddie Exan – convicted of GB's murder and in jail

Barry Jones - whereabouts unknown?

He looked for Frank Martin's telephone number and dialled.

'Oh hello, is that Frank Martin, Sergeant Gibson here, glad I caught you in. Regarding our conversation the other day, I wonder, would you know the whereabouts of one of your father's friends, I mean one of the gang we discussed, Barry Jones?'

'No, I don't think so. I left Regent Park West so

many years ago. I'm not even sure he still lived there when I left.'

'Can you think and anyone that might know, anyone who might have kept in touch with him?'

'No not really. I mean he'll be getting on now, if he's still alive, I mean my Dad was sixty eight when he died last year and that's old for a miner.'

'Oh well, not to worry Mr Martin, I don't suppose you can think of anyone else who might know where he is can you?'

Frank Martin was silent for a moment, thinking, then spoke. 'Sorry, no, can't think of anyone, it's been such a long time since I spoke to anyone from that neck of the woods, I've lost touch completely, sorry I can't help, but if I remember anyone who might know I'll get in touch.'

'Yes please do and thanks for your time.'

'No problem, bye Sergeant Gibson.'

Gibson bid Frank Martin goodbye, then had an idea. *I need to go and interview Freddie Exan anyway, and maybe Barry Jones visited him while he's been inside, so he might know where he is - two birds with one stone. I just need to find out which of her majesty's establishments you're staying in Freddie.*

Gibson checked all the data systems and eventually found the details of the court case and conviction of Frederick Joseph Exan. He was tried on the fourth of March, nineteen eighty five, found guilty of manslaughter and sentenced to twelve years in prison. In sentencing Freddie Exan, the judge said that "he was minded to impose a relatively long sentence as Mr Exan had shown no remorse for his crime, and indeed had never admitted his guilt, and that gave him no choice but to impose a harsher sentence than he might have done otherwise."

So even with time off for good behaviour, it was unlikely that Freddie would be out of prison yet. Better find out where he's banged up and go to see him. Gibson checked the records again and found that Freddie Exan was to serve his sentence at Altcourse Prison in Liverpool. Could have been worse, could have stuck him in one down south, thought Gibson. He picked up the phone to make arrangements to go and see Mr Exan.

'Hello yes this is Detective Sergeant Gibson, Greater Manchester Police CID. I need to arrange an interview with one of your inmates can you put me through to whoever I need to speak to please?'

Gibson got through to the liaison officer in charge of visits, who introduced himself as Officer Blake. Gibson explained the situation. He was kept on hold while he went away to check. Officer Blake came back on the phone.

'You're a bit late Sergeant, he's gone.'

'How do you mean – gone?'

'As in, not here anymore mate, gone, let out in, let's see, yes, let out on appeal in nineteen eighty eight, says here.'

'I thought he was serving twelve years?'

'Dunno mate, don't have anything to do with that side of things, just arrange visits of inmates and that, maybe you could ask the Prison Governor's office, they'd probably know more.'

'Can you put me through?'

'I'll try mate but don't hold your breath, the phone system here's crap.'

Gibson held for quite a while and was just about to put the phone down when a voice came on the line.

'Governor's office, Patricia Denton speaking, can I help you?

Gibson introduced himself and explained the situation.

'Give me a minute and I'll try to find the details.' She sounded efficient.

Gibson held again and eventually she came back on the line.

'Yes Frederick Joseph Exan, originally serving twelve years for murder, but released on appeal after admitting to the crime and expressing remorse etc, etc.'

'When?'

'Let's see, here it is, served two years one month, released April nineteen eighty seven.'

'Any idea where he went to live?'

'No we don't have that sort of information here, but the parole board will probably have those details. I think they monitor prisoners who've been let out early, well in theory anyway, not sure how well it works, an awful lot of them seem to come back.'

He thanked her and hung up. *Damn! That throws a spanner in the works, so he was out when Billy Bowen and Joe Martin were killed. All the more reason to interview the man now.*

Gibson made several calls in an attempt to find out where Freddie Exan was now living. While he waited for a call back from the parole board he carried on with his other work, but he found it hard to concentrate and kept thinking about what motive Freddie might have for killing his old pals Billy and Joe. Based on what he knew, Gibson found it hard to think of any reason why Freddie might kill either man, but he needed to talk him anyway to find out more about the killing of Geoff Brown.

After all, he thought, if the killings were all linked, then Geoff Brown would have been the first, and if Freddie didn't do it, then the real killer got clean away, free to kill again. One problem in linking the deaths, thought Gibson, was that Brown's death was so brutal, whereas the latest two, if they were murders, and if they were committed by the same person, were nothing if not subtle. *Would a killer change his MO so drastically?*

The phone rang and Gibson answered. It was the parole board calling back with the information he'd requested. Freddie had gone to live with his sister in Huddersfield, a Mrs Watkiss, but Freddie Exan had recently breached the conditions of his early release, and so they couldn't say where he was at the present time. They agreed to provide Gibson with contact details of the sister and he wrote it down. He then called the telephone number and after a few rings it was answered by a young child.

'Hello,'

'Hello is your mummy or Daddy there?'

'No,' came the short answer, then silence.

Gibson was just about to ask if anyone else was there when the child said.

'Gran's here,' then in a voice that nearly deafened Gibson, the girl shouted.

'Gran..., someone on the phone.' Gibson held the phone from his ear to recover. A new voice came on the line.

'Hello, who is it?'

Gibson introduced himself, established that he was speaking to Freddie Exan's sister, and explained that he needed to come and talk to Freddie.

'Join the queue Sergeant.'

'Yes I thought you might say something like that, the parole board said that your brother had failed to report in and had breached the terms of his release. Do you have any idea where he might be?'

'What do you want with him?'

'I just want to talk to him about what happened, you know the original offence, the killing of Geoff Brown, get his side of the story, that sort of thing. I'm not from the parole board or anything.'

'Why, why do you want to know after all this time, about the killing?'

'Well two of Freddie's old friends died recently so we're looking into matters in general and your brother may be able to help, provide some information, that sort of thing.'

'Who were they?'

'A Mr Joseph Martin and a Mr William Bowen.'

'How did they die?'

'Officially, an accident and heart attack, respectively.'

'Officially, what exactly does that mean?

'It means that the official cause of these deaths is as I've described, but we just need to check on a few things, that's all and Freddie may be able to help us.'

'You're not trying to pin these deaths on him are you?'

'No Mrs Watkiss, not at all, it's just that, well it's difficult to say anything at this stage, but it might be in Freddie's best interests to cooperate with us.'

There was silence at the other end of the line, Gibson continued. 'Look Mrs Watkiss, there's two ways we can do this, the hard way where we issue an arrest on site bulletin, in which case we'll find him and arrest him and I'll get my interview, but then Freddie will be in serious trouble, maybe go back to jail. Or, you can get him to meet me voluntarily and we can keep matters less formal. At the moment, all he's done is committed a breach of his parole conditions, so not too serious, but if he doesn't cooperate with me on this, then it will be worse for him, do you understand?'

'He didn't do it you know, never laid a hand on Geoff, they were really good friends, had been since they were born practically. If it doesn't sound too soppy, they loved each other – and I don't mean, you know, not like that.'

'Yes I heard he claimed he was innocent at the first trial, but then he relented and in eighty seven, changed his mind and admitted he'd done it.'

'He only admitted to it to get out of that place, but now it's driving him mad. He's innocent, but the only way he could get out of prison was to go to appeal, admit he was guilty and show remorse. So, the only way you can get out of jail is to admit to a crime you didn't commit -doesn't that strike you as a bit upside down Sergeant?'

'I suppose if you put it that way, it does seem a bit ironic.'

'So would it help him if you talked to him, I mean could what you're investigating clear him, prove it wasn't him that killed Geoff?'

Gibson hesitated; they were entering dangerous territory here.

'I'll be straight with you Mrs Watkiss, I couldn't promise that as an outcome. It is possible that our investigations might, and I stress might, just throw some new light on events then, and what's happened since, but until we make more progress I just can't say.'

'If you talk to him you'll have to tell the parole board and they'll pull him in.'

'Yes I would have to report any meeting I had with him, but being blunt Mrs Watkiss, he's going to be caught sooner or later, and if all he's done is miss reporting in when he should have done, then I don't think they'll be too hard on him. I would be prepared to say that he co-operated with us in a police investigation and that wouldn't do him any harm. Incidentally, why didn't he report in as he should have done?'

'Oh I think he's just fed up of being treated like a criminal. Listen I'll try to get hold of him and see what he says. Call me back tomorrow morning after ten and I'll let you know what he decides.'

Okay Mrs Watkiss, but tell him he'd better agree, or there will be trouble.'

The next day Gibson called and Mrs Watkiss said that Freddie had agreed to meet with him at her house. She said he would talk to Gibson but asked if, after they'd spoken, if he would then go to the local police station to help him explain why he hadn't checked in recently, sort of help him out a bit on that score.

Gibson considered it, then thought, what harm could it do?

'Okay, I don't mind doing that. I've got your address so what about later today, say two?'

'He'll be here Sergeant Gibson.'

The drive over the Pennines was uneventful. The M62 motorway was relatively quiet and the weather benign, the sun trying its best to peek through the clouds. Gibson turned off the motorway towards the market town of Huddersfield, eventually finding his way to the address he'd been given. The door was opened by a woman he assumed to be Mrs Watkiss. She greeted Gibson then turned and bellowed up the stairs that Gibson had arrived and that Freddie should come down. Gibson thought idly that he now knew who the phone answering child had inherited her vocal chords from.

Freddie wasn't what Gibson had expected. He was clean shaven, thinning red hair, painfully thin, tall, about six foot, wearing jeans and a green sweater. He looked as if a strong puff of wind could blow him away; perhaps he'd lost weight in Jail Gibson thought. Sadness was etched on Freddie Exan's face, the face of a lifelong victim. Gibson introduced himself and they shook hands. Surprisingly firm handshake thought Gibson. They sat down opposite each other at the dining room table.

'Sally, my sister,' he nodded in the direction of the door she'd just left through, 'she told me about Billy and Joe being dead. Sorry to hear that, they were good blokes, but I haven't seen 'em for years so why do you want to talk to me? Not trying to say I killed them as well are you?'

'No I'm not, but, look, let's just go through some questions and see where we get to, okay?'

'Yeah I suppose so.'

'First off, I'm told that you were a member of a gang, the gang you all belonged to as kids, when you were in Regent Park West?'

'Yeah, it wasn't anything, you know, not a proper gang, not to begin with, we just knocked around together, the others were a bit older than me but they let me join in. We were just some lads who all lived near to each other, that's all.'

'What do you mean, not to begin with?'

'Well there were times when you needed to be in a gang, we had some trouble with gangs from Dutchy Road now and then.' Gibson raised his eyebrows in question.

'Dutchy Road, Salford, they were hard lads, still are, and sometimes they'd come around our area looking for trouble, or girls, or both. It was the start of the Teddy Boy era and you could get in big trouble if you weren't careful. They used bike chains, cutthroat razors, knives, the lot.'

'Did you have any really bad fights with these lads, I mean was anyone ever seriously hurt?'

'No not that I know of, lots of cuts and bruises, but nothing really serious, but there were some bad ones on Irlams o'th Heights and I remember one bloke was killed in a fight, but we never had it that bad where we were.'

'I see, and you all remained friends into adulthood, the members of your gang?'

'Yeah, I suppose we did.'

'And there were five of you?'

'Yes, five all told.'

'I have a list of names here, could you confirm the names are correct?'

'Okay.' Gibson read out all the four names.

'Yourself of course, Billy Bowen, Joe Martin, Geoff Brown and Barry Jones.'

'Yeah, those are all the right names.'

'Did any of the others come to see you in prison?'

'No. I didn't want to see anyone. I think they might have tried, but I told 'em, the prison people, I told 'em I didn't want any visitors, except my sister and her husband.'

'Okay. Would you know where Barry Jones lives these days?'

'No, Barry left the mine and moved away years ago, got married to some girl in Wales from memory, but I don't know where, hang on, Pwllheli I think it was, yeah, he'd been there on holiday, Butlins Holiday Camp. Met this local Welsh bird and got her pregnant, silly git, he was too old for all that stuff. I've no idea if he's still there, not heard of him for years.'

Gibson finished his notes on that subject and flipped a page.

'Okay, now let's talk about the murder of your friend Geoff Brown. What happened that day?'

Freddie Exan breathed in deeply, sighed and began telling a story that he'd obviously told many times before..

'Okay, well we were supposed to meet at the pub for a pint at lunchtime that day. We'd both been miners, underground like, but by then we'd moved up and we worked in the colliery offices, arranging the shifts that sort of thing. Anyway, we both had some holiday leave left so we decided to go fishing, but the weather forecast was bad, so we ditched that idea and decided we'd each catch up on stuff at home in the morning, then meet for a couple of pints at dinnertime, only Geoff didn't turn up.'

Gibson nodded making notes as Freddie spoke.

'I had a couple of games of darts with the fellers in the pub, then when it got to chucking out time I thought I'd go and see why Geoff hadn't turned up.'

'What time was that?'

'About four, they closed for a few hours then. Anyway I decided to walk. It was raining and I could have caught the bus, but I was a bit the worse for drink, I needed the fresh air. It would have taken me about half an hour to get to Regent Park West. I went to knock on Geoff's door but noticed it was open. That wasn't unusual in those days. I went in and shouted but there was no answer, so I went into the back room and there was Geoff, slumped on the settee, in just his vest and underpants, blood all over the place, it was horrible, still gives me nightmares.'

'Was he still alive?'

'I didn't think so to begin with, but he was, just about. I stood there not able to move for a bit, couldn't even speak, my throat wouldn't work, then I walked over to him and he mumbled a bit, maybe he was trying to tell me something, who'd done it to him, I don't know. I put my head down so I could hear what he was saying but no more sound came out, I think he died then. I looked down and there was a knife on the floor. I don't know why, in fact I don't even remember doing it, but I must have picked it up. Anyway, the next thing I know, someone's screaming behind me. It was his wife Brenda, she must have come in just a minute or so after me. I still just stood there but Brenda ran out of the room. I found out later that she went to a neighbour's house, one that had a phone and they called the police and an ambulance. After that everything was a blur. The next thing I remember is being sat in a room with someone reading me my rights and then being arrested.'

Gibson finished writing up his notes then re-read them.

'Can you recall what he mumbled, I mean anything at all, what did it sound like, was it a name or part of a name?'

'I don't know what he said or was trying to say, I don't even know if it was a word, might have been just a noise he made, look the point is I didn't do it. I know what it looked like but I didn't do it?'

'Okay, any idea who did then, anyone have a grudge against him?'

'Yeah, me, I had a big bust up with him about the strike. We came near to blows in the pub a few nights before, but we'd made up the next day. Trouble was everyone saw us have the fight, but no one saw us make up, so it looked bad.'

'What about anyone else, was there anyone else that might have a grudge, might want to harm him?'

'No, not that I can think of, Geoff could be a bit of a pillock at times, can't we all, but he was a good bloke and I can't think of anyone who would have wanted to kill him.'

Gibson looked at his notes again, then asked.

'Why did you eventually admit to killing him?'

'It was either that or stay in jail for another ten years, but now I'm out I'm not sure which is worse, being in there and telling the truth, or telling a lie and being out, with people thinking I killed my best friend.'

He looked Gibson in the eye when he said the last sentence and Gibson thought he knew the truth when he heard it.

'Okay, let's leave that for the moment. Now, can you tell me, have you been back to Regent Park West since you got out of jail?'

'Are you joking? No I haven't.

'Okay, well can you tell me where you were on the third of February this year?'

'Yes why?'

The speed of his reply stopped Gibson in his tracks. *Impressive, to have such instantaneous recall.....*

'Would you like to tell me where then?'

Freddie looked awkward.

'It's a bit, you know, a bit personal.'

'Well it could be important Freddie. Whatever it is I won't be shocked, I'm used to people having, I don't know, things they don't like admitting to, things they don't like people knowing, embarrassing things...'

'No it's not embarrassing, not really, just that, well I was in church, in Huddersfield, St Anthony's. Not all day, but for a couple of hours at least, in the afternoon.

'And how do you know you were in church on that particular date?'

'Because I've been to church every year on that date since Geoff died, well the chapel when I was in jail, but anyway, it's a sort of vigil I think you'd call it.'

Gibson was stunned.

'You mean Geoff Brown was killed on the third of February?'

'Yeah, the third of February nineteen eighty five.'

CHAPTER 11

On the journey back along the motorway from Yorkshire over the Pennines and into Lancashire, the weather gradually got worse. Gone were the fluffy clouds and sunshine of earlier in the day. Now, rain beat down on the windscreen making visibility so bad at times that the traffic slowed to a crawl. Gibson had to use all his concentration to avoid having an accident but kept being distracted; thinking about what he'd just been told. He scolded himself for not checking the date of Geoff Brown's death. He'd read the trial transcript and missed that vital piece of information entirely.

At least now he knew they were dealing with three murders. *Two people killed on the third of February might have been a coincidence, but three, never. Wait till I tell DCI Watson.* Horrific as it was, Gibson had to admit to himself he was excited. It wasn't often a juicy case like this fell into your lap, especially involving a serial killer. Adrenalin coursed through his veins as he relished the prospect of the chase. He knew he would never dare to say that to anyone, but as a detective he knew that these sort of cases that only come your way once in a lifetime. His colleagues would never admit it either, but they would be green with envy.

He was pleased, no relieved, that he hadn't given up on the investigation, even though it had seemed a bit thin at times and he'd had precious little encouragement from the DCI. *Imagine if I'd missed it then someone else eventually linked all the deaths together, what a fool I'd look, but crack a case like this and it could mean promotion – and a reputation, and redemption for the mess I made of the Thornton case.* He felt physically sick when he remembered and tried to avoid thinking about it these days. His instinct on that occasion was right, but he allowed himself to be talked into letting the man go. His colleagues persuaded him that Henry Foster was highly unlikely to be the abductor and said there was no real evidence linking him to the missing child. Well so much for evidence.

That was two years ago now, and he still wasn't over it and knew he never really would be. He'd nearly packed the job in altogether, but his counsellor convinced him that that would be very bad for him in the long run. He took some time off work and then he was offered a transfer to Swinton, near to where he lived. He was reluctant at the time but now he was glad he'd taken up the offer, if he hadn't he wouldn't have met Jill.

So this time, no one's going to tell me I'm wrong, I just know I'm on to something. He felt himself getting carried away and tried to calm down. He spoke out loud to himself.

'C'mon Gibson take it easy, there's a fair way to go yet before the plaudits arrive - plenty of time to ....'

Before he could complete the sentence, a lorry swerved out of the nearside lane directly in front of him. He braked hard resisting the instinct to move right into the next lane to avoid colliding with the rear of the lorry. It was spilt second stuff, the rear of the lorry loomed, but traffic on the right sped past at speed, blocking any escape. He missed a collision with the lorry, but only just, his heart raced as he fought the dual emotions of boiling anger and blessed relief. He hit the horn and kept it pressed down in an angry but futile gesture, the drama was over. He took his hand off the horn and breathed out, dropped back and put plenty of space between his car and the lorry, the lorry driver obviously oblivious of how near he had come to bringing Gibson's now promising career, and life, to an untimely end. Gibson re-laxed and laughed at himself, realising that it was his fault really, and how hubris had made him lose concentration and very nearly, his life.

The next day Gibson was in the office early to update his file notes and prepare a summary statement for approval by DCI Watson. Gibson was certain that in view of what he'd learnt from Freddie Exan, the DCI would want to brief the brass on the possibility, no distinct probability of the existence of a serial killer operating in their jurisdiction. Shortly after nine thirty the DCI walked into CID headquarters. Gibson saw him arrive and met him in the corridor.

'Can I have a word sir, its urgent?'

The DCI looked harassed, 'must it be now Gibson?'

'Yes sir I think it must be now.'

Watson sighed in resignation. 'Okay Gibson but not before I get my coffee, sounds like I might need it.'

They went into the DCI's office and he called down for someone to bring them two cups of coffee, then gestured for Gibson to sit down. There was a knock on the door and a girl brought the coffee in.

'Just down there thanks,' said the DCI. The girl left. He picked up his coffee, took a sip, closed his eyes in appreciation, then opened them and said.

'C'mon then Gibson, let's have it, what's so urgent it can't wait?'

Gibson handed him a two sheet summary. The DCI read without comment until he got to the last few paragraphs of the second page then he straightedge up in his chair and looked at Gibson, drew in a big breath, then exhaled slowly.

He picked up his cup again and drank whilst still reading. He finished his coffee and put down the summary.

'Well Gibson, well well well.'

Gibson couldn't tell if the DCI was disappointed or excited.

'What can I say? Looks like you were right, at least in terms of the probability of these deaths being suspicious.'

'Suspicious sir, a bit more than suspicious, surely?'

'Okay, more than suspicious, have you got the full details of your interview with Freddie Exan there?'

'Yes sir', Gibson took the sheets out of the file and handed them to Watson.

Watson finished reading. 'Hmm, and did you believe him when he said he hadn't killed this Geoff Brown?'

'Yes I did, I don't know why, call it instinct, but I'd bet my life on it.'

'Well it might not be your life, but it could be your career if you're wrong. And about the noise or words the dying man was supposed to have uttered, any clue as to what he was trying to say?'

'No sir, I pressed Freddie Exan on that and he didn't know what Brown was trying to say, so maybe they were just sounds of a man in agony, dying, poor sod.'

'Poor sod indeed Gibson. You realise I'm going

to have to take this upstairs and see what they say.' Gibson nodded.

'I think this will have to go to the Chief Constable. But we need to be sure to hold on to this investigation. I'm not letting this one slip through my fingers. Everyone's going to want a piece of this so I need to be careful how I present it. But leave that to me, I'll make sure we don't get sidelined and that we get to keep the case.'

All of a sudden it's "we", last week it was all a waste of time, well you're not going to grab the glory for this one, you chiselling old sod.

'Of course sir, I'd forgotten all about all those internal politics.'

'Unfortunately Gibson, you can't afford to. There are glory seekers in every walk of life and they'll steal your ideas, your hard work, and claim it as their own without batting an eyelid.

'But don't worry, it isn't going to happen this time. This is could be a big one Gibson, handle this right and we'll be covered in glory, but be careful, there are a lot of pitfalls in a case like this so just think on, and don't get carried away, okay?'

'Yes sir.'

'Now while I think of how to present this, go and decide what you next moves are and come back to see me in a couple of hours, okay?'

'Yes sir,'

Gibson went back to his office, closed the door bunched his fists and let out a roar of rage and frustration. *So I do all the work and you get all the glory, well it ain't going to happen, not fucking likely, no not fucking remotely likely you miserable blood sucking....twat..* He sat down, took some deep breaths and after a while felt calmer. *C'mon Gibson you're better than this, get back to work.*

He took up his pen and began to think, identifying what his next moves should be. He wrote down his objectives, but not necessarily in order of priority.

Locate and question Barry Jones
Meet with the detectives who investigated the murder of Geoff Brown.
Interview the widow of Geoff Brown.
Establish the significance of the third of February.
Look further into the accident at Agecroft Colliery, what date did that happen?
Find out who the 'foreign' man was who visited Joe Martin at the care home?

He leant back on his chair, closed his eyes and tried to clear his mind of anything to do with the case. He turned his mind's eye to their last holiday in Mallorca and Jill lying on the beach in that red bikini, *god she looked gorgeous, the sun was shining, the sea was warm...*

'Whoa', he shouted out loud as he nearly toppled backwards. The near fall brought him rudely back to the present and immediately dispelled the images of his holiday. He straightened his chair and wrote down his thoughts as another list.

All deaths occurred on the same date, so it has to be an anniversary of some event.

All the men murdered had to have been involved in this event.

All the men were miners.

All the men lived on Regent Park West.

Okay, so fairly obvious stuff he thought, but it always helped Gibson to see things written down rather than just have them as thoughts in his head.

But where to start?

He needed to find out where the historical records of local papers were kept, in particular those in circulation at the time of the various events he was interest in, the bombing, the pit accident, the miners' strike etc. Swinton and Pendlebury library was the logical place to begin, although since these previously independent boroughs had now been merged with Salford and Greater Manchester, it was anyone's guess where he could locate the information he needed, but got to start somewhere, he thought.

First he needed to go and talk to his colleagues who dealt with the prosecution of Freddie Exan back in eighty five. He would keep schtum about the prospect of them having possibly convicted the wrong man. No point in pissing on their chips just yet - and anyway, he had to accept that he just might be wrong about Exan and that it was possible, though extremely unlikely in Gibson's opinion, that Freddie was guilty of Geoff Brown's murder.

The various police services in Salford, Manchester and other nearby areas had been merged into one force in nineteen seventy four, and renamed The Greater Manchester Police or GMP. In the process they had established separate sub divisions; each with their own divisional commander. Gibson worked out of the divisional headquarters in Swinton which covered Salford North, the sub division name for Swinton & Pendlebury.

As Geoff Brown's murder had occurred in eighty five, three years prior to Gibson's arrival at Swinton, he had to set about finding out who had handled the original investigation. *Boy are they going to hate me if things turn out as I think they might. Still granny used to say, you can't make an omelette without breaking eggs.*

Gibson eventually established that a Detective Sergeant Todd was the leading detective involved in the Geoff Brown murder investigation, and he'd moved some time ago to take up a post at Salford Central Division in Pendleton. Gibson decided to call a colleague to get some information on D S Todd. He always liked to get a feel for what type of character he was dealing in any situation and he was going to have to be particularly careful in this instance, particularly in view of Watson's reminder about internal politics.

The problem as he saw it was that he couldn't mention the specifics of his own investigation, without inviting a lot of unwanted questions, which he didn't feel would be appropriate to answer at this stage of the game, and which very well might compromise his own on-going investigation.

It would also hinder his enquires if it got out that the murder of Geoff Brown might be tied in with other murders. On the other hand, if and when he established that Freddie Exan was innocent of the murder he'd gone down for, then he, Gibson would be accused of not being up front with the original investigating officers of Brown's death, ultimately leaving them looking like idiots for having banged up the wrong person, and worse still, having let a killer escape to kill again.

Gibson phoned George Mitten, a pal of his in personnel. They'd been to school together and coincidentally had both ended up in the force.

'So what's up Gibbo?'

'Just called to hear your dulcet tones George, see how you were. You know how I worry about your welfare.'

'Yeah yeah yeah, c'mon Gibbo stop taking the piss.'

'Yeah okay, well I need to talk to a D S Todd

about something he was involved with a few years ago and I just wanted to know what sort of bloke he is. He used to work out of here, Swinton, but he moved to Pendleton, Salford Central.'

'Yes I know the name, let me pull his details. Detective Sergeant Roy Todd, yes I remember him. Get results, he's a bit aggressive and sails a bit close to the wind on occasion by all accounts, but there are no formal warnings or reprimands on his file. So, officially, he has a clean sheet and a good arrest record.'

'Okay thanks George, do you happen to have his contact details there by any chance?' George gave him the details.

'So what's happening, anything exciting Gibbo?'

'No, just the usual boring stuff George, see you around. Maybe go for a pint sometime soon.'

'Yeah, providing you're buying, see you.'

There's another one who's going to be pissed with me for not telling him anything. Gibson had planned to go and meet with DS Todd face to face, but now he wondered if that might look too serious, and might suggest to Todd that something heavy was in the offing. *No, better to phone him, keep it light, at least initially.*

'Hello, is that DS Todd, yes, DS Gibson Salford North' Gibson went on to explain what he was calling about and Todd asked him to hold on while he went and got his file on the case. He came back on the phone.

'So what's this all about?'

'Oh just wanted your take on what happened. I need to talk to Freddie Exan about another unrelated matter and I just thought I'd get some background from you before I go to see him',

Gibson grimaced as he spoke. Skirting round the truth was one thing but lying through your teeth was another.

'What sort of related matter?' Todd's interest was piqued, *time for some near truths.*

'Well an old friend of his died recently and the daughter insists there's something funny about his death, maybe something to do with his past, so we're just going through the motions and talking to people who might have known him that's all, there's no suggestion Freddie was involved, just information gathering that's all.'

'Hmm,'

Todd didn't sound convinced, but he went on. 'Well, if you saw the case notes you'll see it was pretty much open and shut, the man, Freddie Exan, was found by the wife of the victim. He was standing over the body of, allegedly, his best friend, with the knife that killed him on the floor at his feet. Forensic tests proved he'd been holding the knife, no doubt about that. He and the vic had had a big row, a fight in the pub a week or so previous, about the strike apparently, everyone knew about the fallout. That was pretty well it.

The vic had been very badly cut and hadn't died quickly, pretty gruesome stuff. There was considerable cruelty in the manner of the killing. Exan protested his innocence but there was no one else in the frame, so he went down for it, good riddance and another fuckin' nutcase off the street as far as I'm concerned.'

'Did this Freddie have any history of violence anything like that?'

'No I don't think so, nothing we found anyway, but so what? You know that doesn't mean diddly.'

'I understand the wife, the wife of the victim, said she didn't believe he'd done it, Freddie I mean, did you ever think he might not have done it, despite the circumstantial evidence?'

'What the fuck are you talking about? Course he'd done it, didn't you hear what I just said, anyway what's that got to do with you "just wanting to talk to him about this other man," is there something going on here that I should know about?'

'No, no sorry, I suppose I was just curious, thanks for taking the time to talk to me. I'll let you know if anything else comes up, thanks again.'

The phone was unceremoniously slammed down at the other end. Todd obviously didn't buy my story thought Gibson, perhaps it had been a mistake to talk to DS Todd? *Better try to talk to the widow now, see what gives there.*

He realised he didn't have Mrs Brown's number, so he called Mary King. She said she'd kept in touch with her and had her number which she gave to Gibson, but she said she'd moved house and knew where it was, but didn't know the house number. Gibson thanked her, rang off and then called Mrs Brown. The phone rang out a few times then went to voicemail. He put the phone down, left it a few minutes and tried again, same result, so he left a message for her asking her to call him as soon as convenient. *Better look at some of the other stuff I've neglected recently, then tomorrow I'll go to the library and see what I can dig up there.*

CHAPTER 12

Pendlebury library had been gobbled up by Swinton library in a rationalisation of the two neighbouring boroughs many year previously, then as both boroughs were eventually subsumed by nearby Salford in some further grand rationalisation plan, the historical record keeping became somewhat complicated and fragmented. So the task of looking up the information Gibson required, became a rather more arduous task than he'd anticipated.

Eventually, with the help of a couple of long suffering, but dedicated library assistants at the Salford library, he was able to find the local newspaper records of the events he was interested in. Details and reports of the miners' strike of eighty four/five were fairly easily found, but the events of the accident at Agecroft Colliery in fifty eight were a little more difficult. Gibson persevered and managed to get most of the information he was looking for, however finding records of the bombing in Regent Park West in forty two wasn't easy at all. It took him the best part of a day to gather up most of the relevant information.

In previous times when newspapers were the main source of news and information, each small town or borough had at least one local newspaper and the Swinton & Pendlebury Journal was one such publication. It contained masses of information on news, local events, job vacancies, weddings, births marriages, deaths etc. and Gibson was fascinated, reading the various articles on a bygone era, so much so that he often forgot what he'd set out to find, life in the forties, fifties and sixties was so interesting and different. However he eventually managed to recover his focus and made copious notes of anything relating to any of the events pertinent to his investigation.

He found quite a bit of coverage on the bombing of the house in Regent Park West in nineteen forty two. One of the reports in the local paper dealt with the back story of the victim's family, and was particularly touching in the way it painted a picture of the hard life that miners endured generally, and the personal tragedy of the particular family destroyed in the bombing incident. The story was penned by "junior reporter" and Gibson was struck by the obvious storytelling talent of the journalist despite his apparent young age.

The article described how the husband, who had lost his wife and children in the raid, had gone out to borrow something from a neighbour just before the raid had started, and couldn't get back to his house until the raid was over. It was extraordinary in the way it drew you into feeling the man's distress and desolation at losing his entire family in less than an hour.

As he looked through the newspaper editions subsequent to the bombing of the houses, he came across an article on the death of four German POWs in a bombing raid which had occurred in the same area, just a week later. This had been penned by a different reporter. On this occasion the article reported that there had been a fire-bomb raid on nearby Trafford Park that night, and the assumption was that a single Luftwaffe pilot had ditched his last incendiary bomb over what he might have thought to be open land, prior to flying back to his base over the channel. Unfortunately for the POWs, the incendiary device reportedly hit the hut where they were billeted and they all perished. The irony of the German air force killing its own German POWs struck Gibson and further reinforced his view on the stupidity and futility of war.

The article went on to pay tribute to the fireman who did their best to put out the fire and rescue the men despite the POW's comrades in the Luftwaffe having bombed and destroyed a local British family the week before. Now, just a short distance away, the Luftwaffe had killed some of their own comrades. The article also contained an interview with the fire officer in charge who confirmed that the remains of four bodies had been found in the fire and that the fire crew couldn't have done anything to save them, the blaze having taken hold well before they arrived on the scene.

The article finished by saying that the authorities would do their best to inform the relatives in Germany, and that the deceased men would be given a Christian funeral and interred together in a single grave in Agecroft Cemetery.

CHAPTER 13

Winter 1942 Pendlebury near Manchester

Shivering in his bunk bed, muscles aching after a hard day's work on the farm, he fought to keep his eyelids from closing, knowing how much he would regret falling asleep and missing the chance to be with Lily. His damaged right leg always ached badly towards the end of the day. He'd been lucky to escape with just a leg wound. Only he had survived when his aircraft was shot down, the rest of his crew had perished. There were many times since, when he wished he'd died in the crash, rather than becoming a prisoner of war and working as a common farmhand. But then he'd met Lily.

Sanding just about six foot tall, the hard manual labour had kept his body toned, but he'd lost weight since his capture, making him thinner than normal. His face was craggy and he looked typically Germanic, with dark blond hair and striking flint blue eyes. The other three had turned in and he was sure they were already asleep. Slowly he got out of his bunk bed, checked again that no one else was awake, knelt down on the floor and pulled the straw stuffed sack out of the space beneath his bunk, placed it on top of the bed and patted it into shape. It would suffice in the unlikely event of the farmer checking they were all asleep in the hut.

He sat down, pulled his boots on and crept silently towards the door of the wooden hut that served as their billet. Originally built to house livestock, the hut still stank of animals. The roof leaked and there were still some gaps in the wall timbers, but they'd managed to plug the worst of the holes using bits of old wood and a mixture of mud, straw and cow dung. They had an outside lavatory of sorts, a corrugated tin construction with boards and a pit. Every couple of weeks or so, they were obliged to dig a new hole and move the tin construction over it. They had no running water and no electricity.

The food was acceptable if somewhat limited in variety, and considering the situation it wasn't that bad, potatoes being the main constituent. The door of the hut was never locked these days, the farmer couldn't be bothered. When they'd first arrived, the farmer would lock them in at night, but after a few weeks he stopped. He assumed the farmer had come to the same conclusion as they had, that if they wanted to escape there was plenty of opportunity during the day, but what was the point?

Gently pulling the door open, he carefully closed it behind him so as not to make any sound. He would only be a couple of hours, and even if one of the others woke and found him missing they weren't going to do anything about it. The night was clear and frosty, with no wind. A three quarters moon hung in the sky, lighting up the surrounding fields. He pulled his jacket tighter in an effort to keep warm, then jogged towards his destination, the frost topped soft earth impeding his progress, its hard crust collapsing with each step. He reached the edge of the field, then pushed through the hedge and on to a dirt lane.

She'd be in much more trouble than him if anyone found out. Fraternizing with the enemy they called it. He turned the word over in his mind. Verbryderung was what they called it back in Germany. He preferred 'fraternizing', it sounded less serious, more like a game. His English was adequate, but she was teaching him more words, and a few other things too. She was older than him and she'd been married, though only briefly, her husband had been killed right at the start of the war. The door opened, she'd been looking out for him.

The hall was in darkness in accordance with the blackout regulations but also useful to avoid prying eyes. They embraced. Few words were said, they both knew time was short. Once in the bedroom they undressed and made love in a frenzy, then afterwards, a second, more gentle lovemaking. They both lay back, satisfied, content, silent, then he spoke.

'Did you love your husband Lily?' he'd wanted to ask her that question for a while now.

'What a strange thing to ask, but if you really want to know, yes is the answer, very much.'

It wasn't the answer he was hoping for, she sensed his disappointment.

'That doesn't mean I don't love you silly, it was just, I don't know, we'd known each other a long time and we were happy together, but he's gone, and now I've met you, and now you make me happy. I can't explain it, but I love you now, so be happy, I am.'

'Then I am too, but doesn't it feel', he searched for the right word, she didn't prompt him and waited, 'odd, strange, to be in love with a German? After all, we, we are enemies, it was us, Germans I mean, who killed you husband.'

'I suppose it does feel strange sometimes, and I suppose I'd be in big trouble if anyone found out about us, but we're not enemies are we? So let's try to forget this stupid horrible war.'

He put his arm around her waist and they kissed. He looked at the clock on the wall.

'It's late, I'd better get back.'

He crept quietly down the garden path, over the lane and through the hedge. Making his way back to the hut, he was just a few yards away when the air raid sirens began their terrifying wail, followed by the unmistakable drone of aircraft, bombers, Junkers Eighty Eights maybe, he thought. He quickly opened the door just as the other men were waking up.

No one said a word as they each tried to judge just how near the bombers were. It was the first raid they'd experienced as POWs. They looked at each other. Gasmasks hung on nails by each man's bunk, but no one bothered putting one on.

'The Luftwaffe is after the railway line' He said, partly to deflect any questions about where he'd been, but he was right.

The railway line was about a quarter of a mile away from where they were billeted and ran along a ridge at the top of the Irwell Valley. A long row of terraced houses ran along the foot of the valley, backing on to the steep embankment leading up to the line. This was where the miners, who worked at the nearby Agecroft Colliery, lived.

'It's going to be a bit close for comfort if you ask me'.

'I just hope they've improved their accuracy' added one of the other POWs.

Just as the last one spoke, the ground vibrated, the wooden hut shook violently, followed almost instantly by the sound, at first a low rumble then the volume increased dramatically to a loud crump, the noise of the first bomb exploding reached them, it sounded very near. Another three explosions followed as more bombs were dropped, but they didn't seem as close as the first. The raid lasted less than ten minutes but it felt like an age. Dust hung in the air of the hut, and they all stood like statues in the ghostly light, provided by the one small candle. No one spoke until the all clear sounded, then shortly after, the bells of the fire engines could be heard getting louder. He was the first to recover his voice.

'Blow out the candle and let's go outside.'

They stood outside and looked at the fires burning in the near distance. Mostly the flames were along the railway line at the top of the embankment, behind the houses, but one fire was raging at a lower level.

'Looks like they hit one of the houses.' said one of the men, 'the locals will not take this well, we need to be careful tomorrow'.

They went back into the hut and got into their bunks, but sleep eluded most of them for the rest of the night. He lay there and thought about home. He'd lied about his age to get into the Luftwaffe, but no one was that bothered, providing you could do the job, and he was an excellent pilot. It was just bad luck to have been shot down on his first raid.

A few months before he'd gone on active duty, he'd met and married Helga. They liked each other, but they weren't in love, at least he wasn't.

It was just something people did then. Helga was fresh, blond, attractive and intelligent and keen to get married. He wasn't sure who suggested it first, but getting married seemed right in the circumstances. You needed someone to come back to, or someone to mourn for you if you didn't make it back.

He came from a military family; his father had been a Major in the army and had twice been decorated for outstanding bravery in the First World War. It was expected that he would go into uniform and he was only too willing to fight for the Fatherland. He wasn't too sure about Hitler though, but you kept your opinions to yourself on that score if you wanted to keep out of trouble.

Now he was in love with Lily. He had watched her most days as she walked her boxer dog along the lane by the farm in the mornings. She lived in a small detached house on the lane flanking the farm. One day her dog had managed to get through the farm hedge in pursuit of a rabbit. She shouted the dog but it was more interested in catching the rabbit. He'd grown up with dogs and was able to bring it back to Lily.

She was very grateful and they chatted briefly as they stood on either side of the hedge. His English wasn't great but good enough to get by. Lily was tall for a woman, she had dark red hair, high cheek bones, a pale completion and sad hazel eyes. He thought she looked aristocratic. He was instantly attracted to her. He thought the feeling was mutual. They said their goodbyes, but from then on he would try to make sure he was working near to the lane at the time she usually walked her dog. Occasionally she would look over in his direction and give him a discreet little wave. If he was able, he would find some excuse to be working near enough to the edge of the lane to be able to stop work briefly and talk to her. From there, one thing led to another.

The next morning the POWs were roused by the farmer, Harry Chapman, a wiry character with a mean face and a sharp tongue. They stood outside the hut being given their duties for the day, then as the morning mist lifted, they could see in the distance the extent of the damage the bombing had caused. On Regent Park West, what had been a house was now just a pile of smoking steaming rubble, an ugly gap in an otherwise row of uniform terraced houses, the smell of damp smoke carried to them on the light morning breeze.

Already, men could be seen clearing rubble from the wreckage of the house, piling it on to the street where it was then loaded on to a lorry. The railway line above was also busy with workers repairing the damaged rail track; the authorities obviously keen that any damage to the railway infrastructure would be short lived.

'Your fucking Nazi air force friends did a lot

of damage last night,' said the farmer as they all took in the scene, 'so I suggest you keep well away from the edges of the fields or someone is likely to have a go at you if they get the chance, and I wouldn't blame them if they did. A mother and her kids bombed to buggery last night. Now get the fuck out there and start doing some work'.

Nearly a week went by and there were no more raids. He hadn't visited her since the night of the bombing. He saw her walking the dog as usual, but they'd avoided any eye contact until today, when she gave him the slightest of nods as she passed by. That night he waited impatiently until the rest of the men were asleep, then re-arranged his bunk bed and slipped out into the night. There was no moon and he stumbled over the uneven ground as he made his way across the field, a fine cold drizzle penetrating his thin jacket, adding to his discomfort.

He crouched low as he approached the gate; it had been left open. The front door opened, he walked swiftly up the path, slipped inside the door and they embraced.

'You're soaking wet my love,' she said.

He let her take his jacket off, and drape it over a chair by the fire. He watched her saying nothing, drinking her in. She turned and the flickering light from the fire lit her profile, accentuating her beauty.

'This is very risky for you now Lily, now that

house has been bombed, people killed, if anyone finds out about us.' Lily put her finger to his lips to stop him talking.

'Shush, I'm not afraid of anything, anything they could do to me anyway, the only thing that worries me is losing you. I've learnt not to waste precious time in this life, you never know what's around the corner, so come over here and hold me.'

They were both dozing in her bed when the distant wail of air raid sirens woke them. Then they heard the drone of the planes, but the sound seemed much more distant than the last time.

'I need to get back to the hut.' He leaned over and switched on small dim table lamp which barely illuminated the bedroom. He got out of bed and started to drag on his clothes.

'Do you have to go, why not wait till it's over?'

'No I can't, the raid could have woken the farmer and he might check on the hut, unlikely but if he does, he'll realize I'm missing, then we'll both be in big trouble and he might send me away to a secure POW camp. Anyway the raid will wake the other men for sure, so I'd better get back. I think they already know I sneak out some nights, we just keep up the pretence so that there are no awkward questions, better that way.'

He kissed her briefly before opening the door and running swiftly out into the black night, across the fields towards the hut.

Lily went back inside, switched of the little light and drew back a small part of the blackout curtains so she could look out over the fields towards the hut. She couldn't see anything, all outside lights were off in line with the blackout rules. The raid, such as it was, seemed to be over quickly, she hadn't heard any noise of bombs exploding- *a false alarm maybe?* Then she thought she heard the all clear, but again it seemed distant.

Lily withdrew from the window and went to make herself a cup of tea. She warmed the pot put in one small spoonful of tea; a precious commodity in such straightened times, and poured the boiling water into the small china teapot. While the tea brewed she thought about her husband and how cruel this war was. They'd only been married for a few months when war was declared but Harry hadn't hesitated and volunteered right away. He joked with her when she fretted about him not coming back.

'Only the good die young Lily and you know what a bad lot I am, so I'll probably live forever'

'Well' she said out loud to herself. 'You were good and you did die young, so it really wasn't a very good joke was it Harry?'

She was pouring her tea when she heard the distant bells of fire engines and they seemed to be getting louder.

Why fire engines?

She went back to the window and carefully

pulled back the curtain just enough to see out across the fields. In the near distance she saw huge fire blazing in the area where the POW's wooden hut was. Her hand went up to her mouth in an involuntary gesture of horror.

'Oh no.' she cried, 'not again, please not again.'

CHAPTER 14

Present day -1990

After completing his search through the local papers and other records, Gibson drove into Manchester and visited the archive department at the offices of the Manchester Evening News. He began by reading accounts of the first bombing raid on Manchester and Salford, known as the Christmas blitz of nineteen forty one. Liverpool had been first on Hitler's north of England hit list. His Luftwaffe bombed the city and docks just a couple of days before they hit Manchester. The Luftwaffe were said to have used the still burning fires from their raid on Liverpool to guide them back up to the north and to nearby Manchester, where they wreaked devastating havoc on the city and Trafford Park just a couple of days before Christmas, killing almost seven hundred people and injuring thousands more.

As Gibson read on, he came across some harrowing individual personal accounts of people missing or killed in the raids. One headed "Two Brothers Missing in First Raid", told of a mother from the Ancoats area of Manchester, who spent two days searching for her two missing sons, twelve and ten years old. The last she'd seen of them was when they left their home to go fishing in the canal. They were never found. There was also a graphic eyewitness account from one of the journalists from the Manchester Evening News, caught up in the first raid. and who lost part of his leg in a bomb blast.

*

Walking along Deansgate, on my way to the pub for a pint and a pie, I heard the sirens begin to wail. I was petrified, the terrifying noise gradually increasing in volume. People were running everywhere. I stood rooted to the spot not knowing what to do, or where to go. I heard another sound, a screaming whistling noise getting louder. I realised it was a bomb, falling to earth carrying its deadly payload.

Then the ground erupted in front of me, the deafening noise of the destructive blast, shrapnel and debris flying through the air, water spurting high into the air from the crater in the pavement, the physical shock of the event caused me to lose control of my bowels and bladder. Miraculously I was still alive, shocked but unhurt, then I heard the whistling sound again as another bomb hurtled down.

I woke up in hospital surrounded by other casualties and counted myself lucky to be alive. I'd lost

*part of my left leg below the knee in the second bomb
blast but when I saw the injuries inflicted on some of
the others, I considered this a relatively minor injury.*
The article went on to praise the firemen who had
rescued him and the doctors and nurses who'd
cared for him in the aftermath.

*

As Gibson carried on reading through the details of that December blitz on Manchester, he
wondered once again at the seemingly unlimited
capacity mankind had to commit such acts of
cruelty and destruction on their fellow human
beings. He shook his head and leafed through the
information until he found more coverage of the
specific event he was interested in, namely the
bombing raid just a few weeks later, on Regent
Park West. It recorded the events in much the
same detail as he'd already found, albeit with a
slightly less parochial slant. The bombing of the
nearby POW's billet a week later, was also reported on and was written with an obvious hint
of poetic justice, perhaps understandable given
the pounding the Manchester area had recently
suffered at the hands of the Luftwaffe.

He then searched for accounts of the miners'
strike in eighty four/five and found a lot more information, including some surprising statistical
information. Gibson was fascinated as he began
to appreciate the scale and impact of the strike,
and particularly its impact on the police. The stat-

istics included 9,808 arrests, more than 10,000 charges, 551 complaints against the police by miners, 1,392 police officers injured, three murder charges and 682 miners sacked for violence and sabotage, the cost of the police operation alone was estimated to be £200 million, a serious amount of money back then.

Ploughing on, he found an article on the accident at Agecroft Colliery in fifty eight, it had been written by Oliver MacMahon, the same person who'd written the touching article about the bombing in Regent Park West in forty two, which he'd read in the Swinton & Pendlebury Journal. *Had to be the same man,* But now his title was chief reporter, so he'd obviously moved papers and up the ranks accordingly. It gave Gibson an idea - *this could just be the person I need to help me to find out more information.*

CHAPTER 15

The next morning there was a message on his desk to go and see the DCI. He went down the stairs, along the corridor and knocked on the half glass door.

'Come on in Gibson.'

As usual DCI Watson was on the phone. He motioned for Gibson to sit down and resumed his conversation.

'Yes, commander, yes I fully understand, in fact DS Gibson has just walked into my office so we'll be having that conversation now. Yes sir and the same to you to, goodbye.'

Watson put the phone down.

'You know Gibson, sometimes, a policeman's lot is definitely, not a happy one.'

'No sir.'

'Well Gibson, we've got them all at it, they're not sure if they want to kiss you or kill you, probably the latter at the moment.'

'Oh, why is that sir?'

'Well, if you're right about these deaths being linked, and it looks as if you could be, then it means that the police will almost certainly have to admit certain errors of judgment. There's the latest death, this Billy Bowen, which now, thanks to your doggedness, we can claim we never accepted was due to natural causes, so that's not too bad. However, the assumption by us, the police in general I mean, that the death of Joe Martin was an accident, would now look as though there wasn't sufficient investigation to establish the correct cause of death at the time. As a consequence, we could be accused of sloppy work at best, or at worst, being incompetent and leaving a killer out on the streets to kill again. Added to which, we then have the potential embarrassment of possibly, no, probably, in the circumstances, of having banged up the wrong person for the murder of Geoff Brown. So it all ends up a bit of a dogs breakfast, do you see that Gibson?'

'Well put like that sir, I suppose it is a bit of a problem, potentially embarrassing I suppose, for the force.'

'It is Gibson, but fortunately, not for us personally.' Watson smiled. 'We, you and I, could end up smelling of roses.' Watson got up and walked up and down the short distance behind his desk. He stopped and looked at Gibson again.

'What sir?'

'You need to find the man in Wales, Barry whatsisname, Jones, find out what's happened to him, if anything. Let's just hope you find him hale and hearty, and not that he died on the third of February. If he did…, well let's not speculate at this stage Gibson, but you can see the potential for this to get even more awkward, embarrassing to say the least.'

Jesus Christ, typical, a bloody maniac serial killer on the loose and all they care about is how stupid and incompetent they'll look when it all comes out.

'Yes sir, I've put a request in to the Welsh police to try to trace him, but the information we have on Jones is a bit sketchy to say the least, but I'll chase them up. I didn't want to go running around Wales looking for him without having some sort of lead on where he is. I've got plenty of other stuff here to follow up on, but I will find him soon, you can be sure of that sir.'

'I'm sure you will Gibson, and don't get me wrong, despite what I've just said, the CC's very pleased and impressed with your detective work so far, and they're anxious for you, us that is, to bring this whole thing to a satisfactory conclusion, so have no doubt Gibson, we're all batting on the same side, it's just that this is going to have to be handled with an eye to the bigger picture. We need to minimise any potential damage to the force, and make sure we come out of this investigation smelling of roses, rather than the stuff you put on them – and I don't mean fertiliser.'

'Yes sir I understand, but if as seems likely, all these deaths turn out to be murders, then there's bound to be blame laid at the door of someone, no matter how unfair or unpalatable that might be.'

'Yes Gibson, I accept that, it's just that we need to make sure that any such damage is minimised that's all. We, you and I, might grab the glory this time, but in the process we could make a lot of enemies for the future if we're seen to be shovelling the shit on to others. People in the force have long memories so we need to handle this carefully. Yes, let's make sure we get the lion's share of the glory, but there'll be plenty left to go round, so we can share a bit, not forgetting of course, that first you need to find the maniac who's killing these people.'

'I' need to find the maniac, then 'we' take the credit - got it.

'So Gibson, you need to be thinking ahead, that's all, you need to keep all these things in mind as your investigation proceeds, especially if and when things get into the press, which they are bound to at some point. So having said all that, the commander wanted me to pass on his appreciation of your efforts so far and he's given me carte blanche to handle the on-going investigation as we wish. Any resources we need we get, as much overtime as necessary. All he wants is a good result, and for us to bear in mind the potential issues we've just discussed, and of course, for us to use our discretion at all times. No talking to the press or making any public statements or answering any questions without prior notice and permission from those on high.'

'Okay, understood sir.' Gibson momentarily thought about telling the DCI about the News of the World reporter, but decided against it, after all Lucy Moore knew nothing, so no point in going there.

'So what resources do you need Gibson? I'm going to want a daily update of progress, and of course I'll be giving you the benefit of my opinions when appropriate, but you've done well so far.'

'Well to be honest sir, I'm not sure I need any help at the moment, other than being able to give all my other work to someone else. That'll free me up to go at this full tilt, but the way things are panning out, I think I'm better working alone until I really need another body to help me do some of the donkey work. I'm not being precious about the investigation, I just think that sometimes you're better and quicker working alone. You know what I mean sir?'

'I do Gibson - he who travels fastest travels alone.'

'Sorry sir?'

'Kipling Gibson, poetry, not cakes, The Winners, learnt it off by heart at school; I can recite the whole poem for you if you wish?'

'Mind if I pass on that sir?'

'I was only joking Gibson, anyway I don't have

problem with that approach for the time being, so clear your desk and give your other cases to Bennett, lazy sod could do with some extra work.'

Gibson smiled. He hadn't realised the DCI had clocked what a slacker Bennett was.

'Will do sir.'

'Okay, let me have an update every day, or let me know immediately if there's a significant development, and we'll go from there. Good luck Gibson.'

Gibson returned to his office where there was a note on his desk saying that a Mrs Brenda Brown had called to say she'd received a message from him and was returning his call. He called her straight back. She answered on the second ring. Gibson introduced himself and explained that he'd been trying to contact her to arrange to meet her for a chat about what had happened to her husband Geoff. She had a not unpleasant, if somewhat gravelly voice with quite a distinct local accent.

'What do you want to talk to me about that now for, it's over five years since Geoff died?'

'Well, it's just that I've been looking into some other matters and your husband's name came up and, well it would be easier to explain if we could meet, if you could spare the time that is?'

'When?'

'As soon as is convenient for you. I could pop over today if you like?'

'I'm on a two ten today so if you could be here before two I suppose....'

Gibson looked at his watch, 'I could come over now, should be there in about half an hour, and I promise not to keep you long, is that okay?'

'All right, you know my address?'

'Sorry no, Mary King gave me your telephone number but she didn't have your precise address, said you'd moved from Regent Park West.'

'I couldn't stay in that house, not after what happened. The council gave me a new place on Hospital Road, thirty four, Hospital Road Pendlebury, see you in half an hour then.'

Gibson had a quick coffee, checked there were no other messages for him, then phoned DS Bennett on the internal phone system but he was out. He left him a message saying he'd like to meet him later in the day with a view to handing over some cases, and to call him back to let him know when it was convenient.

As he drove to his meeting with Mrs Brown Gibson thought about what the DCI had said that morning about the press getting hold of the story. He hoped Lucy Moore was as ignorant of the details as he thought she was, if she wasn't it didn't even bear thinking about and just how bad it would be for him. *I suppose if she looked hard enough, she might just clock that both Billy Bowen and Joe Martin died on the same date.* He tried to imagine what she would do if she then found out that not only did those two die on the same date but at least one other had as well. He saw the headlines in his mind's eye – News of the World exclusive *SEARCH FOR THE THIRD OF FEBRUARY SERIAL KILLER!*

He shuddered at the prospect. She would certainly hang him out to dry now, given half the chance and such public exposure would put impossible pressure on him, and the police in general, to catch the perpetrator. There would be cries from all quarters for the police to bring "the killer to justice". It would also alert the perpetrator that the police were now actively looking for him, and make him all the more difficult to apprehend.

Fumy though, thought Gibson, the killer must want someone to know, to realise the significance of the third of February. So does the killer want to be caught so they can explain, boast even? *No point in meting out vengeance on a specific date like that, if no one ever knows or appreciates why you've done it, is there?*

He'd reached number thirty four. It was a relatively modern, sixties terraced house, built in blocks of four, rendered in sand coloured, pebbledash. As he walked up the front path he noted the small unkempt lawn, in stark contrast to her neighbours' generally tidy gardens. The door opened before he reached it and a woman he assumed to be Mrs Brenda Brown let him in.

She was painfully thin, wore no makeup, and had badly dyed dark brown hair framing a sharp lined face. The house was untidy and smelt of cigarette smoke. He introduced himself. She nodded and motioned for him to go into the kitchen where there was a small square table with a floral patterned plastic table cloth and four wooden chairs. She sat down and Gibson did the same. There was a nearly full ashtray on the table.

'Don't mind, do you?' She showed him the cigarette packet.

'No, no not at all, please feel free, it's your house.' *And your lungs and heart.*

She lit up without offering Gibson one and blew the smoke sideways out of her mouth to avoid it going straight into Gibson's face.

'Sorry, manners, want a cup of tea?'

Gibson looked at the dirty dishes on the draining board and declined, saying he'd had some coffee at the office.

'So Mr Policeman, what's this all about then?'

'I'm sorry to have to bother you like this Mrs Brown, and I apologise if this opens old wounds but I just need to go over what happened that day, when you found your husband Geoff...'

'Again? I don't know how many times you lot want to hear it, it won't change anything.' She sighed in resignation. Left hand still holding her cigarette, she stretched her right hand out in front of her as if to inspect her nails, which

Gibson noticed were painted a deep red and obviously well cared for, in sharp contrast to her otherwise unkempt appearance. She began her account of what happened that day, in a disinterested monotone voice.

'I came home about half past four. I'd been on an early shift, but then I went to do some shopping, bumped into a mate of mine and we were gassing for a bit. Anyway I came home and the door was open so I walked in and found Freddie standing over Geoff. Freddie had a knife in his hand, and Geoff was covered in blood.' Her seemingly indifferent attitude changed and she stopped talking momentarily, drawing heavily on her cigarette before continuing, her right hand now in her lap. Gibson waited, she blew out a stream of smoke. 'And Geoff, all bloody on the settee. I stood there for I don't know how long, trying to take in what I was seeing. My legs went to jelly and I couldn't speak. I leaned against the door and then I must have screamed because Freddie turned round and dropped the knife. He looked, I don't know how to describe it, he looked like a ghost, white as a sheet. I think he'd pissed hisself, he was wet all down the front of his trousers.

I managed to run out of the house, I'm not sure how, I remember my legs still felt wobbly. I went to Betty's house over the road. I managed to tell her there'd been an accident. She sat me down, I think I fainted, not like me really. Then she must have called for an ambulance and the police I think. I don't really remember much after that.' Gibson nodded, having taken down all the details as she'd told them.

'Did you get the chance to talk to Freddie afterwards?'

'No, I haven't talked to him since the...., since it happened.'

'Did he try to contact you, has he ever tried to get in touch?'

'No, not that I know of.'

'I've been told that you didn't believe Freddie did it, is that true?'

'Yes, I still don't.

'Any idea who might have then? Did it, I mean?'

'No, look I've been through all this before and I don't see the point in going through it all again, I mean tell me, what is the point?'

'Well if you don't believe that Freddie did it, then perhaps he didn't.'

Brenda Brown looked at Gibson, took another long drag of her cigarette and seemed to be trying to take in the significance of what he'd just said, then she tapped her cigarette on the ashtray.

'What are you saying? I don't understand, you mean there might be some doubt, about Freddie, I mean, that he didn't kill Geoff after all?'

'I'm not saying anything officially at this stage, but let's just say that some other information has come to my attention that might, and I stress might, just throw a different light on what happened. Now this is me talking, not the police, just me personally at this stage, so don't go running away with the idea that I can prove Freddie's innocence or that I can find out who really did it, but there is a chance, just a chance that things may not have been as they seemed, so anything you can tell me might help. I have to add that if you tell anyone else about our conversation, then it might hinder my efforts, and spoil any chances of any new information coming to light. I haven't mentioned this to anyone yet,' Gibson lied, 'not even Freddie.'

'You've met Freddie then?'

'Yes I have.'

'How was he?'

There was something in the way she asked the question that registered on Gibson's very sensitive antennae.

'Forgive me for asking Mrs Brown, but were you, well, more than just friends with Freddie?'

Brenda Brown straightened up in her chair, her eyes blazing, then raising her voice she replied angrily.

'Sorry, what did you just say, what are you suggesting? You have no right to make..'

Gibson tried to interject, to apologise, when suddenly Mrs Brown stopped talking and seemed to deflate, her shoulders fell, she clumsily stubbed out her cigarette in the ashtray, causing ash and old cigarette stubs to spill out, then she looked down at the table, unable to meet Gibson's eyes, she drew in in a long breath and looked up.

'Oh bugger it, what's the point? Yes' she said, 'yes yes, we were, "more than friends" as you put it, classic story, shagging his best friend's wife, and there isn't a day since Geoff died that I haven't felt like shit for letting him down.'

'And could that have been the real reason for the fight in the pub?'

'No it wasn't, I'm absolutely sure Geoff never knew. I could read Geoff like a book and trust me, he didn't know. We, me and Geoff, we hadn't been, you know, intimate for years, and Freddie and me well, it just happened. We both loved Geoff and I know that Freddie would never hurt a hair on Geoff's head. He felt really bad about me and him, and we'd already, well Freddie he said we should stop messing around, well before Geoff was ....'

Brenda Brown stopped talking and collapsed on the table in a flood of tears. Gibson sat there feeling like a lemon. He never knew what to do when this sort of thing happened. He decided to wait until the flood had subsided. Eventually she got up, took some tissues from the box on the table, and blew her nose, then mumbled something, went through the kitchen door into the hallway. Gibson heard her run upstairs, a door closed, then he heard the lavatory flush. She came down a few minutes later, looking much calmer. She sat down at the table again, took a cigarette out of the packet, then put it back again.

'These bloody things'll be the death of me.' Gibson said nothing.

'You know I've never told anyone about me and Freddie, and I didn't realise what a weight I'd been carting around until now. I know it sounds daft but I just feel so much better having told someone, told you I mean.'

'I'm happy to have helped,' said Gibson. 'So, if you're absolutely sure your, er, relationship, was definitely not a factor in Geoff's death, then tell me, had Geoff fallen out with anyone else, had any disagreements, perhaps over the strike?'

'No, course not, I mean I know everyone didn't have the same view about the strike and there were some big fallouts, but Geoff was always the one who tried to make peace between people. The only time he had a serious argument was with Freddie, and that's because they were so close he expected Freddie to have the same opinion as he did, but no, there was never any serious row with anyone.'

'Okay, what about the accident in fifty eight, when a miner died?'

'What about it?'

'Was Geoff involved in any way?'

'He was working that day and so was Freddie, they nearly always worked the same shifts, but

163

I'm pretty sure they'd finished their shift before the accident happened.'

'Can you think of any reason, any reason at all, why anyone might have blamed them for what happened that day?'

Mrs Brown thought for a moment,

'No definitely not, I remember now, Geoff told me they both went back to try to help but there was nothing they could do. The people at the pit-head, who'd misheard the message and thought the miners in the shaft had moved out, they were shattered, I think the main bloke involved had a breakdown afterwards, he was in a real bad way I heard.'

'So can you think of any event in Geoff's life, no matter how long ago, which might have caused someone to bear a grudge? Think carefully, take your time.'

After a few moments she replied. 'Nope, can't think of anything, can't think of anyone with a grudge, nothing sorry.'

'Okay Mrs Brown, I've taken up enough of your time. Thanks for seeing me, and don't forget what I told you about not telling anybody about what we've discussed today, okay?'

'Yes Sergeant, I understand, and you won't have to mention anything about, you know, me and Freddie, to anyone?'

'No, it stays just between us two, just as long as it never becomes relevant to what happened.' Gibson got up and she followed him to the door.

'Goodbye, Gibson said as he turned to go.

'Thanks for listening' she said and closed the door.

CHAPTER 16

As he drove back to the police headquarters Gibson thought more about the idea he'd had about meeting with the journalist who'd written the piece in the local rag about the bombing of the house, and the later article the same journalist had written about the miners' strike, in the Manchester Evening News, when he was by then, their chief reporter.

Gibson did a quick calculation in his head. *If he was, say eighteen, in nineteen forty two, then he'll be sixty six, so he'll be retired by now, but might as well try to track him down.* Gibson knew that journalists often had information on a story that they couldn't publish for want of space, or because it might be libellous or unsubstantiated hearsay. *Such information might be of interest to me though. The danger is I suppose, that he may still be a journalist at heart and sniff a good story if he gets inkling, but I should be able to handle that.*

He busied himself for the rest of the day writing up the files and preparing a report for DCI Watson. He left his office late as usual and stopped off for a pint at his local on the way home. He needed to unwind and take a break from police work and police conversations.

The next morning he called the Manchester Evening News and spoke to a girl in their personnel department. He established that Oliver MacMahon had, in fact, been the paper's managing editor before he'd recently retired. The girl wouldn't give any more information so he had to pull rank and eventually the manager was called who gave him MacMahon's address and phone number.

'Averill wasn't being obstructive Sergeant, she was just following procedure.'

'Yes I understand, no problem and thanks.'

Gibson took down the contact details for Oliver MacMahon, then immediately called the number he'd been given.

'Mack here, leave a message and I'll get back to you.'

Succinct enough thought Gibson and left a message asking him to call him back as soon as possible. He put the phone down and was about to go down to the canteen to get a coffee when his phone rang.

'There's an Oliver MacMahon on the phone for you.'

'Thanks, put him through please, Detective Sergeant Gibson here, thanks for calling back so promptly Mr MacMahon.'

'Not at all, always happy to help the police, and I'm obviously curious to know why you called, and before you ask, it wasn't me guv.'

'Yes, well I'm not aware that we have anything on you yet Mr MacMahon,' Gibson said carrying on the levity, 'not on this occasion anyway, no I'm just conducting enquiries into something which involves events in the past which you covered as a reporter, mainly to do with Agecroft Colliery and events in the immediate area, and I wanted to ask you about these in more detail.'

'Sounds intriguing, do you want to do this over the phone?'

'No, I think I probably need to come to discuss things face to face, if that's okay with you?'

'Fine by me Sergeant Gibson. Since I retired I'm a bit short on excitement so I look forward to meeting you, when do you want to come?'

'How about today if that's not too short notice?'

'No, no problem for me, roughly what time?'

Gibson consulted his watch, then quickly calculated how long it would take to drive to Southport.

'I should be there about one o'clock, depending on the traffic.'

'Okay, I assume you have my address, so I'll see you later, bye for now.'

Gibson bid him goodbye and put the phone down. He looked out of the window and the weak sunshine. *Might turn out to be a nice day today.* It had been ages since he'd been to Southport and he quite fancied some sea air. The drive had taken him longer than he'd expected, *accidents on the motorway maybe?*. The sudden dramatic change in the weather, with driving rain had created so much road spray, that at times Gibson found it difficult to see more than a few yards in front of himself. He was going to be late and he hated that. Gibson had a bit of a thing about punctuality.

He'd made the appointment for one, so he was a bit annoyed when he arrived on the outskirts of the seaside town and it was already gone one o'clock. When he reached the area where MacMahon lived, the sun was shining again, *good old British weather*. He eventually found the right street and drove along looking for number eight in a line of small neat bungalows. By the time he'd parked he was nearly half an hour late, but he needn't have worried, Oliver MacMahon wasn't in the slightest bit concerned and invited Gibson into his house like an old friend. MacMahon wasn't very tall, but looked fit, and trim, had dark brown hair, no grey in evidence and certainly didn't look like a man in his sixties. He had a warm smile and an open friendly face. Gibson was shown into a large airy kitchen. A black Labrador was lying in a dog bed in one corner. It got up on its two front legs when Gibson came in, obviously curious, but made no attempt to come over to him, and then seeming to lose lost interest, lay down again.

'Please sit down, Sergeant Gibson is it?'

'Detective Sergeant Gibson.'

'Ah, my apologies Detective Sergeant Gibson. Please call me Mack, everyone else does, and that black beast over there is called Monsoon.'

The dog got out of its bed and wagged its tail at the sound of its name but stayed where it was, looking at Mack expectantly, then realising nothing more was in the offing, sat back down.

'I don't know how you are with dogs and I never presume that people always like them, so I've trained Monsoon here not to approach a stranger unless invited, so if you don't like dogs please don't be afraid to say so, I shan't be offended and neither will he.'

'It's no problem. I like dogs, we always had one in the house when I was growing up.'

'Okay then, well come on Monsoon and say hello.'

Gibson held his hand out and the dog trotted over to make his acquaintance, smelling then licking Gibson's outstretched hand.'

'Okay formalities over, back to your bed please' said Mack to the dog and waved him away. It happily trotted back and lay down, eyes firmly fixed on his master.

'Now before we go any further, I was just about to have a bite to eat, which consists of some cheese on toast and a coffee, will you join me? You can wash your hands over there.'

Gibson wouldn't normally accept, but he was starving.

'That would be very nice, Mr, er.. sorry, Mack, thanks very much.'

Mack chatted away as he made the cheese on toast, asking Gibson about his job saying how interesting it must be. He said he always fancied himself as an investigative reporter but rarely got the chance to indulge himself in that regard, nevertheless he said he'd enjoyed his career and still dabbled as a writer on a freelance basis. Lunch was served and Gibson found the food delicious, as was the fresh coffee.

'You said on the phone you want to ask me about some events I've written about in the past, and I'm more than happy to provide any information I can, but normally at this time of the day, weather permitting, I take Monsoon here for a walk along Ainsdale beach, so unless you have any objections, I suggest we go to the beach and you can ask your questions as we walk, believe me, my recall will be much improved by all that fresh sea air.'

Gibson was a bit flummoxed, but this man wasn't a witness or anything, and was giving his time out of goodwill so Gibson felt he couldn't object, and anyway, the idea of a walk along the beach in the early spring sunshine appealed to him. He didn't have quite the right footwear, but never mind he thought.

'Okay, fine by me, do we drive to the beach?'

'No, we'll take a shortcut through the estate.'

Sure enough they were walking along the beach within minutes of leaving the house. Mack let Monsoon off his lead as soon as they got there but the dog stayed by his side until he was told to go and play, then the dog flew off like a greyhound. It was a bit blustery, but pleasant enough and Gibson enjoyed stretching his legs and watching the dog run away then back again, finally settling into a trot alongside Mack. Mack was right, the sea air was invigorating. The beach was virtually deserted, just a few people walking dogs and a horse rider galloping along the distant shoreline. In the far distance Gibson could see Southport pier, stretching far out into the Irish sea.

'Okay DS Gibson, what is it you'd like to know?'

'Well I'm trying to find some further information on events which you've reported on in the past, things that happened at Agecroft Colliery mainly, and I wondered if there were any details that weren't published that might be of interest to me.'

'I see,' said Mac thoughtfully, 'There may well be I suppose, but I'm curious, why would the police be interested in what happened at Agecroft Colliery - in the past I mean? It's probably going to close in the next year or so, so why now, and what events are we talking about?'

This is the tricky bit, obfuscation time... the truth but not the whole truth....

'Well, we're looking into a number of incidents that may have their roots in what happened to certain individuals in the past, people who worked at Agecroft Colliery, miners. It's not a specific enquiry as such, more a question of trying to glean some background information, to see if certain things have any bearing on more recent events.'

'Such as?'

'Well I'm not really at liberty to say. Anything I say could be misinterpreted and I don't want to create a situation where people jump to conclusions. You as a reporter, or former reporter anyway, know what can happen. These things can get out of hand and before you know it, all sorts of things appear in the press. Look I'm not really explaining this very well.'

'On the contrary Sergeant, I think you've made the situation very clear. You need to ask questions about certain events but you don't want to alert the press or anyone else about something that may compromise your investigation. I assume therefore you don't have much in the way of hard facts but more in the way of, to put it crudely, a hunch.'

'Yes well, it's along those lines, yes.'

'I'll tell you what DS Gibson. I'll do a deal with you. I will tell you anything and everything I know, on the record, off the record, about the events you're looking into or anything else that I think may be of help, - and I'll keep my mouth shut. I won't say a word to anyone. I'll go further, I'll find out anything you want to know. My sources are manifold and I can probably find out lots of things that you couldn't. But, the deal is, that if your investigation, your hunch, whatever you want to call it, turns out to have legs and results in a story of substance, I get the exclusive, or at least I get told before anyone else. If nothing comes of your efforts, then we've just had a nice afternoon chat on the beach and that's that. What do you say?'

Gibson thought about it. Strictly speaking he should clear it with his boss, but he decided to take a chance. He liked Mack, there was something genuine about the man. He'd go with his gut instinct.

'I can't see a problem with that.'

'Okay, ask away then.'

'Well let's take things chronologically. The first article I noticed, written by you, was a piece about the bombing of the miner's house in Regent Park West in forty two. Your piece wasn't about the main event but about the husband and father of the family wiped out in the raid.'

'Yes I remember it well. It was my first serious

assignment. I found it difficult to write it was just so horrendous. I was there the next morning when they were taking the bodies out, well what was left of them.'

'That sounds pretty horrific.'

'Believe me, it was, I still find it difficult to put those scenes into words now, even after all this time, I still can't shake the memory of those images.'

'Was there any aspect of the story you didn't report?'

'No, not that I recall, other than I kept the blood and gore to a minimum so as not to upset the immediate family, the husband mainly. Oh, and I didn't mention that the family had only recently swapped houses with another miner's family. They often swapped houses, they called it flitting.'

'Yes I've been told about them doing that, seems a bit strange to me.'

'Maybe, but they often did it to avoid debt collectors and the like. Anyway, I didn't see the point in reporting it, you know, maybe adding to the guilt. As far as I was concerned, it didn't have any real bearing on the tragedy, other than to the unfortunate family who'd perished, and who had 'flitted' only the day before, poor sods.'

'What about recriminations, did anyone blame anyone else for them moving, er, flitting?'

'Not that I knew of, but then grief was the main

emotion when I was there, anger and vengeance tends to come later in my experience.'

As soon as he'd said it, Mack stopped walking and looked at Gibson.

'So I take it that's what you're looking for, a motive for vengeance?'

'Yes it is, something in the past obviously, maybe the dim and distant past, who knows, but I think I have to consider anything and everything. Sometimes people hold grudges for years then something happens, acts as a trigger to make them act on it.'

'Yes, I understand, believe me, I've studied human behaviour on many levels over the years and I know just what you mean.' Mack stood there thinking, then said. 'Look if I'm going to help you, you need to take me into your confidence and tell me the whole story in as much detail as you can, then I can see what I can bring to the party as it were, okay?'

Oh shit, in for a penny.....

'Okay,' said Gibson as they started walking again, 'look I'm not being melodramatic here, but taking you into my confidence means I'm putting myself at risk of an extremely serious reprimand or worse, and don't underestimate what that might mean to my future career as a policeman, okay? So if anything I tell you gets into the press, before they've been briefed formally by our lot, then I'm up shit creek without a paddle, big time.

Now that doesn't mean that I won't tip you the wink on any final developments, but that will be on my terms and my timing, understood?'

'I think you've made the situation clear, and you can rest assured Sergeant, look do I have to keep calling you DS Gibson or Sergeant, or whatever, don't you have a simple name I can use?'

Gibson laughed.

'Just call me Gibson, everyone else does.'

'Okay Gibson, well you can trust me to be discreet and not to let you down. I built my reputation on just that very thing. You'd be surprised what I know and have never told a living soul, so please feel free to tell me anything you like. I promise not to publish or tell anyone else without your express permission or agreement, you have my word on it.'

For some reason he couldn't quite fathom, Gibson trusted the man, and he thought it would be useful to get a completely objective opinion on his theories, especially from someone who had intimate knowledge of the various events relating to his investigation.

'Look Gibson, the sun's gone in now and it's getting a bit chilly, looks like rain clouds over there as well, so why don't we go back, have a another cup of coffee and we can see what I might know that might help your investigation.'

'Sounds good to me.'

They got back just before the rain moved in.

Mack made some more excellent coffee and they sat down again at his kitchen table. Gibson told him the story, more or less from the beginning. Mack nodded on occasion but kept quiet and listened without interruption until Gibson had finished, then Gibson excused himself and asked where the bathroom was. When he came back Mack was still obviously considering what he'd told him.

'Okay so apart from a whole lot of speculation, albeit reasonable speculation, you don't have a case, a suspect or any real leads.'

Gibson was mildly offended at the blunt description of his efforts to date, but had to be honest with himself.

'Yes, correct.'

'However, the fact that three deaths, of people who worked together down the mines and were neighbours for a significant part of their lives - all deaths occurring on the same date, cannot be dismissed as mere coincidence, never. I love it. No, that sounds terrible, callous even, but you know what I mean.'

'I know exactly what you mean,' said Gibson with a smile.

'So these acts of revenge, if that's what they were, and I agree it's hard to see it any other way, were triggered by some event in the past involving these people, and possibly more people that we don't yet know about, such as this Barry Jones feller, whom you've yet to find?'

'Correct.'

'Okay, well I know this might sound a bit daft, but let's not try too hard to find the event as such, let's just talk about anything I reported on in the past that relates to them working as miners or to where they lived. When we had brain storming sessions at the paper, the best ideas would always pop up when we relaxed and just talked around a subject rather than looked too specifically for the story. So, let's go back to your very first observation, regarding me that is, and your very flattering compliment about how my article moved you.'

'Okay Mack, I'm game, so tell me what happened when you arrived at the scene that day, at the bombed out house.'

'Well, the then editor, Henry Goodchild, God bless him, he was old school and I think he'd been biding his time, waiting to throw me in at the deep end. I'd been pestering him to let me do some serious stuff instead of reporting on the local WI events, garden parties and council meetings. I think he'd noticed that I had something about me, but he wasn't the type to say it, in case it might go to my head, so when the reports came in of a German bombing on Regent Park West, he just handed me the information on a scrap of paper and pointed at the door.'

'Go and cover this, and you'd better do a bloody

good job or else.'

'I was beside myself with excitement. That is, until I got to the place and saw the devastation, then I realised it wasn't just about a good story. Even the most eloquent wordsmith can't really describe what it's like seeing real people, or bits of people being picked out of the sort of carnage a bomb can inflict. If you think about it, what you mainly see on news reports is the damage to buildings, which is bad enough, but think about how robust bricks and mortar are compared to, flesh blood and bone.

As a reporter, you do your best, in fact it's your duty to be as brutally honest as you can, try to give an objective account of the way things are. But there are times when that just isn't possible, so in place of describing the gruesome gory details, you focus on the impact that an event has on the nearest and dearest, sometimes that's really the only way you can hope to get it across to people, try to tap into their own emotions, their fears and horror of such a thing happening to them, their children, wives, husbands. Sorry I can get quite carried away. Anyway, that's why I did the piece on the husband. I thought it was the only way I could adequately describe the devastation I'd witnessed.'

'Yes I can understand that, who was the husband, what was his name, I read the article, but I'm ashamed to say I didn't register the name.'

'The family were called Potts, I think the husband was called David, yes David Potts.

'Yes I remember now, David Potts, carry on Mack.'

'Okay, so where were we?, ah yes, I was waxing lyrical about my days as a cub reporter, well after that baptism of fire, as it were, my editor thought me capable of covering more interesting stories, most of which are irrelevant to the topic in hand, but as far as Agecroft Colliery went, there were a few interesting events over the years. There was the accident in nineteen fifty seven or fifty eight, can't remember precisely.'

'It was fifty eight,' said Gibson.

'Oh, so you know about that?'

'Yes, but I only know basic details, so please go on.'

'Right, okay, well one of the miners died as a result of some miscommunication. Someone at the top thinking the men below had left the area. That was a difficult one and whilst I didn't downplay the tragedy of the men who were injured and the one that died, I did try to invoke some sympathy for the man who made the fatal decision to go ahead with blasting. He was the one who would have to live for the rest of his life with the guilt of having caused such a terrible tragedy. The accident made headlines all around the world and my story was syndicated to some impressive publications. Fame at last I thought, but that was nothing compared to the miners' strike in eighty five.

I covered the strike on a daily basis, lived on the picket line day in day out. I know this sounds terrible but they were really quite exciting times. Thatcher versus Scargill. It was a fight to the death, politically speaking that is. Agecroft Colliery was particularly significant in that it crystallised the polarisation of the factions amongst the miners, and the hatred it caused between the ones who wanted an all-out strike and those who thought they were playing into the hands of the government, well you had to see it to believe it. Feelings were running so high, the situation would often erupt into bloody violence, made for some great photographic news I can tell you.'

'Okay, so knowing what I've told you about the current investigation, and given that perspective, is there anything at the time, that any of these three events - the bombing, the accident or the later miners' strike, that could have any bearing on these deaths, and does the third of February date ring any bells?'

'No, nothing comes to mind about reprisals, not anything that I can think of where a grudge would be held for such a long time, but obviously someone has, held a grudge for all this time I mean. As for the date, again, can't think of anything significant but I really need to do some digging through my old notes and check if anything comes to light. That's not to say I won't wake up tomorrow and remember, but at the moment I'm drawing a blank. It's early days though Gibson, and as you said, these three deaths can't be put down to coincidence. Give me time to do some research and let's see what I come up with'

'Okay, well listen Mack, I really appreciate you seeing me today and as you say, when you're not trying so hard to make a connection, things can just come to you out of the blue, so if you remember anything that might have a bearing, please call me, you have all my contact details.'

'I certainly will Gibson.' Mack frowned then smiled, 'Talking of coincidences, I've just remembered one, nothing directly to do with what we're talking about, but when I was covering the strike, there were reporters from all around the world, lots from Europe too. We all used to get together in the pub in the evenings, swap tall stories and generally bullshit each other.

Anyway, I got friendly with this young German reporter. He was a bit shy to begin with, which in itself is unusual in this profession, but we got talking. Anyway it turned out that his father was one of the POWs who'd died in the bombing raid, the second raid on the area, the one that set fire to their hut, the week after the air aid that destroyed the house in Regent Park West.'

'That's quite a coincidence; surely he wasn't there just by chance?'

'I asked him the same question and he told me he'd asked for the assignment so he could visit the area where his father died. He told me he'd never known his father and didn't think his father was even aware of his existence. His mother hadn't known she was pregnant until after his father had left Germany to fight in the war. It was a sad story and I felt sorry for him.'

Gibson had been getting ready to leave but sat back down.

'How did you leave it with this German reporter, did you keep in touch, what was his name?'

'No, we didn't keep in touch. We made all the usual promises but you know how it is? I think he said he was called after his father, from memory it was a typical German name, Hans I think, yes Hans something, I can't remember his surname, but I will. He told me his mother hadn't received details of his father's death until well after the war had finished. Anyway, he wanted to go and visit his father's grave so I told him that I thought he was buried along with his comrades in Agecroft Cemetery, but he knew that already, nothing if not efficient these Germans.'

'Hmm, interesting story Mack, well thanks again and let me know if you think of anything else.'

'Will do Gibson, have a safe journey home.'

The rain had stopped and the roads weren't

too busy so Gibson had a pleasant enough drive back. He pondered the conversation he'd had with Mack, interesting man he thought, *but whether anything will come of the meeting, who knows?* He tried to think what he'd learnt that he didn't know already. Not much really, other than that story at the end about the German reporter. Something tugged at his brain. Could the German reporter have any reason for revenge? He was there about the right time of the first killing, Geoff Brown's murder, but what reason could he possibly have for killing him, or any of the others?

The death of your father would certainly be a strong motive, but it had been his own countrymen who had bombed the hut and killed his father. Try as he might, Gibson couldn't make any connection between the son of the POW and the men whose deaths he was investigating. He felt he was now clutching at straws in his frustration to make some progress, so he decided to put it all to the back of his mind and think about where he would take Jill out to tonight, the cinema and a fish and chip supper afterwards, *sounds good.*

CHAPTER 17

The next morning, he prepared an updated report for the DCI, but he was out so he left the report on his desk with a note asking the DCI to call him on his return, then went back to his own office. In the meantime, he decided to try once again to find the whereabouts of missing gang member Barry Jones. Despite having chased up his request a number of times with the police in Pwhelli, they still hadn't responded with any information. He'd tried to inject some urgency into the request but hadn't wanted to tell them the full story unless he had to. He imagined that any mention of a murder enquiry involving that relatively sleepy part of the country would start the wires buzzing.

A sudden involuntary joke popped into his mind – leaks and Wales, he laughed to himself. They obviously weren't taking the matter seriously enough at the moment and he appreciated that 'missing persons' didn't excite anyone very much, there were just too many of them and they were generally treated as backburner issues.

The detective Gibson spoke to initially in Pwhelli laughed so hard at Gibson's request he couldn't speak for a while. When he'd recovered sufficiently, he apologised to Gibson, but was obviously still on the verge of laughter.

I'm sorry Detective Gibson,' he'd said, obviously stifling the urge to start laughing again, 'it just touched my funny bone, I don't normally react like that, but you're probably aware that the name Barry Jones is hardly unique in Wales and in fact it's my own name - Detective Sergeant Barry Jones, you see, so that's what tickled me, apologies again, please carry on, why are we looking for this Barry Jones character anyway? Any details you can give me that might help us locate him?'

Gibson felt slightly annoyed at the matter being treated with such levity, but tried to appreciate the humour nonetheless. Gibson was able to give his welsh counterpart some more details, approximate age, previous known address, the Christian name of Barry Jones's wife etc.

'Okay D S Gibson, we'll get on to it, I'll let you know when we come up with anything.'

'Thanks, it is a matter of some urgency so I'd appreciate it if you could come back to me as soon as possible.'

'Sure thing.'

Gibson wasn't convinced.

It had been over twenty four hours since he last spoke to DS Jones, so he decided to call yet again.

He got through straight away.

'Hello DS Jones, DS Gibson here, just calling to see if you've had any success yet in locating our man Barry Jones yet?'

'Well not so far Sergeant Gibson, we've had rather a lot on of late, some gangs from Liverpool operating in the area, knocking off some of the larger houses, so we've had a lot of pressure from on high.'

'So have you made any progress at all? This is quite an important matter and I need to find this man as a matter of some urgency now.'

Gibson decided to add something that might get his attention.'

'There's a possibility that the Barry Jones we're looking for, is now dead.'

The reaction was immediate and Gibson smiled, noting a distinct change in the tone of voice at the other end.

'Oh, and why do you think that Sergeant?'

'Well we're looking for him in connection with some other unexplained deaths, not that he's a suspect, more a possible victim, but until we find him we don't know, but some recent developments do give us cause for concern.'

The detective at the other end seemed to be all business now.

'Okay Sergeant Gibson, well that puts a different light on it. Rest assured we'll pull out all the stops on this and try to find him for you, and once again apologies for my initial reaction, just my silly sense of humour.'

'No sweat, just let me know when you get a result and thanks for your time.'

Gibson put the phone down and it rang immediately, it was DCI Watson asking him to come to his office. Gibson made his way to the DCIs office, knocked and went in.

'I've read through your report. Taking a bit of a chance with this reporter aren't you?'

'Yes sir, but I'm confident he'll be discreet, and I've warned him what will happen if anything gets out, so I don't think there's any need to worry, and I think he will be very useful in providing further information for me.'

'Hmm, well let's hope your faith in this man isn't misplaced. Now, there's obviously not a lot more in terms of hard facts but I think you've narrowed down the list of potential events that may have created the motivation for these revenge killings, if that's what they are. The obvious ones are the accident at Agecroft Colliery and the miners' strike. Either situation could have generated strong emotions, capable of driving someone to believe they had just cause to right a wrong, but the date of the third of February doesn't feature in any obvious way, and none of the men whose deaths we're investigating seem to have had any direct involvement in either the miners' strike or the accident at the pit.'

'Yes that's true.'

'What about this story of the young German reporter?'

'What about it?'

'I don't know, just interesting, makes you think about the situation, you know the second raid and the incredible coincidence, a German bomber offloading his last incendiary bomb and hitting a wooden hut containing German POWs before going back to base, ironic to say the least.'

'I suppose it is sir, but these things happen.'

'Hmm, not sure I'd be prepared to accept that so readily Gibson.'

'Sorry sir, I'm not getting your drift.'

'Not sure I'm getting it either Gibson, just thinking out loud I suppose, but I just sense something doesn't quite fit. It's either my sixth sense, or more likely, a sign that I'm going senile.'

'Yes sir.'

'Gibson, you're not supposed to agree with me when I make self-deprecating remarks like that, you're supposed to say something reassuring.'

'Sorry sir, I meant to say I'm sure it's just a sign of your ever increasing brilliance and superb powers of perception.'

'Okay Gibson, no need to take the piss.'

Gibson smiled and said nothing.

'I sense we're losing our momentum here Gibson, happens in most investigations. You make good progress to begin with then the leads just seem to dry up. The clincher would be if you can find this Barry Jones and, God forgive me, find that he died on the third of February. That would put everything we've assumed so far, well beyond doubt.'

'I agree sir and I've chased our Welsh colleagues and asked them to get a hurry up on this and I think they're now taking me seriously, so I expect to hear from them very soon. As soon as I do I'll go down there and can find out what the score is. The Welsh police were highly amused when I initially asked them if they could locate a Barry Jones, possibly living in Pwhelli.'

'Yes I can imagine that Gibson, a bit like asking the police in Dublin if they could locate someone called Paddy Murphy.'

'Yes sir, but like I say, I think they're a bit more serious about finding him now.'

'Good, anything else?'

'Not at this stage, I'll also have a think about the bombing of the POW's hut, but I'm not sure where that's going to lead us.'

'Neither am I Gibson, neither am I, it's just… I don't know.' Watson looked out of the window and was quiet for a while, contemplating.

Gibson had been waiting for an opportunity to ask a favour and he took his chance now.

'You know I haven't had a break for a while now sir, and I'm under a bit of pressure from Jill to get right away from this investigation for a while, just a couple of days, and well I wondered if I could take tomorrow off and make a long weekend of it, the Lakes I think she said. Says it will do me good not to be obsessing about this case all the time, clear my mind, in fact she put it a bit more strongly than that, but I won't repeat what she said, nor very ladylike, you get the drift...., sir?'

Watson, who hadn't shifted in his seat while Gibson had been speaking turned and looked at Gibson.

'Well Gibson, I thought I was your boss, but it seems you have another one, perhaps with a bit more influence than me it seems.'

'In certain departments sir, without any doubt at all.'

Watson couldn't help but laugh.

'Go on you cheeky fucker, take the day off, but it'll cost you, don't forget that, now bugger off before I change my mind.'

'Very kind sir, thanks.'

'Yes well don't come back to work on Monday knackered, don't enjoy yourself too much, you need to get this thing sorted before we're all much older.'

Jill had a couple of days holiday due so it all fitted in. They packed their walking boots, some warm clothes and waterproofs and set off early Thursday morning for the two hour drive to the lakes. They didn't bother booking ahead for a hotel or anything, it was early in the season and so they decided to take their chances, and see what bargains there might be for a casual walk-in booking.

Disappointingly it was quite heavy rain all the way up to the Lakes but it started to ease as they reached the South Lakes turnoff.

'You know it's so easy to forget just how beautiful the British countryside can be,' said Gibson.

'You always say that every time we come to the Lakes.'

'I do?'

'Every time.'

They both laughed and started to discuss where they might stay.

The weekend was over too quickly and as they drove back early Sunday evening along the M6, they were both quiet for a while, Sunday evenings always had that depressing feel about them, thought Gibson, but even more so when you were coming back from holiday.'

'A penny for them,' said Gibson.

'I was just thinking what a nice time we've had, just sorry it's over, but you know what made this weekend extra special?'

'No, but flatter me.'

'No I don't mean that, not that 'that' wasn't, oh stop smirking you're getting me confused, no what I meant to say was, you haven't mentioned work once. I've not even caught you thinking about your case.'

'And you can see inside my head now can you?'

'More or less, yes. I can certainly tell when you are, thinking about a case that is, and your latest one in particular.'

'Well you're right, I haven't thought about it for one minute, and I must say I do feel refreshed, ready for anything.'

Monday morning was all the more of a Monday morning after his long weekend off and although Gibson had passed on his other cases to sergeant Bennett and others, they still needed to refer back to him on various aspects of the investigations he'd been handling. That took up most of his morning and it was lunchtime before he could re-focus on his main case. He decided to read the files again from start to finish, but as he opened the Billy Bowen file his phone rang. It was a call from Detective Sergeant Jones of the Pwhelli police.

'Hello DS Gibson?'

'Hello Sergeant Jones, how are you, some developments I assume?'

'I'm well thanks, and yes developments, but I'm afraid it's good news and bad news. The good news is I think we've found the man you've been looking for, but the bad news is that he went missing a few years ago.' Jones paused.

'Go on.'

'Sorry, just checking my notes, yes, three years ago now, nineteen eighty seven, a Barry Jones went missing at sea. It seems he'd taken over a small one man fishing boat charter business, there's quite a few of them down here. Been going for a few years and was doing okay according to his wife's statement. So the lads who handled the investigation, they ruled out any insurance claim motive, you know suicide made to look like an accident....'

'Yeah, yeah I get it, so what happened?'

'Apparently, he went out one day and didn't come back, simple as that really. His wife alerted the coast guard eventually and they had a good search of the area over the next couple of days but never found any trace of him or the boat, well other than a burst rubber dinghy some days later.'

'Does the report say what the weather was like, was it bad or anything?'

'No, quite good from what the coastguard said. I can get more detail if you want but I thought I'd better call you straight away.'

'Thanks, much appreciated D S Jones.'

'So, D S Gibson, do you think the missing Barry Jones is linked to the suspicious deaths you said you're investigating?'

'Probably not, Gibson lied, 'wrong time frame, sounds like just a coincidence that he went missing, still I'll have to follow it up, my boss will want chapter and verse regardless, i's dotted etc.' *Boy will I have some explaining to do to this man when this is all over, still, can't let the cat out of the bag yet...* so I'm going to have to come down there anyway and dig around a bit more myself. Does his wife still live there?'

'I think so but I'll check and let you know for definite. When were you thinking of coming down?'

'Early as possible, tomorrow probably.'

'Okay it's my day off but I'll change rota with the one of the other lads and meet you here.'

'It's not really necessary DS Jones.'

'No it's the least I can do, and please call me Barry, seeing how we'll be working together, for a short while anyway. I'll call you back when I get more info on the wife, but shall we pencil in a time to meet tomorrow, say midday, give you plenty of time to get down here?'

'Yes that sounds fine and can you fax me a map of where your HQ is please?', Gibson gave him the fax number.

'Oh, and just before you go, when did he go missing, the precise date?' Gibson waited, holding his breath.

'Let's see, it's here somewhere, ah yes, he was officially reported as missing on the fourth of February nineteen eighty eight.' Gibson tried to stay calm. He didn't want to give any indication that the date was significant and invite awkward questions.

'Would a fishing charter boat normally go out in the winter, in February?'

'Depends on the weather, down here we can get

some quite balmy weather at that time of year, so I wouldn't say it was normal, but not that unusual either if the weather's okay, which was one of the comments made by the coastguard, you know, the fact that the weather shouldn't have played a part in the boat's disappearance,' Gibson felt he'd asked enough over the phone.

'Okay, thanks Barry, I'll see you tomorrow.'

'Okay, and what do I call you now we're a bit more acquainted?'

'Everyone calls me Gibson.'

'Okay Gibson, look forward to meeting you.'

The drive down to Wales was pleasant enough, being early in the week there was little holiday traffic to contend with.

DCI Watson hadn't taken the news about the missing Barry Jones very well.

'We've got to find this fucking maniac Gibson, and soon. How in heaven's name have these crimes gone undetected for all this time? When this gets out, the press will have a field day. If they get their hands on the story before we've made any significant progress, we'll be in deep shit. We need to keep it quiet until we have something solid. As it stands, all we've got is multiple deaths, no leads, no suspect, Jesus Christ we'll be crucified in the media. The commander isn't going to be too thrilled about this either I can tell you. I think he may want to bring in a new team, not that we'd lose the investigation, but he may insist we need help.'

'I'd really like to crack this before he brings anyone else sir, and I think I can. It could get really messy if too many people are involved, and stopping the story leaking would be that much more difficult, maybe impossible if we bring more people in. I'm sure the commander would want to avoid that.'

'Good point Gibson, but yet another victim and still no significant progress, no motive, or any idea on who the perpetrator might be. Another thing, if Mr Barry Jones is another victim, and it's hard to see it any other way, then it only adds to the doubt about Freddie Exan's guilt. He could hardly have been involved in Barry Jones's disappearance while he was languishing in jail. If anything Gibson, assuming the killer is out to murder all the members of that original gang, then Exan is a potential target for the murderer, or serial murderer as we should now probably call him.'

'Yes sir, I was thinking along the same lines, so should we consider some form of protection? I mean, the deaths we're now attributing to this killer are historical and occurred prior to us having any knowledge about what might be going on, but if Freddie Exan is killed now, the blame would be well and truly laid at our door.'

"I'll talk to the commander about it and get something organised. Gets more ironic as we go along, the poor fucker gets out of jail where he's been serving a sentence for something he probably didn't do, but in fact it probably saved his life being in there, and he'd be a darn sight safer if he was back in jail. What Gibson? I can hear you thinking.'

'Just a funny thought sir, but he's probably safe until next February.'

Watson laughed. 'Yes you're probably right Gibson, but I don't think we can afford to take the chance. Now you get down to Wales and establish the facts about the disappearance of this Barry Jones. Report to me as soon as you get back.'

Gibson drove along trying to organise his thoughts, running all the facts through his brain again until he just couldn't think any more. He had just bypassed Chester then crossed the English Welsh border. It was a three hour drive in total so he figured he had plenty of time to think later. He decided to give his brain a rest and started to take in the scenery.

He arrived at the seaside town of Pwhelli more or less on time, finally locating Ala Road and the police station, which had a signpost hanging at the front in welsh, HEDDLU, then underneath in English, POLICE. It was a pleasing looking yellowish brick building, but looked more like a house than a police station really, and eminently preferable to the monstrous edifice he worked in he thought. He found a parking place and walked through the front door of the police station. Chatting to the desk Sergeant was a slight man of around thirty five, sharp featured face, dark hair, dressed in civilian clothes. He looked up as Gibson entered the station.

'D S Gibson?' he enquired.

'That's me.' Said Gibson.

'Pleased to meet you at last, Barry Jones as you've probably guessed.'

'Nice to meet you too Barry.' They shook hands and Sergeant Jones led Gibson to his office.

'Nice building,' Gibson said making small talk as they walked along the narrow corridor.

'Yes, lots of history here, it was the former home of some famous Welsh opera singer, Megan Jones I think she was called, no relation. They reached Jones's office.

'Please sit down, would you like a coffee, tea, anything to eat?'

'I'll just have a cup of tea if that's okay.' Jones picked up the phone and ordered two teas.

'I hope you don't mind, but I assumed you'd want to meet Barry Jones's widow, so I've made an appointment for us to see her at one o'clock, she lives just over the other side of town, not too far away.'

Gibson had anticipated that such an appointment would be made, and that the Sergeant would try to get involved. Curiosity was part of a detective's make up and Gibson would have done the same in his situation. He was ready with his response.

'That's very kind of you thanks, er Barry, but I really need to see her on my own on this occasion. I think it might be a bit too intimidating being interviewed by two officers.'

Jones's disappointment was obvious but there was nothing he could do about it.

'Yes of course if that's what you think best. He turned to his desk and found the piece of paper he was looking for.

'This is her address and I'll draw a bit of a map for you. It's not difficult to find, so you shouldn't have any problem.'

'Thanks Barry.'

'Listen Gibson, I've been thinking, and please don't take this the wrong way, but you seem to be putting a lot of effort into something you say you don't think is relevant to your other investigation. If there is anything in this missing Barry Jones situation, you know you can trust me, I can be very discreet, and I'm not a blabbermouth.'

Gibson felt extremely awkward and felt terrible lying to a colleague, but he just couldn't take the chance.

'No Barry, it's not like that, like I say my boss DCI Watson, he'd jump all over me if I don't do things his way. He's a real pain in the backside and a stickler for detail, so it's not as though I have a choice. He'll expect me to be thorough even though it a waste of time.' *I'm not fooling this bloke at all...*

Just then the tea came and saved Gibson having to say more. Barry Jones looked disappointed but dropped the subject and they chatted for a while about police matters in general, then Gibson got up, excused himself and asked to use the lavatory before setting off to see Mrs Jones.

As Sergeant Jones had said, Mrs Jones house was easy to find. It was a modern red brick semi on a small estate just by the sea. She'd been expecting him and showed him straight into her front room. She was dainty, had short dark hair and small pixie like features. Anxiety was etched on her pale pasty face giving her a haunted fragile look. She was obviously eager to find out what this was all about and Gibson detected a glimmer of hope in her manner, making him feel like a fraud.

They sat down and she asked if he'd like some tea but he declined. Then a phone rang somewhere and she excused herself and went out of the room to answer it. Gibson got up and looked the many pictures on the wall and on the sideboard. They all showed the same man in each, Barry Jones he assumed, together with various groups of people, always with the same boat in the background. They invariably displayed catches of fish with all the people smiling broadly at their piscatorial achievements. Mrs Jones came back and apologised for the interruption, her voice trembling a little despite her efforts at trying to appear calm.

'So is there something new?' Mrs Jones asked as she sat down, a mixture of fear and hope in her voice.

Gibson had prepared a story to cover the real reason for his visit.

'No not really I'm afraid, well not directly, it's just that we're looking into the death of one of your husband's old acquaintances. His death occurred some time ago, in nineteen eighty five, but circumstances have arisen lately that have caused us to re-examine matters, routine really, just a procedural matter, but it came to our attention that the deceased, Geoff Brown, may have been in contact with your husband before his death, so we're just covering all the bases.'

Mrs Jones looked confused.

'So you're not here about my Barry's disappearance?'

'No, not as such, tragic as it is, we can't see how it would have any bearing on the matter of Mr Brown's death, but as I say, we're covering all the bases. Tell me did he, your husband, ever mention the murder of his old friend Geoff Brown?'

Mrs Jones looked at Gibson unsure of where this was going. Gibson tried to maintain an air of detachment.

'Yes he did, you mean the man who was killed by his best friend, that one I assume? Barry knew both of the men involved, he was very upset. Geoff Brown had been the only one of his old friends to keep in touch, could write a nice letter could Geoff, not often mind you, but even so…'

'I don't suppose you have any of Geoff's letters do you?'

'Yes, think I know where Barry kept them, he was a bit of a hoarder you know.' She hesitated then realised. 'Oh, I suppose you'd like to see them?'

'Well if you don't mind, I mean they probably won't have any bearing on the matters I'm looking into but my boss will expect me to cover all the bases as it were.'

She looked at Gibson in a resigned manner then spoke.

'Yes, okay well I can't see what difference it's going to make to me, or Barry now, I'll go and get them.'

She left the room and went upstairs and was back down in a couple of minutes. She handed the small bundle of letters over to Gibson.

'Do you mind if I borrow these Mrs Jones, I'll send them back to you in a few days' time?

'No, take them, I don't mind. You know, I still think my Barry's going to come walking through that door any minute, large as life….,' her voice faltered and she took a moment to compose herself. Gibson waited saying nothing until she'd recovered her composure.

'Perhaps you could tell me a bit about Barry, how did he end up here with his own boat, it's a bit different than working down a mine?'

'We met in nineteen seventy five. Barry had come down for a holiday at Butlin's holiday camp with a couple of his mates in the August. I was working as a chalet maid, you know cleaning the rooms, helping out with the entertainment and looking after kids.'

'Was Geoff Brown one of these 'mates' he came down with?'

'No, Geoff wasn't with him on the holiday, but he came to our wedding later, so that's when I met him. Anyway Barry didn't see much of his mates on the holiday because we met just a couple of days after he arrived, fell for each other, love at first sight it was, and well, we became lovers I suppose is the way to describe it, not just randy sex I mean, we really were in love. Anyway when Barry left to go back we both cried and he swore he was going to give up his job down the mine and come back and marry me.'

'And presumably that's what happened?'

'Yes, although probably a bit sooner than we both thought, you see I found out shortly after Barry left that I was pregnant. I told him and he didn't hesitate. He packed in his job and came down here to find work. He was lucky and found a job helping one of my Dad's friends out on his boat, fishing charters. He was part time to begin with, but the owner of the boat was getting on a bit, so Barry did more and more, and that's how he came to own the boat eventually. The man who originally owned it left it all to Barry when he died. Anyway, we'd already got married shortly after Barry came down here, and we moved in with my Mum and Dad until we could get a little place of our own. Megan was born a few months after Barry and I were married, she's twenty four now and lives in London, got a good job, doing really well she is.'

'So let's move on to when Barry disappeared, what happened, anything unusual about that day, I mean apart from…, well him going missing, or in the days before he disappeared?'

'No, there was nothing unusual, well other than the weather was very mild for the time of year. We'd had a nice weekend, been out on the boat ourselves that Sunday, then Monday he was doing some work on the boat, getting it ready for the season, tidying it up, a bit of painting, varnishing and all that stuff. Boats need constant attention Barry always said, just like a woman. He was always joking comparing his boat to me, the two loves of his life he'd say, three including Megan of course.'

'The detective who originally investigated Barry's disappearance told me that he had just one charter client that day, tell me how that came about, I mean, wouldn't he normally take out groups of fishermen, not just one person?'

'Yes he would but Barry said this bloke had wandered up to him on the Monday, while he was working on the boat, and asked if it was possible to go fishing the next day. It was a bit unusual, a bit early in the year to be going out, but the weather forecast was good and we were having like a false spring they call it, so he said he told him if the weather held he didn't see why not. Like you said, normally there'd be a party of people, three at least, the boat could take up to six comfortably, a couple more with a squeeze, but I think Barry thought it was extra money so why not.'

'Did you see this man at all?'

'No, I never saw him.'

'Did Barry describe the man, say what he looked like or tell you a name?'

'I think he did tell me his name, but I've never been able to remember it. All I can remember is that he said the man was a foreigner, spoke with a foreign accent.'

This was new information to Gibson. He was annoyed that this hadn't been mentioned in the notes he'd seen of the investigation to date.

'Did he tell you anything else about this man, was he old, young, short, tall, anything unusual?'

'No, if he did I can't remember. I wasn't taking that much notice really; it was just another fishing charter. I made up the lunches as normal, flask of hot coffee and sandwiches, plus some fruit.' She looked more intensely at Gibson.

'You seem to be taking an awful lot of interest in Barry's disappearance for someone who says this probably has nothing to do with Geoff Brown's murder?'

'Well the thing is, until we have all the information, we just don't know if there's any link. At the moment, there's nothing to associate the disappearance of your husband and the murder of Geoff Brown, other than they were friends in the past, and that's a tenuous link at best.'

Gibson hated himself for lying to this woman but he just couldn't risk telling her about the coincidence of the dates. The woman was clearly not convinced, but shrugged her shoulders.

'What else do you want to know?'

'Just tell me the rest of the story as it happened, when did you start to get concerned that something was wrong?'

'Well as you know the days are very short in February and he needed to be back around four o'clock, maybe a bit later, it soon gets dark after that, but I wasn't too worried for a while. I thought maybe he'd gone for a beer in the pub afterwards. He sometimes did that but not often. Anyway I waited until half past six and then I got worried so I called the pub and no one had seen him, so I went round to see if the boat was moored up and nothing, no sign of the boat or Barry.

That's when I really got worried, so I called the coast guard.

They'd heard nothing, no distress call. They said the weather had been good, calm seas all day, so they were at a loss to think what might have happened. They'd spoken to Barry when he headed out in the morning and he'd told them which wreck he intended to fish over, given them the co-ordinates, and that was the last they'd heard from him. They tried calling on his VHF but got no response so they launched a boat to search the area. They wouldn't normally do that until the morning, but it was a full moon and the seas were still calm so they didn't hesitate, but they found nothing.'

'So that was, what date?'

'It was Tuesday the third of February when he went missing, then Wednesday when they officially declared him missing, the fourth of February.'

'What about the customer, the person who chartered the boat?'

'Nothing as far as I know, no one reported anyone missing to my knowledge, the police might know different.'

'And that was it, nothing more?'

'Not quite, the dinghy, Barry's dinghy, an inflatable little boat. Every big boat has one, they call it a tender, don't know why, always struck me as a strange name for a boat, anyway they found it on a beach a few days later. It was popped, burst. They said it had blown in with the wind and tide.'

'What did the coastguard make of that, or the police? Did they say what they think happened, I mean why the dinghy ended up on the beach?'

'Nothing, they never said anything about it really, I think they were mystified by the whole thing, like I was. I mean Barry was a really good captain, lots of experience, it was a nice day, so no good reason for him and his boat disappearing like that. There's never been a satisfactory explanation about what might have happened. But you turning up today asking these questions, it's making me wonder.'

'I'm really sorry if I'm opening up old wounds Mrs Jones, I don't mean to cause you any distress.'

'You couldn't 'distress me', as you put it, any more than I've been distressed since Barry disappeared. I'll be honest with you, Sergeant Gibson is it?, if it wasn't for Megan, I'd have ended it all by now. You just can't imagine what it's like, one minute I had the life I'd dreamed of. Not a lot of money, but we were okay. But I had a man who loved me, and I loved him. And the next minute, he was gone, just like that.'

Gibson nodded and looked away, not knowing how to respond to such raw emotion. Mrs Jones carried on speaking.

'Look I'm no fool Sergeant and I can tell there's more to this that you're letting on. I suppose you must have your reasons for not telling me. You seem like a decent man, so I'm not going to kick up a fuss. All I'll say is that if you find out what happened to Barry, you let me know before I or Megan, read about it in some crummy newspaper. In the meantime, if there's anything I can do to help you find out what happened, then you can call me, okay? Now if you'll excuse me I'd like you to go now.'

'Okay, Mrs Jones I'll leave my card in case you want to get in touch, goodbye.'

Gibson left, feeling guilty, he felt as if he'd played some sort of trick on a grieving woman. She was a smart perceptive person and he was impressed by her ability to deal with the whole tragedy in such a dignified way, and it only made him further resolve to get to the bottom of these murders.

CHAPTER 18

He drove away from the house and after a couple of miles he came across a McDonald's and pulled into the car park. He took the bundle of letters off the passenger seat and untied the string. There were only five letters. He read through the first one. Geoff Brown did indeed write a nice letter, neat handwriting and few spelling mistakes. The content was less interesting from Gibson's perspective, just stuff about old friends, who was doing what, questions about how Barry was enjoying the change from being underground to being out at sea with all the fresh air, but nothing enlightening.

Gibson speed read through the remaining letters but learnt nothing of interest. He put them back on the passenger seat deciding to read them again in more detail later on at the station. He pulled out of the car park and resumed his journey. On the drive back, Gibson switched on the car radio to distract himself, but couldn't find anything he wanted to listen to and switched it off again. He went through everything again in his mind again and tried to simplify things.

Just concentrate of the basics, he told himself. *One, what is the significance of the third of February? Two, there has to have been an event that all the murdered friends were involved in. Three, all the murdered people lived in the same street and worked in the same mine, at least in the early part of their lives. Four, a 'foreign man' features in at least two of the murders. Okay so what significant events do we know of that all these people were involved in? One, the bombing of the houses in Regent Park West in forty two. Two, the pit accident of fifty eight. Three, the miners' strike in eighty five, and that's it. Any one of these events could have involved a situation that might have caused someone to seek revenge. Two of the events involved the untimely death of loved ones, loved by someone at any rate.*

It was no good, his mind was beginning to seize up. He switched the radio back on and listened to the afternoon play on BBC Radio Four. It was an adaptation of one of Le Carre's George Smiley stories, The Spy Who Came in from the Cold, all about an East German double agent. A couple of hours later he drove into the car park at police HQ in Swinton and hurried to his office. He sat down at his desk opened his file, found Mack's number and dialled.

'Hello Mack, Gibson here, no, I'm not feeling great if I'm being honest,' Gibson said in response to Mack enquiring how he was.

'I've just come back from Wales where I've been talking to the wife of a man who went missing at sea some years ago, a Mr Barry Jones.'

'Please don't tell me he went missing on the third of February?'

'Yep, three years ago, nineteen eighty seven. He was officially reported missing on the fourth of February, but that was after, you know, the search, and when they didn't find him....'

'Unbelievable, and was there anything that might give you a lead, any investigation, did they find his body, the boat, anything?'

'Nope, it was just recorded as missing at sea, so no real investigation and nothing ever found, other than a small rubber dingy from the boat, found some days later, blown in by the wind and tide they said, it was popped. Doesn't take a genius to work out what happened, knowing what we know anyway. He had a passenger, the man who chartered his boat, a foreigner his wife said. Jones ran a little fishing charter business out of Pwhelli.'

There was silence at the other end of the line as Mack absorbed the information.

'This is one resourceful serial killer.'

'You said it Mack, now I don't need to remind you about confidentiality do I? 'Cos this is just piling on the pressure, this gets out and all hell will break loose. The brass are crapping themselves. Bodies piling up and no real leads, nothing. Anyway I've been thinking, which is the main reason I'm calling you. Can you dig up all you can on the bombing and the fire that killed the German POWs in forty two? And can you write down all you can remember on the young German reporter you met while you were covering the miners' strike, the son of one of the POWs who got killed in the air raid?'

'Yes, not a problem, may I ask why?'

'Well I know this is a bit of a reach, but an unknown 'foreigner' visited Joe Martin in the care home some time before he died, and then, the man who chartered Barry Jones's boat was described as a foreigner, so for foreigner, you could read 'German'. Now before you say anything, I appreciate that it's difficult to see why this German reporter would have any grudge to bear against the people whose deaths I'm looking into, and I appreciate that it was his own countrymen, the Luftwaffe, however innocently, who caused the death of his father, and the other POWs, but I just need to look at this man in a bit more detail. More than likely, he wasn't even in the country when these deaths occurred, although he was obviously here when Geoff Brown was murdered in eighty five, because that's when you met him, but I just need to absolutely rule the man out if nothing else, and that means I've got to get as much information on him as I can, maybe go and see him, talk to him, depends, so let me have as much as you can get, okay?'

'Yes, I understand, and consider it done. But with respect Gibson, I have to say I think it's a waste of your valuable time, but you're the boss. I'll work on it right away and get back to you.'

'Thanks Mack, and while you're at it, can you look for any event, no matter how small or insignificant, that involved the date of the third February, any year, for Agecroft pit, the miners, or the POWs, anything? I'm clutching at straws here Mack, but I need something.

'I realise how serious this is Gibson, and I'll do my best to help.'

'Thanks Mack, much appreciated, I'll call you back tomorrow and see what you've managed to dig up.'

He put the phone down and wondered. *I really am clutching at straws here, that bloody radio play getting me going about Germans and subterfuge, maybe I'm losing it?, why would this German reporter have any reason to bear a grudge against anyone other than the German bombers who caused his father's death. Still him being around at the time of Geoff Brown's murder, it's another coincidence that needs rationalising away, at the very least.*

Gibson called DCI Watson's office. He needed to bring him up to date about the missing Barry Jones, and see if he had any ideas on where to look next. The DCI said he'd be free in about ten minutes so he used the time to call Sergeant Jones at Pwhelli police station to give him an update on his meeting with Mrs Jones. He kept the details to a minimum and tried to impress upon DS Jones once more, the need for complete discretion and to keep all information relating to the case completely confidential. Gibson tried to get over the consequences that would result if anyone was found to have been the cause of any leak to the press, or anyone else for that matter, but he tried to do it without it seeming to be him issuing a threat.

Nevertheless, he made it clear that the potential embarrassment of them missing a possible murder would have serious consequences for the Welsh police and for Jones himself, in case the disappearance of Barry Jones turned out to be more than just another boat missing at sea. It was a difficult conversation and he could tell Barry Jones was upset about not being told the whole picture.

'I hear you loud and clear Gibson, I understand, like I told you, I'm not a blabbermouth, and neither am I a fool. I know there's more to this than you're letting on, but I'll trust my instinct and assume you have good reason for not taking me into your confidence, so don't worry, but do have the good grace to tell me what this is all about when the time comes, okay?'

'Yes, okay Barry, and thanks for your patience and understanding.'

They said their goodbyes then Gibson made his way to the DCI's office.

'Sit down Gibson.' The DCI was on the phone as usual. He finished his conversation and put the phone down.

'Okay Gibson I can see you're anxious to tell me something, I hope it's good news.'

'Not really sir.'

'I was afraid you'd say that, c'mon then let's have it.'

'Well we have another victim, Barry Jones. As you're already aware sir, he went missing at sea, but you won't be too surprised to know the date he went missing.'

'I think I can guess, the third of February. What year?'

'Eighty seven.'

'Jesus Christ, this just goes from bad to worse. Do the Welsh police know the significance of the date?'

'No sir and neither does the widow. I felt a bit bad about not telling them, but I don't see how I could without spilling the whole can of beans.'

'That's an interesting mixed metaphor Gibson, but makes the point well. So, any good news?

'Well, not good news exactly but I do have some more thoughts about who we're looking for.'

'Oh, tell me more.'

'Well remember the lady at the care home in

Eccles, where Joe Martin stayed? Well she mentioned he was 'different' after a visit from a 'foreigner'.

'Yes I remember you telling me that, go on.'

'Well Barry jones had a small fishing charter business and his wife told me that a 'foreigner' hired him to go out fishing on the third of February and that's when the boat and Barry Jones disappeared.'

'And do we have any idea who this 'foreigner might be, any clue, a name anything?'

'No, regretfully, but maybe he was German?'

'German, why German?'

'Well this is where my theory get s bit, well maybe a bit fanciful, but do you remember the German POWs, the ones who died in the fire caused by a German firebomb hitting the hut where they were billeted?'

'I do, Gibson I know I'm getting on a bit, but my memory's still functioning reasonably well.'

'Yes sir, I didn't mean to imply..., anyway, suppose for one reason or another, someone, this killer, blames the people who he's murdered, for the deaths of the German POWs?'

Watson's eyebrows arched up in an expression of *where are we going with this one?*

'Go on,' he said to Gibson in a slightly exasperated manner, 'for the sake of argument, let's say that that's the case, so who might this person be?'

'Well Mack, you remember him? The journalist

who's helping me with the historical research.'

'Yes Gibson, I remember him as well, are your questions a sort of memory test, to see if I'm going senile or something?'

'No sir, sorry, anyway, well he met this German ....'

'Yes, I remember that too, the German reporter, son of one of the POWs, right, so you're surmising that this reporter could have decided to avenge the death of his father?'

'Yes, well other than his father was killed by the Luftwaffe, so why would he blame the miners?'

'Quite so Gibson, so why are you pursuing this line of reasoning?'

'I don't honestly know, but it's just like a jigsaw that almost fits but some of the pieces are from another jigsaw altogether.'

The DCI looked at Gibson and raised his eyebrows again.

'Let's put the jigsaw to one side for the moment Gibson, have you got anything yet on the significance of the date of the third of February?'

'Sorry sir, can't make that fit anywhere yet either.'

'Hmm, okay then. So where do you think this German reporter is now?'

'No idea sir, but I think there's a distinct possibility he's back in Germany.'

'Can you put him anywhere near the area of the

deaths on the any of the dates in question?'

'Only the first one at the moment sir, nineteen eighty five, the miners' strike and the killing of Geoff Brown.'

'And are you saying that you want try to find this reporter and interview him, even though we can't think of any cogent reason why he would want to kill the people that have been murdered?'

'Sounds a bit daft when you put it like that, but I do think it might be useful. He certainly has good reason to feel aggrieved at the untimely death of his father, but logically, he could hardly hold responsible the people who've been murdered, nevertheless I feel he's a sort of loose end that needs tidying up.'

'Are you sure you're not just grasping at straws here Gibson?'

'My own thoughts exactly sir, so yes I suppose I might be, but the way I see it is that someone has murdered four people we know about, possibly more, but assuming it's just four, then we have, in anyone's judgement, a serial killer at large. I appreciate that we haven't established a solid motive, nor do we have any real physical evidence of murder, other than Geoff Brown's killing, but all these men, connected in other ways, murdered on that same date, is just too compelling and I'd challenge anyone to claim these deaths are just coincidence and not connected, so we have to follow up anything and everything that relates to any circumstances involving these people, no matter how tenuous. It's our duty to do everything we can to try to get a lead on this person before he kills again - sir.'

'That's quite a speech Gibson.'

'Sorry sir.'

'Don't apologise Gibson, passion's a good thing as long as it's not misplaced. And I agree with your sentiments in general, but I think we need to stand back a little and re-think the whole situation in relation to our focus on this 'gang', as it were.'

'How do you mean sir?'

'Well, we've sort of taken it for granted that the murderer wants to kill all five member of this so called gang, and by definition, that includes the remaining member who's still alive, Mr Freddie Exan, but that may not be necessarily so. I mean just because all five were members of some childhood, or youth gang, it doesn't follow that all five are the murderer's target list, as it were, does it? It could easily be that the four people already killed are all the people he wants to kill for some other reason, on the other hand, it could be that there are ten people he wants to kill, or maybe has killed more than four already, just that we haven't picked up a different link?'

'Yes, I see what you mean, but the fact that all the five gang members lived together in the same street and worked down the same mine, surely that's too much of a coincidence not to be the link?'

'Maybe Gibson, maybe, but I think we have to be careful not to get tunnel vision on this. We need to keep an open mind.'

'Yes, I see what you mean sir.'

'Nevertheless Gibson, I accept what you say about this German chap being a loose end, so I'll have word with the Commander, prepare the ground for a possible trip to Germany, okay?'

'Yes sir.'

'And find this fucking murderer before there are any leaks of this investigation, the CCs on the verge of a nervous breakdown, thinking of how this will look if we don't get a result soon. He's due to retire next year and unsolved serial killings is just what he doesn't want to be remembered for, and for that matter neither do I, so get your finger out Gibson and find the bastard.'

'Gibson went back to his office, ordered a coffee and thought about what the DCI had said. *Get your finger out, what the fuck does he think I've been doing, lazy fat pig, one of these days....*

Nevertheless, he thought, he had a point about him making assumptions about the 'gang of five' being the killer's target group, an assumption which seemed reasonable in the circumstances, but when looked at objectively, it could be a bit open to question. *I really need to establish the motive for the killings. Find the motive, find the killer. All I've really got at the moment in cold hard facts, is one undoubted vicious murder, plus two of the murder victim's friends having died, officially by accident, or by natural causes, and one other friend missing at sea, presumed dead. But most significantly, all deaths occurred on the same date but in different years. Jesus Christ, please send me some inspiration.*

He finished his coffee picked up the phone and dialled.

'Hello Mack, Gibson here, glad I caught you in,'

'Only just, I was halfway out of the door on my way to the beach, pissing down today but who cares, Monsoon's raring to go so if you don't mind I'll call you back in about half an hour or so.'

It was nearer an hour before Mack rang him back but it had given him time to refine his thoughts and questions.

'Hello Gibson, I was going to call you later today anyway. I've done as you asked and written down all I can find and/or remember about the German reporter, and I've looked again at all the stuff I ever covered relating to that area, the miners, Regent Park West, the first bombing, the subsequent bombing of the POW's hut, the accident at the pit, the miners' strike, everything seems pretty straight forward on the face of it.

As far as the POW's hut fire goes, the Luftwaffe were targeting Trafford Park generally at that time as it had a number of factories involved in weapon production and various other industrial activities that the Germans perceived as making a significant contribution to the war effort. They also targeted supply lines to the park, in particular railway lines, which they assumed carried goods to the park, hence the bombing raids on the line adjacent to Regent Park West. As you know, the house was bombed by accident, just too close to the railway line unfortunately, and a combination of bad luck and a bad aim. The POW's hut was slightly different in that there had been a firebomb raid on Trafford Park that evening, and it was assumed that the Luftwaffe pilot had one bomb left that he hadn't dropped for some reason, then decided to ditch it before returning to base, so he dropped it, on what its presumed, he thought was open land, but unfortunately for the POWs, it hit their hut and set it on fire.'

'Yes that's more or less what I understood to have happened, but going on from that, could there be anything, anything at all, about the hut setting on fire, that might give rise to someone bearing a grudge against anyone, apart from the obvious, that being the Luftwaffe bomber pilot of course. I'm obviously looking for something that might give someone a motive, in particular your German reporter friend, but I'm struggling. I can't come up with any reason why he would want to take revenge on the miners, when the Luftwaffe were obviously responsible for his father's death. But, the proximity of the miners who've been murdered, to the fire that killed his father in forty two, then his visit to Agecroft Colliery years later, at the time of the miners' strike and the murder of the first miner, just, I don't know, it just rankles.'

Mack was silent for a few moments.

'I know what you mean, but looking at it another way, apart from his father being one of the POWs who was killed in the fire, why would he be any kind of suspect, I've remembered his name by the way, it was Hans Konig.'

'Oh right thanks Mack, Hans Konig.' Gibson made a note in his file.

'So where do you go from here?'

'Good question, truth to tell, I just can't think who else might have such a strong personal motive for revenge. I think it has to have been something deeply personal for someone to commit these murders, plus as I said before, a foreigner's been mentioned in relation to Joe Martin's death and to Barry Jones's disappearance and presumed death.

'I can sort of see the connection your making, and I hate to cast doubt on your deductive powers Gibson, but I'll say it again, I find it hard to see why you think Herr Konig would have killed these people, the pilot of the plane that dropped the bomb on the hut where his father was, maybe, but these miners – why would he?'

Gibson sighed in frustration.

'Yes I suppose I agree, but I would still like to speak to this Hans Konig, interview him properly and see what transpires, you just never know. The one thing I do know is that the killer will want people to know, at some stage, that he did it, and why he did it, otherwise why commit all these murders on the same date? It's a message of some sort. Apart from the first murder, the others were done in such a way as to make them look like natural deaths or accidents, so in my opinion, whoever it is, wants to complete his revenge killings before revealing the reasons.

Now it might be that he intends to claim responsibility anonymously and hopes to walk away without being caught, but committing the crimes on the same date seems pointless to me unless this person is going to reveal the reason to someone at some stage – as in, "I killed these people on the third February because...", if you get what I mean?'

'Yes I do, and I agree it seems pointless unless you intend to say why you killed these people and on that particular date. Presumably the killer feels he has good reason to exact revenge in this way and on this date, but I've looked through everything I can, and I can't find anything of significance happening on the third of February in the years preceding nineteen eighty five. I went back over all the events we've discussed, to do with the area and the mine, to make sure I covered all the possibilities and I can't find anything that stands out.'

'Okay Mack, well I'd appreciate it if you could keep looking, there just has to be something of significance, probably staring us in the face. Anyway, going back to our friend Mr Konig, do you think you can trace him?'

'Yes, it shouldn't be too difficult, I'll dig out my notes again, I'm pretty sure he worked for Der Spiegel at the time and he might still be there, but even if he's moved on they'll know who he went to work for, so a few phone calls should sort it. I'll get on to it and call you back when I've got a result.'

Gibson thanked Mack and told him to keep a record of any expenses he incurred and the police would refund him accordingly.

On the way back home Gibson had to stop to buy the food for dinner. Jill was working late and in a moment of weakness the night before, Gibson had promised to make the evening meal tonight. He decided on steak and chips preceded by a prawn cocktail starter, *I'm nothing if not original.* He bought two sirloin steaks and a bottle of burgundy, he had all the other ingredients at home already. He got back and prepared everything ready to assemble and cook when Jill arrived home. He was glad of the opportunity to concentrate on something different and forget his obsession with the miner's murders, for a short while anyway.

Everything was ready so he thought it was his duty to try the wine to see if it was up to standard. It was, and as he took a couple of mouthfuls he felt more relaxed than he had for a while. He switched the TV on, then off again, nothing on. He put a CD on, Chopin's nocturne in E, and sat down on the sofa and closed his eyes. He was lulled by the music and was almost drifting off to sleep, when his mind turned back to the case.

What about the accident at the pit in fifty eight? One man died, but how many more were injured? I need to get more information. Just then he heard the key in the door and Jill's voice.

'I'm home and hungry so I hope you haven't forgotten your promise?' she shouted from the hall.

'Steak and chips,' he shouted back.'

'You're a star, pour me a glass of wine, I'm just going to get some slippers on. I'll be there in a minute.' Gibson smiled and looked forward to an evening of good food, wine and who knows what else he thought?

CHAPTER 19

G ibson drove to the office early to miss all the rush hour traffic and got to work straight away on researching the accident in fifty eight at Agecroft Pit. He re-read his notes taken at the library and the archives of the Manchester Evening News but couldn't find out any more than he'd already discovered in his initial research.

An underground explosion had killed one man and injured twelve, trapping them at the bottom of the shaft nearly two thousand feet under the ground. The accident was caused by a misunderstanding in signalling when men at the top misinterpreted a message that the men at the bottom of the shaft had left the pit, and so they commenced the planned demolition, sending tons of debris and rock down the shaft.

Getting more detailed information, thirty two years on, who was killed and who was injured was difficult. He established that the dead and injured were not miners, but construction workers who were constructing new shafts in the mine. He sat and thought, *I need to speak to someone who was working at the mine at the time – and of course Freddie might just be that person?*

*

Gibson had already checked back with the DCI on what, if any, security arrangements could be made to protect Exan, but the Commander had said that without an explicit threat he was powerless to provide any formal protection and the best he could do was to request the local police to keep a close eye on Exan's sister's house, where he was staying. Gibson thought that it might have been better if he'd asked the police to put him back in jail for breaching his parole terms, rather than asking them to go easy with him. Anyway he needed to go and speak with Freddie so he called ahead and made plans to go to see him.

He drove over to Huddersfield the following morning. He hadn't slept well and had gone over his last meeting with DCI Watson in his mind time and time again until he was exhausted, yet he was still unable to get to sleep. His restlessness was keeping Jill awake, so much so that she complained, and so he spent the rest of the night tossing and turning in the uncomfortable single bed in the spare bedroom. He wasn't in the best of moods when he met Freddie, who was still living at his sister's house. Freddie on the other hand, seemed brighter to Gibson this time, less stressed.

Freddie Exan opened the door and led Gibson into the dining room. He offered him a cup of tea or coffee, which he declined. They sat down and Freddie spoke first.

'I appreciated what you said to the police about me the last time you were here, I think it helped a lot, you know, telling them I was helping you with your investigation and all that. They just gave me a ticking off and told me not to miss checking in with them again, like I'm supposed to, so thanks for that Mr Gibson.'

'Detective Sergeant Gibson, or Sergeant Gibson to you Mr Exan, if you don't mind?'

Freddie looked surprised and confused at Gibson's apparent change of attitude.

'Oh sorry, yes Sergeant Gibson, so what do you want to see me about this time?'

'Before we get into that I want to warn you about something.' Exan immediately looked alarmed.

'Nothing to worry about really, just that whatever we discuss in these interviews must remain confidential, between us two. That means you don't tell anyone about anything we talk about, right, not even your sister or brother in law, no one, do you understand?'

'Yes I understand, so why did you want to see me today?'

'Well first off I wanted to tell you to be careful.'

'Careful, how do you mean?'

'Well I found out where Barry Jones lived, but it turned out that he went missing some years ago. Now it could be all just coincidence, but I just think it would be wise for you to be a little more alert, like I say, be a bit careful.'

'Careful, Barry, missing? What the fuck's going on? First Geoff, then Joe, then Billy, and now Barry, Jesus Christ, coincidence, are you fuckin joking?'

Freddie got out of his chair and ran his hand through his thinning hair whilst walking up and down in the small room. Gibson sat, waiting for him to calm down.

'You mean someone's killed them all don't you, and I'm next on the list?'

'No I don't mean that.' *Thank god you don't know about them all dying or disappearing on the same date.*

'No, all I'm saying, is that if you didn't do it, kill Geoff Brown, as you claim you didn't, then obviously someone else did, and as the others have all died recently or gone missing, it would just be as well if you were to exercise caution, that's all, there's no specific reason to think anyone is out to harm you, okay?'

Freddie Exan sat down. He was quiet for a while, then spoke.

'So what you just said, that means you believe me when I say I didn't kill Geoff?'

'Well that's a bit hard for me to say, after

all there was another reason why you and Geoff Brown might have fallen out wasn't there?'

Freddie Exan looked at Gibson as if about to ask, what reason, then he realised.

'So you know about me and Geoff's wife? Jesus Christ, I know it looks bad, but I, well, we'd finished anyway. Look, all I can tell you is, I didn't do it, no matter what had happened between me and Bren, or how it looked.'

Freddie looked distraught and near to tears. Gibson decided.

'Look Freddie. Off the record, and this is just my private opinion. But, for what it's worth, I don't believe you killed Geoff Brown. But I'll deny ever saying that, if you should ever tell anyone, clear?'

Freddie Looked up and stared at Gibson trying to take in what he'd just said.

'Why? I mean, why do you believe me?'

'Let's just say it's instinct.'

'Thanks Mr, sorry, Sergeant Gibson. That means more to me than you could ever know.'

'Yes, well let's just leave that there for the moment shall we? What I really wanted to talk to you about today, is the accident that occurred in fifty eight. Were you working at the mine then?'

Freddie Exan's face expressed consternation at the abrupt change of subject. He hesitated, recalling events, then spoke.

'Yes I was, that's one day I'll never forget. I

was on the early shift and I'd just come out of the showers when someone yelled about the accident. We'd heard the explosions but that didn't mean anything, blasting went on quite often.'

'Was there much blame attached to the people who were involved, I mean any recriminations, any anger displayed or felt against the man who gave the order to set off the charge?'

'No, not that I'm aware, everyone pulled together to help the rescue and I never ever heard one person try to lay blame on anyone. When you work down a mine you know that accidents happen, it's part of the job and everyone knows there are risks, why're you asking?'

'Nothing, just wondered how people perceived the accident and whether it caused any bad blood, grudges or anything.'

'No definitely not, if anything there was sympathy for the bloke who gave the order, he were devastated, never worked again I heard.'

'Okay, well maybe people weren't as benevolent about him as you think, but anyway, another change of subject. Going back further, a good few years, what do you remember about the day the hut was bombed on Chapman's Farm, when the German POWs died in the fire, the week after the house on Regent Park West was bombed?'

Exan seemed surprised by the question.

'What's that got to do with anything?'

'Never mind that, just answer the question.'

'Well I think I was only fourteen or fifteen at the time. We were all at the funeral of the Potts family, the ones that died in the first bombing the week before, everyone from the street was there, and a lot of other people too. It was in the afternoon.'

'What happened when the hut went up in flames, when was that?'

'I don't know, sometime in the evening. It was dark and it lit up the sky.'

'Did anyone go to help?'

'Help, how do you mean?'

'You know, as in try to get the men out, put out the fire, that sort of help.'

'You must be joking, the thing was blazing like buggery, you wouldn't have got anywhere near it, no one would have survived, anyway it wasn't like today, no one had cars or anything and it would have been quite a hike across the farmland.'

'So you all just watched and did nothing?'

'That sounds like an accusation, it wasn't like that, we all knew the fire engines would be there soon enough and they'd be the only ones who could do anything, what are you trying to say?'

'What was the general feeling about these Germans dying in the fire?'

'I don't know, but we'd just buried a family killed by German bombers, and we were at war with them if you remember,' Freddie added sarcastically. Gibson ignored the jibe. 'But anyway, I don't know, no one said anything as far as I can remember, but truth to tell, I was drunk, and well out of it. There was some homemade booze, horrible stuff and I wasn't used to drinking anyway. I must have fallen asleep 'cos when I woke up, everyone had gone outside to look at the blaze. I got up and went out. The hut was about two farmer's fields away but I remember, you could almost feel the heat. Anyway like I said, I remember going outside, feeling dizzy and puking up, then going back inside, and I think I must have fell asleep again.'

'Were your mates all there, the members of your little gang?'

'As far as I remember, yes I think so'

Gibson looked again at his notes and concluded this was about as much as he needed for the moment.

'Okay Freddie that's all for now.'

Gibson closed his notebook and reminded Freddie again about the consequences of repeating anything they'd discussed with anyone else. He left and headed back to headquarters.

Having stopped at the motorway services on the way back for a barely edible sandwich and a lukewarm coffee, Gibson finally arrived back at police HQ in Swinton. He sat down at his desk and saw a note telling him someone called Oliver MacMahon had called. He phoned Mack back.

'Afternoon Mack, Gibson here returning your

call.'

'Thanks for calling back; well I've managed to track down Herr Konig, our German reporter. Took me a while as his previous employers in the Fatherland had little idea of where he'd moved to, and as he had no immediate family to ask, it was a bit of a job to find out where he ended up. In the end I managed to talk to a cousin of his, a Frieda Brandt, who he'd given as a contact to his last employer. Thankfully she spoke reasonable English and was able to tell me where he is at the present, as far as she knows anyway.'

'Not moved to Siberia I trust?'

'No, but the weather where he's moved to is notoriously bad, said to rain most of the time.'

'Sounds like Manchester,' Gibson joked 'come on Mack let's have it.'

'You won't believe this Gibson but that's precisely where he is, Manchester, moved there in, let's see, nineteen eighty six.'

'You're having me on?'

'Nope - seems he met a girl in Manchester when he was over here, covering the miners' strike in eighty five, when I met him, and apparently he came back a year later to be with her, permanently as it were.'

'Bloody hell, Mack that's a bit of a turn up, any idea what he does for a living?'

'Last known to be teaching German studies at Manchester University. I found details and it's a very well thought of course, specialising in German history, the language, linguistics, media, films and such.'

Gibson stayed silent as he tried to take in this new information.

'Hello Gibson, you still there?'

'Yes, sorry Mack, just trying to think what implications this has on things in general.'

'Well the most practical implication, it seems to me, is that you can now go and talk to the man without too much of a problem.'

'Yes, you're right of course. Thanks Mack you've been a great help and I very much appreciate you finding all this out for me. I'll go and have a think how I approach Herr Konig, as you call him, so thanks again. I'll call you when I've spoken to him, let you know how I've gone on.'

'Yes please do Gibson, and good luck.'

Gibson called DCI Watson and told him about Konig.

'Well there's a turn-up Gibson, the Commander will be pleased not to have to fund a jolly to Germany for you. I assume you'll go and see this Konig as soon as?'

'Yes sir, I will. This of course means that his presence in the area at the time of all the killings does give us one more of the elements needed to make him a suspect though, 'opportunity', so theoretically he has both the means and the opportunity, but as yet no direct motive we can link to the men killed.'

'Yes Gibson, I'd worked that out all by myself, so go and talk to him as soon as you can and report back to me on your conclusions, and good luck Gibson.'

'Thanks sir.'

Finding Hans Konig turned out not to be as simple a Gibson had assumed.

Gibson called the university, and asked if a Mr Hans Konig was a lecturer there and if he was could he speak to him. He was put on hold and eventually an authoritative tetchy sounding man came on the line.

'Yes, can I help you?'

Gibson hadn't said who he was initially, now he decided become a bit more formal.

'Yes you can, I'm Detective Sergeant Gibson from the Greater Manchester Police and I would like to speak to a Mr Hans Konig, who I am led believe is employed as a lecturer at Manchester University.'

'Oh Lord, what's he been up to now?'

'Sorry, who exactly am I speaking to?'

'Professor Colin Hall, Hans Konig's boss for my sins. How can I help you, er Sergeant Gibson is it?'

'Detective Sergeant actually, but you can refer to me as DS Gibson professor.'

'My apologies D S Gibson, no offence intended, I'm just a bit weary of dealing with the various messes left by the juvenile behaviour of a once very able and capable man, so as I asked before, what has he done now?'

'Nothing as far as I'm aware, I was merely calling to make an appointment to see him about a matter I'm looking into, nothing directly to do with his behaviour in any way, but from your response I assume he's in some sort of trouble, would you care to enlighten me?'

'Strictly speaking I don't think I should be giving this sort of information over the phone, but as you're from the police I suppose it will be okay. Mind you, I'm surprised you don't already know Mr Konig if you're with the GMP?'

'We are a large force sir and I'm not with the central Manchester division, I'm based in Swinton and so I wouldn't know what goes on in the vicinity of your university.'

'Yes of course, forgive me. Well Konig was one of the best lecturers I've had the pleasure to work with, until he went native that is, sorry I shouldn't speak in riddles. I don't know how much you know of his background, but he came to us a few years ago having previously had a very successful career as a distinguished journalist, then last year he started missing lectures, then we wouldn't see him for days and then when he did come in he was as much use as…, well no use at all really.'

'And the reason for this drastic change in behaviour?' asked Gibson.

'The usual, a woman, well girl more like, plus drugs.'

'So where is he now?'

Good question. As far as the University's concerned, he's on sick leave, with a final warning that if he doesn't sort himself out by the end of this month, then he's finished here, which would be a tragedy for all concerned, not least for his lovely wife and two children.'

Just what I need, thought Gibson.

'So any idea where I might find him now professor?'

'No, I'm afraid I have no idea. I can only suggest you try his wife, she might know.'

'Okay, well can you give me her contact details please?'

'Well again I shouldn't really, not without some sort of authorisation, but I'll give you her phone number, and if you do get to see him, try to talk some sense into him will you? He has a great talent for teaching and it's such a waste. Hang on a minute.'

The professor came back to the phone and gave Gibson the telephone number. Gibson thanked him and the professor wished him good luck.

The phone rang out for five rings and Gibson was about to put the receiver down when it was answered.

'Hello' said a breathless voice, Gibson could hear children in the background laughing hysterically.

'Is that Mrs Konig?'

'Yes it is, who is this?' She was well spoken and Gibson could tell she'd been laughing herself.

'Detective Sergeant Gibson Greater Manchester Police, I'm calling to see if I can come and speak to your husband Hans Konig - and before you ask, it's not in connection with anything he's done, I'm just investigating a matter which he may be able to help me with, to do with his time as a journalist, so is he there please?'

Her voice lost its jollity, replaced with annoyance.

'No, he isn't here and I don't know when he will be. Have you spoken to the University?'

'Yes I have.'

'Okay then you probably know what he's been up to. I haven't seen him for over a month now.'

'Any idea where I might find him?'

'Not really, Deaths Door maybe?'

Gibson was confused by her reply, which seemed casually framed as a question. Did she mean she hoped he was going to die, if so she seemed hardly bothered.'

'I'm sorry, I don't understand, do you mean he's ill?'

'No, sorry I thought you'd know, being a policeman. I mean, it's a club in Manchester, you must know about it.'

Gibson explained yet again that he wasn't with

the central Manchester division.

'Oh, well I suppose that explains it. It's a club he goes to, supposedly a bar, but drugs seem to be the main things on offer, from what your lot have told me, your colleagues in the Manchester police I mean. He seems to spend most of his time there, in fact he's been arrested there, I only know 'cos they came to me to tell me, as if I was somehow responsible for him. He goes there with his young tart apparently, so you might find him there, other than that I can't help you I'm afraid.'

'Any idea where this club is?'

'No but I'm sure your colleagues on the drug squad can tell you. Look I have to go, it's my son's birthday party and I have a house full of screaming kids. If you do talk to my husband let him know he missed his son's third birthday,' She hesitated then added 'and tell him what a fucking miserable self-centred selfish, two timing bastard he is, will you?' And with that she slammed the phone down.

Gibson made a mental note to remember the precise message. *Does this make him any more of a suspect than before? Is it an interesting development, or just a time consuming distraction? Better go to talk to the man and try to find out, so where to start*? He called Central Manchester Drug Squad. He decided to keep things simple so as to avoid the questions that would inevitably arise if he told them why he was looking for this particular individual, questions that would then result in more questions requiring more answers than he was prepared to give at his stage.

The phone was answered. He introduced himself, asked for the drug squad and was put through to a Detective Constable Gareth Edwards. He introduced himself again and asked DC Edwards if he was familiar with a club or bar known as Deaths Door. Edwards laughed, then said in a broad Manchester accent.

'Ay, difficult to be in the Manchester drug squad and not know that place, so what is it you want to know?'

'Well, for starters, where it is, plus opening times, and any other useful information you can give me.'

The DC obliged and gave Gibson the address. It was located on Princess Street, near China Town.

'As for opening hours, most of the time really, apart from say nine in the morning 'till about eleven, a real twenty four seven place as they would say these days.'

'Don't they have to conform to particular licencing hours?'

'I suppose they should, but to be honest, we leave it pretty much alone from that aspect. We work on the basis that we know what's going on there and where certain people are so it's useful.'

'Yes, I can see the logic of that.'

'My boss says if we busted the place and closed

it down, we'd disperse the dodgy bastards all over town, and to boot, we'd lose a number of readily available sources of information on all sorts of activities, so we turn a bit of a blind eye, unofficially that is, but you know how these things work, babies and bathwater as my boss says.'

'Yes I suppose so, a bit different in central Manchester than out in the sticks.'

'Dare say, any particular individual you're looking for Sergeant?'

Gibson decided to give Konig's name to see if it registered.

'Konig, rings a bell, just a minute.' Gibson waited. 'Yes German bloke, busted for possession with a Marcia Halpern, let off with a caution. Not what you'd call one of our real villains from what I can see here.'

'When was that?'

'Let's see, couple of months ago. We do raid the place now and then, keep up appearances and all that. They were caught up in the raid, but nothing serious, just possession.'

'Of what?'

'Oh, let's see, cannabis and cocaine, but small quantities, personal use amounts, so not much point in prosecuting.'

'Okay, well thanks for your help DC Edwards.'

'No problem DS Gibson, and good luck with your enquiries.'

Gibson sat and thought. It was going on for six,

so he decided to pay the club a visit, get a look at the place and find out what time Konig usually pitched up there.

He drove to Manchester against the prevailing remains of the rush hour traffic, found a parking space in the car park in the middle of China-town and walked the short distance to Princess Street. Deaths Door was easy enough to find. Gibson showed his warrant card to the doorman and went in. He went through the door, down a flight of stairs and through another doorway. It was as he expected, gloomy to the point of hardly being able to see your hand in front of you. Gibson stood by the door for a short while until his eyes adjusted to the gloom, then went over to the bar and ordered a coke. The shaven headed, surly barman served him and took his money. Gibson had the feeling he knew he was police, either by instinct, or the doorman had communicated the information by some means.

Gibson, pulled up a bar stool, sat down and looked around. The club was much bigger than he'd assumed it would be. Low ceiling with some metal girders and pipes running along the ceiling painted out in black. Hidden wall lights gave out an eerie yellow glow and provided the only illumination other than the down lights behind the bar. The furniture was basic, with false red leather, deep buttoned padded booths around the walls, providing privacy of a sort for the 'clientele', as his colleague had described them. There were just a few people in the place, it was early, only just after half past six in the evening. Muzac played in the background, some sort of jazz tune which Gibson didn't recognise. He turned back to the bar and looked for the barman who was chatting to a girl at the other end of the bar. He caught his eye and signalled him over. The barman reluctantly left the girl.

'Yes, another coke?'

'No thanks, information. Do you know a customer by the name of Konig, Hans Konig'

'No.' the barman answered without hesitation and made to walk away.

'Come back here, I haven't finished.'

The barman sighed and came back to stand in front of Gibson, defiant.

'Gibson got his warrant card out, opened it and shoved it in the barman's face.

'There are two way we can do this, one is where I start to look into matters to see, if you've breached any of your licence conditions, then bring in the drug squad, dogs maybe, to see if there are any traces of illegal substances in this dump, then I'll probably have the place closed own. Or two, you can stop fucking about and give me the answers I want, is that clear enough for you?'

The barman mumbled a response.

'Sorry I couldn't hear you.'

'I said yes okay.'

'Well?'

'You mean the German bloke, yes he comes in here, he's a regular, comes in with his girlfriend.'

'Every night?'

'Yeah, most nights, sometimes in the day as well, depends?'

On what?'

'I dunno, ask him.'

What time does he usually come in, in the evenings I mean?'

'About nine usually.'

'Okay, What's your name?'

'Bobby, Robert Pearson.'

'Okay, Bobby, what does Konig look like?'

The barman looked as if he was about to give a smart answer, then decided against it.

'Tall, just over six feet I guess, thin, grey hair, not long, not short, glasses, always dresses in black, that's about all I can remember.'

'Okay, so listen Bobby, I'll be back later and if I find out you've warned Konig or told him I've been asking about him, there'll be big trouble for you, understand?'

The barman gave the briefest nod, sullen again. Gibson raised his voice.

'I said, do you understand Bobby?'

'Yes, yes I understand, okay?'

Gibson gave him a hard stare to reinforce what he'd just said, got off his stool and walked out, up the stairs and into the street, the fresh air a relief after breathing the stale smoky air of the basement club.

He decided to go back at ten. It was too long to hang around so he drove home, grabbed something to eat, had a coffee and watched the news for half an hour, before heading back out to Manchester. He made sure he had his mace, cuffs and his personal radio in the car before driving back into the city. He parked his car, put the cuffs in his coat pocket, radio on his belt and mace in the other pocket. He hoped he wouldn't have to use any of them, but nothing worse than going in unprepared, then looking like a complete plonker when someone got the better of you because you couldn't be bothered to tool up.

The doorman nodded him through this time without asking to see any identification. As he walked down the stairs Gibson felt, as much as heard, the music. *How could anyone communicate with this racket going on? Then again, if you're out of your mind on some substance or other, does it matter?'* The same barman was still on duty, but he was now accompanied by another barman and two bar girls. It was just after ten and the place was filling up. People were arriving and the combined noise of the music and shouted conversations at the bar added to the general cacophony. Gibson signalled the same barman over and he reluctantly acknowledged Gibson with a hand signal indicating he'd be with him in a moment.

Bobby, the barman came over and shouted to Gibson, asking if he wanted a drink. Gibson declined and shouted back asking if Hans Konig had shown yet. The barman nodded in the direction of a dark corner booth on Gibson's right. Gibson walked over and spotted Konig sat next to a girl. They seemed to be having some sort of disagreement, but he couldn't hear what it was about with all the noise. *Going to be a bugger trying to interview the bloke in this place.*

Gibson stood over Konig and caught his attention. Konig looked at him then turned back to the girl. Gibson took his warrant card out, waved it in front of Konig's face, and raised his voice to shout over the noise.

'Hans Konig, I'm a police officer and I want to talk to you, outside.'

Gibson put his right hand thumb up and gestured towards the door with it. Konig took a minute to take this in then replied.

'Ich spreche kein Englisch.' Which Gibson took to mean he was claiming not to understand English.

Gibson was beginning to feel foolish, the girl was giggling and other people nearby had stopped what they were doing to watch. He put his hand on the arm of the booth, leaned over and spoke directly into Konig's ear.

'Don't fuck about Konig, outside now.'

'Ich spreche kein Englisch.' Konig said again with a smile on his face and his hands in a held out in a gesture of helplessness. The girl laughed louder.

Gibson grabbed Konig by the arm and hefted him to his feet. He got Konig halfway up, but Konig resisted and swung a fist at Gibson. Gibson wasn't particularly big, but he was strong and had excellent reflexes. He let go of Konig, and at the same time leaned back. Konig's fist went flying harmlessly past his face. It was what Gibson wanted, an excuse.

'Okay matey.'

Gibson quickly grabbed the arm Konig had just swung, and using the momentum pushed Konig into the back of the booth, twisting his body, then brought Konig's arm up his back. Konig screamed in agony and slid own with his front pinned to the seat of the booth. Gibson put his knee on the seat and turned Konig all the way round and pulled his other arm round his back, transferred his knee to Konig's back took his cuffs out of the back of his belt with his free hand and cuffed Konig's wrists together. It all happened so fast that no one had the chance to react, but now the doorman came rushing towards the fray. He saw what had happened, looked at Gibson and backed off. The girl had stopped laughing.

Gibson pulled Konig on to his feet and led him outside. Once he was on the street, he radioed in for a car to come and get Konig. While he waited, he formally arrested Konig for obstructing the police in the course of their duty and assaulting a police officer, He read him his rights and just as he finished, a police car came screaming round the corner, siren on full blast. A little crowd had gathered. The car stopped and two burly officers got out.

'Want some assistance do we?' said the first one smiling broadly.

'Yes, thanks.' Gibson got his warrant card out and showed the policemen.

'Out of towner ay? Well always happy to help our mates from Swinton, what do you want me to do with him?'

Konig stood there in a daze, all the bluster gone.

'Can you put him in a cell for the night? I'll come along with you now to sort out the paper-work, if you can give me a lift back when we've finished so I can pick my car up, then I'll come back tomorrow morning, decide how I want to proceed, Bootle Street is it?'

'Yes jump in, Bootle Street it is. If you could come and claim him before ten thirty tomorrow that would be good.'

On the drive back home, Gibson smiled to himself. He was pleased with the result. He could interview Konig on his own terms and in his own time now he was under arrest. *I quite enjoyed the action too, nice to know I haven't lost it. Might ham it up a bit for the lads at the station – and Jill of course.* He laughed out loud.

Gibson arrived at Bootle Street Police Station at nine thirty the following morning. He went through the formalities with the station Sergeant and told him he was unlikely to proceed with any charges relating to Konig's arrest, but that he needed to interview Konig whilst he was still under caution so anything he said could be used if necessary. Konig was transferred to an interview room.

Konig sat at the bare metal table, looking forlorn, pale, ill and dishevelled, but stood as soon as Gibson entered. The grey walled room smelt faintly of disinfectant, not quite masking another more unpleasant odour and was lit by two naked neon tubes suspended from the stark white painted ceiling. Gibson could have sworn that Konig gave him the archetypal German greeting, standing with a straight back, then making a slight bow. He sat back down. The officer accompanying Gibson switched on the recording equipment, and then went through all the necessary formalities prior to Gibson asking any questions.

'I'm obliged to inform you, Mr Konig, that you can have a solicitor present at this interview, one of your own choosing or we can arrange for one.'

'No thanks.'

'Are you sure?'

'Yes, I'm sure.'

'Okay, anything you need before we start, coffee tea, water?'

'No, nothing thanks,'

'You understand you are still under caution?'

Konig had hung his head as if in shame whilst he'd been talking, but now he looked up.

'Yes, look, I wish to apologise to you, it was you, last night wasn't it?'

Gibson nodded, realising at that moment that one of his theories had just gone out of the window, Konig spoke perfect English without any trace of a foreign accent. *Shit, why didn't Mack mention that when I suggested that this man could be the 'foreigner' we were looking for?*

'Okay, well you seem to be in a more cooperative mood today, so let's get on with it. I'm looking into a situation which involves some events in the past, and one of those events has a very loose connection to a subsequent incident. I'm referring to the bombing in which your father died in nineteen forty two.'

Konig was thrown, surprise showing on his pale pasty face.

'Sorry, what about last night, am I not in trouble for resisting arrest or assault or whatever it was I was charged with?'

'Let's say that if you cooperate with me on these other matters, then we might be able to forget about your behaviour last night.'

Konig looked confused but relieved.

'Okay, so what is it I can help you with, my father's death you said, why is this of interest to anyone, especially now, after all this time?'

'I'm looking into some recent matters, which have a possible, if tenuous connection to some events in the past, and it's really just a matter of tying of some loose ends, you know, just for the record as it were. There's no inference or implication that the manner of your father's death has any direct significance at all to the matters we're looking into.'

'I see, well I think I do.'

'And, if you had just cooperated with me yesterday evening, this would have been dealt with in a much less charged atmosphere, but you chose to become violent.'

Konig looked ashamed.

'It's the drugs; I was confused, I'm really very sorry. Anyway please carry on, ask any questions you want and I'll try to help you if I can.'

'Right, okay, well in view of your change of attitude, and now that you're willing to be reasonable and cooperative, I think we can dispense with the formal interview under caution.'

Turning to the officer, Gibson asked him to switch off the recording equipment and asked if he could arrange for Hans Konig to be let off with a formal caution when he'd finished with him. The officer said he'd sort it out, switched off the recording equipment and left the room.

Gibson took out his notepad and pen.

'Thank you,' said Konig.

'Okay, I understand that the first time you visited this area, or the UK at all possibly, was in nineteen eighty five, to cover the miners' strike at Agecroft Colliery, for the German newspaper Der Spiegel, and that you had requested this assignment partly because of your Father's death which …' Konig put his hand up to stop Gibson.

'Sorry to interrupt, but I'm curious to know how you found out this information?'

'Well, in the course of our investigations into another matter I'm looking into, I spoke to an English journalist by the name of Oliver MacMahon, who I understand you met on your visit over here in eighty five.'

'Oliver MacMahon…., oh you mean Mack, yes I see, how is he, he must be retired by now I should think.'

'Yes, he is retired, but still doing some free-lance work I think. Anyway, what I want to ask you, was, did you find out any more about your father's death when you came over to cover the miners' strike, or since for that matter?'

'I'm afraid I didn't really find out much more than I knew already. I don't know what I was hoping to find, as it all seemed quite straightforward, if you can call be killed by your own air force "straightforward", friendly fire, I think they would call it these days. I've always thought that term a little incongruous to say the least. Anyway as you said, I'd asked for the assignment to cover the strike, both in Yorkshire, and in particular in Agecroft as my father had lost his life in the immediate area. I was naturally curious to see where it happened, but unfortunately the farm where he was billeted no longer existed, having been taken over by the colliery when it expanded after the war.'

'You said you didn't find out 'much more' than you already knew, but what did you find out, anything at all?'

'Nothing of any significance really. As I said, I'm not even sure what I was looking for, somebody that might have known him perhaps? I don't know, you see unfortunately my father probably never knew he had a son, never knew of my existence. My mother wrote to him of course, to tell him about me. They'd been married just before he left to go to war, but her letters were returned. I suppose I thought it might be possible to find someone who knew him, someone who'd talked to him, met him, I don't know.

My mother died in nineteen seventy nine. She was only sixty years old. I don't think she ever got over losing my father, particularly because of the way it happened.'

'And did you find anyone who had known him?'

'No, I knocked on a few doors. There were some houses near the area of where the farm had been, miner's houses as they called them, and another little estate of other houses nearby. I spoke to a few people. What I wanted to find was someone old enough to remember those days, someone who might have memories of that time, maybe even the bombing when my father died, but I couldn't find anyone. I did go to see his grave in Agecroft Cemetery of course.

It wasn't easy to find but I found it eventually. He was buried along with the other three German prisoners of war who died with him. I found that very sad. It really brought home to me in a very personal way, the futility of war and the stupidity of the human race. Anyway,' said Konig taking a deep breath, 'I suppose I am hardly in a position to engage in a philosophical discussion on the self-destructive qualities of the human race.'

'Weren't you ever curious about the way the incident happened; I mean the fact that it was attributed to a stray bomb from a German plane?'

'Yes of course, the irony didn't escape me, and I looked into the matter in some depth, in fact I talked to an old Luftwaffe pilot who'd been on similar bombing missions during the war, and asked him what the chances were of that sort of thing happening. He told me it was unusual and that if the pilot had problems getting rid of his entire ordinance, which did happen on occasion, then the pilot would normally try to ditch it over the sea, rather than over open land. Whatever, he would want to get rid of it before landing back at base anyway.'

'After your assignment covering the miners' strike, you came back to live here, why was that?'

'The usual reason Sergeant, a girl. I'd met and fallen in love with an English girl, so we kept in touch, then I came back and we got married and now have two wonderful children.'

As Konig said this his voice broke with emotion. Gibson was unmoved and put his notebook and pen in his pocket. As he stood up to go, he said.

'Oh yes, I spoke to your wife and she gave me a message should I be speaking to you.'

'Oh, what message?'

'She said to tell you that you are a, let me get this right, a selfish, two faced, miserable, no that's not quite right, yes I remember now, she said that you have missed your son's third birthday, and that you are a fucking miserable self-centred, selfish, two timing bastard, yes that was it, pretty well verbatim.'

Konig looked shocked and seemed if he were about to burst into tears, but then got a hold on his emotions.

'I suppose I deserved that,' he said.

'I guess you do, but that's not my concern. I see people like you all the time, chuck their lives away for booze, drugs etc., though I have to say, they're normally a bit thick, not much education, but you, well ......, anyway you're free to go now, but I need to know where I can get hold of you if I need to talk to you again, do you have an address?'

'At the moment I live in a squat, but I've had enough. I'm going to go home now and beg to be taken back, so you'll either find me there, or at the university.'

'You that confident either will take you back?'

'No, but I'm going to try.'

'Well good luck Mr Konig, I think you'll need it.'

'Thanks.

CHAPTER 20

As he drove back to Swinton, Gibson reflected on the last twenty four hours. Eventful for sure, but productive, not really, in fact he was back again to square one in many respects, just one loose end less, and still no clue as to the identity of the murderer, or what his motive was.

He got back to his office and there was a note on his desk to call a Lucy Moore, a reporter from the News of the World. Gibson sat down in his chair and his shoulders slumped.

Oh shit, please don't tell me the press are on to it... Gibson hesitated then picked up the phone and dialled.

The phone was answered simply 'Lucy Moore.'

Direct line? Yes, Detective Sergeant Gibson here, I've got a note here asking me to call.' Gibson tried to make his voice sound neutral and authoritative.

'Ah, yes thanks' for calling back so promptly Sergeant.' Her voice became soft, almost seductive.

'No problem, what can I do for you er, Miss Moore?'

'Well, just a little information actually, I believe you're investigating the deaths of two men, and I thought you might want to tell me why you're linking two deaths, which I believe were previously thought to be unsuspicious.'

Gibson feigned the need to take another urgent call to give him time to think. 'Sorry Miss Moore, a call on my other line; I'll get rid of it, just hang on.'

Gibson held the receiver with his hand over the mouthpiece while he tried to think.

Someone's blabbed, but who? She says two deaths, so it isn't anyone who's up to date. Who would be pissed off enough to blab, who only knows about two of the deaths....? D S Pollitt. The bastard, he's done a deal, information in exchange for her going easy on him if it turns out he was wrong....

'Sorry about that Miss Moore, you were saying, two deaths, which two deaths are we talking about?'

'Playing dumb are we Sergeant?' she said, still in a friendly manner 'okay, well how about William Bowen and Joseph Martin.'

'Oh, those two yes, well we always look carefully into any unexpected deaths, and I think we did find a tenuous link between the two men. As I recall, I think they were friends from childhood, and were both miners as well, but apart from that .....'

263

'So are you telling me you're not investigating the deaths of these two men?'

Gibson decided to dodge the question and call her bluff at the same time. 'Investigating them for what Miss Moore? If you're saying you have some information that suggests these deaths were suspicious in any way, then I needn't remind you that you have a duty to inform us, the police, so what it is that you know about the deaths of these two men Miss Moore?'

'Okay Sergeant Gibson,' her voice had hardened up now, 'I get the message, but I'll be watching and If I think you've misled me in any way, I'll take great pleasure in hanging you out to dry.'

'Goodbye Miss Moore, it's been a great pleasure speaking to you today.' He put the phone down and realised his hands were trembling. *Christ, just what I need now, the press on my back, especially someone like her.*

The call niggled away at him all afternoon. He kept replaying the conversation over in his head to see if he'd slipped up. He was sure he hadn't. Maybe she'd just go away, but he doubted it somehow, didn't sound like the type. *Should I tell the DCI?* He decided not to, on the basis that it might hasten him losing control of the case.

He left the station at five thirty feeling the need for a drink. He went to his local, one drink led to another and he felt good, better than he had for a while. As he relaxed he realised just how tense he'd been. More drinks followed and the pressure lifted completely. The conversation flowed, funny stories and jokes, great craic. Suddenly it was closing time and someone suggested going back to his place for a few more drinks, why not?

Gibson woke up unaware of where he was. He was fully dressed and lying on the floor. The lights were still on. He tried to get up and the room spun. He lay down again and he hurt all over. His head felt as if it were going to explode. He felt sick, nauseous and knew that this wasn't going to pass for some time. He tried to gather his senses, will power that's all that was needed. He managed to get to a standing position and looked for the lavatory. The first door he tried led to a bedroom with someone snoring loudly, the next door was the kitchen. He suddenly realised how thirsty he was and went over to the sink and turned on the tap. He found a cup and drank the cold water greedily, two cups, then another. He stopped to breathe. He felt better, then worse. God he needed the lavatory which mercifully he found behind the next door he tried.

He woke up to the noise of someone banging on the door. He'd fallen asleep sat on the lavatory and someone wanted to come in. He pulled up his trousers and flushed, then staggered to the door, unlocked it and mumbled an apology to the next user as he exited. Finding his way back to the living room, he collapsed on the settee and slumped, not moving until he felt he could. Fresh air, he'd feel better with some fresh air. He got up slowly, found the front door and walked out into the street, it was still dark.

He had no idea where he was or what time it was, but there were no people around. The air was cool. He walked, slowly, unsteady to begin with. The fresh air made him feel better and he began to walk a little faster. He still felt quite ill, but definitely better, but he knew he wasn't really going to feel much better until tomorrow. He began to remonstrate with himself. *How old am I, how on earth did I allow myself to get in this state, me, me, the one who was holier than thou about drug addicts and drunkards a few hours ago? Completely out of control, anything could have happened while I was in that state, God what an idiot .....*

He got to a main road which he vaguely recognised. No people, no traffic. He looked at his watch and focussed, it was five thirty a.m. He carried on walking, then a noise, and a taxi came into view. He flagged it down, the driver wary of stopping until he could see what type of person he might be picking up at this time in the morning. He stopped. Gibson opened the door and fell into the back seat. The latent smell of curry, donna kebab and vomit, overlaid by sickly air freshener made him heave. Gibson took a deep breath through his mouth, gave his address and ignored the attempt at conversation offered by the Sikh driving the car.

He opened the front door as quietly as he could and crept upstairs to the spare room. Disrobing he crawled into the small spare bed and fell asleep. He woke light streaming through the gap in the curtains. He looked at his watch on the bedside table – nine thirty *shit,* he got up and immediately regretted having moved so quickly, he sank back into bed, gave it a minute and tried again, more gingerly this time.

He showered dressed went downstairs and made some toast and tea, then realised his car would still be at the pub. He found his keys. *Surely I couldn't have been stupid enough to drive last night, could I?* It was a couple of miles to the pub and he was relieved to see his car still in the car park. He drove away, the mantra repeating itself in his head *never never again, never never never again......*

He went into work, but the day was a write off. He tried to write up his report on his interview with Konig but eventually gave up. *God what did I drink last night and how much*? It suddenly crossed his mind that he was probably still over the limit when he drove this morning, *great.* He struggled on till five then went home. The awkward explanation to Jill was still to come when their paths crossed. He hoped she was on lates today. He ate some eggs on toast and watched the news on the TV, still no Jill by nine, so he went upstairs. He used the spare bedroom again, and was in bed and asleep by nine thirty.

He woke early the next day and marvelled at the recuperative power of sleep. He felt good and wanted to preserve the feeling. The door to the main bedroom was shut. Presumably Jill was on lates and still asleep. He showered, shaved, had some cereal and coffee and was out of the house for seven thirty and at his desk for eight fifteen He felt remarkably fresh and alert, almost as though his night's drinking had somehow washed away the confusion in his mind. He brought his records up to date with details of his interview with Mark Konig, then once again he read through all the files.

He sat back and pondered. *Let's go back to the beginning, not the murder of Geoff Brown, not the deaths of any of the others, not the missing boat, the beginning, the bombing of that house.* He picked up the phone and dialled. The phone rang out then he answered.

'Mack, glad I caught you in. Fancy a trip down memory lane?'

'Well…. I suppose so, would you mind elaborating?'

'No, not at all, glad to. I met with your friend Mr Konig, or Herr Konig as you call him, and however hard I try, I can't figure him as the murderer. Oh and by the way, why didn't you tell me he doesn't have a German accent?'

'Oh, doesn't he, hmm sorry, though to be fair I think he did have a bit of an accent when I met him. Maybe it's worn off, you know living here for all this time.'

'Yes could be I suppose, but it's not him anyway, so that means I'm back to square one, which is where I would like to begin again.'

'What, square one?'

'Precisely, all the people involved, the victims, the missing man, were all present, in one way or another, at the various events we've discussed previously. The first event being the bombing of that house in Regent Park West, so I'm going to start with that event and look at it in detail, then move on to the next event and so on. I want you to come with me to look at where this first event took place and we'll start from there.'

'Okay, don't quite know what you're up to, but I'm game, when do you want to do this?'

'Tomorrow, if you're free.'

'I'll have to see if my friend Celia will look after Monsoon, but subject to that, I should be okay. I think the train might be my best bet. I don't drive much these days, so can you pick me up from Oxford Road Station, Manchester, I think that will be the nearest to you?'

'Yes, no problem, call me back with what time you arrive, the earlier the better for me.'

'Will do. So tell me about your meeting with Hans Konig, did he remember me?'

'Yes he did, and when I said I met with him, it was a bit more complicated than that, I ended up having to arrest him, he was a bit the worse for wear at the time. It's a bit of a long story, so I'll tell you all about it tomorrow when I pick you up, but let's say it was a useful meeting, even if it only served to eliminate him as any kind of suspect.'

'Sounds intriguing, can't wait to hear about it all. I'll call you back as soon as I know the train times, toodle-pip.'

'Yes, bye for now, see you tomorrow, *toodle-pip, haven't heard that one for a long time.*

Gibson picked Mack up the following morning from the station at ten, and they drove out to Regent Park West. On the way Gibson told Mack the story of his run in with Hans Konig and his subsequent interview. Mack expressed his disappointment to hear his old colleague was into drugs, but was fascinated by the events in the club and the manner of Konig's arrest.

'I wish I'd been there, sounds like something out of Starsky and Hutch.'

'Oh I wouldn't go that far, said Gibson, 'Magnum maybe...'

'Yeah..., Magnum, I can see the resemblance now,' Mack said with a straight face.

Gibson smiled. 'You think?'

They drove in silence for a while.

'So we go to Regent Park West now and see if we can pick up some vibrations from nineteen forty two?'

Gibson laughed 'Not quite, but I do need to change the way I'm looking at this case and I need to make some serious progress, one, before it drives me insane, and two, on a more practical level, before they take the case off me.'

'Oh, you think they might do that?'

'No, I know they will. I submitted my report on my interview with Hans Konig to my boss DCI Watson and he discussed it with his boss, the Chief Constable, and they've decided that they're going to bring in another team to take over the investigation.'

Mack turned in the passenger seat and looked at Gibson.

'They told you that?'

'No not exactly, but I know the signs, and one of my close colleagues told me there were mutterings on the bush telegraph, nothing specific, they still want to keep this tight. They're terrified of anything getting out before we make progress, which is why they've left me to it until now, but I can sense they think I'm not making enough headway, so they'll be looking at alternatives.'

'Right okay, how much time do you have before they do something, I mean take it off you or whatever?

'Who knows, but it doesn't matter because you and I are going to get to the bottom of this.'

'We are?'

'Yes we are.'

'All of a sudden you seem very sure of yourself.'

'I think you could say it's the confidence of the dammed, but I do have the feeling we've missed something obvious, I don't know what, but let's get there and see what happens.'

'You're the boss.'

'Hmm.'

'Oh and by the way, I had a journalist on to me a couple of days ago, News of the World, Lucy Moore, she knew something, but not much.'

'Oh shit, she's got a reputation of being a bit of a terrier, when you say she doesn't know much, how much...'

'Well she knew the names of the first two men whose deaths started all this thing off, Billy Bowen and Joe Martin, and she knew we were linking the deaths in some way, but I'm pretty sure that's all she knew.'

And how do you think she got her information?'

'I'm pretty sure it was from the detective who handled the Joe Martin case. I think he's now a bit windy Martin's death might not have been an accident and he's covering his arse by giving information to this Lucy Moore, my guess being, she's agreed not lay the blame on him if it turns out Joe Martin wasn't killed in an accident.'

'So how did you leave it?'

'Well I just bottled her, so she promised to hang

me out to dry if she found out I was holding anything back.'

'Well you can bet your cotton socks she's busy trying all her contacts to find out if there's anything to find out, and someone's going to say something, even without realising it, so she'll be back, you can bet on it.'

That's comforting to know Mack, all the more reason to get this cracked.'

'Amen to that Gibson.'

They arrived at Regent Park West and parked outside a small corner shop situated at the end of the right hand terrace of houses. They got out of the car and looked around. Gibson turned his face to the sky and for the first time in months he could feel the warmth of the sun.

'Do you know Gibson, this shop was here when I came to cover the bombing in forty two, still here after all these years, must be one of the few left that Tesco hasn't killed off.'

'C'mon Mack let's walk up the street and see if it invokes any other memories of your past life. Give me the historical tour.'

'Okay, well up here on the left is the gap left by the bombing. The house has obviously never been rebuilt which is a bit surprising, mind you all these houses are probably now owned by some absentee landlord. In the sixties and seventies, you could buy whole streets of terraced houses at auctions, with tenants, and for very little money.

The way things were then meant that tenants on fixed rents were more of a burden than an asset.

'Really, why?'

'Well you couldn't increase the rents, you couldn't get rid of the tenants and the tenants could pass their tenancy on to their husbands, wives, sons' daughters, uncle Tom Cobbly and all, so the chances of realising the value of these houses as assets, was virtually nil.'

'And that little estate of houses over there, they look different.' Said Gibson pointing.

'Yes, they were. They were all individual tenants from what I remember, whereas the houses in Regent Park West were virtually all occupied by miners. That road over there was a dirt lane that ran alongside Chapman's farm.' Pointing further over, past the houses, Mack continued. 'Over there was the old pit, which later became Agecroft Colliery, which as it expanded gobbled up the farm and all the fields surrounding it. Shame really, it was a nice bit of countryside.'

They stopped walking.

'When you covered the story of the bombing, you know, when the house was destroyed, I assume you talked to a lot of the residents on this road?'

'Yes, well quite a few anyway, why?'

'I just wondered, do you think there'd be anyone left living here who was living here at that time?'

'Maybe, but they'd be getting on a bit now, I mean, let's see it's nineteen ninety now so forty two from ninety is forty eight, so exclude children because I didn't talk to anyone less then say eighteen years old, but even so, they would now be, what sixty six? Anyway why do you ask?'

'Oh I don't know, I suppose I was thinking, wondering if there was some old biddy who knew everyone's business? There's always one in every street, but that wouldn't be an eighteen year old.'

'Hmm, well there was actually someone of the ilk you're talking about, but she was a bit more than an "old biddy" as you put it'

'Go on.'

'Well she was quite glamorous and single. I don't know what had happened to her husband, but she had a son called, let me see, Mickey, that was it, and she was called,' Mack frowned dredging his memory banks, 'sorry can't remember. She was a character though. She drank a bit, and I remember, the other women didn't like her. I think she 'entertained' quite a few of the local men.'

'You mean she was …on the game?'

'Oh, I don't know about that. I was only here a couple of days on that occasion, but I did talk to her, and she was a mine of information. Knew everyone's business it seemed.'

'Which house did she live in, can you remember?'

'As it happens I think I can? I'm pretty sure she

275

lived two houses up from the shop we just parked beside, but she must have been, let's see, well no younger than thirty I'd guess. Having said that, remember I was only a lad myself then, so anyone over twenty five seemed ancient to me then, and people those days were much older, younger, if you know what I mean?'

'Yes I think I do. So if she was thirty in forty two then she'd now be.... seventy eight, is that right?'

'Yes, maths isn't my strong suit Gibson, but I think you're right.'

'So she could still be alive?'

'Well yes, I suppose she could be.'

'She might be interesting to talk to if she is, and if she's still compos mentis.'

'Nothing to lose in asking, shall we knock on the door?'

'I've got a better idea,' said Gibson, 'let's go and ask in the shop, they'll know everyone on the street I should think.'

The shop, more an Aladdin's cave crossed with a Tardis thought Gibson as he entered. He marvelled at the size of the inside of the shop compared to the impression from the outside. The huge array of goods of goods on offer was impressive, someone had incredible organisational ability. Fruit and veg, booze, cigs, canned goods, newspapers, magazines, toiletries, sweets, even a blood pressure machine. The name over the shop was 'Richards' but if the owner was the dark complexioned young man standing behind the counter smiling, Gibson doubted his real name was Richard, Mohammed or Krishna maybe, he thought.

'Can I help you? Anythin' in particular you're lookin' for mate?'

Gibson was thrown and glanced at Mack who looked back; he was obviously caught off guard as well. The man spoke in broad Lancashire, not a trace of the expected Indian accent.

'Yes, I'll take some of these bananas please,' Gibson replied.

As the man tilled up the price, Gibson asked him.

'Have you had this place long?'

'No not very long, took over about six months ago.'

'Oh, I was hoping to speak to someone who'd known the area for a while.'

'You can speak to my Dad if you want, he was here for donkey's years, only retired when I agreed to take over. I used to do the markets see, but I'm getting a bit old for that so I agreed to take this place on, best thing I ever did.'

'Right, so where is your Dad now?'

'He's in the back, I'll go and get him.'

Gibson and Mack exchanged looks, Mack shrugged his shoulders and smiled.

An elderly Indian man appeared. He walked

slowly with the aid of a stick, wore a turban and a full beard. What you could see of his face resembled dark brown crinkled parchment. He was getting on, but had bright sparkly intelligent brown eyes and a big smiley face.

'Yes,' he said, 'my son says you want some information?' This time the accent was as expected.

'How long have you lived here, I mean how long ago did you take over the shop?'

The old man looked behind him, pulled a small wooden stool across and sat down. Once he was comfortable he replied.

'In nineteen sixty three I believe it was, why?'

'I imagine you got to know most of the people around here?'

'Yes, I did, sometimes I got to know them a bit better than I wanted to.' He laughed, then coughed a bit.

'There was a lady who lived two doors up from here, number five, my friend here knew her many years ago but can't remember her name. I, we, just wondered if she was still living there, she'd be getting on a bit now if she's still alive?'

'Ah you mean Dolly.'

'That's the name,' said Mack, 'I nearly had it, yes definitely Dolly, great name.

'Is she still there?' asked Gibson

'No she moved away few years ago, couldn't cope by herself, went a bit gaga. I think she's still alive though.'

'Any idea where she went to?'

'No, but Mrs Pennington at number thirty can probably tell you, I think she was the one got social services involved. Nice lady, keeps an eye out for us old fogies.'

With that he started to laugh but the laugh turned into another coughing fit and he struggled to get his breath. The son came over with a glass of water and held it to his father's lips.

'Stubborn old bugger, still smokes twenty a day.'

Gibson waited until the old man regained his breath.

'Are you okay?' enquired Gibson before going on.

'Yes, as my son says, I'm a silly old bugger. I shouldn't smoke for many reasons, not the least that I'm a Sikh and it's against the teachings to smoke or swear, so I'm probably a lost soul.'

He smiled and resisted the obvious urge to laugh again, no doubt fearing another coughing fit.

'Are there any other old residents still living on the street, I mean people who've lived here since the war maybe?'

'Oh I wouldn't know really, but since I moved here a lot of the old people have died. There was old Billy, he died not long ago. He must have been one of the last ones from that era I should think.'

'Do you mean Billy Bowen?'

'Yes that was his proper name I think, old Billy everyone called him round here. Had a bad chest like me and it killed him in the end, but you have to die of something I suppose.'

'Come on Dad, time for a nap.' said the son.

'Sorry,' said Gibson 'didn't mean to keep you, thanks for the information.'

'My pleasure young man, always happy to help the police.'

And with that the old man got off his stool and allowed himself to be led away to the back room by his son. Gibson and Mack bid their goodbyes and went outside.

'Got all his chairs at home that one,' said Mack. 'You never said you were police but he'd clocked you anyway.'

'Yes I got that, nice man. Let's go and see if Mrs Pennington can tell us where we might find your Dolly bird.'

The door was answered almost before the first 'ding' of the doorbell had finished chiming, dong. She wore Dame Edna Everage glasses, but there the comparison with the Australian housewife character ended. She was small, birdlike, tiny even, and looked as if a stiff wind would blow her over.

'Mrs Pennington?'

'Yes, and who might you be?' She had a surprisingly refined voice.

Gibson introduced himself and Mack. She was

obviously concerned at a visit from the police so Gibson quickly reassured her that he was just looking for information and told her that the man at the corner shop had said she might be able to help them locate a Mrs...... at this point Gibson realised he didn't have a surname, just Dolly.

'We were hoping you might help us to locate a lady who lived at number five, a lady by the name of Dolly, I'm sorry but I don't know her surname.'

'Millar, and the man at the corner shop is Mr Banji.'

'Right, thanks, yes Dolly Millar, and it was Mr Banji who told us you might know where she is, said you got social services to help when she was ill.'

'Yes I did. Look I was just on my way out, will this take long?'

'No, not long, perhaps we could come in for a minute?'

'Oh yes, sorry, please come in.'

She showed Gibson and Mack into the kitchen. Her house was spotless, neat and tidy, just like the lady herself. They all sat down around a pine kitchen table.

'So what is it you want to know?'

'Mr Banji told us that Mrs Millar was going a bit, well gaga was how he described it, and said that you got social services involved.'

'Yes that's true. I was concerned, Dolly was getting more and more forgetful and I was afraid she would end up having an accident, she really wasn't fit to be on her own, so I called them and they arranged to move her into a home. That was three years ago now. I visit her now and then, when I have the time. She's quite sprightly still, but as Mr Banji said, quite gaga at times.'

'And the home is where?'

'Not far, Newlands, it's called, on Rivington Road Pendlebury, I've got a card here somewhere.'

She scuttled off and came back with a card with all the details on.

'Here have this, visiting times are very lax, you can go there any time really, now I really have to go, so….'

'Yes of course, sorry to have delayed you and thanks for the information.'

Mack and Gibson said their goodbyes and left.

'Want a banana Mack?'

'Thanks, we're off to see Dolly now I assume?'

'Yes we are, but if you attempt to sing or even hum 'Hello Dolly' I'll kill you on the spot.

'The thought never crossed my mind Gibson.'

They found Rivington Road and pulled up outside a large old Victorian house with a sign saying, Newlands Lodge and underneath in smaller letters, 'Dignity in Care'. Gibson pressed the bell and they were subjected to scrutiny by a video camera, then a metallic voice asking them who they were. Gibson spoke into where he assumed the microphone was, then showed his warrant card to the camera. They were buzzed in and the voice told them to wait in the hall and someone would be with them shortly.'

A short slim man in crisp white trousers and a white jacket came out of a door, introduced himself as the care home duty manager. He asked if he could help them. He was bottle blond, slender and held one hand over the other at mid chest level. As he spoke, he fixed Gibson with an unwavering friendly stare making him feel slightly uncomfortable.

'Yes, sorry, we believe you have a resident here by the name of.., sorry I'm not sure if this is her proper first name or a sort of nickname, but she's known as Dolly, Dolly Millar.'

'Yes you're right on both counts, em.....officer?'

'Oh, sorry, Gibson, Detective Sergeant Gibson and this is Mack.'

'Nice to meet you both I'm sure, I'm Steve, and yes we do have a resident by the name of Dolly Millar, and Dolly in her case I can tell you, is short for Dorothea.'

'Dorothea, repeated Mack raising his eyebrows.'

'Yes, a bit much for this neck of the woods, can't blame her for changing it to Dolly. Anyway I assume you want to see her do you?'

'Yes we'd like to have a chat with her. It's informal, just some information gathering really, stuff about the dim and distant past. She's not in trouble or anything' Gibson rushed to say, 'just

283

that she might be able to throw some light on what happened to some people a long time ago.'

'Right, well she'd probably enjoy talking about the past. Life in here can be a bit dull.'

'Before we go to see her, can I ask you how she is,' said Gibson, 'I mean I understand she was brought in because she wasn't able to cope at home, is she, and I don't want to say the wrong thing here, but someone described her as being a bit gaga.'

Gibson hoped he hadn't said anything offensive but he needn't have worried, the man laughed as he replied.

'I think gaga is probably about right, having said that, she's bright as a button sometimes. She's quite a character you know, tells me all sorts of stories, some of them quite naughty. Makes me blush sometimes. Anyway here I am again I gabbling on, I'll take you to see her now, before they have lunch.'

Gibson looked at Mack who was smiling broadly.

'Sounds like this is going to be an interesting Gibson, I'll take my own notes as well if you have no objection.'

They followed Steve through to a large airy lounge with a number of residents resting in comfortable looking armchairs. They were all women. Some seemed to be dozing, others knitting, a couple of them were chatting to each other and a few were watching the television at the far end of the room. As they followed Steve, he turned to them as he walked and told them that Dolly was a bit unsteady on her legs sometimes and spent a lot of time in bed these days, so he'd be taking them to talk to her in her room. As they continued walked down a narrow corridor he told them that she did have regular visits from the physio to try to keep her legs working and so on, but she was getting on now and not all that interested in walking.

'Sleeps a lot of the time now as well' he said as they came to a door on the left.

'Just wait here a mo and I'll make sure she's decent.'

Steve came back after a couple of minutes and waved them in. There were four beds in the room, but only one occupied. The room itself was a cross between a bedroom and a hospital room, quite pleasantly decorated and bright, with a view of the garden through the two large windows that came down, almost to floor level. Dolly was sitting up in bed land seemed a bit sleepy, but she looked smart with her silver grey hair neatly permed. She smiled at Steve, not taking Gibson or Mack in.

'These gentlemen have come to see you Dolly, so be nice to them. I'll see you later.' Dolly looked at them and the smile faded. Steve turned to Gibson and said, 'Just push that button there if you need me, but she should be okay.

Gibson spoke first.

'Hello Dolly.'

As soon as the words were out of his mouth he realised and looked at Mack who just smiled raised his eyebrows but said nothing.

Dolly looked at one then the other.

'Who the devil are you?' She said in a feeble voice.

Gibson was a bit concerned that she might be frightened of him being a policeman so he introduced Mack to avoid the issue. He increased the volume of his voice and spoke.

'This is Mack. Mack has met you before, a long time ago, when you were just thirty, in nineteen forty two, during the war.'

'There's no need to shout, can I have a drink?'

Gibson looked round, there was a glass on the top of her locker and a jug of water.

'This?' said Gibson pointing at the water jug.

'No, a drink, a proper drink, brandy.'

'I'm sorry Dolly I don't have any.' She tutted and Mack stifled a chuckle, he took over.

'I don't suppose you remember me Dolly, but we met the day after the bombs hit the house on Regent Park West and killed all those people. I was a reporter and I interviewed you, we had quite a chat and I mentioned your name in the newspaper.'

'Poor devils, bad that was, very bad, I was

frightened; we were all frightened by the bomb. It shook my house. I remember a young lad, asking lots of stupid bloody questions.' She squinted and looked at Mack. 'Was that you?'

Gibson and Mack looked at each other wondering if she really could remember.

'Swinton and Pendlebury Journal was it?'

That put it beyond doubt. Gibson had heard about old people who lost their short term memory, but could remember things in the distant past without any problem, still he was amazed.

Mack laughed, 'Well I'm glad I made such a good impression,' he said.

Dolly suddenly seemed agitated.

'Where am I, why am I in bed, where's my Mickey, has he gone out, will he be back soon?'

'You're in a care home Dolly, they look after you. I'm not sure about Mickey, he's your son isn't he?'

'Of course he's my son, who else would he be, where is he? Who are you?'

'I told you, we met years ago during the war, in Regent Park West, when the house were bombed, remember?'

'Of course I remember, with the local paper weren't you?'

Gibson jumped in. 'Did you know the family, the people that died in the bombing?'

'Course I did, Pottsy. He were okay, she were a bit flighty though.'

'Flighty, how do you mean?'

'What?'

'You said Mrs Potts was flighty.'

'Oh 'er, tallyman told me about 'er'

Gibson was lost, but he decided to pursue her line of answering and see where it went.

'The tallyman and Mrs Potts'

'Ay rum bugger 'e were, 'ad a few of 'em, including me, better than paying up.'

Then she laughed so hard Gibson thought she would have a seizure. Once she'd calmed down Gibson thought he might as well ask the direct question.

'So the tallyman took favours, I mean took payment in sex in place of money.'

Dolly had gone into a trance like state and stared ahead into the middle distance.

He tried again.

'So the tallyman would ask for sex instead of money?'

'What, who are you?'

Gibson looked at Mack, hands held out in a gesture of frustration.

'Here, let me have a go, but let's assume the answer to your question about the tallyman was yes, I mean I don't think it was that uncommon. They were desperate times. And there's something else I've remembered.

'What's that?'

'I'll tell you in a minute, just let me just ask

Dolly something.'

Dolly's arms were outside the covers and Mack took one of her hands gently in his and stroked the back of it. She came out of her trance like state and looked down at her hand, left it there, looked up at Mack and smiled.

'The tallyman, the one you knew when you were in Regent Park West, can you remember his name?'

'E were a rum bugger.'

'He sounds it Dolly, did you like him?'

'Oh yes, randy git 'e was, and cheeky with it.'

'What was his name?'

'Charlie, poor old Charlie.'

'Why poor old Charlie Dolly... why poor old Charlie?'

'E killed 'im.' Mack turned and looked at Gibson who motioned for him to carry on.

'Someone killed Charlie?'

'Pottsy, don't blame 'im.'

'So Pottsy killed Charlie?'

'Who are you?, where's my Mickey, I want my Mickey.' Her voice started to rise in volume and she started to cry, repeating that she wanted Mickey, getting more and more distressed. She was wailing now.

'Jesus Christ Mack, do something.'

Mack looked around, then remembered what Steve had said. He went round to the other slide of the bed and pressed the button. Gibson tried to calm Dolly down then Steve the nurse came in.

'Oh dear, what's the matter Dolly? Don't worry darling Stevie's here now sweetheart.'

He made soothing noises patting her hand and reassuring her. He looked at Gibson and Mack and motioned with a nod of his head that they should leave.

CHAPTER 21

They let themselves out of the care home and got into the car. Gibson turned to Mack.

'So, what was all that about Mack, Charlie the tallyman?'

'Well, if I'm right, I think we might have found the answer, or at least half the answer, to what happened to a man who went missing nearly fifty years ago.' Mack stopped talking and closed his eyes, obviously thinking.

'Come on Mack, what man?'

'Well, I'm trying to remember the sequence of events, but I'm pretty sure. See, a tallyman by the name of Charles,' Mack stopped talking again and frowned then smiled, 'Rollison, that was his name, Charles Rollison, he went missing, and I'm sure it was shortly after the bombing that destroyed the house in Regent Park West.'

Gibson sat there pondering this new information, then said.

'Right, so we assume this Charles Rollison, is Charlie, too much of a coincidence not to be, and he was killed by 'Pottsy' and we're assuming that by Pottsy, Dolly means Mr Potts, bereaved husband of Mrs Potts who died in the bombing, and whom Dolly implied, was having it off with this Charlie Rollison?'

'Hard not to see it that way, yes, his name, the husband, was David, David Potts, the man I did the interview with, the one that so caught your imagination when you read my story in the newspaper archives.'

'Well bloody hell, how about that?' Said Gibson trying to process all he's just heard, and the implications it had to his case.

'Where did they find the body of this Charles Rollison?'

'That's just it, they didn't, his body was never found, at least as far as I know.'

'So, would David Potts have killed Charles Rollison just because he'd been knocking his wife off?' I suppose he well might, but extreme' said Gibson answering his own question. 'And if he did kill him, what did he do with the body, and, what impact does this new discovery have on my investigation into the deaths of the miners? Holy Moly Mack, life just got a lot more complicated. Are you sure this Charlie went missing after the bombing, and not before?'

'Yes, I'm ninety nine per cent sure it was after the bombing. I was on the story, and in fact the police established Charlie Rollison was seen on his collecting rounds on the day of the bombing, because at one point they wondered if he'd been killed in the bombing, you know if he'd been at that house, collecting money. Regent Park West was one of his regular rounds.

'So is this anything to do with my case Mack, or just serendipity? Have we just come across a completely unrelated crime, I mean in the sense that it's not directly part of the other crimes?'

'I think it could well be Gibson, I can't think at the moment how it would fit with the other murders. This was a crime of passion if Dolly's to be believed, more than likely spontaneous, whereas the others were premeditated and well planned executions, well at least two of them were. Hang on; I've just had another thought.'

'Please don't make my life any more complicated Mack.'

'Think about this Gibson, Our friend Charlie could well have been one of the reasons they moved house, flitted, to try to avoid paying him. If that's the case then you could reasonably assume that the husband might have blamed the tallyman for being indirectly responsible for them being bombed, ergo, they moved to avoid the tallyman so the tallyman was indirectly responsible for the deaths of David Potts's family, possibly having also been messing round with Mrs Potts to boot, Now you have two very powerful motives there Gibson.'

'Yes, extremely powerful, if that was the case, but are you saying that this Charlie character took sex in place of payments, but then still wanted paying anyway - as well?'

'Yes, the sex would have been accepted for extending the credit as it were, delaying the payment. The debt would still be there, but sex would be accepted for the missed payment, not in place of the payment as such.'

'Jesus Christ Almighty, I never cease to wonder at people, I really do. So where to go from here? My boss will have kittens when I tell him it looks like I've discovered another murder. Having said that, at least we have a probable motive, and a suspect for this one. So, to make sure we're not on a flight of fancy here Mack, I need to question this David Potts, which then poses the question, where is he now, if he's still alive that is?'

'Yes, I was thinking the same thing. Maybe we need to go back and see Mr Banji, or maybe Mrs Pennington, see if either of them knows where he might be?'

'Good idea, but I've just had a thought. I mean we're taking it for granted that Dolly's story about Charlie being killed by Pottsy as she calls him, is true. I mean how would she know that Potts had killed this Charlie character?'

'It was a very close knit community; I doubt you could fart without your neighbours knowing about it.' Mack suddenly realised what he'd just said and looked at Gibson. 'Bad example perhaps?' And they both burst out laughing. When they'd recovered Gibson asked.

'You said that this Charles Rollison had gone missing and they didn't find a body, but suppose he just went missing, maybe he had reason to disappear, maybe he reappeared eventually?'

'Yes, that's a possibility. From what I remember he was married and might have had a child, or children. I can check through the newspaper archives, see if I can find out details of his wife and child, then maybe we can trace them and you check if he ever turned up again?'

'Right, so which first, Rollison or Potts?' Gibson pondered. 'Tell you what Mack, you go and see what you can find about Charles Rollison in the newspaper archives and I'll go back to Regent Park West and see if I can get a lead on where David Potts might be, dead or alive as it were. What time's your train back to Southport?'

'Seven this evening, but I really would like to stick around, see what happens, it's all getting quite interesting, so if it's okay with you, drop me off at the bus stop on Bolton Road and I'll get the bus to Salford library and look up the stuff on Rollison. Should be easy enough, I've got the dates, then I can go on to Manchester and hook up with some of my old friends at the Manchester Evening News, go for a couple of pints with them and stay over. Then I can be back with you tomorrow and see how things go?'

'Sounds like a good plan Mack.'

Gibson dropped Mack off then made his way to Regent Park West. *Mrs Pennington would be the better bet, probably lived there a bit longer than Mr Banji.* Mrs Pennington didn't answer her door so Gibson went to see Mr Banji at the corner shop, but unfortunately he was having a late afternoon nap and his son wouldn't hear of disturbing him. Gibson sat in his car outside the shop. He didn't really want to go back to the station until he'd made some progress on the latest developments. If he told DCI Watson about this possible additional murder, it might be the final straw and accelerate the introduction of a new team to oversee the investigation.

Gibson was sure that this was being actively discussed at the top level, but he thought that maybe Watson would prefer to keep him on the case, at least for the time being. There would be a much better chance of Watson grabbing the glory if he, Gibson, cracked it. No chance of that if the investigation was handed over to a new team. *That said, I won't have much longer on this case in any event, unless I come up with something pretty soon.*

Gibson decided to go back to the police station anyway but would try to avoid bumping into the DCI if he could. He would come back tomorrow and see if Mrs Pennington had known David

Potts and where he lived now. In the meantime he would try to get hold of Mack and see if he'd had time to find out anything useful on Rollison's wife and child or children.

He arrived at the headquarters and managed to get to his office without the DCI knowing he was in. He phoned the Manchester Evening News offices and asked if Mack was there. There was a delay while he was located but eventually Gibson was put through to him.

'Hello Gibson, I'm glad you called, we're off to the pub shortly, catch up on old times and all that, but I have managed to find some stuff on Rollison. He had a wife, name of Susan and a daughter. Carol. There's no record of him turning up, at least nothing obvious, but that doesn't mean he never did reappear, but if he did, there was no big fuss, nothing in the papers as far as I can see.'

'Anything on where the wife and daughter might be now?'

'Yes, thanks to investigative expertise of a hack friend of mine here, we've managed to ascertain that a Carol Rollison resides in Wilmslow, Cheshire. She's the right sort of age for the daughter and it's not that common a name, so she could be the one, worth a try anyway.'

'Still the same surname, so she never married, lucky for us.'

'Don't jump to conclusions Gibson, a lot of professional women keep their old surname these days and some go back to their maiden name when they get divorced, so it's anyone's guess on that score.'

'Yes I suppose so, look do you want to come with me to see this Carol Rollison tomorrow?'

'I would like to yes, what time can you pick me up?'

They agreed on nine thirty and Mack gave Gibson the details of where he was staying the night.

'Give me the address details of Carol Rollison anyway, and I'll try and call her tonight and see if she can see us tomorrow morning.'

It turned out there was no phone number listed in the telephone directory for a Carol Rollison. A call to directory enquiries confirmed that she did have a phone number, but it was ex-directory but they wouldn't release it to Gibson unless he made a formal application and then they said they would consider it. He had no time to go through that process so he decided they had no choice but to wing it, and trust to luck she'd be in when they called.

Gibson picked Mack up the following morning from the Red Lion hotel in Manchester and they drove out to Wilmslow, Mack navigating. They soon found the house on the outskirts of Wilmslow where a Carol Rollison lived, they just hoped it was the right Carol Rollison. The door was opened by a small elderly woman, who wisely had the safety chain on. She looked at them through the gap in the door.

'Yes?' she said in a wavering voice.

Gibson explained who they were and showed his warrant card, but the lady didn't look as if she was going to let them in.

'We'd like to speak to a Carol Rollison, does someone by that name live here?'

'Yes,' she said again, giving nothing more.

'Is she at home?'

'No.'

Gibson looked at Mack who was stood to the side of the door, and raised his eyes. Mack made a thumb screw motion. Gibson tried to keep a straight face.

'Are you Mrs Susan Rollison by any chance?'

'Yes I am, Carol is my daughter, but she's not in, she's at the shop.'

'Oh, what shop is that?'

'She has a dress shop in Wilmslow, Catwalk, on Water Street.'

'What number Water Street?'

She gave them the number. Gibson now knew they had the right Rollisons and was about to ask her about her husband Charles Rollison, but then thought better of it. She was obviously on her own and she might get upset, or worse, so he left it.

'Thanks Mrs Rollison, nothing to worry about, just some routine enquiries we're making and your daughter may be able to help us, that's all.'

They left and were soon parking outside Catwalk. It looked pretty exclusive, a couple of manikins in the window were wearing some stunning feathery creations without any price tags. They got out and went into the shop. There was just one customer, being attended to by an assistant. Another, older woman, in an expensive looking black dress came over to them right away.

'Are you the policemen who've just been to my house?' She asked in an annoyed manner.

The mother had phoned.

'Yes we are, well I am.'

'You frightened my mother half to death, what do you want bothering a harmless old woman like that?' Haughty, Gibson thought

'We didn't frighten her, well, we certainly didn't intend to,' he said 'we just asked if we could talk to you. I assume you're Carol Rollison?'

'Yes I am, what do you want?'

Gibson showed her his warrant card and introduced himself and Mack, who he referred to as his assistant.

'So do you have anywhere private we can talk?'

She took them into a tiny office at the rear of the shop. There was a small desk and only two chairs, Mack elected to stand. Gibson started without preamble.

'You're the daughter of Charles Rollison who disappeared in February nineteen forty two.'

Taken by surprise at what Gibson had said, she

suddenly sat bolt upright in her chair and drew her breath in, her hand going up her mouth in shock. Gibson waited, she found her voice.

'Yes I am, surely this is not about my father, not all these years later? 'Don't tell me you've found him after all this time?' She went on without waiting for an answer to her first question.

'No we haven't, but we do have some information which we are still checking, which may help us to find out what happened to him, I stress might. Sorry, is it Mrs or Miss?'

'I prefer Ms.'

'Well Ms Rollison, as I was saying, it's pure speculation at this stage, for various reasons, which I'm not at liberty to go into, the witness we have couldn't be described as entirely reliable, but, there is a possibility we will find out what happened to your father.'

'So he is dead?'

'I'm simply not able to say that at the moment, in fact the main reason we came to speak to you was to establish that he hadn't reappeared into your life.'

'No he never reappeared. I was only three when he disappeared, mummy had to pick up the pieces once she realised he wasn't coming back. She thought maybe he'd run off with one of his fancy women, as mummy called them, but he just disappeared without trace.'

'You seem to have done okay for yourself.' Mack

said.

'Er, yes, well Daddy, who was a bit of a reprobate in other respects, turned out to be quite clever financially and left mummy and I well provided for.'

'Wouldn't there be a problem, I mean proving he was dead and not just missing, I mean for the will to be executed?' Mack asked.'

'I believe there was a problem and mummy had to wait five years before she could go to court to have him declared legally dead. I was eight years old by then. We'd had to live quite frugally up to that point; basically we lived on the cash Daddy had hidden under the mattress, then later, well we were able to get the money he'd left us in his will.'

'Do you know if the police came to any conclusions at the time, about what had happened to him?'

'No, mummy says that it was wartime and people had lots of other things to worry about, and a missing tallyman, of all people, wasn't something they were going to spend a lot of time on. She says that they also thought he'd run away with a woman, or that he'd been robbed and killed by one of his clients. A tallyman wasn't exactly the most popular person in society. Look, is there any great need to speak with my mother about this? She's quite old and very frail and if you start dragging up memories of Daddy, well she loved him very much. I think it might make her ill.'

Gibson thought about it.

'I'll tell you what, I won't interview your mother yet, I don't want to cause her any unnecessary distress, and we've got more or less what we came for, which was to establish that Charles Rollison never reappeared, so just promise me you'll discuss his disappearance again with her, in as much detail as possible, and if she says anything you think might help us find out what happened then you let me know, okay?'

'That sounds reasonable, Sergeant ..?'

'D S Gibson will do Ms Rollison. Gibson gave her a card with his details on and asked her to contact him if she found out anything more. She shook hands with both of them and they left.

CHAPTER 22

'Where to now kemo sabbe?' Asked Mack as they drove away from Wilmslow.

'Well, it seems to me that the stage is set for a good chat with Mr David Potts, so let's hope Mrs Pennington is in and that she can help us to find where he is, assuming he's still alive that is.'

'Okay, but I'm going to have to be back in Southport by this afternoon to relieve my dog sitter, and as much as I'd like to accompany you for the rest of the day I can't, so I'd be grateful if you could drop me off in Manchester, we've got to go that way anyway, and I'll get the train back, but please call me later to let me know how you went on.'

Gibson dropped Mack off as near to the station as he could, then took the road to Pendlebury. He passed Irlams o'th Height, turned off Bolton Road into Agecroft road then right into Regent Park West where he saw the diminutive figure of Mrs Pennington walking along on the other side towards her house. He stopped, got out and caught up with her.

'Hello Mrs Pennington, sorry to bother you again but I wonder if you could help me with some more information.'

'Gosh you made me jump' she said as she stopped and turned round to face Gibson.

'Oh, sorry.'

'If it's about Dolly, I've told you all I know about her,' she said 'I don't really know any more.'

'Sorry, no, different subject. I wondered if you knew a David Potts, he lived on Regent Park West during the war. His was the house that was bombed, you know where the gap is in the houses just down there.' Gibson pointed down the road.

'No sorry, I didn't know him; he'd left before I moved in here. Poor man lost his family in that bombing I believe?'

'Yes he did. I don't suppose you have any idea where he went to live or anything?'

'No I don't, but you could ask his sister in law, she lives on the estate over there.'

She pointed at a small estate of houses running at right angles to Regent Park West.

'Any idea what her name is and an address if possible?'

'Well, I think her first name is Maggie, but I don't know her surname. The only reason I know her, is that she helped out in the shop for a while, when Mr Banji's wife died. She told me about the bombing when we were chatting one day. It was her sister that died, she was married to this David Potts you're asking about.'

'Right, well thanks, I'll go and see Mr Banji, thanks again Mrs Pennington.'

Gibson got in his car and drove to the end of the street and parked outside the shop again.

'I'm sorry Sergeant but my father's out, gone to the hospital for some tests.'

'Not to worry, sorry I don't know your name?'

'Krishna.'

'Not to worry Krishna, maybe you can help me. I'm looking for a lady called Maggie who helped out in the shop when your mother, em, passed away.'

'Maggie Lomas you mean?, Is everything okay, she's not in trouble or anything?'

'No, nothing like that, I just need to ask her something, do you have her address, I believe she lives on the estate over there.' Said Gibson, pointing in the general direction of the houses.

'No problem, hang on, I'll just go and get it.'

He came back out and gave Gibson the address, and directions of how to find her house. Gibson found the house, a pre-war style semi. He parked outside, went up the neat path lined with a small privet hedge and knocked on the door. A child opened the door, quickly followed by a matronly looking woman who Gibson guessed to be in her sixties.

'How many times have I told you not to answer

the door Michael, you don't know who it might be.'

'Sorry Gran', said the youngster smiling, his face full of mischief.

The woman looked at Gibson.

''Sorry, I didn't mean....'

''No that's okay, good advice,' then looking down at the child Gibson said. 'You should listen to your gran, there's lots of people out there you wouldn't want to let into your house.'

Looking back at the woman he quickly introduced himself and showed her his warrant card.

'Sorry to bother you but I'm looking for Margaret, Maggie Lomas, is that you?'

As with most people suddenly confronted with a police detective on their doorstep, she was alarmed and unsure how to react.

'Oh, is there something wrong?'

'No, no nothing wrong, I'm just trying to locate a Mr David Potts, who used to live on Regent Park West. I believe he's your brother in law.'

She looked flustered.

'Why, sorry, why, what for?'

'I just need to talk to him.'

'What for?' she asked again

Gibson was getting fed up with her prevarication.

'Look can we go inside Mrs Lomas, I don't think it's appropriate to discuss this on your doorstep.'

Mrs Lomas looked uncomfortable. She hesitated.

'Is there a problem?' asked Gibson.

'No, I suppose not, you'd better come in.'

Mrs Lomas told the child to go upstairs and play with his toys. The front door opened into a small hallway and off to the right another door opened into a small sitting room with two chairs, a sofa, a huge 'room dominating' television and a false coal fire burning brightly. On the sofa sat an old grey haired man, asleep, snoring gently. Gibson looked at Mrs Lomas.

'Is this David Potts?'

'Yes, he couldn't manage on his own any more, so he came to live with us about six years ago. My husband, we divorced a long time ago,' she said in answer to an unasked question.

'He's really not very well, dickey heart, diabetic, arthritis and some other problems, which is why I didn't want you coming in and upsetting him.'

'Why do you think I'll upset him?'

'Well you're a policemen aren't you? And a visit from you lot usually means trouble, of one sort or another. Can you tell me now what you want to talk to him about?'

The old man was stirring even though they'd both been speaking very quietly.

'Look, I'll be as gentle as I can with him but I have to ask him some questions about the past, something that may have happened shortly after your sister was killed in the bombing raid, it was your sister wasn't it?'

'Yes, her and her three children, lovely kids they were.' She filled up. 'Sorry it still upsets me.'

Gibson gave her a minute to compose herself.

'Would you like a cup of tea or anything?' she asked.

Gibson declined the offer and was about to ask Mrs Lomas to wake the old man up when he woke up by himself and looked around, slightly confused.

'It's okay Dave, this gentleman's from the police and just wants to ask you a few questions.'

He looked apprehensive and spoke in a croaky rasping voice He coughed a couple of times before he could speak properly.

'What about, what?'

Gibson sat down on the chair opposite.

'Amongst other matters, I'm investigating the disappearance of a man called Charles Rollison. He was a tallyman and he went missing in nineteen forty two. I have reason to believe you knew this man. Regent Park West was one of the areas he operated in.'

The old man couldn't hide his discomfort, he looked sacred. Gibson knew he'd struck home.

'Before I ask any questions, I want to tell you that I know about the bombing in nineteen forty two, when you lost your wife and family, and I appreciate what a traumatic event that must have been for you.'

The old man nodded, waiting.

'So can I ask you to confirm a couple of things, first did you swap houses, flitting I think you called it then, did you swap houses with Joe Martin and his family, and had you moved into the house the day before it was bombed?'

'Nay lad, I can't remember what happened yesterday, let alone all that time ago.'

Gibson knew he was lying, you couldn't forget an event like that.

'I'm going to ask you again, and this time I want a proper answer, do you understand?'

'Yeah, all right,'

'So, did you swap houses with Joe Martin and his family, and had you moved into the house the day before it was bombed?'

David Potts hesitated, then spoke.

'Yes.'

'And can you tell me why you'd moved, was it mainly to avoid the tallyman, a Charles Rollison?'

The old man looked worried and glanced at his sister in law.

'You don't have to say anything Dave.' Gibson shot her a warning look.

The old man looked at the floor, then replied

'Yes, but we just knew him as Charlie.'

'Did you see this Charlie again, soon after the bombing?'

The old man's shoulders slumped, his head bowed. Gibson thought he heard a sob. He waited.

'Not sure, can't remember.'

Gibson was losing patience; his voice now had a hard edge to it when he spoke.

'I want answers Mr Potts and I want honest answers, we can do this down at the station if you prefer, see if your memory improves when we get there. I'll ask you again.'

'Did you see the tallyman, Charles Rollison again, after the bombing, yes or no?'

The old man was silent, then just as Gibson was about to lose his patience completely, the old man spoke.

'Yes.' He said, still looking at the floor.

'Now it's important you tell me the whole truth here Mr Potts. Did you suspect that your wife and Charles Rollison had been,' Gibson searched for the least hurtful way of putting it... 'intimate?'

The old man was wringing his hands, still looking at the floor as he answered. His voice was very faint. Gibson knew he would ideally have this man under caution while he asked these questions but he didn't want to interrupt the flow.

'Yes.'

Gibson thought carefully about the next question.

'Did you blame the tallyman, Charles Rollison, for having to move your family into the house that was bombed, and indirectly, did you blame him for the death of your wife and children?'

The sob was undoubted this time. Gibson waited. The old man raised his head and looked at Gibson, tears streaming down his face, mixed with mucus from his nose. Mrs Lomas moved from where she was standing to sit by his side, put her arm around his shoulders and passed him a wad of tissues. He blew his nose then wiped his eyes. Mrs Lomas looked at Gibson.

'Can't you see how you're upsetting him, he's not well, can't you leave him alone, it's bad enough having gone through that once without having to go through it all again.'

Gibson said nothing and looked straight into the eyes of the old man.

'Well?' Gibson asked, ignoring the hostile stare of the woman. No one spoke, then the old man's shoulders slumped.

'It's alright Maggie, had to happen one day,' he turned towards her and patted her on the knee as he spoke, 'and they can't do much to me now.'

He turned back to Gibson. 'I'll save you some time Mr Policemen, I killed him, the day after my wife and kids were killed - and I'm not sorry, he deserved it.'

Gibson breathed out not realising how long he'd been holding his breath.

'Okay Mr Potts, I'm going to formally charge you now, then I'm going to have to take you to the station for a further interview and to ask you to make a formal statement.'

The old man nodded, Mrs Lomas broke down in tears, as Gibson went through the formalities.

Down at the station Gibson booked Mr Potts in and asked for a doctor to be brought to ensure that Potts was fit to be questioned. While that was being attended to, Gibson called DCI Watson and told him about the new developments. Gibson was keen to impress upon his boss that this didn't represent any direct progress in the matter of the killings of the miners and he urged him to keep this under wraps for the time being. Watson agreed and asked Gibson to come and see him as soon as he had secured a formal statement from David Potts.

Gibson himself felt that the interrogation might well reveal links to the main case he was working on, but he kept that to himself for the time being. He thought about calling Mack, but he didn't know if he'd be home by now. I'll call him later he thought. He checked that the doctor had given the all clear to proceed, and then asked to be accompanied by another officer to comply with regulations.

David Potts had decided to accept the offer of a duty solicitor, who was seated by his side at the metal table in the interview room. Potts looked up as Gibson entered with the other officer. He looked pale but seemed calm. The solicitor was smartly dressed in a blue pinstripe suite, black slick hair, parted to one side giving him an old fashioned look. A small moustache added to his slightly shifty appearance. They both sat down on the other side of the desk and as Gibson took out his notebook and pen, the other officer commenced setting up the recording equipment, stating the time, date, the names of those present and other necessary details.

He nodded at Gibson to confirm they were now ready, and Gibson made the formal introductions. He then stated David Potts's full name, date of birth and address, and asked him, for the benefit of the tape, to confirm that these details were correct, which he did. He then addressed David Potts directly.

'You have now been formally charged with causing the death of Charles Rollison on the twenty fifth of January nineteen forty two and you have agreed to make a statement to that effect.'

The duty solicitor held up his hand to stop the proceedings.

'I am advising my client to say nothing. I understand that his previous conversation with you Detective Sergeant Gibson, was before he'd been cautioned, so anything he said would be inadmissible as evidence. I suggest therefore, that we keep this interview to the bare minimum so Mr Potts and I can leave here and I can then consult with my client in private and advise him further?'

Shit, I thought this might happen.

'Is that what you want Mr Potts, or would you prefer to get it all off your chest once and for all?'

David Potts looked at Gibson, then at his solicitor. He drew in a deep breath, exhaled, and then spoke directly to the solicitor.

'I appreciate you're trying to do your best for me, but I've had this hanging over me all these years and I'd just like to get it all over with now.

'I strongly recommend you reconsider Mr Potts, I really do, for your own good.' The solicitor replied.

'I'm really sorry to have wasted your time, but I've made up my mind. I want to get the whole thing sorted, no more lies, no more worrying, I've had enough,' he turned to Gibson, 'please ask your questions and let's get this over with.'

Gibson got up and poured some water into a glass and placed it on the table next to the old man.

'Thanks' he said.'

The solicitor looked miffed, but kept quiet. It was obvious the man had made his mind up.

'Okay then.' Gibson consulted his notes. 'You've already stated that you killed the tallyman Charles Rollison the day after your house had been bombed, on the,' Gibson checked the date of the bombing in his notes, 'on the twenty fourth of January nineteen forty two. Just to be clear, the bombing was on the twenty fourth January, and you say you killed Charles Rollison the following day, the twenty fifth of January, is that correct?'

'That's correct yes.'

'Would you recount the events of that day, in as much detail as you can please?'

Davis Potts straightened up in his chair, looked upwards, breathed out heavily and began speaking.

'I don't remember much about things before he knocked on the door. With all that'd gone on, I was in a bit of a daze, when I look back. Anyway I was staying at the Martin's house, the one we'd moved out of only a couple of days before. They'd gone out, the Martin's, to sort something out with the police and fill in some forms and things, to do the wife and the kids, I wasn't up to it. I think I was asleep, I don't know what time it was but it was mid morning, around elevenish I'd guess. Anyway I hears this knock on the door and when I opened it, there he were, big smile on his face as usual.'

'What you doing home Dave, no work today? Heard you've had a bit of excitement down here.'

I couldn't believe anyone could be so, what's the word, so unfeeling, callous, then the penny dropped. He thought we were in our own house as usual, he wouldn't have known we'd flitted to the house that'd been bombed. I remember starting to think then how it was all his fault. If it wasn't for him always wanting his money, every penny on time or else, then when you'd paid it all off, he always managed to talk you into another loan, well he did with the wife at any rate, always talked her into borrowing more than we could afford to pay back.' The old man stopped talking and took a drink of water, then carried on.

'I'd heard that he sometimes took advantage of women as well, you know, if they couldn't pay, he'd like say he would make an exception if they were, well you know what I mean.'

Gibson interrupted.

'Sorry Mr Potts, but we need to be clear, what you mean is Charles Rollison would sometimes ask for sex with women if they weren't able to pay what was due that week, is that what you meant?'

'Yes, sorry, anyway I'd heard that sort of thing went on and I thought maybe he might have taken advantage of Betty, my wife, I mean I know there were weeks when we didn't have the money to pay, so.... So anyway, there he was rabbiting on about I don't know what, and there I am, my wife and kids just been killed 'cos we'd moved house, 'cos of him, 'cos of all the money we owed him and couldn't pay. I said to him, my wife and kids are dead because of you. He just stood there and laughed at me, said what are you talking about? I told him we'd moved house to avoid him pestering us for money we hadn't got. He could see I was very angry and I think he was scared. He stopped talking and went towards the door, but

I got there first and I wouldn't let him out, not before I'd given him a good hiding anyway. He backed off, then kneed me in the balls, took me by surprise. I fell down near the fire grate. He came back and stood over me and kicked me in the kidneys. He was shouting at me then, I can't remember what he was saying, but I reached out, got hold of the poker which was next to the grate and I rolled over and hit him as hard as I could in the shins. I caught him a good one and he went down, screaming that I'd broken his leg. I had too.

He was writhing in agony holding his leg, but it was bent at a funny angle. I got up off the floor. I was so angry and I couldn't help myself, I kept thinking about Betty and the kids and how they'd been killed 'cos of him. I hit him on the head, I don't know how many times but there was blood and like pulp stuff all over the place by the time I'd finished.'

David Potts stopped talking, seemingly horrified by the recollection of his own violence. Gibson said.

'We'll have a little break here and re-commence shortly.'

The constable switched the tape off having given the time and reason for the break. Gibson took the opportunity to call DCI Watson and bring up to date with events. He'd already told him in brief about David Potts, but was now able to confirm they now had a solid case against him for the killing of Charles Rollison.

'Well done, one down and one to go Gibson eh?'

'Yes sir.'

'Do you think this has any direct link to the other murders?'

'No indication of that yet, but I'll be in a better position to tell you that later sir, when I've finished the rest of the session with Potts. I'm just going back in now, so I'll call you when we're finished.'

'Okay.'

Gibson went back in and sat down. The duty solicitor was sat across the table, stony faced.

'The officer switched on the tape and formalities over, Gibson asked the next obvious question.

'Following on from what you said previously, there you were, in the Martin's house with the body of the man you'd killed and all the mess, blood etc. What happened next?'

'I remember going into the back kitchen and washing myself. There was blood all over me and I took my shirt off, went back into the other room and tried to mop up as much as I could, but it was a waste of time. Then Joe Martin and His wife walked in. They didn't know who it was I'd killed at first, he was, was unrecognisable I suppose. I don't think I was making any sense but I remember Irene, Joe's wife giving me some hot sweet tea and how good it tasted.'

'Anyway I told them what had happened and they made me go and have a bath, told me to take off all my clothes. After that they made me go to bed and told me to stay there until they said I could come down. I think I must have zonked out because it was dark when I woke up, I mean dark outside. I found some fresh clothes they must have left for me on the chair, so I went down and they'd cleaned up everywhere. Joe was sitting on the settee reading the paper and listening to Tommy Handley on the wireless.'

'I asked him what they'd done with Charlie's body and Joe told me not to worry, it was all taken care of. That I should try to forget what had happened and that I shouldn't talk about what had happened to anyone, not even him. I was in a state, I kept thinking about my wife and kids and then the tallyman and it all got a bit too much for me, I didn't know what was real and what wasn't. I stayed at Joe's for the rest of the week, until the funeral.'

David Potts stopped talking and looked down at this hands clasped together on the table top, as though in prayer.

'Tell me about the day of the funeral Mr Potts.'

'The funeral, well I'm sorry, but I don't remember much of that either. I couldn't believe they'd gone, in those wooden boxes, three wooden boxes. I remember bits of course, the church, the cemetery. When I saw the graves it reminded me of what I'd done, killed someone. I couldn't believe I'd actually killed someone. It made me feel, I don't know, it made my grief feel less, less genuine than it should be, I can't explain. On the way back I remember asking Joe what he'd done with Charlie's body. He said again it was all okay and I shouldn't worry, they had it all worked out.'

Gibson interrupted

'They had it all worked out, who did you think 'they' were?'

'I don't know, he didn't say.'

For the first time Gibson thought David Potts was lying.

'You must have had some idea of who he meant though, was it your old chums, Joe's gang?'

'I told you I don't know.'

If you're trying to protect them, your old friends, the gang, it's a bit late for that, they're all dead, well other than Freddie, and he was too drunk to know what was going on that day. Oh and Barry Jones, but he went missing at sea, years ago, so it's a fair bet he's gone as well.'

'Barry, gone?'

'Look Dave, I know you're not telling the whole truth here, so let's not waste each other's time. You've confessed to the killing of Charlie Rollison, so why not tell us what happened to his body? I met Charlie's wife and daughter yesterday and they still don't know what happened to him. Don't you think they deserve to know, I mean, you lost your nearest and dearest so you must know what they've been going through all these years? Even if Charlie was a bit of a shit, his wife and daughter deserve better surely?'

The old man sat there, obviously torn, then seemed to come to a decision.

'This is the truth, I don't know what they did with the body, but I think they burnt it.'

'Why do you think that?'

'Cos Joe said Charlie was an evil man, a loan shark, a, a parasite, that's the word, who preyed on poor people, and that he'd burn twice, once on this side and again in hell.'

'That was quite a speech.'

'Yeah it was, I memorised it, the bit about him being evil, made me feel better. Joe had a way with words, he was clever, could have gone a long way if he hadn't been born poor.'

Gibson thought about the implications of what Potts had said.

'I assume Joe and all the others in the street attended the funeral?'

'Yes, I'm certain of that, Joe was one of the pall bearers, I think Billy Bowen was another.'

'I also assume you know they were part of a gang, there were five of them?'

'Yes, I know, tight knit they were, always together, up to no good, not that they were really bad or anything, just a bit rowdy.'

'Why weren't you part of the gang?'

'Dunno, just the way it was, I was always making models, collecting train numbers, that lot weren't interested in stuff like that.'

'Were the rest of the gang at the funeral?'

'As far as I remember, yes.'

'You had a wake afterwards, were the gang at that, did they all come to the wake?'

'I think so but I can't remember, there were a lot of people there. I wasn't interested in seeing who was there, I didn't care.'

'Okay, do you remember later that day when the hut went up in flames, the German POW's hut, on Chapman's farm?'

'Course I remember it, couldn't have happen to nicer people.'

'You were glad they'd been killed then?'

'If you want an honest answer, yes, I was glad, we all were, and all the better that they were killed by their own lot, though we didn't know at first, I mean that they'd all died in the fire, we only knew that afterwards, but yes it made us feel better at the time.'

'And now?

'What are you asking, you mean, how do I feel now about them being fried like that? I don't think about it, but they started it didn't they so I don't feel sorry for them if that's what you mean, anyway why are you asking about them?'

'Just covering all the bases. What did Joe Martin say about the German POWs, I mean not on the day of the funeral, just generally?'

'He said what we all thought, that it was an insult to have them there on our doorstep, especially after the bombing that killed my family, and that they shouldn't be allowed to work on a farm, that they should be shot.'

'Okay, so going back to the hut being on fire, what time were you first aware of it?'

'I'm not sure, maybe about seven, half past, maybe later, I'm not sure.'

'Was the wake still going on then?'

'Yes, but quite a few people had gone by then I think.'

'Was Joe Martin there, when you saw the hut on fire, did you speak to him about it?'

'No I don't remember seeing him, maybe he'd left already. The only person I spoke to was my sister in law, Maggie.'

'And finally, did you hear the German planes, the one that supposedly dropped a bomb on the POW's hut?'

'No, I don't remember hearing one, but I wasn't really all there at the time.'

'No I can appreciate that, so how did you get to know it was a German bomb that set the hut on fire?'

'Em, I'm not sure, someone must have told me.'

'Okay Mr Potts, that'll do for the time being. They'll take you back to the cells now and I'll come and see you later, okay?'

Gibson left the interview room and went back to his office and sat reading over his notes from the interview when his phone rang. It was Mack.

'Hello Gibson any progress?'

'Yes, quite a lot, I'm just reading through my notes prior to reporting back to the DCI. We now have a formal confession from David Potts for the murder, well probably manslaughter of Charles Rollison.'

'Wow, that was quick.'

'Yes, I think he was relieved to tell me, get it off his chest after all these years. I don't think he's an evil man, just got provoked beyond endurance and snapped.'

Gibson went on to tell Mack how David Potts's story unfolded.

'So you didn't have to mention Dolly, her saying he'd killed the tallyman?'

'No, I thought about it, but bearing in mind her mental state, I knew she wouldn't be a credible witness if push came to shove, so I thought I'd see if he would own up, and fortunately he did. Like I say, I think it's been on his conscience all these years. The only thing that bothers me a bit, is how she knew. I mean they seemed to have played it pretty close to their chests.'

'Look Gibson, in a street like that you'd be hard put to keep anything a secret. Maybe one of the gang was seeing her, you know, pillow talk.'

'Hmm, that's a point, Mack I think you've given

me an idea.'

'Go on, what gem of wisdom have I just imparted, unknowingly?'

'Okay, well this is a bit speculative, but Potts said Joe Martin implied he would burn Charlie's body, but even burning a body doesn't get rid of it. And it isn't that easy to find somewhere you can burn a body without attracting attention, agreed?'

'Yes, absolutely, go on.'

'Well suppose you're planning to have a big fire anyway and you think that you'll just add Charlie's body to the blaze and no one will ever know it's him.'

'Sorry Gibson, you've lost me. Who was planning to have a big fire…. hang on, not the POW's hut?'

'Why not? Suppose the story of a German bomber is all baloney, and I have to say I've never really bought the bit about a stray German bomber ditching some unused ordinance plonk on top of the POW's hut. If you dismiss that, then you might come up with a more simple explanation, which is that the hut was set on fire purposely, motive, revenge.'

'Christ, that would really put the cat amongst the pigeons. But hang on, I'm thinking, there are a few ifs and buts to this theory.'

'Give me some objections then, play devil's advocate.'

'Okay, well there was a raid that night, by German bombers, on Trafford Park, not a million miles away from the area.'

'Agreed, but put that down to just good luck, for the arsonists I mean, fortuitous.'

'Okay, but what would their cover story have been, if they weren't able to blame the fire on the Luftwaffe?'

'I've thought about that and they wouldn't need one really. All they would need to do would be to alibi each other and say they were all at the Potts's family wake. As long as they stuck together, the police would never be able to prove they'd set the place alight. They might have a bloody good idea, but there's a world of difference between thinking you know who done it, and proving it.'

'And by "they" I assume you mean the gang, some or all of them?'

'I'm not sure who I mean, but I suppose that's the logical assumption you might make.'

'Okay, so what you're suggesting, in plain language, is that one or more of David Potts's friends perpetrated an act of arson and murdered those prisoners of war by burning their hut down?'

'That's what I'm suggesting might have happened.'

'Right, lets run with that for a minute then, so if you're right, and he... hang on a minute, there had to be more than one person.'

'Now you're getting there Mack, yes there had to be more than one person. One person couldn't get Charlie's body to the scene of the fire, trap the POWs inside, start the fire and all that that entails, it had to be more than one, and my guess is it was four, the gang less one member, Freddie, who was too young and very drunk and incapable at the time.'

'Jesus Gibson, Jesus Christ, I've just realised where this is taking us, the motive for the killing of your miners, whoa.. something's wrong.'

Gibson smiled, he'd been through the same process in his mind just before Mack called.

'Don't tell me Mack, not enough bodies.'

'Quite, four bodies found to have been in the remnants of the fire. Course, it could be that you're just wrong about the tallyman's body being disposed of in that fire, or any fire for that matter, they could have buried him, or maybe thrown him in the canal.'

'I agree, but something in my gut tells me they did dispose of Charlie's body in the fire.'

'Hang on Gibson, they must have known that the remains of five bodies would be likely to have been found after the fire, so wouldn't that have raised suspicion in the minds of the police?'

'So what?, the police wouldn't have been able to find out who the bodies belonged to, and we're back the alibi scenario I mentioned before, it still ensures that they couldn't be charged, even if there was any suspicion they were involved in some way, there just wouldn't be sufficient evidence or grounds, but as it was, there were only the remains of four bodies found at the scene, which begs the question, if Charlie's body was incinerated in that fire, whose body wasn't, in other words, did one of the POW's escape?'

Mack was quiet for a while.

'Jesus Christ Almighty Gibson, if you're right, then you now have a suspect with a solid gold motive for revenge.

'Yup, just one small problem though, presuming I'm right that is. I haven't got a clue which POW he is, or where he is.'

'Well you know he's one of four people, he's male, and he's German and you can guess his approximate age, but as for where he is, yeah I can see that's a bit of a problem, so what's your next move?'

'Well I have to bring my boss up to date, run my theory past him and just hope they don't bring someone else in on the case. That really would be a pisser at this stage of the game. Look, can you try to dig up as much information on the four POW's names, ages, anything?'

'Yes of course, I'm in the wrong place, but now I've been properly reacquainted with my old friends at the Manchester Evening News, I think I can get them to see what they find. I'll call you later with anything I can find out.'

Gibson went to see DCI Watson and laid out the latest information, and told him his theory on what might have happened. The DCI listened intently to what Gibson had to say, without interruption, elbows on his desk, hands clasped together, chin resting on his thumbs. He stayed in that position long after Gibson had stopped talking, then spoke.

'I've been instructed to take you off the case.'

Gibson felt as if he'd been felled by a punch in the stomach.

He heard his own voice, wavering as he replied, it didn't sound like him it sounded weak, whiney.

'They can't do that.'

'They can and they have.'

'But I….'

The DCI held his hand up palm towards Gibson, Gibson stopped mid-sentence.

'When I next see you, I am to tell you to hand over all you have on this case to D S Roy Todd, he's based in Pendleton, do you know him?'

'Yes I know who he is sir.'

'You know, you're looking a bit peaky Gibson, decidedly ill, do you feel okay?'

'Well considering what you've just told me, I can honestly say I've felt better, look sir…'

'No, I think you definitely look off colour to me, probably overdoing it Gibson, maybe you need a few days off sick?'

The DCI picked a file up from his desk and

began to read it as though Gibson wasn't there. Gibson wasn't sure. The DCI looked up.

'You still here?'

'No sir.'

'No, I didn't think so.'

The DCI went back to reading his file and Gibson left.

So two, maybe three days at most to get a result, no problem. Now where did I put that magic wand......?

Gibson went to his office and collected all the files he needed, to carry on working from home. That wasn't too big a deal as he already had an office of sorts in the spare room. Once back home he called Mack who answered right away.

'Me, get anything?'

'Yes Gibson, and it get curiouser and curiouser. As it happens, there was quite extensive coverage of the bombing of the German POW's billet in the local rags. I wasn't assigned to that particular story, my colleague at the time, Ian Jackson covered it for the Journal. He's dead now, but apparently he wrote it up in some considerable detail. Now this is the strange bit, it seems that all German soldiers wore dog tags which had their unit ID number, and each soldier's personal ID number.'

'Okay so what's so strange about that?'

'Well there were four of them found in the remains of the fire, four German soldier's dog tags.'

'Oh shit, well there must be some rational explanation for that, I'm not giving up on my theory, in fact I can't. I've just been told they want to take me off the case, bring someone new in, so it's this or nothing, and anyway, I just know I'm right.'

'So if you're off the case, what can you do?'

'Well for once, my miserable git of a boss has given me a bit of rope. I don't think he wants to lose this case either. Officially I'm now on sick leave for a few days, so it's last chance saloon time.'

'Right, so how many days is that d'you think?'

'About three before they get ants in their pants and insist I give over the stuff, even if I'm dying.'

'Do you want me to come and help? I can probably get Celia to take Monsoon for a few days.'

'Well if you can, I'm going to need all the help I can get now.'

'No sweat, I can stay with Nigel, one of my old pals from the paper, he lives your side of town, so that won't be a problem.'

'Okay well it's time I was out of here, so call me later at home and let me know what time your train gets in and I'll pick you up.'

Gibson gave Mack his home number.

'Before you go, did you get any more details of the POW's names, ages etc?'

'Oh sorry yes, got a pen and paper?, here goes, Eric Muller, born nineteen twenty, aged twenty two at the time, Hans Konig born nineteen twenty two, aged twenty, Fritz Meyer born nineteen nineteen, aged twenty three and Karl Fiedler born nineteen twenty one aged twenty two.'

'What a waste, so young.'

'Yes, tragic, but that's the price of war Gibson.'

'Yes I suppose, oh, I had another thought, could you try and find out if Harry Chapman, the farmer, if he's still alive, and if he is, where he is?'

'That's a tall order but I'll give it a go. By the way, I've got someone looking to see if he can get any more information on the POW's from the German Embassy.'

'Good, the more info the better. By the way, your colleagues at the paper seem to be helping out a lot, I assume there's going to be a quid pro quo required at some stage?'

'There is, but I haven't let anything slip, I promise, I just hinted there may be something worthwhile for them if they help. They get the drift, so we can rely on them to do everything they can, within reason.'

'Good stuff, see you tomorrow Mack.'

CHAPTER 23

The following morning Gibson picked Mack up outside the Oxford Road train station at eight thirty.

'Any brainwaves overnight?' Mack asked as they drove away from the station.

'Not really, some thoughts and theories which I'll tell you about, but we need to focus on potential sources of information, if that isn't stating the bleeding obvious. What I mean is, we have a limited number of people who possibly have knowledge of what happened at the time of the bombings. I think it's fair to say that the bombings, one way or another, are the catalyst for everything, all the deaths, murders etc. So, who do we have who has knowledge of those events, who is still alive? We have Freddie Exan for one, Dizzy Dolly, two, three David Potts, four Mrs Pennington, but she wasn't there at the time, and then the only other person we know of, is of course the farmer, Harry Chapman, who could be an invaluable source of information, if he's still alive and not gaga, that is.'

'Well when we get to where we're going, your house I assume, I'll call the boys at the paper and see what they've come up with.'

'Okay said Gibson.' They drove along in silence for a while; the road was still quite busy even though they were heading out of Manchester and against the prevailing morning rush hour traffic. They drove along Chapel Street then past Salford Crescent, passing Salford University campus, then onwards towards Gibson's home in Worsley. Gibson broke the silence.

'So how did you end up living in Southport? Not that isn't a nice place mind, just wondered, why Southport?'

'It's too corny for words really, but it's where I met the love of my life. I'd never had any intention of getting hitched. I'd had a few girlfriends over the years, even moved in with a couple of them for a while,' he laughed, 'not at the same time you understand, 'but they didn't last. Then I met Mandy. I'd gone to Southport in seventy four to do a story on Red Rum. If you remember, he'd won the Grand National, twice, once in nineteen seventy three and again in seventy four. He ended up winning again a few years later I think.

Anyway, I was getting on a bit, fifty two, and getting married was the last thing on my mind. I was destined to be a lifelong bachelor. Then I was sent to do this piece on the Red Rum's trainer, Ginger McCain, a very interesting man, said to be the most successful Grand National trainer of all time. Mandy worked at his stables, helped train the horses and so on. I first saw her when I went to see Red Rum on a training ride on Southport beach, she was riding one of the other horses. We met later at the stables, began chatting and I ended up taking her for a drink that night.'

Mack closed his eyes as he remembered.

'You'll need to leave early in the morning, and I mean early,' said his editor.

'Four o'clock isn't early, it's the middle of the night!' he'd protested, though not too much, he really wanted the assignment.

Leaving his flat on the outskirts of Manchester, he drove north, and eventually along a more or less deserted motorway, the light pollution of the city dropped away and the absence of road lights on the M6 rendered the sky jet black a with a backdrop of shining stars. He switched the radio off and enjoyed the silence and solitude. As he came off the motorway and headed towards Southport, the sky gradually changed colour as dawn broke with bars of pinkish light, slowly appearing on the horizon.

'Park over there' said the man who'd let him into the stable area, 'and jump in here quick.'

Mack climbed into the battered green Land-over and they drove through the deserted country lanes then the empty early morning streets of Southport and finally through some sand dunes on to the large flat wide Southport beach which stretched for miles, as far as the eye could see. The sky was now a deep blue colour. The jeep stopped and they both got out, the cool morning air smelt of salt and seaweed.

"Ere,' said the man, unscrewing two plastic cups from the top of his thermos, filling them with coffee and handing one to Mack, 'there's not many mornings as sweet as this.' The man said. Mack looked around at the newly minted March morning, no argument there he thought.

'Ayeup, 'ere they come' said the man.

Mack looked to his left and saw three horses and riders approaching in the distance. As they came nearer Mack could hear the rapid clumpety sound of the hooves as the horses were whipped into a gallop by their riders. They passed just yards in front of them, Red Rum in the lead he assumed. Flaring nostrils rapidly expelling and inhaling steaming air, a fury of limbs, sinew and muscle thundering along, the ground beneath them shook as the horses sped past, sand flicking up behind their hooves.......

'You okay Mack?' asked Gibson

'Yes, sorry, I was just remembering, where was I?'

'You were telling me how you ended up taking the love of your life for a drink.'

'Yes, well she was quite a bit younger than me, but we hit it off and six months later we were married, and I moved to Southport, been there ever since.

'So where is she now, what happened?'

'Well technically, she's still my wife, but as for where she is, I've no idea. Three years after we married, she ran off with a stable hand, Spanish bloke, would you believe called Manuel?'

'Oh shit, sorry to hear that.'

'Don't be, we had three good years and then, well looking back I can understand it, we should never have got married, the age gap was just too much. I think I'm much better off with Monsoon.' Mack laughed. 'So... you?'

'Well I was adopted, as was my sister Sophie. We had great parents, both now dead, sadly.'

'Well at least you have a sister, I was an only one, so when my parents passed away. I had lots of friends, but no wife, no children and no siblings. It's a strange feeling to be the only one left of a family.'

'Yes, I can imagine, but when my Dad died, it affected my sister so badly that she wasn't much of a comfort either. His death somehow made her desperate to find her real mother, you know, her biological mother.'

'And did she?'

'Yes, it wasn't too difficult. Our parents told us at a relatively early age that we were adopted and that they'd lodged details of our biological parents with the family solicitor, well as much as they knew anyway. They told us we could get the information any time we wanted to.'

'So you both found out who your real parents were?'

'No, I wasn't interested, I'm still not. As far as I'm concerned I was more than happy with the parents I had, but Sophie, well she went the whole hog and managed to contact her biological mother. It didn't turn out well.'

Gibson stopped talking briefly to curse at a driver who'd strayed into the lane in front of him, forcing him to brake. He recovered his composure.

'Anyway, she eventually found her mother in a hostel, a sort of drug rehab place, but I gather she was a pretty hopeless case. She wasn't interested in Sophie so there was no emotional reunion. It turned out she'd been working as a prostitute when she'd had Sophie and hadn't got a clue as to the father was. Sophie went really downhill then, became very depressed.

Then she gave up her job in Manchester and went to London, just like that, and the next thing I knew she was working as a hostess in a nightclub. I went to see her of course, tried to persuade her to come back up to Manchester. But she'd changed, she'd become cynical, said she would use her good looks to earn lots of money. She said she was working the top end, as she called it, Saudi Princes all that sort of crap. We had a bit of a row and that's the last time we spoke, haven't heard from her since, must be going on for three years now, probably doesn't even know I got divorced and remarried.'

Mack stayed silent for a while, he could tell the memories were upsetting to Gibson. He decided to change the subject.

'So what did your folks do, for a living I mean?'

Mum was a housewife, Dad was a musician in the NDO, don't know if you remember it, the Northern Dance Orchestra?'

'I do Gibson, always on the BBC. Their conductor I remember, he was called Bernard Herrmann. I was a Hitchcock fan, still am, but I got really confused because the composer who worked with Hitchcock, did all the music scores for his films, he was called Bernard Herrmann, and I couldn't square it, him being the conductor of the NDO as well. Then of course I realised they were two entirely different people.'

'Yes, I think a lot of people got confused about that, but the NDO Bernard Hermann lived in Swinton. My Dad told me that Bernard, that's the NDO Bernard, was once sent a cheque by mistake, for royalties earned by the American Bernard Herrmann. It was a small fortune compared to what he was paid by the BBC, he sent it back of course.'

'And you, when did you join the police?'

'I joined in seventy four, the same time you met

your wife in Southport. I made my way up the ladder and became a detective constable, then DS a couple of years later, and then in eighty seven I made a real bollocks of a case I was on, and as a result, a child died. I nearly left the force then, nearly left the human race if I'm honest, I don't think I've ever felt so, so utterly wretched and useless.'

'That bad?'

'Yeah, that bad. A child, he was just nine years old, went missing and we'd interviewed a suspect, I was convinced he was lying and possibly, no probably, the kidnapper. He had form, but we had no evidence and I was persuaded to let him go. We found the boy, two days later, dead. It took us another two weeks to pin the death on that same man, the man we'd had in custody when the boy was still alive. I swore that day that if ever I came across another situation where my instinct told me I was right, I'd trust my instinct.'

'Like now?'

Yes, like now, yes, but at least a child's life isn't at stake this time.'

'I think I remember the case now, Wilson, wasn't that the boy's name?'

'No, close, Wilkinson, Graham Wilkinson, a name I'll never forget. Anyway that's when I met my wife, well just afterwards, and actually, my second wife, Jill. I'd been married before, for two years, but it didn't take, then I met Jill and we're still together and very happy, touch wood. This is it, we're here, welcome to Gibson Towers.'

They went in and Gibson showed Mack where the phone was, then went to make tea. Mack called his contact at the Manchester Evening News, and after a couple of minutes asked the person he was speaking to hold on while he found a pen and some paper to take notes. He spoke for quite a while, writing down the information, then put the phone down and in between sips of tea, filled Gibson in on what they'd been able to find out.

'Right, well the German Embassy was willing to provide information on the general area where each of the POW's came from, but they wouldn't give precise addresses. When it was explained to them that one of the POW's may have escaped and may still be alive, they said they would be happy to give further detailed information on the precise addresses and next of kin information insofar as they could, but it would need to be on the basis of a formal application by the British police. My friends have got details of their contact at the German Embassy if you want to do that, but I don't suppose we have the time now?'

'No we haven't, but I'll need it if and when I have to hand over the case to someone else.

'Okay, well I've got it written down here. Now as far as Harry Chapman is concerned, this might be more promising. They managed to dig up some stuff on when the farm had been bought, which was done to enable Agecroft Colliery to expand. Apparently it was the source of an aggravated dispute with Harry Chapman with him refusing to move. Then the land became the subject of a compulsory purchase order and bailiffs had to move in to dislodge Harry. The records showed that Harry Chapman then bought another farm in Stafford, Mack looked at his notes, 'Yew Tree Farm, I've got the address here, anyway the place is still owned by a Harry Chapman, so he either had, or has, a son with the same name, who's taken over, or, less likely, the original Harry Chapman is still farming himself.'

'Hmm, if he's alive, how old Harry Chapman would be now?

'Let's see,' Mack said consulting his notes again, 'yes, in one of the articles reporting on his evictions he was reported as being "the thirty nine year old farmer", so if he was thirty nine in forty six and it's now nineteen ninety.'

'Eighty three.' Said Gibson, 'not impossible he's still going, a good age, but you never know, good old British farming stock, could well be.'

'So what now Gibson?'

'First off, we need to decide what our prime objective is, then we need to prioritise who we go to see first. I just can't afford to waste any time chasing around willy nilly.'

'So what's our first job, finding out the identity

of the missing POW?'

'Yes I suppose so, but lets' do a little bit of theorising first. I couldn't sleep much last night so I spent a lot of time thinking about how the missing POW might have escaped. Now I appreciate that some of what I say will be obvious, but bear with me and chip in when you feel like it.'

'Okay professor, carry on.'

'Right, well assuming I'm right about Charlie, the tallyman's body being disposed of in the fire, then..' Gibson stopped and looked at Mack, 'what?'

'Nothing, but you're sure about the tallyman's body being in the fire?'

'No, I can't say I'm sure, but I've thought about this until my head felt as if it would explode and nothing else fits. I start from the premise that the miners, well four of the so called gang, that is, decided to exact revenge for the bombing of the house and the deaths of the Potts family, by setting the POW's hut on fire in the evening of the day of the funeral, okay, so let's just run with that.'

'Okay, carry on?'

'So, let's also accept that the story about the lone Luftwaffe pilot conveniently dropping a bomb on the POW's hut is made up, intentionally or unintentionally, but I've never really bought it myself, just too remote a possibility.'

'Okay.'

'Now we have the tricky bit. How did one of the POW's escape, because if my theory about the miners burning the hut down, and disposing of the tallyman's body in the fire is correct, then one of the POW's had to have escaped as there were only the remains of four bodies found in the burnt out hut.'

'And four German dog tags,' said Mack.

'Yes, and I admit that's the one small flaw in my argument, but it is only a dog tag after all, and there could be lots of reasons why it was there, for instance, if you were a German POW and you were planning to escape, logically, you wouldn't take your dog tag ID with you, would you?'

'Okay, fair point, although that presupposes that the escapee knew something was going to happen, which you must admit is unlikely. But nevertheless, carry on, what next?'

'Well, assuming my scenario is correct, then we now have the perfect candidate for the revenge killings, the escaped POW.'

'Right so where did the POW go to? It would have been impossible for a German to blend in in Pendlebury, he'd have stuck out like a sore thumb, but if he's your man, then he had to have stayed somewhere in the area for years, in order to have been able to commit the murders, so tell me Gibson, how the hell did he manage that?'

'Well, he must have had help, someone helped him, hid him, and I need to find that someone, if they're still alive that is.'

'Hmm, interesting theory Gibson I have to

admit.'

'Well I've lived with this for some considerable time now Mack, and It's the only theory that fits, plus I can't think of another one. Oh I nearly forgot, I also think we've missed something important, the grave.'

'Sorry, whose grave?'

'The POW's grave, at Agecroft Cemetery.'

'And what do you think that will reveal?'

'Absolutely no idea, but in an abstract way, it's central to the whole thing, and something we should at least go and look at, even if it's just out of morbid curiosity?'

'I thought you said you hadn't got any time to waste?'

'I haven't, but I just think it would be remiss not to go and have a quick look.'

'When?'

'Well it seems to me that Dolly is the nearest person on our list of people we need to talk to, so we could go to see her. She might know something about the POWs. Then we could go to Agecroft Cemetery, it's only a couple of miles on from the care home.'

'Sounds reasonable, so when do we go?'

'Let's go now Mack, we don't have time to fart about.'

'Fine by me, but shouldn't we call the care home first?'

'I thought about that and decided there isn't

much point. I mean it seems to me you take you chance with Dolly, whether she's lucid or not when you go to see her, and based on our previous experience that can change from minute to minute, so I think we'll just take a chance and see what happens.'

'So is that the cemetery first or the care home first?'

'Care home.'

Okay, well lead on Macduff.'

They left Gibson's house and arrived at the care home some fifteen minutes later. They went through the same security procedure, Gibson showing his warrant card to the camera, but this time it was a woman who let them in. She was quite small, dressed in a nurses blue uniform and seemed to be quite stern to begin with, but then she smiled, introduced herself as Mrs Ilene Kendall and explained that she was today's duty manager. Gibson asked if Steve was around, but she said it was his day off. Gibson had to explain again why they wanted to see Dolly Millar.

'How is she today?' Mack asked as the lady took them through the same resident's lounge towards Dolly's room.'

'Oh much the same as usual is, here one minute, gone somewhere else the next, well in her mind anyway, you know what I mean?'

'We certainly do Mrs Kendall,' said Mack, she turned and smiled knowingly.

'Here we are, just wait there a minute will you?' and she left them standing in the hall.

The door opened. 'You can come in now.'

They went in and this time Dolly was sitting up in a chair by the side of her bed, looking down at her hands in her lap. Mrs Kendall had thoughtfully moved a couple of chairs near to Dolly's bed, facing her. She looked much the same as before, perhaps a little more alert, thought Gibson. He was just about to speak, when he stopped and looked at Mack, who was grinning, waiting for Gibson to say it. Gibson smiled, shrugged and made a face at Mack. They both sat down. Gibson couldn't think of an alternative way to greet her.

'Hello Dolly.'

She looked up and noticed them for the first time.

'Oh hello, are you the doctor?'

'No Dolly, I'm,' he decided not to say he was a policeman, 'I'm Mr Gibson and this is Mack, we came to see you last week, remember, Mack knew you all those years ago, in Regent Park West?'

'She squinted at Mack.'

'Oh yes, I remember, are you the doctor?' she asked Mack. Mack looked at Gibson smiling.

'Mack is a reporter, worked for the local newspaper, do you remember, he wrote about you once, mentioned you in the papers, when the house was bombed, in the war...'

He stopped talking, Dolly had been nodding as

he was speaking giving the impression she knew what he was talking about.

'I remember, what do you want?'

Gibson was unprepared for that response and hesitated trying to think how to frame the question. Try the direct approach he decided.

'Do you remember the German prisoners of war Dolly; they worked on Harry Chapman's farm, in the war, remember?'

'Course I do, why?'

'Did you ever meet any of them?'

'Course I did, Fritz was my favourite though, shame it was.'

Mack looked at Gibson and raised his eyes in amazement.

'What was a shame Dolly?'

'What?'

'The German prisoners, what was a shame; you said it was a shame?'

'What was a shame?'

Gibson rubbed his forehead, thinking what to ask next.'

'Were you friends with any of the German boys, the prisoners of war, the ones who worked on Harry Chapman's farm?' asked Mack.

'Shh,' dolly put her finger up to her lips, 'I liked Fritz, he was very handsome, said he'd marry me if he could, but he couldn't, then he went … in the fire…they shouldn't have done it.'

'Who shouldn't have done it, done what Dolly?

'What?'

'You said they shouldn't have done it, what did you mean, who shouldn't have done what?'

'Can't remember.' Dolly said, suddenly looking frightened.

Gibson took over and tried again but Dolly wouldn't respond. He gave up after a couple of more questions. Dolly had retreated into another world and was just staring at her hands again.

'C'mon Mack,' said Gibson getting up, ' I don't think we're going to get any more out of her, today anyway, might be worth another visit sometime though.'

'Yes, could be, but hard to know what's fantasy and what's real.'

'Yes I know, come on, let's go to Agecroft Cemetery, see if we get any anything from there.

'Looking for answers from beyond the grave are we now Gibson?'

'At this point in the proceedings I'll take any answers I can get, from beyond the grave, or anywhere else for that matter.'

'Right, well we could try holding a séance, you know, one knock if you're a dead German POW, two knocks if you're a murdered tallyman. They both laughed at the weak joke, needing to relieve the growing tension. 'I mean there's desperate and there's really desperate, Gibson.'

'Well put me in the really really desperately desperate category then Mack, 'cos that's where I am at the moment, c'mon, let's go.'

As they drove the few miles to the cemetery they discussed Dolly's responses to the questions.

'I know she's a bit out of it,' said Gibson, 'but nevertheless she gave us some interesting if somewhat oblique answers. I think it's pretty certain she knew at least one of the prisoners well enough, Fritz. I don't see how she would know his first name unless they'd been friendly, maybe even intimate, him promising to marry her and all that, but maybe that last bit might be fantasy, what do you think Mack?'

'I agree, and she might have known the others as well, or at least one other. She said Fritz was her favourite, and you can't have a favourite if you only have the choice of one, can you?'

'Yeas, good point, she also mentioned the fire, and what was it, "shame" and "shouldn't have done it" too vague to know what she really meant, but you could easily interpret those remarks support my theory. Then that was peculiar, how she clammed up when I asked her about the fire, saying she couldn't remember. It was as though she could remember, but was frightened of saying anything.'

`Yes, but as you say, all a bit vague. Look Gibson, on the right, that's where Agecroft Colliery used to be, beginnings of some sort of business park now by the looks of things. And over there,' Mack pointed across the road in the opposite direction, 'that's where Agecroft power station was, powered by the coal direct from the mine. A long conveyer belt took the coal straight from the mine, over the road and into the power station.'

'Hmm, impressive.' said Gibson.'

'Not by today's standards maybe, but in its time it was quite innovative. Slow down, isn't this the cemetery, coming up on the right?'

'Well spotted.' They slowed and drove through the old iron gates attached to two large grimy sandstone pillars, cautiously making their way along a long gravelled drive to a building that looked like a chapel, with another small building next to it. They parked and got out of the car.

The first thing that struck Gibson was how quiet it was, and how the atmosphere contrasted with the immediate area outside the cemetery. Gravestones and old mausoleums were interspersed with trees; the only noise to be heard was birdsong. There was a pleasant peaceful calm about the place. They both stood there in the weak sunlight looking around, then a loud voice made them both jump.

'Yes gentlemen, can I help you – oh, sorry did I startle you?' the man said, when he saw their reaction. He was small, portly and bald, smartly dressed in a white shirt with a black tie, grey trousers, but incongruously wearing a brown overall.

'No need to apologise,' said Gibson, 'I think we were both away with the fairies for a minute, it's so peaceful here.'

'That it is, you wouldn't believe you were in the middle of all this busy commerce, there's even a prison here now, just over the road.'

'Yes, I know,' said Gibson 'you could say I'm partly responsible for keeping it filled with customers.'

'Oh, right, a policeman then?'

'Correct, I'm Detective Sergeant Gibson and this is a journalist colleague of mine, Mack.'

They all shook hands.

'Well nice to meet you both, I'm sure. I'm George Baker and I look after the place, caretaker, manager, whatever title you want to give me, I still get paid the same.' He laughed at his little joke.

'So, how can I help you gentlemen?'

'How far do your records go back George?'

'How far back do you want them to go?'

'How about nineteen forty two?'

'No problem, I thought you were going to ask me for something difficult?'

'Right, well we're looking for details of the internment of four German prisoners of war who perished in February nineteen forty two, on a farm not far from here. They're all buried together in a communal grave I believe.'

'Okay, you need to give me few minutes to go and look up the records but I've been asked for this before I'm sure, a few years ago, it's quite an unusual request, I remember things like that.'

'Yes, we think we probably know who asked you,' said Mack.

'Okay, well feel free to roam about while you're waiting, the older gravestones are quite interesting if you like that sort of thing, fascinates me and I've read most of them several times over, back in a jiff.'

'A bit of a character isn't he?' said Mack, when he'd gone.

'I suppose you have to be a bit quirky to look after a graveyard,' said Gibson, stroking his chin, deep in thought.

'You know Mack, I've just thought of something.'

'What?'

'About when the POWs were killed, well more about when they were buried.'

'What about it?'

'I think I know why the third of February is important, I mean important to the killer.'

'Go on.'

'No, let's wait for George, see if I'm right.'

'You're becoming very enigmatic Gibson.'

'Sorry, just bear with me. C'mon, let's go and look at the gravestones.'

Gibson walked towards the headstones nearby and Mack followed. They wandered through the graves, reading the brief stories of people's lives etched into the headstones.

'You know when you read these epitaphs, makes you realise just how short life is, and how insignificant we all are, just here for a few moments of time really, in terms of the life of the universe I mean.'

'Whoa Gibson, not going all philosophical on me are you?'

'Sorry, no, not at all, just that sometimes you get a completely different perspective on things, know what I mean?'

'I suppose so, look, here comes George and he's looking pleased with himself.'

'Here's the record of the internment, February nineteen forty two, come into the office and you can sit down and read it properly.'

They followed George into his office. He put the big brown hard backed record book down on the desk. Gibson sat down on the chair and Mack stood behind him, looking at the book over his shoulder.

Gibson ran his finger down the entries until he came to the right one. He looked back at Mack, a triumphant smile on his face.

'I thought so Mack, the funeral, the effing funeral, look at the date.'

'Bloody hell, the third of February! 'You clever bastard Gibson, full marks..., but where does it get us?'

'Unfortunately, Mack, absolutely nowhere, not in terms of catching him anyway. What it does tell us though, is that our avenging angel, well more like, devil I suppose, chose the funeral date as the date for his murders, but apart from that, we're not much further forward.'

'Still clears the mystery of date thing, as to exactly why....?'

'Yeah, well, as for the logic, I could theorise, imagine even, our perpetrator attending the funeral and making some sort of macabre solemn promise to kill the people who set fire to the hut.'

'That could fit, maybe one more piece of the jigsaw Gibson, so where do you go from here?'

'Well it seems to me that a trip to Stafford has got to be my next move, how are you for time, do you need to get back?'

'Unfortunately, I do, and just when things are getting interesting, I'm sorry Gibson, pig sick, but Celia's got to go to her mothers and I don't have anyone else to look after Monsoon so I've got to get back, but please call me later and let me know what happens, okay?'

'I will Mack, and thanks for all the help so far, I've really appreciated it.'

'No problem, Gibson, I just wish I could stay and help some more, listen just drop me off at the main road and I'll find my way back to Manchester, there's lots of buses so no problem, then I'll get a train back home. Call me later or tomorrow and let me know how you went on, okay?'

'Will do.'

'He dropped Mack off, then made his way out of Manchester, towards the M6 motorway then drove south, stopping briefly at Knutsford services to fill up and get a sandwich, then back on to the motorway, leaving it at junction thirteen. The roads got narrower and soon he was driving down roads so narrow Gibson wondered what would happen if he came face to face with another vehicle. There were passing places, but they were so few and far between that someone would need to reverse for a considerable distance to let any oncoming traffic through. If that happens, what's the protocol for who backs up and who goes through, thought Gibson? Fortunately the road widened after a while, without him coming across any other vehicles, and soon after, he took a right turn down Chanter Lane and came to Yew Tree Farm.

He parked in the dirt yard, beside an old rusting Massey Ferguson tractor that had seen better days. To the right of the handsome sandstone brick farm house was a large corrugated tin roofed barn containing other various farm vehicles, plus ploughing and harvesting contraptions. On a large field opposite were sheep, some of them with early spring lambs sticking close to their mothers. Hens walked freely around the yard, scratching and pecking the ground in search of food.

He was walking across the yard towards the

small gate in front of the path leading to the farmhouse front door, when a new looking tractor drove into the yard at speed, dispersing the chickens in flurry of feathers and squawking. It came to a sudden halt and a sprightly old man climbed down from the cab. He was small, wiry, black hair flecked with grey and a weather beaten face that looked like old leather. He came towards Gibson with a frown on his face and before Gibson could open his mouth the man started speaking.

'Whatever you're selling I don't want one, and if you're from that bloody DEFRA outfit, you'll have to wait for the forms, 'cos I haven't filled 'em in yet, so whatever it is, you can piss off and leave me to get on, I'm a busy man.'

And with that he turned and walked towards the barn.

Gibson recovered from the verbal onslaught and walked after him.

'Excuse me Mr Chapman, I'd like to have a word with you.'

The man stopped and turned round.

'Are you still 'ere, don't you understand English or what, now fuck of, is that clear enough for you?'

He turned and was about to carry on walking away when Gibson decided he's had enough and raised his voice.

'Mr Chapman, or whoever you are, I'm Detective Sergeant Gibson and I need to ask you some questions, so come back here, NOW!'

The man stopped and turned round.

'Oh, police, well why didn't you bloody well say so?'

He walked back towards him.

'You didn't give me much of a chance, now is there somewhere we can talk?'

Gibson was now able to get a better look at him. He was one of those people whose age was difficult to guess, but from his manner it was obvious he owned the place and Gibson thought it was possible he was the original Harry Chapman.

'Ay, well you'd better come in, follow me.'

Gibson followed him through the small gate. He opened the front door of the farmhouse and bellowed.

'Betty, visitor, can we have some tea? Come in here, sit anywhere you want.'

He showed Gibson into a pleasant farmhouse kitchen. It had a high ceiling with exposed wooden beams. In the centre of the room was a large old wooden table with ten chairs around it. An old sheepdog lay in front of a traditional brick fireplace, complete with wooden logs laid on an iron dog grate ready to be lit. Comfortable looking threadbare chairs with high arms were situated on either side of the fireplace.

Gibson sat down at the table. The farmer took his wellingtons off and left them on a mat at the door, then walked round the table and sat down facing him.

'Like I said I'm busy so you'll have to excuse me being blunt, but I've got a farm to run and two men off sick, so whatever it is you want, can we get on with it?'

Gibson introduced himself properly, then a woman came in.

'Did you say tea?'

'Ay, might as well while I'm talking to this man, he'll have some as well,' turning to Gibson he said, 'so, ask away?'

'Are you Harry Chapman, who used to own a farm in Agecroft Pendlebury?'

'One and the same, but what the devil do you want to know about that place, all this time later?'

'We'll get to that in a minute, but tell me, how old are you Mr Chapman?'

'I'll be eighty two next birthday, why?'

'I had you down as eighty three, but nevertheless, impressive running a farm at your age.'

'Well, never did hold with this age thing, the day you stop working is the day you start dying, I've seen it happen a lot. I've seen what happens when farmers retire, they don't know what to do and before you know it, you're going to another funeral, not for me, anyway. I feel as fit as a flea and I get the lads to do the real hard graft these days. But anyway, I'm sure you didn't come here to discuss my health so what's this all about?'

Just then Betty came in with the tea and put

a tray down with a china teapot, milk jug, china cups and saucers, sugar dish and a plate of biscuits. She poured each one of them a cup without asking, put a cup in front of each of them and said, 'Help yeself's to milk an sugar.' Then she left the room.

Gibson reached for the milk. The farmer waited until Gibson had poured milk into his cup, then did the same and sipped his tea.

'Ahh, that's better, now, like I said I'm busy.'

'Yes, well we're looking into a matter which may be connected to the fire that destroyed a hut on your farm in Agecroft, in nineteen forty two and in which, some German prisoners of war died.'

'And?'

'Well I assume you recall the event.'

'Yes, course I do, but what do you want, surely you're not investigating that all these years later?'

'Well sort of, it may be that the fire, the deaths of those Germans, may have some bearing on some recent matters we're investigating, so what I'd like to know is, what exactly happened that night.'

'Right, let me think.... well I remember the first thing I knew about the fire was when one of the farmhands, who lived in one of the cottages near to the farmhouse, he came banging on my door shouting about the prisoner's hut being on fire. By the time I got to it, it was well alight and the fire engines arrived just after we did, but it was too late, nothing could have survived in that.'

'Why wouldn't the POW's have tried to escape, were they locked in at night?'

'They should have been, but I stopped locking them in a few weeks after they arrived. They weren't bad lads and it seemed silly to me to lock 'em up at night. If they wanted to scarper they could easily do it during the day, but they'd be caught in no time and get carted off to a place much worse than a farm. They knew that and so did I so I stopped locking them in.'

'Okay, was there any evidence of them having been locked in that night, possibly by someone else?'

'Don't know but I shouldn't think there'd be anything left that would tell you, one way or the other after that fire.'

'What do you think caused the fire?'

'Dunno, no idea, well not really.'

'What about this supposed German bomber that came over that night?'

'What about it, scared the bejesus out of me I can tell you.' Gibson's heart sunk.

'So there was a German bomber?'

'Yeah, came right out of the blue, so bloody low I thought it was going to crash, no warning siren, I could only hear the one further away, see Trafford Park was being bombed, but we had no warning where we were, none of the local sirens sounded at all.'

'So the story about the hut being set alight by an incendiary bomb was true?'

'No, was it buggery, the plane was long gone by then.'

'How can you be so sure?'

'Well the only way it could have set the hut alight is if it had a very slow burning fuse, the plane came and went at least an hour before.'

'This is very important Mr Chapman, you're sure the hut wasn't set alight by an incendiary bomb dropped by a German bomber?'

'I'm sure, yes.'

'Okay, you said before, when I asked you what you think caused the fire, you said, you had "no idea, not really", does that mean you might have some idea, a suspicion rather than actually knowing for sure?'

'Well all I know is that the fire wasn't started by a German bomber and I don't see how it could have started by accident. Yes they had candles for light, but I don't believe they would be that careless, I just don't. Then a couple of week later I found a jerry can round the back of another old derelict brick building not that far away from the hut. It smelt of paraffin. It wasn't one of mine, I know that, and I just thought...'

'Did you tell the police?'

'I mentioned it, yes, told the local bobby next time I saw him but I don't think they were that interested; there was a war on, people had lots of other things to worry about, and they were krauts after all, and the week before the fire a mother and her two kids living in the miners houses had been wiped by German bombers, so...' Harry Chapman shrugged his shoulders, then took another sip of tea.

'Any idea who might have wanted to kill these German POW's?'

'Ay lad, you're supposed to be the detective not me, but it doesn't take a genius to work that one out does it?'

'You think the miners did it then?'

'I didn't say that, how would I know? I'm just using common sense, that's all. Look I'm going have to get back to work, cows need milking, sheep need feeding and that won't happen on its own, so I'm sorry but I'm not sure I can tell you any more.'

The farmer got up to leave.

'Okay Mr Chapman you've been very helpful, please give me your phone number and I'll call you if I need to come and talk to you again, but this is a serious matter I'm investigating and I do have to ask you a couple of more quick questions before I can let you go.'

The farmer looked as if he was going to object, but sighed in resignation and stayed still.

'Okay, but make it quick.'

'The remains of four bodies were found in that

fire, but we have reason to believe that one of those bodies wasn't one of your prisoners.'

'Well bugger me.' The farmer sat down again.

'What?' said Gibson.

'Well that solves a bit of a mystery. I knew I wasn't seeing things. I've got a bloody good memory, never forget a face. I saw the bugger, about two weeks after the fire.

'Saw who?'

'One of the prisoners.'

'Where?'

'I was driving through the estate, the little housing estate just near the farm, and I thought I saw one of them, but he disappeared into a garden and I thought I must have been imagining it. Thinking about it now, I think he must have seen me just before I saw him.'

'I don't suppose you know which one, the prisoner's name?'

'No I can't remember, I never forget faces, names is a different matter altogether, can't remember the wife's sometimes.' He laughed at his own little joke.

'Okay, one last question and then you can go and feed your chickens or whatever.'

'Sheep.'

'Sorry?'

'Sheep, not chickens.'

'Oh yes right. Now, did the prisoners ever, you know, sneak off anywhere? I assume they weren't supposed to leave the farm, but did they?'

The farmer weighed the question up.

'Well it was like this, like I said they was Germans, the enemy if you like, but individually they weren't bad lads really, so I admit I did turn a blind eye sometimes when they nicked off at night, it wasn't that often, they didn't push it like, and it wasn't like a proper camp with guards and that sort of thing, so I had to be a bit, realistic you might say.

Anyway, you can't expect to keep young men locked up all the time, otherwise you'll end up getting more trouble than it's worth. I know a bit about people and in many ways they're not that different to animals, in some respects anyway, so yes is the short answer.'

'Any idea where they went to?' asked Gibson thinking he probably already knew the answer.

'Well there was one particular lady who lived not that far away, who, well shall we say, liked to entertain men, very friendly if you get my drift.'

'Would that be a lady by the name of Dolly by any chance?'

'Ay lad I'm impressed, you have done your homework after all, so if you knew, why did you ask me?'

'I wasn't sure, you see the information wasn't that clear, not from what you might call a reliable source, so this lady "entertained" all four prisoners did she?, I don't mean at once.'

The farmer laughed, 'No lad, it wasn't like that, the lads would only nip off very occasionally and never at the same time, and I don't think they knew that I knew, but I did, not much gets past me I can tell you. If they'd been going out every night see, I'd've had to do something about it. Anyway, they knew they had to be careful as well, if the locals had found out, there'd have been ructions and God knows what would have happened then?'

Gibson thought about his last remark, prophetic maybe? The farmer carried on talking.

'As for all four though, Dolly I mean, that wasn't the case, one of them had a thing going with another woman, he didn't think I knew either, but I saw him a couple of times.

'Oh, any idea who this "other woman" was?'

'Oh yes, a widder, lived in a house right near the farm, had a dog she used to walk down the lane every day, sometimes twice a day, that's probably how they met, her and whatever he was called.'

'So you can't remember his name either?'

'No, like I said, faces yes, names no, but what I can tell you is that he was the same one I saw after the fire, the one on the estate.'

Gibson paused to think about the significance of what he'd just been told, then he asked.

'I don't suppose you knew what her name was then, this widow?'

'No, but I can tell you which house she lived in.'

'Oh, what was the number?'

'No idea, but it was the only one on its own, detached, might still be there, Dairyhouse Lane it was called then. Now sorry, but I really must be going, let yourself out, have another cuppa if you want.' With that, he put his wellingtons on and left.

Gibson let him go, poured another cup and sat there thinking, processing all this new information. He was much closer now, he thought. He was excited, more than excited, but he had to plan his next moves carefully, this could be the breakthrough he needed, but time was running out, for him at least.

CHAPTER 24

I t was late afternoon and the traffic on the return journey was getting heavy as the rush
hour started to build on the M6. Gibson decided he would drive straight to Dairyhouse Lane
to see if he could identify which house Harry
Chapman was talking about. It should be easy,
he thought, being the only detached property on
the road according to the farmer. Gibson made
good time but dusk was fast approaching and the
temperature had plummeted. He wondered about
coming back in the morning, but that would
mean a loss of valuable time.

He eventually drove down Agecroft Road, into
the same little estate of houses where he'd arrested David Potts only a couple of day before.
He found Dairyhouse Lane easily enough, then
slowly drove along it until he came to a detached
house. He slowed down a bit more to get a good
look, then decided to drive the full length of the
lane for completeness, and to find a convenient
pace to turn round, but before he reached the end,
he came across a second detached house.

Bugger, I'm sure Chapman said there was only one detached house, what to do now?
The first house had been in darkness, so Gibson assumed nobody was home, the second one, the curtains were drawn to, but had lights on. Direct approach I think? Gibson parked, killed his lights and switched off the engine. He was about to open his car door, when the front door of the house opened and out stepped a figure, turning briefly to bid goodbye to whoever was still in the house, then pulling the door to. The person started walking down the garden path to the small gate leading on to the lane. Gibson could see his breath as it vaporised in the cold air.

It was quite dark so it was difficult to see the man's face, but Gibson's brain registered a mixture of recognition and incongruity as it does when you see something or someone vaguely familiar, but in entirely the wrong setting. Gibson sat and watched, trying to figure out why this person seemed so familiar, then as the figure turned back to close the gate, his features were briefly illuminated by the eerie yellow glow of the street lamp on the opposite side of the road. *'What on earth is going on here? What the fuck is Freddie Exan doing coming out of that house?'*

Exan turned and walked down the lane in the opposite direction and away from where Gibson was parked. He sat there, not moving a muscle, his mind whirling. He was tempted to drive after

Freddie and ask him what he was doing there, but something told him he needed to think things through before taking any action. He decided on a plan, got out of the car and walked back to the semi-detached house next door but one to the detached house, number fifty five, he saw as he got closer. He walked up the path and knocked on the door. A young man opened it. Gibson showed him his warrant card.

'Hello, sorry to bother you. I'm Detective Sergeant Gibson, Greater Manchester Police, and I'm investigating reports of some attempted break ins around the area, and I'd like to ask if you've seen any unusual activity or suspicious people hanging around, that sort of thing?'

'Eh, no don't think so, better ask me mam though, come in.'

Gibson followed the young man into a small living room where two people sat in front of a gas fire, watching the television.

'This is a policeman, detective, and he wants to know if we've seen anything.' The boy gave up. 'sorry mate you'd better ask, I can't remember what you said.'

Gibson introduced himself to the older woman as the younger one had completely ignored his presence and remained glued to the television. He gave the woman the same made-up story.

'No love, haven't seen anything dodgy, well no more than usual anyway.' Sorry can't help.'

'Not to worry, perhaps your neighbours might be able to help me, the people next door…?'

'Oh, Mrs Hobson and her daughter Alice, well maybe, but they haven't said anything to me and I talk to them nearly every day, so I'm not sure.'

'Hmm, what about the people next to them, in the detached house?'

'You'll get nowt out of him, deaf mute, well not deaf, just mute. Funny bugger though, understands what you say but can't speak, poor devil. I suppose you should be sympathetic but he's such a dry stick, know what I mean? Anyway, Alice knows more about 'im, well her mam does.'

Gibson had the information he wanted so he thanked the woman, told her to keep an eye out for anything suspicious going on and left, letting himself out as it was obvious no one was going to get up and see him out. The young man and woman, now both glued to the TV set, completely unaware of his departure, or existence, he thought.

He knocked on the door of the house next door. It opened and this time the person had had the wit to put on the security chain.

'Yes love?'

'Mrs Hobson is it?,

'No, Mrs Bailey, my married name, I used to be a Hobson, you probably want my mam, Nora Hobson?'

'Well, it probably involves both of you, nothing to worry about though, I'm Detective Sergeant Gibson Greater Manchester Police,'

He showed her his warrant card and trotted out the same story about attempted break ins etc., she let him and showed him into a sitting room, similar to next door, but thankfully the television was switched off.

'Sit yourself down, mam's upstairs, I'll get her, she loves a bit of excitement. If she hasn't seen anything though, she'll probably make something up, she can't help gilding the lily if she gets the chance.' She laughed and went to the bottom of the stairs.

'Mam come down here there's a policeman to see you.'

'Mam', turned out to be a sprightly, bright eyed lady, short in stature and wide in girth. She had bright red, rather than ginger hair, wore a white and bright blue flowery dress, and all in all looked quite eccentric. She seemed pleased to see Gibson and thrust out a podgy hand after Gibson had introduced himself and explained why he was there.

'Please to meet you I'm sure, won't you sit down.' She said indicating a comfy looking armchair. Gibson sat down and felt the warmth of the coal fire. The daughter excused herself saying she had to pop out to the shop for something and it was only open till nine, so she said goodbye to Gibson and went. The mother sat down on the sofa opposite Gibson.

'So burglars is it?' said Mrs Hobson

'Well yes, there have been a couple of break ins round the area recently, so we're just checking up, see if anyone's seen anything out of the ordinary, that sort of thing.'

'Well I can't say I've seen anything out of the ordinary, I wish I had, it gets a bit boring round here, Happy Valley some people call it, no pubs or clubs, you have to walk miles to get to one, unless you have a car, but then you can't drink. The buses are useless... oh I'm prattling on aren't I, what was it, oh yes burglars.'

'Okay well I'll assume from what you've just said that you haven't see anything unusual recently. Gibson wondered how to direct the conversation towards next door, this lady was just what I was hoping for, she'll know everything there is to know about whoever lives in the detached house next door.

'I was going to see the people next door to you as well, but your neighbour at number fifty five said it's a man who lives on his own and something about him being a deaf mute?'

'Yes, never recovered poor lamb.'

'Oh, recovered from what?'

'Shell shock, he can hear all right, just can't speak, writes it down if he wants to tell you anything, we've all got used to it over the years, course it didn't matter when Lily was alive but now, well…., mind you, he manages quite well, gets most of his shopping from Mr Banji these days and they're very patient with him.'

'This Lily, was his wife I assume?'

'Oh no, she wasn't his wife, no, his cousin, or was she his auntie, no cousin I think, anyway, one or the other. He came to live with her during the war, he'd been injured apparently, on the front line, not serious, I mean I don't think he had any physical injury or anything, but he had this shell shock, like I said and he was never able to speak again.'

'What happened to Lily, I mean when did she die?'

'It was very sad, she passed away in eighty four, no, eighty five, I think it was. They were so close, went everywhere together, seemed very fond of each other, you'd have thought they were married if you didn't know better.'

'So how did it happen, I mean how is it that they came to live together?'

'You seem very interested in him; you don't suspect him of being a burglar, do you?'

'Oh no, just curious, that's all, what did you say his name is?'

'I'm not sure I did, but it's Walter, Walter Fraser, but everyone calls him Mr Fraser, he's never been that friendly so you could call him by his first name, not that he's been nasty or anything, just not friendly somehow. As for how he came to live there, well like I say, he was injured in the war, and tragically all his family were killed in an air raid, so Lily told me, said they'd all been killed in the blitz in London.'

'And Lily, she wasn't married or anything?'

'She had been, but her husband was killed at the start of the war, volunteered she said, she tried to stop him, but she said he thought it was his duty, such a shame.'

'Hmm, tell me, if you were here during the war, you probably remember the bomb that was dropped on Regent Park West, destroyed a house and the family inside?'

'Yes, course I do, you don't forget something like that, a whole family wiped out, well most of them, why do you ask?

'Oh, just curiosity again, we were talking to someone round here recently and they were telling us all about it. I knew they'd bombed Manchester and Trafford Park, but I hadn't realised they bombed anywhere round here.' Gibson lied.

''Well, they did, and we were terrified I can tell you, and it wasn't just the once either, we had another do about a week later.'

'Oh really, did they do any damage that time?'

'Well they killed a load of German prisoners that were working on Harry Chapman's farm, seemed like poetic justice to a lot of people round here, not many tears shed for them I can tell you.'

'Really, tell me, was that about the same time

that Lily's cousin turned up?'

'Sorry, what's that got to do with the price of fish?'

Gibson had heard the expression before and it always made him wonder where on earth such sayings came from.

'Let's just say I'm being curious again, so was it, around the same time?'

'I don't think so, let me see,' Mrs Hobson closed her eyes briefly and concentrated.

'No, I can't remember, why are you asking all these questions about the war?'

'Nothing really, just caught my interest that's all, but you're sure, sure you can't remember, try again, was it before, or after those prisoners died in the fire.'

'Well let's see, I remember we were coming back from Mass when we first saw him. He was walking down the road with a little suitcase, then he turned into Lily's house and she opened the door and let him in. It's not that I'm nosy you understand, but I was curious I must admit. Now let me think.' Mrs Hobson put her forefinger to her lips, concentrating, then her eyes lit up and she took it away. 'Got it, it wasn't a Sunday, it was mid-week, and we don't normally go to mass midweek, so it must have been a saints day... no, it was Ash Wednesday, it was, I remember now, seeing him walking down the lane with a small suitcase, yes Ash Wednesday, definitely.'

'So Ash Wednesday would have been when, quite a while after those prisoners died in the fire on the farm I guess?'

Gibson had spoken out loud rather than meaning to ask Mrs Hobson the question, but she answered anyway.

'Yes I suppose it would have been, Easter's normally in March or April isn't it, although it can be as early as the end of February some years, so I couldn't say, depends how Easter fell that year. But I still don't understand, what have those prisoners dying got to do with Mr Fraser coming to stay with Lily?'

'Nothing at all, nothing at all Mrs Hobson, and thanks for your time, maybe I'll just go and call on Mr Fraser, make sure he's not seen anything suspicious either.'

Mrs Hobson was still looking at Gibson trying to fathom out what was going on. Then she shrugged her shoulders and said.

'I'm not sure he's there at the moment, goes away quite a bit, they never said, but I think they must have another house somewhere, holiday home, maybe a caravan or something.'

'Oh, why do you think that?'

'Well, like I say, they used to go away quite a lot, and it would have cost them a fortune in hotels or even staying in a boarding house these days, so I just assumed they had another place somewhere, but we never did find out where. Not that I'm nosy, just curious, like you I suppose?' She smiled at Gibson, pleased with her own little witticism.

Gibson got up to go, he had enough information to consider his next move.

'Just one more thing, does Mr Fraser have many visitors?'

Mrs Hobson looked at him again, frowning, obviously wondering why Gibson was now interested in who visited Mr Fraser.

'No I don't think so, I have seen a man visit a few times, no idea who he is though.'

'Okay Mrs Hobson, thanks for the chat and don't forget to keep a lookout for anything suspicious. Don't hesitate to call us if you do.'

'Yes, I will, bye,' she said as he left her at the door still frowning. The door closed behind him. Gibson walked down the garden path and on to the lane. He stood by his car pondering his next move. *I should probably call in and speak to the DCI, but then, have I really got anything of significance to tell him? More speculation yes, but nothing concrete. Freddie Exan visiting this house is decidedly strange and the man himself, well I obviously need to see what gives there. Could he be the missing German? Time scales seem a bit iffy, but I suppose there's one way to find out - go and ask him.*

Gibson checked his watch, a bit late to be making house calls warning about burglars, *but I can't wait until tomorrow. The man might not be there tomorrow, so here goes*. He went up the path, pressed the illuminated doorbell and heard a loud chiming from inside the house. The window curtain twitched as someone tried to see who was knocking on the door, then the door opened, no security chain on this time.

The man was of indeterminate age, but Gibson would have guessed he was in his mid to late sixties. He was grey haired, quite tall, slim and looked fit. He also looked familiar, where have I seen this man before? Gibson showed him his warrant card and repeated the spiel about burglars in the area. The man didn't look convinced and put his hand up to Gibson indicating he should stay there. The man came back quickly with a card on which was written in large capital letters.

"I CAN HEAR YOU, BUT I AM UNABLE TO SPEAK DUE TO A MEDICAL CONDITION".

Gibson was determined to interview the man regardless of any impediment he may have.

'Yes, your neighbours did say you had a erm, communication problem, and I'm really sorry to bother you, but the matter is important so I'll try not to take up much of your time, but I do have a few things to ask you, so could we go inside please, I think it will be much better than standing here freezing on your doorstep?'

The man looked annoyed and Gibson thought

he was going to refuse to let him in, then in an obvious change of heart, he stood back and signalled for Gibson to go into the living room which was situated directly off the small hallway.

'Thanks,' said Gibson. There was a roaring fire and he went and stood in front of it warming his hands. 'Lovely fire, a bit nippy out there isn't it?'

The man nodded and sat down on the sofa. This was going to be tricky thought Gibson.

'You don't mind if I sit down do you?' And he sat down without waiting for an answer. 'Well as I was saying.....' Gibson started but was interrupted by the chiming of the doorbell.

The man looked startled, uneasy, but made no move to answer the door.

'Erm, your doorbell, Mr Fraser...'

Fraser drew in his breath and reluctantly got up, went to the door, opened it and immediately a voice said.

'Sorry Hans, I was halfway up Agecroft Road when I realised I'd forgotten.......' The visitor stepped into the hall but stopped talking as he saw the warning look on the other man's face. At the same time he turned and saw Gibson who had got up and was now standing at the open living room door.

Shock registered on Freddie's face. 'Jesus Christ, what the fuck's he doing here?' screamed Freddie, pointing at Gibson. Then house shook with the force of him slamming the front door shut behind him. Gibson looked at Freddie's contorted face, instantly registering just how badly he'd misjudged this man's innocence.

Hans replied, his guttural voice angry at the implication of any fault on his part. 'He said he was warning people in the area to look out for burglars, said there'd been some break ins, but he was plainly lying, he knew something.....' Hans stopped speaking, there was little point in arguing now. They all knew cat was well and truly out of the bag. All three of them stood motionless, each one deciding what to do next. Gibson was weighing up his chances of arresting both of them and knew he was on a bummer, but he thought he might just get away with it. He took a deep breath and summoned up all the authority he could muster, then spoke.

'I'm going to have to ask both of you to come down to the station and answer some questions,' and reached for the radio on his belt.

Freddie was the first to move and almost dived at Gibson, but it turned into more of a shoulder charge. Gibson was knocked through the door and over an armchair, landing awkwardly against a wall. It knocked the wind out of him and in the process he lost his grip on the radio, it dropped to the floor. Freddie was on top of him now and the two of them struggled in the confined space to get an advantage over the other. Gibson managed to shove the chair away with his foot and rolled over at the same time ending up facing Freddie on the floor.

He reached out with his left hand, his right arm partially trapped underneath him and got a hold on Freddie's throat. Freddie's face contorted in agony as he used both of his hands to try to prise Gibson's hand away, but Gibson had now freed his right arm and had brought his other hand round to reinforce his grip. Freddie's face was going purple as he struggled in Gibson's stranglehold, they rolled over sideways, then Gibson felt a hefty blow to the back of his head and everything went dark.

Gibson woke, but wished he hadn't, the pain in his head was worse than anything he'd ever experienced before, not helped by the fact that he was sitting in a kitchen chair with his hands tightly tied behind him. He felt something viscous trickling down the nape of his neck. *What the fuck did he hit me with, probably a poker.* He slowly moved his head from side to side to see what happened, *sweet Jesus that hurt.* He stopped, then felt as if he was going to be sick, but managed to gasp in some air and waited until the worst of the nausea had passed.

He took some more deep breaths and weighed up the situation. The two men, Freddie Exan and the man he now knew was called Hans, were standing on the other side of the kitchen table. They were discussing the situation and Gibson knew he was in deep shit. At least one, or possibly both of these men, had killed before, of that he was certain. *What a fucking idiot I was not to have radioed in, at least to say where I was. No one has the foggiest where I am. As far as everyone's concerned, I'm on sick leave, Jill might be a bit worried, but she won't do anything until I've been missing for quite a bit longer – and probably much too late.*

Gibson tuned into their conversation. They were obviously unconcerned if he heard them or not, which didn't bode well he thought. Freddie's voice was croaky from the effects of his near strangulation.

'So what the fuck do you suggest we do now Hans, I mean how was I to know he'd be here having a cosy chat with you? Talk about bad timing, Jesus Christ.'

'Calm down Freddie,' the other man almost shouted, his German accent only too obvious now, 'Look, I'm not blaming you okay, we just have to stay calm and sort this out. First, if he was with anyone else, they'd be knocking on the door by now, so he's on his own. Go and check. He must have a car outside, take his keys out of his pocket and find out which one it is, then come back and we'll decide what to do with him, but be careful, make sure there's no one else around.

Freddie went through Gibson's pockets and retrieved the keys without saying a word. Gibson spoke the utterly useless cliché.

'You'll never get away with this Freddie, you don't think people don't know where I am do you?'

It sounded like a very bad line from a B movie, thought Gibson and the sneer on Freddie's face in response only made him feel more hopeless and impotent. His only satisfaction was the obvious damage he could see he'd inflicted on Freddie's neck, the bruising already starting to show. Freddie went out to check the car as instructed. The man called Hans sat down opposite Gibson and stared at him saying nothing. Gibson spoke.

'I know you've probably killed already, and you've got away with it, until now that is, but killing a policeman, well that's a whole different matter.'

'It's no different,' said the man, 'unplanned yes, but no different, we will improvise, and we will get away with it, so please be quiet, I have no wish to discuss anything with you.'

Gibson ignored him and carried on talking. 'He called you Hans and from memory there was only one prisoner called Hans, Hans Konig, so that's you, isn't it?'

The man remained quiet and stony faced. Then the penny dropped with Gibson, of course he looks familiar, he's the spit and image of his son!

'You obviously escaped the fire, then presumably killed the people who you thought were responsible for setting fire to the hut and killing the others, but why did you wait so long, why wait all those years, did Freddie help you?' The man stared back at him, saying nothing.

The front door opened and Freddie came back in. 'No one outside, found his car, what now?'

'I've been thinking about that. There's little doubt that this man's colleagues will eventually find out that he was round here knocking on doors on the lane, and that he probably came to this house. So we, well, I, will just have to say that he came here and warned me about burglars in the area, but then went away, and that's all I know. Me being dumb, will help. I'll write it all down for them. No one likes to think badly of someone with my problem, and they're always embarrassed talking to me, so they'll go away soon enough.'

'Okay, but what do we do with him though, how do we get rid?' said Freddie nodding in Gibson's direction. Gibson's mind was racing, trying to think of how to escape, but listening at the same time.

'I think I have the answer. When I worked on the farm, there were some old mine workings on a field next to the farm. They were part of the original Agecroft coal mine, the farmer told us. They were sealed, but not very well, so he pointed them out to us, said they were dangerous and said we should be careful to avoid them. Naturally we prised the wooden planks away to have a look inside a couple of them, but never went very far in. The farmer said they sloped down, then the shaft suddenly becomes almost vertical, he said they were very deep and full of water. If they're still there, I think I can probably find them again.'

Freddie smiled. 'Sounds perfect, but what if the mines have been filled in, or you can't find them?'

'Then we'll just have to think of an alternative method, but don't worry Freddie, we're not going to get caught. 'Look you stay here and I'll go and try to find the shafts, then we'll dispose of him, they'll never find his body. When we've finished dumping him we'll take his car and park it a good few miles away, that should do it.'

Gibson tried to stay calm but he was finding it extremely difficult being spoken about as though he was already dead. He thought about Jill, and pictured her in at his funeral, Assuming they ever find my body that is. Freddie rifled through a kitchen draw and came out with a large knife. Gibson could only describe the manic look in Freddie's eyes as bloodthirsty, but the cool calm way the German talked about disposing of him was even more terrifying. The German got up to go.

'It's a good night for this work, no moon. There are plenty of gaps in the fence so no big problem, I'll be about twenty minutes maximum, so don't take your eyes off him and don't cut him, I don't want any blood in this house, okay?'

'Okay, Freddie replied with obvious reluctance.

And sat down on the chair the German had just vacated.

Gibson tried frantically to think how he could change the circumstances to his advantage. The thin plastic rope holding him was too secure, no chance of wriggling free, plus his hands were going numb due to the tightness of the bonds tying his wrists. The only thing he could do now was talk, try to persuade Freddie it wasn't worth taking the risk of killing a policeman.

'Look Freddie, there's still a chance you can stop this madness, you know what it'll be like, kill a copper and they won't stop till they find out who did it, and they will, despite what your friend Hans says. Do yourself a favour and untie me, I'll put in a word, tell them you saved me, it would make things easier for you.'

'Shut the fuck up, or I'll cut your tongue out, and don't think I won't "Detective Sergeant Gibson", that's what you told me to call you wasn't it, course that's when you thought you were in charge wasn't it, eh, the big man, not so big now though. Had you fooled good and proper, didn't I? You believed all that shit I fed you, some fuckin detective you are'

You can say that again Freddie, I'm a really great judge of character, that's for sure.

Gibson gave Freddie a few moments to calm down, then tried another tack.

'Okay, well at least tell me why you killed Geoff,

supposedly your best friend. I presume it was you who killed him? Your sister said you loved him.'

'I did' Freddie mumbled.

'Sorry?'

'I said, I did love him okay?' his voice thick and emotional.

'Then why did you kill him, such a vicious attack?'

'He had it coming, he lied to me, all those years he'd deliberately lied to me, I knew they'd done it but whenever I asked what happened *that day*, Geoff would always laugh and say nothing happened, that I was being stupid, and said why should I care anyway, called me a Nazi lover and worse.'

'So the argument you had in the pub, the week before you killed him, is that what that was about?'

'Yeah, I overheard him talking to some bloke in the pub about the sixty six world cup, when we beat Germany. Geoff was drunk and started boasting saying he'd scored four nil against Germany in the war. When the bloke asked what the fuck Geoff was on about, he told him about when him and his mates had torched four German POWs in the war.'

'Then he started singing four nil, four nil at the top of his voice and laughing, then he saw me and knew I'd heard what he'd said and turned on me asking what the fuck I was bothered about, and calling me names. Said they'd left me out 'cos they knew I hadn't got the bollocks for it. I hit him in the face with my fist and we ended up being pulled apart by the blokes in the pub and I was chucked out for starting the fight. That was it.'

'Then the week after, you killed him?'

'Yeah, and I don't regret it, I enjoyed it, made me feel great, I loved Bren as well, and he treated her like shit, but she'd never said, never complained, but I knew. She really loved me, it wasn't just sex. Geoff found out but he didn't say anything, not to her, just told me to finish it. I told him, said he didn't love her, never been near her for years. He told me it was none of my business, she was his property, that's how he thought about her, she deserved better....'

Gibson thought this was progress, Freddie seemed much calmer, a bit more rational. Perhaps he would now respond better to another appeal.

'Look Freddie, you can end all this now, I'm not going to say you won't do some time, but if you stop it now, you're going to be looked on as having acted responsibly, even if a bit late in the day, but you'll do a lot less time, and you can still have the chance of a life when you get out.'

'Do I look stupid, what about all the other murders, you saying they'll just say, oh forget about those Freddie, you helped this nice policemen so we'll call it quits? You must think I'm a fucking cretin.'

He had a point thought Gibson, *but time's running out, what the fuck do I do now?* Gibson felt a trickle of sweat running down his back, despite the cool temperature in the kitchen. *Keep talking maybe something will come to me but keep the bugger talking, maybe I can find something to make them fall out with each other.*

'So Freddie, how did you get to be on such good friends with Hans? Who killed the others, was it just him or did you help him?'

'Doesn't matter, they deserved it, they all deserved it, it wasn't revenge, it was justice, Hans said. No one else was going to punish them for what they did, so we had to.'

'But why were you involved, how did you get to know Konig?'

'Aunty Lily, she, well her husband, he died at the beginning of the war, then she met Hans, while she was walking the dog. He was a prisoner of war and worked on the farm, when it was over there.' Freddie nodded his head in the direction of the fields over the road. 'Anyway they fell for each other. Then when that lot burnt down the hut, Hans escaped 'cos he was with Lily that night, so he hid in aunt Lily's house, this house, until they came up with this plan, to pretend he was her cousin who couldn't speak 'cos he had shell shock.'

'I got to know him as Harry Fraser to begin with, but one day I walked in through the back door and Harry was speaking to Lily. Aunty Lily had no choice and told me everything. Hans was worried I'd talk but Aunty Lily, she knew she could trust me, she virtually brought me up when mam died. Hans was okay and I liked him. Everything I'd been told about Germans being bad, well Hans was just like us, no different.'

'Your mam was Lily's sister?'

'Yeah, died when I was a little kid. Aunty Lily was great, looked after me. Dad had to work a lot so she fed me and looked after me....' He stopped talking.

Freddie's mood had changed considerably as he'd talked. He'd become subdued, the vicious bloodthirsty look in his eyes had gone and he looked confused. Gibson knew he had to do something before the German returned. Lily was obviously Freddie's emotional weak point so Gibson tried another tack.

'And do you think your aunty Lily would approve of what you've done, what you're going to do now, she wouldn't would she? Now why not just cut me free with that knife and we'll go outside. I'll call the station and you can give yourself up, what do you say Freddie, think about what your aunty Lily would want you to do.'

Freddie seemed to be thinking about it, Gibson thought maybe he just might do it.

'Nice try policeman.' Gibson and Freddie had both been so absorbed in their conversation they hadn't noticed Hans Konig come back into the house.

'I found one of the mine shafts, so let's go. We need to gag him, but keep him able to walk, easier than a dead weight.'

Freddie didn't move.

'What are you waiting for Freddie, get him up, there's no time to waste here, it's dark and there's no one around, let's get this done.'

'I've been thinking Hans, you know, the others, well they deserved it, they killed your friends, but this man, he hasn't done anything and he's a policeman. He says they won't stop looking until they find out what happened and I believe him.'

'You fool, he's lying to you, you'll go straight back to jail whether we kill him or not. There are only two choices here, we kill him now and hide his body, or we give ourselves up and go to jail, it's that simple. Do you really want to go back to jail Freddie, spend the rest of your life behind bars?'

Gibson spoke, 'Freddie, you've done some bad things but...'

Gibson's speech was cut off by a sudden blow to the face. He was knocked over with its force, still in the chair and landed awkwardly on his face and shoulder, hands still tied behind him. The pain was excruciating and seemed to emanate from every part of his body, his nose spurted blood on the parquet floor, and he spat out a tooth together with more blood. The German rubbed his knuckles and screamed at Freddie.

'You fucking idiot, look what you've made me do, his blood's in the house now, just do as I say and get him up off the floor, wipe the blood off him and gag him, I'll find something to wipe the floor, now Freddie!'

Gibson was stunned but still conscious. He could see Freddie deciding what to do, then he came over to where Gibson lay and roughly heaved him and the chair up off the floor. Gibson tried to resist but he was groggy and weak from the blow and too well tied to the chair to do anything effective. Freddie brought his face close up to Gibson's.

'You nearly had me fooled then, spouting all that crap. Hans is right, I'm not going back to jail for any fucker, so it comes down to you or me pal, and that means, I'm not going back to jail, and you're going down the mine.' Then he laughed hysterically at his own joke.

Gibson took the opportunity and spat a mixture of blood and mucus directly into Freddie's face. Freddie stopped laughing and his face contorted.

'You fucking twat, you fucking, I'll fucking show you....' and he looked around for the knife he'd put down on the table a few minutes before. He found it and raised it over his head and made to plunge it down towards Gibson neck. Gibson tried vainly to kick out but just as the knife was on its downward arc, it was suddenly stopped, knocked away by the German.

'What did I tell you about not cutting him, more blood, do you want more of his blood in the house, do you want us to get caught? Now just do as I say, get him up and let's get him out of the door, gag him now.'

Freddie went to a drawer and pulled it out so hard it came all the way out and landed on the floor, then he did the same to another and another until he found the one with some kitchen towels in. He grabbed a towel and put it across the front of Gibson's face then tied it hard behind his head. Gibson nearly passed out with the pain as the knot bit into the open wound at the back of his head. Freddie bent down and picked up the knife he'd dropped earlier and put it on the table.

The German was standing at the front door with it partially open, looking out.

'Bring him now Freddie, no one around, quickly.'

Freddie stood Gibson up with his knees bent and slid the chair from between his back and tied hands, then grabbing the knife in one hand, he half carried Gibson across the room to the front door. By now Gibson was semi-conscious and in no state to resist. Once they were out of the front door the German took Gibson's other arm and the two of them half carried, half dragged Gibson, down the path and on to the lane.

The cold night air revived Gibson a little, but he was still in no condition to do anything effective, the best he could do was to try to be a dead weight, but it seemed to make little difference. He began to wonder what it would be like, being thrown down a mineshaft into the black water, and hoped it wouldn't take too long for him to die. He was afraid, terrified, more scared than he'd ever been in his life. He didn't want to die. He blacked out, then he could hear a Scottish voice talking to him, Dr Forbes-Mackay's friendly tones were anything but reassuring.

'Aye son, people don't realise just how quickly you can die of hypothermia, your blood pressure increases dramatically, and you usually suffer cardiac arrest within three minutes or so.'

'That quickly?'

'Aye, never worry about drowning in freezing water, the hypothermia will get you first, every time.'

He regained consciousness and felt himself being dragged along, through a gap in a wire fence and into a field, then after a few more yards the German spoke.

'I think we're far enough in now to use the torch,' and a small yellow beam appeared on the ground in front of them and found the recently trodden down grass path. The two men were grunting and breathing heavily now as they dragged him through the fields, stopping every now and then to catch their breath. Gibson was slipping in and out of consciousness and losing all sense of time. Finally, the German spoke.

'Here Freddie, over there look, I've already pulled the wood panels away. We just need to walk him along the passage for about ten, fifteen metres to the edge of the vertical shaft, then just a quick push and we can go back and clean up, okay?'

A new voice spoke out of the darkness and simultaneously three strong torch beams lit the scene.

'No it's not okay.'

Gibson felt both men let go of him, he dropped to the ground and passed out.

CHAPTER 25

Words were penetrating his consciousness then fading again. Someone calling his name, his father, no….

'Gibson you silly sod I'm not your father, wake up man, wake up.'

There was no mistaking Watson's voice now.

'You okay Gibson? Is he okay?'

'I think so, vital signs are all good, probably suffering from shock and concussion, he's got a nasty head wound, broken nose and bruising to his face, dislocated shoulder and a few other cuts and bruises, but apart from that, I'd say he's okay.'

'Hear that Gibson, hardly anything wrong with you.'

Gibson tried to raise himself off the pillow but his shoulder didn't work properly and his head felt as if it would fall off, he lay back down again.

'Jesus Christ, that hurts, where am I?'

'In an ambulance, don't worry, you're not going to croak.'

Gibson passed out again.

He regained consciousness and guessed he

couldn't have been out of it for long as he was still in the ambulance.

'Back with us Gibson?'

'Yes.'

'Shoulder feeling any better?'

'Hard to say with all the other pains but yes, I think it is, why?'

'Well while you were out just now, I helped the medic here get your shoulder blade back where it should be.'

'What can I say sir, I'm very grateful.'

'That's better, a bit of respect for your olders and betters. I think there might also be some thanks due for pulling your arse out of the fire, or mine in this case. What do you think Gibson?'

'Yes sir, probably, but you left it a bit late didn't you?'

'Well there's gratitude for you,' Watson said, addressing the paramedic tending the hapless Gibson. Then turning back to Gibson, he became more serious.

'If you'd had the common sense to report in to me from time to time I wouldn't have had to play find the policeman now would I? I appreciate we agreed that you were on "sick leave" to give you a bit more time to crack this, but that didn't mean you had to drop off the radar so completely. You're fucking lucky I'm such a good detective Gibson, otherwise you'd be at the bottom of a very deep mine shaft, in your own very private swimming pool.'

'I'm very grateful sir, I can't thank you enough.'

'I see, taking the piss again are we Gibson, well at least I now know you're getting back to normal.'

'Where are they now sir, I assume you collared them?'

'Not quite, least not both of them. The one, the other man called Freddie chose not to go back to prison. I assume that was Freddie Exan, the one you thought was innocent?'

'Yes, a bit of bad judgment on my part I'm afraid. How do you mean, chose, what choice did he have?'

'Well put it this way Gibson, you know that private swimming pool I mentioned a couple of minutes ago?'

'He didn't?'

'He most certainly did, his final words were along the lines of "if you think you're sending me back to that fucking shithouse of a prison, you can think again"'.

'Poor sod.'

'Save your sympathy Gibson, he didn't go without stabbing one of our lads as he was trying to arrest him.'

'Oh shit, how bad?'

'Bad enough, stabbed in the neck, he went in the first ambulance.'

'What about the other one?'

'The other one, well he made a more pragmatic choice and is presently waiting to be interviewed, so as soon as I see you into your comfy hospital bed, I'm off to have a long chat with Mr Fraser, but I doubt that's his real name.'

'I'm really not feeling that bad now sir, so what say we both go to interview Mr Fraser, whose real name, I can tell you, is Hans Konig.'

Watson looked sceptical.

'Is he up to it?' Watson asked the paramedic who'd been listening to the conversation.

'I wouldn't recommend it, but I can give him some more strong pain killers which will help. He really should see the doctor first, but I can't stop you. My responsibility ends when I deliver you to the hospital, so it's up to you, once we get there.'

'Look sir, I'll come straight back to the hospital once we've talked to Konig, but it wouldn't be right for me not to finish the job, and anyway there are some questions I need to ask him.'

'How long before we arrive at the hospital?' Watson asked the paramedic.

'About ten minutes, now we've switched the siren off.'

'Okay Gibson, lie down and rest, then we'll see what you're like on your pins once we get out of the ambulance. Okay.'

'Fair enough sir, but how did you find me?'

'Well as you hadn't bothered to check in with me for such a long time I took it upon myself to try to find out where you were. I knew your reporter pal Mack had been helping you but I didn't know where to get hold of him, and as you had the files I had no phone number or anything, so I looked around on your desk and fortunately, amongst all the other scribblings on your pad, was his name and number, so I called him.

'But he didn't know where I was.'

'I know that Gibson, let me finish'

'Sorry sir, please carry on.'

'Well your friend Mack, told me he'd found out where the farmer, Chapman had moved to, and you were going to see him. Finding a number for farmer named Chapman of Yew Tree farm wasn't that difficult, so I called him and he told me about your conversation, and the prisoner he thought he'd seen after they were all supposed to have died in the fire. He also told me about the widow one of them was visiting, and that she lived in a detached house on Dairyhouse Lane, he said it was the only detached house. Anyway I put two and two together and decided that's where you'd be haring off to, and fortunately for you I decided I'd better see if you were okay.

'Just as well sir, but he was wrong, there are two detached houses on the lane, good job you found the right one.'

'That's just it, I didn't, I sat in my car outside the wrong one for ages, wondering where you were and questioning my powers of deduction, then I decided to have a drive further up the lane and I saw your car parked. Two detached houses, not one. I drove past, parked, walked back and waited in the shadows, not much light in the lane, so it was easy. I was about to go and knock on the door when matey came out, the man I now know as Freddie.'

'He checked your car in a suspicious manner, then went back in, so I gave it a few minutes, then another man came out and went through the hedge on the other side of the lane. I told you I used to live round here so I know, or at least knew, all the fields at the back here, played in them when I was a kid, so I followed the man, and he eventually came to one of the old disused mines.'

'Then he pulled some wooden planks away from the entrance. It didn't take a genius to work out what he was doing that for, so I waited until he went back then radioed for backup. The lads arrived just after they'd dragged you out of the house and through the hedge, so we followed. And that, as they say, was that.'

'But I might have been dead inside the house by then.'

'You might have, true, but I thought probably not, harder to move a dead body than a live one.'

Gibson was trying to think of an appropriate response, when the ambulance came to a halt, they'd arrived at A & E. Gibson made a superhuman effort to appear normal when he stepped out of the ambulance. The paramedic helped him down the steps and then let him stand on his own two feet. Gibson just about managed to remain upright.

'You look dreadful Gibson.'

'Thank you sir, but I feel fine.'

'Yes, of course you do. Now, providing you don't fall over before we get over to that car, you can come and interview our German friend, I assume he is German?'

'He is sir, most definitely German.'

'Okay, come on.'

'Just one thing sir. When we get to the station, and before we talk to Konig, I need to make two phone calls. Won't take me long.'

'Is it that important Gibson, I can get someone to call Jill and tell her you're okay?'

'Yes sir, it is important. And don't worry about Jill, she'll be alright.' Watson raised his eyes to heaven,

'Whatever Gibson, whatever,' and they walked slowly over to the police patrol car that had been following the ambulance.

CHAPTER 26

Konig sat at the metal table in the centre of the stark windowless white painted room, a plastic beaker of water in front of him, his head bowed as if in prayer. He looked up as the three men entered the room. Gibson and Watson sat down opposite him and the third, a uniformed officer, fiddled with the controls of the recording equipment, then spoke into the mike, confirming the date, time and those in attendance. Watson took the lead.

'You understand that you're still under caution, so anything you say now can be used in evidence against you in a Court of Law.'

Hans Konig nodded and smiled. The uniformed officer spoke into the mike confirming that Konig had nodded, indicating he understood.

'In future, please answer the question properly, no nodding or other gestures please. And for the tape, please confirm that you have been offered the services of a duty solicitor, but that you have waived your right to have legal representation.' Hans Konig nodded again.

'Please speak Mr Konig and answer yes or no.'

'Yes, I understand and I waive my rights to legal representation, okay?' Konig said in a clear, strong, belligerent voice.

'Now I believe you've already met DS Gibson, in shall we say less favourable circumstances, less favourable for him that is. D. S. Gibson will now take over the questioning.'

'Okay, can you confirm that you are Hans Konig, a former German prisoner of war who worked on Harry Chapman's farm in Agecroft, Pendlebury, in nineteen forty one and two?'

'I am he.'

'And can you also confirm that you are the same Hans Konig who was presumed to have died in a fire on Harry Chapman's farm in January nineteen forty two?'

'I confirm that, yes.'

'We have reason to believe that you and Frederick Joseph Exan conspired to cause the deaths of Geoffrey Brown, Joseph Martin and William Bowen, and further, were instrumental in the disappearance and probable death of Barry Jones?'

'I was not involved in the death of Mr Brown, but the others, yes.'

'Could you explain why you killed these people?'

'Yes, they deserved it, they killed my comrades, in cold blood, locked them in their hut and set fire to it, it was murder and none of them were going to face justice for their crime, unless I carried it out.'

'And how can you be certain it was these people who killed your comrades?'

'Freddie, he always thought he knew who'd done it, so before he killed Brown, he forced him to tell him who else was there that night, who helped him burn down the hut.'

'Now please describe the sequence of events leading up to the alleged crime, that is the destruction of the hut where you and your fellow POWs were billeted, on Chapman's farm, and the subsequent events involving the deaths of Geoffrey Brown, Joseph Martin, William Bowen, and Barry Jones?'

Konig looked weary and Gibson thought he was going to refuse to give any more details, but then he seemed to have a change of mind.

'Okay, I'll tell you everything, I'm tired of all the pretence, I just want to be left alone, so I'll tell you just this once, then do your worst, as I think your expression goes. First though, may I have a cigarette, I haven't smoked for many years, but I would like a cigarette now please?'

Gibson looked at Watson. Strictly speaking, there was no smoking allowed, but they weren't going to let a petty rule spoil the chance of a confession. Watson turned to the uniformed officer.

'Turn off the tape Robinson.'

The officer recorded that they were taking a

break and switched off the machine.

'Go and get a few fags from one of the lads in the station will you Robinson and make it quick please. Robinson returned with some cigarettes, a plastic lighter and an ashtray. He put them on the table and Watson nodded at him to start the tape again. He spoke into the mike confirming the resumption of the interview. Konig picked up a cigarette, lit up and drew in a lungful of smoke, then exhaled slowly.

'I was seeing a lady, a widow, Lily, Lily Turner. Her husband had been killed early in the war, a brave man, a volunteer. We met when she walked her dog along the lane near the farm and we became lovers. She lived nearby in the house, well you know where that is.'

Gibson interrupted and confirmed the address of the house in Dairyhouse Lane for the tape.

'Please carry on.'

'I would sneak out some nights and spend time with her. I was with her when the first raid happened when the German bombers destroyed the house on Regent Park West. Then about a week later, I was with Lily again in her house, and we heard sirens, then German bombers again, but far away. We thought it was going to be another raid, so I left Lily and went back to the hut on the farm where we slept, our quarters.

As I got near to the hut I saw some men, they were dragging a body towards the front of the hut. I had no idea what they were doing, so I waited in the shadows. Then they opened the door of the hut, pushed the body inside and at the same time they threw bottles with rags stuffed in the tops, they were alight, I assume they contained gasoline, Molotov Cocktails.

I saw them bolt the door and run away, then the hut exploded in flames. I couldn't see the faces of the men who'd done this and had no idea who they were, but I guessed they were taking revenge on us for the bombing the week before, when the house was destroyed. They didn't see me. I thought about trying to rescue my comrades, but it was no good, the hut went up very quickly, so I stayed where I was and watched. As the flames died down a bit I heard the fire engines coming so I left, but before I did, I took off my dog tags and threw them into the flames.'

Konig stubbed his cigarette butt out in the ashtray. Well that clears up the mystery of the dog tags, thought Gibson.

'Where did you go, when you ran away?'

'Back to Lily's, I had nowhere else to go. Lily had seen the fire and thought I was in the hut, she was very upset and couldn't believe I was still alive, she'd lost her husband and then she thought she'd lost me.'

Gibson thought he could guess what happened next, but he asked Konig to carry on.

'We thought everyone would think I had died

in the fire, especially as I had thrown my dog tags in. but we were mystified about the other body, nothing was ever said about that, and so by chance they found the remains of four bodies, not five as they should have done. I couldn't figure that out, but I did find out later, when Freddie talked to Brown, before he killed him.'

'And for the record whose body did Geoffrey Brown say it was?'

'Some money lender, I don't remember a name, they lend you money then charge you a lot on top when you pay back, we have the same thing in Germany, Geldverleiher we call them, they often got killed in Germany too.'

'Okay so what happened next?'

'I hid in Lily's house. It wasn't difficult, we just had to make sure there were no obvious signs of an extra person in the house, no more than normal groceries, milk, that sort of thing but it wasn't that difficult with rationing anyway. We thought of the plan about me appearing one day as her cousin, but there was the problem of my accent, which you will notice I still have quite strongly. So we decided Lily would say I'd been invalided out of the British army with shell shock and that I couldn't speak. It was easy in a way, but difficult not to respond when someone said good morning and things like that, so we tried to keep ourselves to ourselves. It worked, and gradually people got used to me not talking and left me alone.'

'So how did you manage, I mean for money, you wouldn't have been able to get a job with your so called shell shock, being struck dumb etc?'

Konig laughed derisively.

'You underestimate me Sergeant, you people you are so…. so dumb,' he laughed again at his little joke, then continued, obviously keen to show them how clever he was.

'Lily had her pension but it wasn't really enough, but we managed for a couple of years, then as the war was drawing to an end, we had the idea of advertising in the papers for German translations, written work only to begin with. We had replies sent to a box at the post office, so it was all anonymous. Lily would collect them, and I used a false name of course, actually one of my fellow prisoners of war who was murdered by your miners, Fritz Mayer, we didn't think he would mind.'

'Then eventually, after the war ended, I was invited to go to London to do some simultaneous translations for various German organisations, visiting business leaders and so on, so I ended up making a very nice living, and in London, Lily and I could be ourselves and I could speak freely. We had a great life but then eventually Lily became ill and then she died and that was it for me, my life was over.'

'Okay, I have to leave shortly,' said Gibson, but a

couple of final questions before DCI Watson takes over the interview.'

Konig nodded. Just then there was a knock on the door. A uniformed officer came in, went over to Gibson and put a folded piece of paper on the table in front of him. Gibson read it and refolded it.

'Sorry about that, now, why did you wait nearly forty four years before you started taking your revenge, to start killing the people who'd set fire to the hut?'

'The timing was accidental in some ways, I mean I had sworn to avenge my comrades when I went to their funeral, well my own funeral as well I suppose it was. Can you believe that, how many people can say they went to their own funeral? I went with one of Lily's husband's hats on as a disguise, but I needn't have worried, apart from the minister, there were only a couple of old people there. Anyway, as far as my revenge was concerned, it was a bit of an empty threat, in that I didn't know the identity of the murderers, and I had no way of finding out who they were, but then fate eventually decided things for me.

Freddie was Lily's nephew and like me, he adored her. She introduced me to him as her cousin, with the story we'd concocted and all was well. I got on well with Freddie despite my not being able to talk to him in the normal way. He liked me, but I suppose that was partly a reflection of how much he loved Lily. But one day, in the summer, Lily had left the back door open and Freddie walked in while I was talking to Lily. The game was up as far as Freddie was concerned anyway, he now knew I could speak and had heard my accent, so we had to tell him everything. After that Freddie and I, we used to talk a lot, Freddie was a lonely boy and quite sensitive in many ways. He'd always suspected that his friends had set fire to the hut and killed the German prisoners, something he didn't approve of, even before he met me, but afterwards, he was even more angry about it, but he could never find out if they'd done it or not.

I told him about my vow to avenge my comrades and to kill the people who'd set the hut on fire, and that I intended to kill them all, one at a time, each on the anniversary of the funeral, my funeral, February the third, but of course, I didn't know who they were. Then one day, Freddie heard his friend Geoff Brown, boasting about how he'd killed some German prisoners during the war, torched them, I think he'd said. They had a fight about it in the pub. Everyone thought it was about the miner's strike, but it wasn't.

Freddie was already upset with his friend Geoff Brown, because of his wife, He'd been seeing her, he was very fond of her, said Brown treated his very wife badly. Anyway, Freddie told me later, that he realised the third of February was the following week, so he decided to kill Brown. I don't think he really intended to do it, but he went drinking and just became so angry, he decided to go and see Brown and find out the whole truth about the fire. So he got a knife from somewhere, maybe Brown's house I don't know, but he cut him until he admitted to setting fire to the hut, then Freddie made him tell him who else was involved, and by then he'd cut him so badly he died.'

'So what about the others, was that you, did you kill them?'

'Yes, I killed them. After the trial, I went to see Freddie in jail and he told me who the others were. I decided to take my time and kill them one by one, on the same date as the funeral, but in a way that wouldn't be detected. I wanted to kill them all, and then wait until I was ready to tell everyone what they'd done and why I killed them, to get justice.'

Gibson and Watson looked at each other, Gibson spoke.

'Even after all that time, you were still prepared to kill them, why didn't you just tell us, tell the police what had happened?'

'How could I prove it, and anyway, I'd made a promise to my comrades, and I was going to keep it.'

'I'm still surprised you could find the will to commit such ruthless crimes after all those years had passed.' said Gibson.

Konig laughed briefly and looked directly at both detectives.

'I believe you also have the expression in English revenge is a dish best eaten cold. Well I can tell you, it's true.

'And your wife Lily, was she aware of any of this?'

'No, my wife died in nineteen eighty five, just after Freddie went to jail. She had been unwell for some time, but I think the strain of Freddie's trial and conviction finished her. I'm not sure I would have killed those men if Lily had lived, not because I didn't think it was right, but I loved Lily and wouldn't have done anything to offend or upset her, but once she had died, I really had nothing to live for, no family, no friends apart from Freddie and he was in jail, so what had I got to lose, even if I was caught? You see that's why I'm prepared to tell you everything now, I have absolutely nothing to live for, so you can throw me in jail, do anything you like, and it won't mean a thing to me.' Konig folded his arms and smiled at the two detectives.

'Hmm, well I am going to have to go now, I need to get some treatment for the battering you gave me. The DCI will take over and question you about the details of how you went about killing your victims, but I think we already have enough to secure a conviction for premeditated murder. You're going to spend a long time in jail Mr Konig, in fact you'll probably die in jail.'

'I'm sure you're right Detective Gibson, I'm sure you're right, but as I told you I really don't care.

'Well, I wouldn't be too sure.'

Gibson leaned across to Watson and whispered in his ear. Watson looked back and nodded in assent.

'What is going on, why did you say I shouldn't be too sure, what are you up to?'

'In some ways, I feel sorry for you Mr Konig.'

Konig smiled, 'Oh I don't think you should feel sorry for me detective. I'm beyond pity, you see nothing matters to me as I said.'

'Switch off the tape will you please Robinson?' said Gibson

'Now, I want to bring someone in to see you, someone you didn't know existed, and when you meet him you'll know why I feel sorry for you.'

'Bring who in, what are you talking about?'

'Hans Konig, that's the name of the person I'm going to bring in to see you. He's your son.'

The blood drained from Konig's face. 'What trick is this, I don't have any son, what are you trying to do....?'

'Not only do you have a son, but you have a daughter in law and two grandchildren.'

'That can't be true, Helga...'

'It is true Mr Konig. Helga your wife, was pregnant when you left to go and fight in the war. She wrote to you, but her letters were returned, they never got through. You see Mr Konig, you really did have everything to live for after all.

ΔΔΔ

EPILOGUE

The adrenalin that had sustained Gibson since the beginning of his ordeal, and through his part of the interview with Hans Konig, evaporated. Within a couple of minutes of getting into the back of the police car taking him back to hospital, Gibson began shaking so much, he couldn't speak. The driver turned round to see why Gibson wasn't responding to his pleasantries, took one look, hit the 'nee naw' button on the dash and floored the accelerator.

Three days later Gibson woke up, he'd been taken in intensive care for twenty four hours as a precaution, then slept, more or less for another two days. Loss of blood combined with shock and concussion had taken its toll. On his departure from the hospital, he was issued with some potions and pills and a confusing schedule of when to take what. The doctor came to see him before he left and gave him strict instructions to go home and rest for a few days before going back to work.

Gibson made his way outside on slightly

rubbery legs, got a taxi and went straight to police headquarters in Swinton. He was greeted by some complimentary comments and the odd pat on the back from his colleagues as he made his way to his office. Some joker had left a deerstalker hat on top of a pile of newspapers on his desk. He sat down and rifled through the papers, speed reading the headlines and various articles on how the serial killer had been caught and endless subsequent analyses of why and how such monsters came to be. There was also mention of the 'mystery' of the missing Charles Rollison being finally being solved, but it had been largely side-lined due to the 'big' story coverage about Hans Konig, serial killer.

Gibson smiled as he saw that the interviews were mainly with his DCI, together with some pictures of him, but he noted Watson had not entirely forgotten to give him a fair bit of the glory. There were comments from the Chief Constable and pictures of him looking grand and stately in his uniform - and smug, pension and glory on his forthcoming departure now assured.

Gibson asked one of the girls to get him some coffee and he couldn't help noticing a little more respect in the way she talked to him. I could get to like this – celebrity. Once he'd drunk his coffee he felt a bit more human and made his way to the DCI's office.

'Well look what the wind's blown in?' Said Watson as Gibson entered his office, 'had a nice rest Gibson?'

'Very nice sir thanks, I see you got your picture in the papers.'

'Not only the papers Gibson, TV, radio, you name it. I saw your friend Mack managed to get the drop on the rest of them, I assume you gave him the nod?'

'Yes sir, it was part of my agreement, for him helping me, I assume that was okay, I mean we'd agreed he wouldn't do anything until I told him it was okay, so I called him once it was all in the bag.'

'Fair enough, so anything planned Gibson, I think you deserve a few days off, go and take Jill off on a little trip maybe?'

'Maybe, but before I do anything or go anywhere, tell me what happened, the interview with Konig I mean. How did he kill Joe Martin and Billy Bowen and what happened to Barry Jones?'

'Take a seat Gibson.' Gibson sat.

'Obviously you can read a full transcript of the interview in your own time, but in the meantime, I'll give you the potted version. Barry Jones was Konig's first. He knew his general whereabouts then from the information Exan had extracted from Geoff Brown and passed on to him, he knew that Jones had a fishing charter boat business in Pwllheli, so he said finding him wasn't that difficult.'

'He chartered his boat for a day's fishing and

when the opportunity presented itself, he hit Jones over the head with a large spanner he'd found on the boat. He weighted him down then turfed him over the side. He knew a little bit about boats apparently and opened the sea cocks to scuttle it, then got back to shore using the inflatable. He popped it so that whoever found it might conclude it had been damaged at sea, and not used by someone to get back to shore.'

'Poor bugger, at least he wouldn't have known anything about it.' I promised to tell Mrs Jones what happened to her husband before she read it in the papers. I'm probably a bit late for that but at least I can give her some details that haven't been released yet, at least I assume you haven't released the details yet sir?'

'No Gibson, none of the details have been released, in fact I don't think we've formally released any of the victim's names yet, other than William Bowen, which is the killing we've arrested him for, initially that is.

'Okay, well I'll call Mrs Jones when we've finished, so what about the others?'

'Joe Martin, was murdered by Konig as you suspected. He went to see Martin at the care home, didn't say who he was, just told him that he knew he was one of the men who set fire to the hut and killed the POWs. He said he wanted Martin to suffer. He said he didn't threaten him as he didn't want him running off to the police, just wanted to worry him.'

'Then he watched Joe and got to know his routine over the following weeks. He had planned to knock him unconscious and push him into the canal anyway, to drown him, but then the freezing weather came along as a bit of a bonus and he knew no one could survive for long in water that cold, so he did just that, followed him one day when he went on his walk and wallop, that was that, nice and simple.'

'Hmm, I know one copper that's going to be really pissed with me.'

'Oh who's that?'

'One Detective Sergeant Pollitt, the officer who dealt with Joe Martin's death, put it down as accidental and when I spoke to him, I didn't think I could say anything about Martin's death possibly being linked to the others, so now he'll know I knew and didn't tell him. Boy is he going to love me.'

'Never mind Gibson, when you've got as many enemies as I have on the force, you can start worrying. So, next was the killing that started your investigation, poor old Billy Bowen, mostly thanks to his daughter's refusal to accept it as a natural death, oh and of course, your undisputed intuition Gibson.'

'Yes, well, I suppose it was easy to imagine how he killed the others, but Billy Bowen, go on sir, how did he do it and manage not leave any clues?'

'Plastic bag Gibson, nothing if not resourceful our Mr Konig. Watched the house, saw where the keys were hidden and the rest...'

'Oh Jesus, poor sod, he would have known what was happening. The daughter, well she's going to be distraught when she finds out. Who's going to tell her?'

Watson looked at Gibson meaningfully, eyebrows raised.

'Oh shit, me you mean?'

'Maybe not Gibson, I might do that one for you, seeing as how I was so dismissive of her in the beginning.'

'That's big of you sir, thanks. So, what did Konig say when he came face to face with the son he didn't know he had?'

'I have to admit, I've seen a lot of things, but I've never seen anything quite like that. Konig senior aged twenty years in twenty seconds. The likeness was astounding and there was no room for doubt. I thought he was going to pass out at first. The son was obviously very upset as well and there were lots of tears on both sides, it was difficult to watch.'

'Was anything said?'

'Not a lot, I think the son said something along the lines of "what have you done, all this time and now...." I can't remember all of it, but it even touched a hard bitten old copper like me, and even though the father has done some truly evil things.'

'Well I'll go back to my office and call Barry Jones's widow, then I'll go and see the Rollisons, then home.'

'Okay Gibson let me know when you're coming back in won't you?'

'Yes sir, tragic isn't it, I mean the whole thing, funny how wars don't just stop, the reverberations carry on through the generations.'

'Not going all philosophical on me are you now Gibson?'

'No sir, just thinking out loud, well I'll be off now sir, how much leave do I have?'

'Oh I think you deserve a week Gibson, see how it goes, you might get bored.'

'Oh right sir, thanks.'

'You're welcome Gibson. Mind how you go.'

Before he left, he went back to his office, phoned Barry Jones's widow and told her all he knew. She thanked him but sounded drained of all emotion. Gibson sensed that what he'd told her came as no surprise.

'So, I won't even get to bury my husband it seems. You say this man was acting out of revenge for something my Barry did when he was young?'

'Yes, I'm afraid so, but I can't go into any detail about that, but you will get to know more soon enough.'

'Can you at least tell me, was it something really bad, I mean did Barry kill someone?'

Gibson didn't know what to say.

'I really can't say any more than I've told you Mrs Jones, I probably shouldn't have told you as much as I have, but if it helps, and off the record, then yes, that's what he's alleged to have done, but it wasn't just him and I'm not making excuses for him or the others involved, but there was a situation he was caught up in which was highly charged, some innocent people had died and some other people took it upon themselves to exact revenge, and, well Barry got involved.'

'So, Barry and these others, as you put it, they took revenge for someone who'd been killed, then this man, this man you've arrested, he killed Barry in revenge for the killing which Barry was involved in?'

'I really shouldn't comment, but let's say it's a fair description of what probably happened, yes.'

'We never learn do we Sergeant, I mean people, the human race, we just never seem to learn?'

'No, at times it does seem that way Mrs Jones.'

'Well thank you Sergeant, I know how difficult it is to deal with these matters, so goodbye and thank you for letting me know.'

'You're welcome Mrs Jones,' he said and put the phone down. He hoped she would eventually get over her husband's death, but he doubted it.

He called Ms Carol Rollison at her dress shop in Wilmslow and made an appointment to meet with her and her mother at their home in an hour. He wanted to tie up all the loose ends before he went home. They let him in and offered him coffee or tea, which he declined.

They were all sitting in the very nice living room with French windows looking out on to a beautiful garden. Mother and daughter were seated side by side, the daughter holding her mother's hand. Gibson came straight to the point.

'You will know by now that we arrested a man for the murder of your, er husband and your father' Gibson said looking at each of them in turn.

'Yes we know that much,' said the daughter.

'A Mr David Potts has confessed to the killing, but more than that I can't tell you for the moment, but what I did want to tell you was what we believe happened to Mr Rollison's body. After he was killed, his body was burnt in circumstances that were, shall we say unusual, but will be revealed to you in time.'

Gibson stopped. He didn't want to upset the old lady and wanted to give them the opportunity to stop him if they didn't want to know any more details.

'I assume you want me to tell you about all this, at least as much as I can tell you at the moment?'

'Yes please go on Sergeant, let's get it all over, it's been a long time now' said the old lady.

'Okay, well as I say more details will be revealed in time, but for reasons I can't go into at the moment, your husband's body was mistaken for that of a German prisoner of war.'

The old lady let out a cry, Gibson stopped talking.

'A German prisoner of war, you mean a German soldier?'

'Yes Mrs Rollison.'

'My God, well...but how...Charlie mistaken for a German soldier...?'

Then the old lady took her hand out of her daughter's and buried her face in the handkerchief she'd been holding. Gibson thought she was crying until she put her head up and he realised she was laughing hysterically. Her daughter looked at Gibson then back at her mother.

'Please, mother.'

'Sorry dear, said the mother and dabbed at her eyes with her handkerchief. 'My apologies Sergeant, do please carry on.' Gibson looked at the daughter who shrugged her shoulders in resignation.

'Well, I'm afraid that's not all; Mr Rollison was interred together with three other German prisoners of war, soldiers, in a single grave in cemetery in Agecroft Pendlebury.'

That set the old lady off again and it seemed she'd never stop. Gibson felt embarrassed and looked at the daughter who now had a face like stone. Gibson waited until the old lady calmed down. She coughed, then blew her nose delicately on her handkerchief.

'You probably both think I've gone batty or something, but I just found it so funny. I assume it's a Christian cemetery?'

'Yes as far as I know, yes it is.'

Gibson thought she was going to start again, the daughter looked totally confused.

'You see there's something I have to tell you, you too Carol, I've never told anyone else, but Charles Rollison wasn't Charlie's original name, he changed it by deed poll. He was afraid his real name wouldn't go down too well with his, well, clients.'

'His family came over from Eastern Europe just before the war. Charlie's real name was Ruben, Ruben Finkelstein. The Finklesteins used to deal in diamonds and money lending, mainly the latter. They came over here to escape persecution. Being Jewish and money lenders didn't make them very popular.'

'So the idea of Charlie being interred with German soldiers in a Christian grave, well you really couldn't conceive of anything more inappropriate could you?'

She still seemed on the verge of laughter as she spoke. The daughter remained silent, dumbstruck Gibson thought.

'I suppose you could apply to have his body exhumed Mrs Rollison, but after all this time it might be a bit tricky to say the least.'

'No, no Sergeant, they've all been together for such a long time now, any differences they had, are buried along with them all, so let it be.' Turning to her daughter she said, 'I think I'll go and lie down now dear,' she looked back at Gibson and smiled weakly, 'goodbye Sergeant.'

'Goodbye Mrs Rollison,' he replied. Carol Rollison got up and helped her mother out of her chair, then turned to Gibson and said,

'Goodbye Sergeant, please see yourself out will you?' Then she took her mother by the arm and gently walked her through the door, into the hall, and up the stairs Gibson let himself out, went to his car, got in and sat there quietly for a minute. He shook his head, turned the key and started the car. He put his seat belt on, then said to no one in particular,

'You couldn't make it up!'

****

DEAR READER

I enjoyed writing this book. I hope you enjoyed reading it. I like to write a mixture of fact and fiction

*

Thanks (and review request)

And thanks for taking the time to read my book. I hope you enjoyed it. I love hearing from all of you and I take the time to read all the emails and reply. I also love reading your reviews. If you enjoyed this work, I'd be very grateful if you would leave a review and rate this book. Why? Because reviews help others find my work and that in turn helps me to keep on writing. And also of course, I love knowing that someone has enjoyed my work. Bless you!

Kerry Costello

DEDICATIONS

For my wife Lyn and our sons Andrew
Timothy and Alexander

AFTERWORD

In the latter half of the nineteenth century, coal mining and cotton spinning thrived in the north west of England. As a result, Manchester became a major industrial city. Most of the coal mines are now closed, but you can still see many of the original spinning mills, dotted around the North West, and even some remaining rows of terraced houses, built to accommodate the workforce for both industries.

Situated a few miles to the west of Manchester, are the towns of Swinton and Pendlebury. Typical of areas that relied largely on coal and cotton for their existence. This location provides the setting for this book and covers the period from the middle of the Second World War, 1942 to 1990.

△△△

German POWs

As late as 1946, after the end of World War Two, nearly half a million German prisoners of war (POWs) were still being held in Britain. There were POW camps on the outskirts of most towns at that time. Up to one fifth of all farm work in Britain was being done by German POWs, in this post war period.

ABOUT THE AUTHOR

Kerry Costello

Kerry Costello was born in England but is of Irish heritage. In his late twenties he started his own successful travel business, eventually selling out to focus on enjoying life - traveling, fishing, cooking, and writing novels. Costello says he feels more Irish than English and is very much at home in America where he and his wife Lyn have had a home for many years.

"The Irish are great story tellers and poets," says Costello. "James Joyce, Samuel Beckett, Oscar Wilde, W B Yeats, Edna O'Brien, Brendan Behan, the list goes on. I don't claim to be in the same class as these writers, but I just enjoy writing and entertaining people with my stories.

BOOKS BY THIS AUTHOR

No Way Back

Jack's in the wrong place at the wrong time. It could happen to anyone – it could happen to you! One beautiful sunny morning in May, Jack Brandon takes his dog Bess for their usual early morning walk in the Cheshire countryside, and suddenly Jack's pleasant and peaceful world turns into a violent nightmare. A chance meeting changes his life forever. Jack now has a secret or two, and is pursued by some powerful people who want answers - they'll stop at nothing to get what they're after.

Florida Shakedown - Gibson Series, Book 2

Jack paid the ransom, but they executed Rick anyway!

"An exciting read, with a terrific ending that

won't disappoint"

Retired ex British detective Gibson travels to Florida to recover from a tragic family bereavement. All he wants is peace and quiet, but Jack, a resident of the holiday condo he's staying at, has other ideas. He persuades Gibson to look at the death of his business partner in bizarre and brutal circumstances. Gibson is hooked, and against his better judgement, agrees to help. He's soon drawn into a violent corrupt and terrifying world where his very own survival is at risk.

Florida Clowns - Gibson Series, Book 3

Lorna's life depends on Gibson believing her incredible story. He knows anyone in her situation would lie. in just a few short weeks, Lorna faces execution by lethal injection.

Ex British detective Gibson returned to Florida to find work as a Private Eye, but didn't expect his first assignment to be so tough. He's tasked to rescue a fellow Brit from death row. Lorna claims she's been set up. Does Gibson believe her, or is Lorna sending him on a wild goose chase? Will Gibson find the truth out in time – and what evil might lurk behind a clown's painted smile? Find out in this spine-chilling thriller.

You Owe Me - Frankie Armstrong Book 1

Mafia thugs. Sunken treasure. Can an ex-soldier solve the case before he's dragged under?

Frankie Armstrong's skills in combat never prepared him for his wife's rejection. Desperate and depressed, the former British soldier gets just the distraction he needs when the American who saved his life calls in a favor. But shortly after arriving on Florida's sun-soaked coast, a simple search and rescue mission gets tangled up with lowlifes and murderers

Joined by a loyal stray dog, Frankie races to stay a step ahead of the police force, a rival PI, and ruthless mafia henchmen. But when he learns that his old pal left out a million-dollar detail, he fears his furry companion is the only one he can trust.
But will Frankie's attempt to repay an old debt cost him his life?

Condo - Frankie Armstrong Book 2

After attempting to rescue a woman attacked by a gator in an otherwise peaceful Florida condo community, ex British soldier Frankie Armstrong becomes suspicious. Was it a freak accident, or was it something more sinister?

The more he looks into the lives of his fellow condo residents, the more troubled Frankie becomes. Nothing and no one are as they seem. Using all the resources at his disposal to expose the truth, he attempts to hunt down the killer and bring him to justice… But will he succeed, or will the killer find him first?

CONDO is an edge-of-your-seat crime thriller. If you like fast-paced storytelling with twists that keep you guessing until the end, then you'll enjoy this gripping tale.

Irma - Frankie Armstrong Book 3

This crime thriller will blow you away!

When Detective Sam Randazzo discovers the un-reported theft of priceless jewels in the aftermath of violent Hurricane Irma in 2017, he has serious concerns. His suspicions are aroused.
Assisted by British security expert Frankie Armstrong, their investigations unearth an astounding possibility. Could these be the same jewels, stolen in a notorious and audacious raid in 1907? If so, how on earth have they found their way to Naples Florida in 2017? And what, if anything, do these stolen jewels have to do with a horde of invaluable works of art plundered by the Nazis in WW2? Lieutenant Detective Sam Randazzo wonders if this is the ultimate cold case.

The risks are many as Randazzo and Armstrong seek to uncover long buried crimes. Just how far will those involved go to prevent them succeeding?

Copyright © 2018
Kerry Costello

WRITERS NOTES

In the latter half of the nineteenth century, coal mining and cotton spinning thrived in the north west of England. As a result, Manchester became a major industrial city. Most of the coal mines are now closed, but you can still see many of the original spinning mills, dotted around the North West, and even some remaining rows of terraced houses, built to accommodate the workforce for both industries.

Situated a few miles to the west of Manchester, are the towns of Swinton and Pendlebury. Typical of areas that relied largely on coal and cotton for their existence. This location provides the setting for this book and covers the period from the middle of the Second World War, 1942 to 1990.

△△△

German POWs

As late as 1946, after the end of World War Two, nearly half a million German prisoners of war (POWs) were still being held in Britain. There were POW camps on the outskirts of most towns at that time. Up to one fifth of all farm work in Britain was being done by German POWs, in this post war period.

Printed in Great Britain
by Amazon